A Russian Requiem

Also by Roland Merullo

Leaving Losapas

A RUSSIAN REQUIEM

A NOVEL

ROLAND MERULLO

LITTLE, BROWN AND COMPANY
BOSTON   NEW YORK   TORONTO   LONDON

First Edition

This novel is a work of fiction. Names, characters, places, and incidents
are either the product of the author's imagination or,
if real, are used fictitiously.

Library of Congress Cataloging-in-Publication Data

Merullo, Roland.
    A Russian requiem : a novel / Roland Merullo. — 1st ed.
      p.   cm.
    ISBN 0-316-56789-2
    I. Title.
    PS3563.E748R87   1994
    813'.54 — dc20   93-22526

                    10   9   8   7   6   5   4   3   2   1

                              MV-NY

              *Published simultaneously in Canada
              by Little, Brown & Company (Canada) Limited*

            Printed in the United States of America

For Anatoly Ivanovich Lezhnyov
friend and brother
PROPAVSHII BYEZ VESTI

// AUTHOR'S NOTE

THIS BOOK grew out of a long-standing affection. Between 1977 and 1990, I lived in the Soviet Union for twenty-eight months, mostly outside the tourist axis of Leningrad–Moscow–Kiev. The people I met and worked with there — Soviet and American and European — have served as inspiration for much more than these few hundred pages of fiction. But fiction, with its hidden layers, insufficiencies, and occasional bursts of beauty, seemed a proper vehicle for trying to express what I have long wanted to express about those people. It seemed to me one way of trying to penetrate the mysterious affiliation between suffering and love — Russia's great secret.

This story is set mainly in the Russian provinces during the two weeks preceding the failed coup of August 19, 1991. The events depicted here are, in many cases, based on actual events, though the characters are fictional. There is a city called Vostok in Russia, but it has nothing in common — geographically, politically, or physically — with the Vostok presented here. As for USCA, it can be considered a Federal Agency of the Imagination, borrowing a bit from USIA, USAID, and USDA, but completely consistent with none of them.

A note for those unfamiliar with Russian names: In place of middle names, Russians use a patronymic, a variation on the father's first name. A woman called Lyudmila Bessarovich whose father's name was Ivan would be called Lyudmila Ivanovna Bessarovich. Her brother Maxim would be called Maxim Ivanovich Bessarovich, and might be referred to as Maxim, Maxim Ivanovich, or simply Ivanich.

// ACKNOWLEDGMENTS

MY THANKS to the Blue Mountain Colony, and to all who read the manuscript and offered their advice, especially: Marion Abernathy, Peggy Leith Anderson, Tracy Brown, Dean Crawford, J. Michael Harvey, Bruce MacMillan, Eileen Merullo, David Payne, Joyce Rothschild, Andrea Rutherford, Nadya Shokhen, Janet Silver, Sarah Stearns, Volodya Tokarev, Sergei Vinogradov.

Special thanks to Amanda for her unflagging love and support, and to Cynthia Cannell, Peter Grudin, Joe McGinniss, Michael Miller, and Alan Williams, whose aid and encouragement went beyond the ordinary bounds of friendship.

What foolish things we do to cover ourselves,
and by doing them are uncovered.

— Alan Paton
Too Late the Phalarope

In the terrible years of the Yezhovshchina
I spent seventeen months in the prison queues in Leningrad.
Somehow, once, someone "identified" me. Then a woman standing
   behind me
with blue lips, who, of course, had never heard my name,
awoke from the stupor to which we'd all succumbed
and whispered in my ear (we all spoke in whispers there):

     — And this, can you describe this?

     And I said: — I can.

Then something like a smile slipped across what
had once been her face.

— Anna Akhmatova, *Requiem*
(*trans. by R.M.*)

// PROLOGUE

THERE ONCE was a place called the Union of Soviet Socialist Republics, an idea incarnate. The Union of Soviet Socialist Republics was born in blood, suffered through a starving and terrified adolescence, then, in its youth, its prime, endured a war in which twenty million of its people perished. After the Great Patriotic War, there were a few years of relative middle-aged calm before the country began sinking into an early senility haunted by unspoken and unspeakable memories.

In its sixty-eighth year the USSR brought forth from its heartland a native son, a man bearing a bloodstain, who would lead his country, remarkably, to its almost bloodless dissolution.

This is not his story, nor the story of the USSR. What follows is only a paragraph in the ten-thousand-page history of that nation, two weeks in the lives of a few ordinary men and women, some Soviet, some American.

As the story begins, on a mild August night in 1991, politicians of the right and left are assailing the beleaguered Soviet president. The nation is wobbling under the weight of strikes, demonstrations, resignations. There is hunger in the provinces and treachery in Moscow. The Union of Soviet Socialist Republics — so thick-skinned, so heavily armored, so much like a person who has lived behind row upon row of mask and defense — is splitting open along a hundred subterranean faults.

One of these fault lines runs through Vostok, an industrial center six hundred miles south of Moscow, a smoking engine of a place. In Vostok on this mild August night, Nikolai Phillipovich Malov, patriot, stands at a dark window on the top floor of Party Headquarters, looking down on a park with a statue of Lenin at its center. Lenin is facing the street with one arm outstretched (hailing one of Vostok's notoriously elusive taxis, some say), and between his back and Party Headquarters mills a crowd of seventy or eighty workers holding banners and placards and one crude crucifix made of two-by-fours. On the edge of this crowd, close to the front of the park, five men and a woman sit on a canvas tarpaulin, starving themselves.

For a long time, Malov stares down at the hunger strikers, at the cross, at individual faces in the crowd, but, obsessed by the past as he is, held in the past's embrace, he does not realize he is seeing the future. The ragged gathering looks to him like mere defiance and disrespect and disorder, things no patriot abides.

He stands there in the window, bitterness collecting in his blood, until an idea comes upon him. An idea. A sparkle of thought in one dark mind. Of such small occasions is human history fashioned.

A RUSSIAN REQUIEM

// CHAPTER 1

NOT FAR from Party Headquarters stood the monument to those who died in the Great Patriotic War, and Nikolai Malov sat there for a time, in homage, trying to calm himself. It was an unusually clear night for Vostok, with a full yellow moon sailing in the east, and couples were petting and kissing on the nearby benches. A pistol hung in a leather holster against Malov's ribs, and in the leather gym bag on the bench beside him was a silencer for that pistol, a paintbrush, and a towel wrapped around a jar of paint he'd appropriated from the storeroom at the Council of Commerce and Industry.

Malov studied the quavering eternal flame and the shadowy granite monument above it — soldier, partisan, peasant woman with a sheaf of wheat. He recalled coming here as a schoolboy and laying flowers at the base of this monument, standing guard here as a Pioneer, being driven here with his first wife on their wedding day and paying his silent, solemn tribute to the Motherland. Twenty million men and women had given their lives in defense of the Soviet Union, and now the country they'd saved was being torn up and trampled by a few radicals and religious fanatics. People were waving crucifixes in Lenin's face, standing all day on the lawn in front of Party Headquarters instead of working, kissing each other on park benches while enemies conspired and maneuvered everywhere.

After sitting there for more than an hour, Malov stood and walked east across the grassy hillside above the river. He could make out two freighters tied up at the terminal downstream, and what appeared to be a forklift jerking back and forth in the glaring lights of the quay.

Someone out late, he thought, stealing.

Farther along he came in sight of a cluster of golden cupolas gleaming in the moonlight, their crosses throwing curving shadows, elongated and menacing. The churchyard gate squeaked. Malov crouched down and moved along inside the fence until he was standing in the shadow of the bell tower. One light shone inside the church, and from time to time he saw a silhouette pass across the windows, but there was no singing or praying to be heard, no parishioners queueing for a late-night blessing. Malov himself had arranged for Father Alexei to be moved to an apartment on the far northern edge of the city, where he would be unavailable for late-night blessings. Only Tikhonovich would be in the church now, dusting icons, whispering incantations, planning his Christly sub-versions and trysts.

Malov screwed the silencer into place, snapped in a clean clip of bullets, and crept toward the nearest grave. The headstone was surrounded by a spiked iron fence, and, resting his forearm on the fence's crossbar and tilting his arm up, Malov aimed and fired three times, hitting the mark twice and listening to the bell's metal echo fade. In a few seconds the church door was thrown open and Tikhonovich appeared in a box of yellow light, crossing himself like a monkey.

The watchman came slowly down the creaking stairs and walked backwards into the churchyard, his face lifted toward heaven. Malov was squatting fifteen meters behind him. He could see Tikhonovich's muscular back, and a small, shining bald spot on the top of his head. He could hear him muttering, *"Gospodi pomilui, Gospodi pomilui, Gospodi pomilui,"* and the singsong prayer thrust Malov up against a sudden vision: his own mother, rocking on her heels in the little wooden church in Ozerskoe, begging the mercy of a merciless Lord. *Gospodi pomilui.* Malov could actually hear the village priest droning out his lifeless liturgy, drowning the congre-gation in guilt and superstition. He could feel old women pressing close around him, smelling of garlic and soap. He could see the raw skin of their hands as they swung them from forehead to breast to shoulder, their eyes cast down, their attention fixed on a realm he had never been able to imagine.

As if impelled by the details of this vision, Malov raised his pistol and took aim. From this distance, the Lord's mercy notwithstand-ing, he would send Comrade Tikhonovich to heaven with one squeeze of a finger.

He felt the butt of the pistol jump back against his thumb. He heard a sound like a bare hand slapping concrete, and saw Tikhonovich pitch soundlessly forward in the churchyard dirt, the soles of his peasant boots twitching like the paws of a sleeping dog.

When Tikhonovich lay still, Malov straightened up, slapped the dirt off his knees, and approached the wall of the church. From his leather bag he brought out the brush and paint, and in ragged red letters printed a verse from his own liturgy:

THE PARTY IS THE MIND, HONOR, AND CONSCIENCE OF OUR ERA!

// CHAPTER 2

SERGEI SERGEIEVICH PROPENKO dreamt he was cutting open a pineapple. He was sitting at a plain white table, steadying the fruit with one hand and holding a kitchen knife in the other. Behind him stood his wife, daughter, and mother-in-law, and as he brought the knife down lengthwise through the pineapple, the women began to cheer. In the dream he could feel a smile pinching the muscles of his face, he could see sticky juice on the tabletop, he could hear, above the applause, the voice of his daughter, Lydia, urging him to hurry. Propenko clamped the halves of the pineapple together with his thumb and middle finger, twisted the fruit ninety degrees on its axis, brought the knife down through it a second time, and let go. The four sections fell away from each other in an eruption of succulent yellow flesh and rocked back and forth on the table's sticky surface, a triumph.

Then, somehow, the applause turned into sobbing. It took Propenko a moment to understand. Sobbing, slippers scratching the kitchen floor, the soft explosion of stove gas, a spoon ringing in a teacup, more sobbing. He heard his daughter choke out a word that sounded like "saint," and he wondered how celebration could turn so quickly to sorrow in the land of sleep. But it was no longer the land of sleep: kitchen noises were joined by street noises — creaking bus brakes and twanging trolley wires — and all sense of celebration faded. Propenko kept his eyes closed and tried to cling to the remnants of his dream, tried to recall the last time he'd held a piece of pineapple on his tongue.

The year, if memory served, was 1963.

His feet and ankles were dangling over the end of the mattress, as always, and he felt Raisa squeeze his big toe through the sheet. "Sergei, seven-thirty. You have a meeting at nine."

"What's the tragedy in our kitchen?"

She sat on the mattress, against his hip, an old Russian terror twirling beneath her face. "The caretaker at the church was murdered last night. Lydia's friend."

Propenko pushed himself up onto his elbows.

"Shot," Raisa said. "Here." She pointed a finger at the back of her head. "One of Mother's friends came by a few minutes ago and told her." She pressed her lips together, and what had been beneath her cheeks rose and reddened the surface, a thing Propenko had seen before. The kettle shrieked. Lydia went on weeping in the kitchen. Raisa squeezed his hand and left him.

He sat on the side of the bed, listening, assaulted by a twenty-year-old memory. He was alone with his infant daughter in the two-room apartment in Makeyevka — Raisa and Marya Petrovna were at church — and Lydia started to cry and wave her tiny red fists in the air. Babies were a mystery to him — he'd grown up in a household without them — and as the crying grew worse it began to sound to him like choking, as though something had gone wrong with Lydia's lungs. He went to the crib and rubbed one hand gently back and forth on the front of her body, covering her from neck to knees, feeling the hard belly puff like a bellows. When this didn't help, he lifted her and held the weightless bundle on his shoulder as he'd seen Raisa do, and paced the living room patting Lydia's tiny spine. She would not stop. She squirmed and squalled and fought for breath, dribbling tears and spittle onto the back of his undershirt and filling the small apartment with misery. He rubbed her backside, he sang and rocked her to and fro, he took her to the window and let her look out at the billowing, roiling smoke from the concrete panel plant. Nothing worked; the terrible sadness persisted, piercing him.

He had felt accused then, and he felt that way now.

He washed and dressed and made his appearance at the breakfast table. Lydia sat with her head bowed, tears dripping into her kasha, hair hanging straight down so that it hid both sides of her face. Her grandmother was watching, red-eyed herself. Raisa stood at the stove, listening over both shoulders.

Propenko put a hand on one of his daughter's bare arms, and his touch brought on a fresh wave of sobbing.

"Lydia."

She looked up, her face contorted, all the beauty wrung out of it so that it had become a vision from her father's recurring nightmare: Men were breaking down the door of the apartment, intent on raping her. Raisa and Marya Petrovna were screaming for him to do something. And he was lying in a bed that was too small for him, unable to move or speak, a wooden giant.

"He was a fine person," Propenko said, though he'd never actually met Tikhonovich, only listened to Lydia's reports about him night after night, and been jealous. Tikhonovich helping to arrange the orphanage project; Tikhonovich convincing his tough miner friends to come to church services; Tikhonovich helping her with her English lessons — a friend almost twice her age, a mentor; Tikhonovich and Father Alexei kneeling together at prayer for hours at a time.

"Go to the church," Propenko suggested, because he believed it was his duty to suggest something. "Talk to Father Alexei."

"He's in Moscow," Lydia said, and another fit of sobbing shook her.

Propenko squeezed her shoulder gently, but there was no getting through. She fled to the bathroom, and the adults made a show of chewing bread and sipping tea while listening to the water run. After a minute, Lydia reappeared, gave her grandmother a clumsy hug, and went out the door. They heard the elevator gate bang open and closed and the twang of cables in the shaft.

"She was like a daughter to him," Raisa said.

Propenko coughed on a sip of tea, recovered, asked if there were suspects.

"The *chekisti* will invent suspects," his mother-in-law told him, insisting on using the old word, as if it held more venom. "They have a long line of suspects in their torture cells, anxious to step forward and confess. Very anxious."

Propenko nodded without looking at her. He did not need death and torture with breakfast this morning. Three hard-boiled eggs sat steaming on his plate, but there was no sausage to go with them, no butter for the bread, no sugar for the tea, no guarantee that, after his nine-o'clock meeting, there would even be a job to provide the money to buy whatever food might still be available next month, and the month after. He was a Party member with no sausage on his plate; death and torture were the last things he needed this morning.

"Bessarovich is flying down from Moscow," he said, to change the subject.

Raisa changed it right back. "Because of this?"

Propenko frowned, bit off the top of the first egg, and washed it down with tea. "People are saying she's coming to break up the Council. Move us all to Moscow."

"I'd go," Raisa said, too quickly. "I'd go tomorrow, Sergei. Lydia has been at the church almost every night all summer. She's been seen there. Some of her things will be found there. They'll torment her now the way they tormented my father."

"Not that subject this morning, please."

"What is to stop them?"

"Me."

"You?"

"Me."

"Sergei, these people are animals, they have no —"

"It won't happen," Propenko said. "That's all."

Raisa looked away. Marya Petrovna was watching him as she'd watched him for twenty-three years, still not sure he was the right husband for her daughter. She forked off a piece of stale cake but did not lift it to her mouth.

"It could have been robbers," Propenko suggested.

"Nothing was taken."

"These days it could have been anyone."

"With a pistol? Once in the back of the head? Speak the truth, Sergei."

"It was the *chekisti*," Marya Petrovna said, speaking the truth for him, at him. Rubbing his face in the truth.

"Lydia won't be hurt."

"She's *already* been hurt," Raisa said. "She was close as a daughter to this Tikhonovich, I'm telling you."

"She gave us a history lecture," Marya Petrovna added, crossing her arms and flapping her elbows, letting Propenko know what he'd missed by staying in bed on such a morning. "The university student gave us a class in history. Stalin, Dzerzhinsky, Yezhov, Beria. Crying like a cloud. The 1930s all over again, she said."

Propenko had finished his eggs and was still hungry. His women were miserable, haunted by history, disappointed in him. He reached across the corner of the table and sliced his butter knife down through Marya Petrovna's half-eaten cube of cake, slid the tip of the knife under the morsel, lifted, brought it back across the table and slipped it into his mouth.

Marya Petrovna reached out and slapped him on the shoulder. Raisa's lips moved as though she might smile.

"I dreamt we were getting ready to eat a pineapple," he said, watching them. "I was slicing it like a surgeon. There was yellow juice on the table. You were all standing around, cheering."

They were both smiling now.

"Where did you get it?" Raisa wanted to know.

"It was just there."

"Just there," Marya Petrovna said wistfully. She pushed her plate toward her son-in-law, and he finished the cake in two bites.

// CHAPTER 3

ANTON CZESICH opened the hotel's casement window and leaned out, his thighs pressed to the sill for balance, the thumb and middle finger of his right hand working to bring a piece of central Moscow into focus. Framed in his viewfinder was a corner of the Kremlin enclosure — gold church cupolas gleaming in a mustard, late-afternoon light — and beyond and above it, a rumpled purple quilt of clouds advancing on the city. A westerly wind was gusting against the open window, causing the frame to strain and squeak on its hinges and stinging Czesich's hands with specks of grit. He held his breath and pressed the shutter release, then put the camera down and stood for a time, just looking. From ten stories up, even Moscow, bedeviled as it was by intrigue and insufficiency, seemed at peace.

On the sidewalk in front of the hotel, all the vices of the free world were in evidence: a pair of prostitutes leaning against one of the concrete pillars, laughing; a slinking black marketeer; a busload of German tourists — smirking, muttering, complaining — watching two sweaty, white-haired Russian porters struggle with their luggage and a metal cart. Taxi drivers smoked and talked in little knots of arrogance, and behind them, parked squarely in the middle of the drive, sat a black Zil limousine with Ministry of the Interior plates.

Czesich stood near the door for a time, observing, as was his habit, from a distance. The prostitutes ignored him, but he noticed the cab drivers and black marketeer carrying out their own inspections, making their calculations, ogling his umbrella, his shoes and

suit, his colorful American tie and new leather briefcase. After a
few seconds of this prurience, one of the drivers sauntered over.
"*Kuda?*" he demanded, running his eyes from Czesich's hairline to
his shoelaces and back again. "Where to?"

"American Embassy."

"*Dvadtsat dollarov.*" The cabbie squeezed his lips around the
filter of his cigarette and considered Czesich through the smoke.
Twenty dollars. It was a twelve-minute ride.

"A pack of *Marlbara*," Czesich countered.

"Let's go."

The taxi stank of gasoline but the driver appeared not to notice.
He flicked the butt of his cigarette out the window in the general
direction of the ministry limousine, lit another, jammed the stick
into gear and rocketed away from the hotel toward the traffic on
Nogina Square. Ahead, Czesich could see slivers of lightning cutting a bruised sky.

"Took you for a tourist," the driver said apologetically.

Czesich rolled down his window to get a better look at the city.
A few large droplets were already marking the street and sidewalk, and in front of the Children's World store, where a huge
crowd of unofficial salesmen and traders of various sorts had
gathered, he could see umbrellas sprouting like mushrooms. Moscow's air seemed fouler than he remembered it. Canvas-colored
trucks and double-length buses spewed diesel exhaust at the stoplights, and with the rain clouds swirling low and dark above, the
column of army recruits moving double-time along the curb, and
men and women trading boots for meat a few yards away, the city
offered the momentary impression of a burning, hungry, wartime
capital.

In true Russian style, the driver raced away from the light and
cut madly back and forth across the four-lane thoroughfare. "How
do you come to speak the language like a native?" he asked between puffs.

"My father's parents left Moscow at the start of the Revolution."

"*Pravilna,*" the driver said, nodding. The word meant "correct,"
but the man's inflection adorned it with shades of admiration and
approval. "And moved where?"

"America."

"*Pravilna, pravilna.*" He mashed the horn with the heel of one
hand and chased a dented Zhiguli out of his lane. "They did the

right thing, your people. I wish my grandparents had left. I'd be driving a cab in *Menkhettn* now."

"You'd enjoy it," Czesich said. A clap of thunder sounded directly above them, and the rain came all at once. He rolled his window tight. "Any chance you could put out that cigarette? I'm worried about the gas fumes."

The driver laughed and explained he'd been smoking in fumes like this — worse than this — for eighteen years now and nothing had happened. On the contrary, it was good luck. The fumes improved his mood, made him forget how much better things had been in the Brezhnev days. He took a deep drag and filled the front seat with smoke. They were flying along Kalinin Prospekt at fifty miles an hour, rain drumming the roof and hood and windshield. Every ten seconds or so the driver would run his wiper blades back and forth once to clear the flood.

"How's perestroika doing?"

The cabbie snorted and skidded to a stop at another set of lights. He flung his elbow over the back of the seat and turned to see if his passenger was joking. "See this?" he said, holding up the pack of Marlboros Czesich had slipped between the seats. "For this, the prostitutes pay me thirty rubles. I take the thirty rubles to the garage and I give five to the mechanic so my cab will still have a battery in the morning, five to the dispatcher so he won't check the meter too close, ten to Comrade Director. By the time I'm done I have ten rubles left — out of every thirty — and I've fed all their families. See this shirt?" He pinched the fabric of a plain work shirt and pulled it away from his chest. "A hundred and eighty-seven rubles." He snorted again, turned forward, and said, "Perestroika," as if he were saying "Shit." After a moment something seemed to occur to him. *"Korrespandyent?"*

"Deeplamat," Czesich said, though, technically, it wasn't true. He held a diplomatic passport, and the usual, unnecessary, security clearance, but he was an ordinary civil servant, a bilingual bureaucrat, United States Communications Agency, Grade 14, Step 3. "I'm here with the food program."

"You're selling American food?"

"Giving it away."

The driver nodded, suddenly solemn. "Puchkov's speech."

"Right." Boris Puchkov was the new interior minister, a rising Stalinist star. Not long ago he'd given a speech in which he'd warned that the planned Western food shipments would be tainted

with radioactivity and chemicals, the distribution personnel linked
to the CIA. The speech had embarrassed Gorbachev, of course, and
sent Western reporters and intelligence-gatherers scurrying about
for evidence of an impending right-wing insurrection, but it was
nothing new. In the last six months, perestroika had come to seem
like a prescription for starvation. The President's adversaries had
gone high-profile. To the right, the army and KGB were growling
like chained attack dogs. To the left, Yeltsin strutted about, making
proclamations. Gorbachev, once so vibrant and optimistic, was
now a fading sun around which enemies and rumormongers or-
bited.

"You're probably a spy then," the driver said over his shoulder.

"Of course. Why else would I want to give away food?"

There was a slight delay before the driver chuckled. He turned
onto the Garden Ring, drove a quarter mile, then performed the
famous *raz*, crossing the double yellow line and making a sweeping
U-turn in front of four lanes of wet oncoming traffic.

Instead of pulling up to the embassy door, which would have
landed him in plain view of the pair of KGB officers standing guard
there, the driver stopped thirty yards away and flipped the shift
into neutral. "You wouldn't have anything to sell, would you?"

"Food?"

"Food, dollars, T-shirts. Anything."

"The food is already on its way to Vostok," Czesich told him.
"And I'm afraid the other things are illegal for us."

"Vostok? You're giving away food in *Vostok*? My wife has a
cousin in Vostok who makes beautiful wooden dolls. We could
arrange a trade!"

"I don't think so," Czesich said. By way of consolation, he
reached into the right pocket of his suit jacket — his gift pocket —
took out a cigarette lighter etched with the coat of arms of a Vir-
ginia country club he'd never seen, and handed it forward. "A sou-
venir."

The driver turned the lighter over twice in his tobacco-stained
fingers, and pushed his cigarette out the top of the window. He
reached into his own gift pocket and presented Czesich with a cal-
endar, two inches by three, one side showing the months of a year
long past, the other a blond woman with enormous bare breasts.
The woman was kneeling with her hands on her thighs, squeezing
her breasts between her elbows like pale balloons. The driver
smiled, showing a silver front tooth, and said, *"Glasnost."*

// CHAPTER 4

PROPENKO trotted down the three flights of stairs and went out into the Vostok morning riding a wisp of good humor, but the mood had no foundation, and he knew it, and he was not surprised to feel it slip away as he drove toward the Council of Commerce and Industry Building. He parked in the side lot, stopped by his office, then went to the conference room, sat alone with the life-sized portrait of Vladimir Ilyich, and contemplated the specter of unemployment. The killing of Lydia's friend floated in the air beside him, not quite real.

After a few minutes, Nikolai Malov sauntered in and took the seat to Propenko's right, a head shorter, even sitting down. "Our boss woman from the capital honors us with her presence," Malov said sarcastically. The skin near one corner of his mouth twitched as he spoke. Hung over, Propenko guessed. "Why now, do you suppose?" Malov asked him.

"You know better than I do, Nikolai."

Malov seemed offended. He rubbed his bad ear. "How would *I* know, Sergei? I have no connection with this woman. To me she's just another Moscow bitch."

Propenko shrugged and looked at the door. Malov's Moscow bitch could walk into the room in a few seconds and turn the Council of Commerce and Industry to ashes with two sentences.

"You heard about the church worker?"

Propenko nodded stiffly.

"A terrible thing, no?"

"A tragedy," Propenko said in a neutral way. Malov sounded sincere enough, but you could never tell. He was a man of many duties, a dozen masks and voices. There were rumors that, in addition to his job at the Council of Industry, he worked nights at Party Headquarters advising the First Secretary, or in the *chekisti* cells interrogating political activists with cattle prods; that he had friends high up in Moscow; that he and the First Secretary shared a mistress.

"Murders, hunger strikes, rapes. What would our fathers say if they were alive, eh Seryozha?"

"They'd say our socialist purity had been polluted by bourgeois decadence."

"Exactly," Malov said, in an approving way. Propenko averted his eyes.

By the time Lyudmila Bessarovich made her grand entrance, heels clacking, hips shifting, Propenko and Malov had been joined by the group of men Raisa called Our Generals. Volkov was there — the Council's nominal director and Propenko's nominal boss, a kindly drunkard, still half-asleep. Victor Vzyatin, chief of militia and a friend. Mladenetz, chief fire marshal. Leonid Fishkin, another old friend, and head of the Central Exhibits Pavilion. Ranishvili, the Council's food manager. Ryshevsky, chief of customs. An assortment of assistants and transportation specialists. There were the usual fawning welcomes. Only Volkov remained sleepy and aloof, lost in a fog of his own making. Bessarovich began the meeting by dropping a stack of brown folders on the table, which silenced the Generals and roused the Council's director from his vodka dream. "Comrade Volkov," she said, fixing her bright green eyes on him and almost smiling. "We await your opinion with great interest."

Propenko watched Volkov's rectangular head tremble, watched him straighten his back and draw in his pointed jaw. With the index finger of one hand, Volkov pushed his eyeglasses tight against the bridge of his nose, then he tugged at the cuffs of his shiny suit jacket until they covered the base of his thumbs. Awake at last, he cleared his throat and met Bessarovich's gaze. "Lyudmila Ivanovna," he began importantly, in a tone befitting a Director. "My opinion is this. . . . My opinion is that we should follow the Leninist course in this matter. We should act for the good of the people."

As if impressed, as if hoping for more of this wisdom, Bessarovich lifted her eyebrows and turned down the corners of her mouth.

Volkov sneaked a glance around the room and shrugged modestly. He placed his left hand on the edge of the table and covered it with his right. "After all, who are we to quibble with the strategies of Vladimir Ilyich himself?"

Again, Bessarovich's brows arched. She crossed her lips with two fingers and nodded several times, then, shifting her attention from Volkov to the group at large and bringing her hands together twice, she elicited a round of energetic applause. Volkov appeared puzzled for a moment, and then, like a good communist, joined in.

The commotion died down. Lyudmila Ivanovna let her smile slowly fade and said: "I understand people are being murdered in Vostok these days."

The Generals examined the backs of their hands. Propenko's own large hands had been coated with sweat since Bessarovich walked into the room. He slipped them beneath the table.

Chief Vzyatin broke the silence. "There was a shooting last night, Lyudmila Ivanovna. A man was killed outside the Church of the Sacred Blood. A caretaker. Forty-one years old."

"And?"

"I have my three best detectives on the case."

"My information is that he was shot with a nine-millimeter pistol."

Vzyatin glanced at his knuckles. "Correct," he said.

"And my understanding is that nine-millimeter pistols are the caliber used by our government law-enforcement officials."

"Also correct," the Chief said. Propenko saw Malov's fingers drumming the tabletop; his face was twitching again. Bessarovich glanced about and let her eyes come to rest on Lyubov Mikhailovna, Council secretary, the only other woman in the room. The sight of Lyuba's round, peasant face seemed to cheer her. "Of course," she said, "law enforcement has always been a masculine province, eh Lyuba, so perhaps we shouldn't meddle."

The secretary quivered and tried to nod.

"But something smells rotten, wouldn't you say?"

"If you say so, yes, I think so, Lyudmila Ivanovna."

"And it would be a shame to invite a Westerner to Vostok and have this rotten smell spoil his visit, wouldn't it?" Bessarovich moved her eyes from General to General, a stern second hand clicking around a clockface, and Propenko saw that she was tapping the blunt end of her pencil on the table, she and Malov beating out an angry duet on the oak veneer. "We have an international operation coming to Vostok next week, were you aware of that, Giorgi Arkadevich?"

They watched Ranishvili shake his fine gray head.

"We'll be receiving a shipment of American food. Flour, canned vegetables, beans, powdered milk. Have you heard about it?"

Ranishvili shook his head again.

"You haven't heard that the Germans, French, and Americans will be feeding us?"

"I hear it now for the first time, Lyudmila Ivanovna," Ranishvili said with his charming Georgian smile.

"And as director of the Council's Restaurant Services Collective, what do you think of the idea?"

"A disgrace!" Malov burst out before Ranishvili had a chance to answer. Malov had made both hands into fists and was pressing them down against the table. Propenko was astonished. He could not remember ever seeing him this way. Malov's specialty was tricking other people into behaving like this, while he sat back with his arms crossed, smiling or faking sympathy, watching like a camera.

Bessarovich stared at him a moment. "Disgrace or no, it seems to be a fact. The trucks are en route. Some have already crossed the border checkpoint at Brest."

"We don't need it!" Malov said loudly. "We don't need their food and their chemicals and their conceit. We've lived a thousand years without them!"

Propenko could see Malov's wrists trembling against the wood. Even for a man with Malov's connections — whatever they actually were — raising his voice to someone like Bessarovich was unprecedented, the act of a drunk, or a lunatic. Professional suicide.

But Bessarovich's face showed only amusement, as if Malov's outburst were a piece of provincial theater, no more dangerous or significant than Volkov's morning nap. "Nikolai," she said calmly, "I believe the decision was made at a level somewhat higher than your own."

Malov opened his mouth to respond, then clamped his teeth together and began working his jaw, stoking a furnace Propenko could feel a meter away.

"I cannot understand why," Bessarovich went on sarcastically, "but there seems to be some concern in the West about whether this food will be fairly distributed, whether it will serve the good of the people — as Comrade Volkov has suggested — or fall into the hands of individualists who might try to profit from it." She paused and ran her eyes once again around the table. "Accordingly, we are not going to be given the food all at once. The Americans, French, and Germans are sending representatives to three Soviet cities to accompany and monitor three small initial deliveries. If everything goes well, if we behave, there may be more free food in our future, enough to make some kind of significant difference, even. Bananas and pineapples and canned pork steaks, no doubt." She put both hands flat on the tabletop, as if holding down a swelling private anger. "In any case, it is Vostok's good fortune to host the American representative, beginning on Thursday of next week."

There was a quiet shifting of position around the table. Propenko let out a breath, still employed. He and Leonid Fishkin held a brief conversation with their eyes: Less than a week to prepare for a high-level American visitor.

"Your American" — Bessarovich checked a sheet of paper on top of her pile of folders — "is called Anton . . . Chez-zik. He will have a suite in the Intourist Hotel and a small office in the Central Exhibits Pavilion, and he will spend his days supervising the deliveries, investigating, taking photos, writing reports, and so on. From what I understand, he is of Slavic ancestry and speaks fluent Russian, so there will be no need for translators. Questions?"

No one moved. Propenko supposed everyone in the room was feeling exactly what he was feeling. On the one hand it was a relief — the city would have more food, badly needed, and the Council was not being disbanded; on the other, it was a supreme humiliation, Western charity, exactly the kind of patronizing gesture Vostok did not need.

"Will there be foreign press?" Leonid had the courage to ask.

"At some point."

"But not at first?"

"Not that I am aware of." Bessarovich handed the stack of folders to Mladenetz, and gestured for him to send them around the table. "We've prepared some information about these shipments — exact quantities, description of contents, a list of distribution sites, and so on." She sipped from a glass of water, made a face, and held the glass up to the light. "I'm sorry we weren't able to give you more warning," she said, but Propenko thought she did not sound sorry at all. She was about to go on when she was distracted by the sight of Anatoly Volkov nodding off again. Propenko did not know whether to laugh or weep. His boss was a communist of the old school — affable, alcoholic, unprincipled but crafty, lacking even the semblance of an original idea. But Volkov's wife had been a cousin to Andrei Gromyko, and that flimsy link to the top rung of Moscow politics served as a kind of safety line even now. Bessarovich observed him with a mixture of affection and pity.

"Since Comrade Volkov will be in Romania for two months," she said, "mapping out next year's cultural and business exhibitions there, the person charged with directing this operation in Vostok will be Sergei Sergeievich Propenko. He will assemble a small Council staff as he sees fit, and he will, of course, report to and receive the complete cooperation of the Moscow office. Questions?"

Propenko felt as though the normal coordination of his ears and brain had broken down. There were no questions, none that he was aware of, at least. With the exception of Volkov, who raised his chin as though having heard his name spoken, not so much as a hair moved on any of the fifteen heads.

"I will speak with each of you individually later in the day," Bessarovich said, waving a hand to dismiss them. "Sergei Sergeievich, remain here with me a minute."

There was a shuffling of papers, a scraping of chair legs. On their way out the door, both Leonid Fishkin and Chief Vzyatin caught Propenko's eye and winked their congratulations.

The door bumped softly, leaving Propenko alone with Bessarovich in the large room. He took the seat beside her and endured a brief inspection. He could see grains of talcum powder on her cheeks, and fine scarlet threads crossing the whites of her eyes, but the rest of the room was a whirling blur. Bessarovich smiled warmly. "I can see you are surprised, Sergei."

"Shocked."

"This is no ordinary undertaking."

Not knowing what else to do, Propenko nodded.

"Do you understand what I'm trying to tell you?"

Propenko nodded again, though he did not have the slightest idea what she was trying to tell him. He could not remember ever having had a private conversation with Lyudmila Ivanovna; he was mildly surprised she even knew his name. He was Volkov's assistant for foreign visitors, stalled three-quarters of the way up the Council ladder, and she was a legend among Moscow progressives, linked, according to various sources, with Shevardnadze, with Yakovlev, with Yeltsin himself.

"You look baffled, Sergei."

"Shocked," he repeated, and Bessarovich laughed a hearty laugh, exposing a flash of gold molars.

She rested a hand on his forearm as though they were old friends. "You will be something of a public figure these next few weeks. A Director now, working with the Americans. You may find the position complicates your life in ways you cannot imagine."

"I understand."

"You'll be moving into a different weight class," she went on, and Propenko flushed. It was a compliment of sorts, an acknowledgment of his glorious socialist past. She had done research on him. "Should you begin to feel overwhelmed, I want you to contact me without hesitation. Call me regularly, two or three times a week, at least. And if something arises that you don't feel comfortable discussing over the phone, fly up to Moscow and we'll speak in person. Agreed?"

"Agreed," Propenko told her, but he was responding like a robot, waiting to be excused so he could go out into the hall and explore the boundaries of this dream. A Director! Working with Americans! He imagined calling Raisa and giving her the news, or surprising the family later that evening at the dacha.

"My single piece of advice would be this: Free yourself of all preconceptions."

"All preconceptions," Propenko repeated. It was eerily similar to advice he'd been given so many times in his boxing days. The mind should be empty, alert, free of expectations. "Expectations inhibit reflex." He nodded at Bessarovich now the way he'd so often nodded at his trainer, but his mind was elsewhere.

"Sergei," Bessarovich said sharply, bringing him back. "What do you know about this church watchman?"

At first, Propenko did not understand the question. He stared at Bessarovich, seeing the surface of powdered skin and green eyes and curled brown hair, but sensing something underneath as well. Already he was aware of certain preconceptions giving way. "Nothing at all," he said.

"But your daughter was very friendly with him, wasn't she?"

He felt a sliver of pain cross his forehead, temple to temple. It occurred to him that the whole meeting might have been a charade, a ruse intended to bring him to this point — to a betrayal he would have to endure until his last breath. Maybe Lydia was right: It was the thirties all over again, parents forced to denounce their own daughters.

Bessarovich was watching. Propenko nodded without breaking eye contact.

"And are you aware of what has been going on at the Church of the Sacred Blood?"

"Services, I suppose. I'm not a churchgoer, Lyudmila Ivanovna."

"Meetings," Bessarovich said. "Of a political nature."

"Impossible."

"Not impossible, Sergei. A fact."

"And Lydia was involved?" The words had simply flown out of his mouth, erupted. *And Lydia was involved?*

"You're asking me?"

Propenko hesitated only a second. There was no point in caution now. "If she was involved," he said, "I support her completely."

"You do? Are you certain?"

He felt the muscles around his throat constrict, trying to keep the words from escaping, turning his voice hoarse. "One hundred percent."

For perhaps five seconds, Bessarovich sat back in her chair and studied him, but it seemed to Propenko like days, months, half a lifetime. Her face was perfectly without expression. The woman was giving nothing away. Finally, she said, "A loyal father," in a tone he could not read, and ended the interview with the smallest of smiles. "This is a difficult assignment, Sergei. I wish you well."

Propenko left the conference room in a state of monumental confusion. It occurred to him, across a great, dreamy distance, that Bessarovich had said almost nothing about the particulars of his duties. He supposed that information was contained in the folder — which, along with his briefcase, he'd left behind on the conference table. He wandered down the corridor, found the rear door, and stepped out into the wind and sun.

Across the street from the Commerce and Industry Building was a small workers' cafe. The food was inedible — limp cucumbers in watery sour cream, soup that tasted like it had been seasoned with dirt — but not long ago Ranishvili had let it be known that a bit of cognac might be had there, even before one o'clock.

You were supposed to ask for Vadim at the back door and mention Ranishvili.

Propenko managed to thread his way through the traffic on the Prospekt. At the back door of the cafe, for ten rubles, Vadim obliged him with a mineral water bottle half-filled with diluted cognac, and Propenko stood behind the building, looking out at the flat wheat fields beyond the river, having at the liquor in quick hits.

After a few minutes, he placed the bottle carefully on the ground and, assuming the correct posture, shuffled his feet and threw a series of rights and lefts into the August air. He feinted with his jaw, threw a straight right hand, thought, *Director!* and sliced the sky with a combination of beautiful jabs and crosses. A short uppercut. *Volkov to Romania!* Two left jabs to the head, a hard right to the belly, a lightning left hand, one final, beautiful right cross, and he was standing over his opponent, caught in the steel gaze of a *babushka* taking a shortcut across the parking lot. The woman was holding tightly to the hand of a four-or-five-year-old boy, and they were both staring at him as if he were the Antichrist, a large-sized lunatic, father of political insurgents.

"*Boylnoi,*" the woman explained quietly to her grandchild. "Sick."

// CHAPTER 5

CZESICH was met at the embassy door by one of the gray-
uniformed KGB guards, who demanded his passport, and
then, since it was raining, spent an extra minute thumbing the
stamped pages, comparing the actual Anton A. Czesich — chilled
and unamused beneath a dripping umbrella — to the photo on the
first page. Thunder boomed and echoed and rain whipped around
them, but the game went on, part of a long-standing tit for tat even
glasnost had not been able to push aside. Czesich held the new
briefcase against his chest to keep it from getting wet. At last, the
guard handed the passport back, gave a sharp salute, and swept his
arm toward the entrance in a parody of welcome.

Inside, things were not much better. Ten feet from the entrance
was another set of doors that could be unlocked only by a Marine
standing in a glass booth. Opposite the booth stood the gray arch
of a metal detector, and in front of it an agitated crowd of Armenians who'd come seeking permission to immigrate. The Marine
guard was shouting at them in indecipherable South Carolina Russian: "PROHADITYA CHAIREZ METALICHISKI CONTROL!" Then in
English: "THEW THE MATAL DETAICTOR!" Then in a mixture of
the two: "GO THEW THE METALICHISKI DETAICTOR, GAWDAM-
MIT!"

The Armenians stood mute and puzzled before the arch of this
cold new world. Choice salamis and bottles of cognac protruded
from their raincoat pockets — bribes for the consular officials —
and they seemed to be wondering if this might be the time to hand
them over.

Czesich slipped forward, offered a translation to the couple at the head of the line, then presented his passport to the Marine and stated that he had a 6:00 P.M. appointment with the political affairs officer. The Marine made a phone call and buzzed him through, and Czesich was met beyond the doors by a handsome, blond-headed foreign service type who provided a name he failed to catch. It was a real problem of late, this thing with new names, part of a more general collapse. All his old strengths seemed to be abandoning him in middle age. He and his escort passed along the building's shabby, smoke-damaged corridors, mounted its uneven stairs, and ascended to the eighth floor in a grinding, thumping, plywood elevator. "Place is still a wreck," Czesich said. "That never changes."

His escort smiled a toothy, Ivy League smile, and said, "A mirror of our host country's hospitality," and Czesich disliked him immediately. "They're sending you into the swamps, I hear."

"I just came from the swamps," Czesich said. He'd meant Washington, with its equatorial Julys, but his companion took it wrong, frowned, looked at him as though he might be a closet anti-American, the type to sell missile secrets to the KGB.

His escort deposited him in a small waiting area and coldly wished him well, and Czesich sat there, hands clasped between his knees, sweating like a teenager on a date. There was a box of Italian nougat candy in the briefcase, but, as a gift, it seemed suddenly insufficient, less than what he felt, less than what he wanted to say. The scenario he'd been nourishing for the last month seemed impossible here in this broken-down building, a fantasy and nothing more.

At ten past six the door opened and Julia Stirvin appeared with one arm held straight out in front of her like a sword. "Wonderful to see you," she said.

Czesich thought, at first, it was Julie's idea of a joke. Keeping him waiting fifteen minutes when there was no one else in her office. A businesslike handshake instead of a kiss and a hug. All across the Atlantic he'd been picturing something quite different.

Julie's office, too, was more sterile and controlled than he'd expected, twelve feet by fifteen, with a plain blue carpet, a bulky desk on one side, and a sofa and two hard chairs on the other. She'd decorated the walls with portraits of American Indian chieftains, though, and their faces, so fierce and certain, touched him with a faint breath of hope.

Julie sat him on the sofa and took one of the chairs. Twenty-three years ago, they had been enthusiastic lovers, and she had been the startling beauty of the Photography USA staff. She was tall and elegant, still wonderful-looking at fifty-one, with large, pale eyes and dark hair swept severely back from her forehead and temples. Even in a prim, blue, knee-length dress with a short jacket, and even constrained by the posture of this office, her body moved with a lightness and ease that had nothing of the arid bureaucracy about it.

She crossed her legs and folded her hands in her lap, and for a few minutes Czesich was content just to look at her. "Do we have a little time?"

"I'm receiving a group of business types at the Ambassador's residence at seven, so we have half an hour or so. Care to join us?"

Czesich made a face, trying to get his balance back, waiting for the strange, sleety discomfort to thaw.

"Nothing in common with the American business community?"

"With any community." He let his eyes travel the room again.

"Family well?"

"The same," he said. "The situation hasn't changed since Upper Volta."

Julie smiled and he resisted the urge to ask about her family life, even more barren than his own, brothers and sisters strewn along the eastern seaboard like historical markers worthy of a few minutes' attention if you happened to be in the neighborhood, plus one wealthy, recent ex-husband playing golf somewhere in the bayous of the American South.

"Marie still hasn't found anyone else?" she said.

"It's not in her makeup."

"And you?"

The question sent a little pulse of feeling up through Czesich's chest and cheeks, but he shook his head and it passed.

"Is Michael well?"

"Fine." He shifted his eyes to the window. A few deft strokes, three questions, and she'd stripped him almost naked. Almost. As though it were a touchable thing, he could feel the meringue of diplomatic chitchat and clever office conversation clinging around him. His act. It occurred to him that he might be here — in this country and in the presence of this woman — because they were the only two places on earth where he knew how to scrape that soft protection away.

"Michael's out in Reno," he went on, measuring her, deciding how much to reveal. Julie's eyes and mouth seemed locked in an expression of polite interest, a diplomat's mask, a face to meet the faces that you meet. Czesich held his tongue.

Something between a sigh and a laugh escaped her. "Nevada," she said wistfully, looking over his shoulder at the stormy Moscow dusk. "A different planet."

"In some ways."

This always happened, Czesich reminded himself. Their first meeting was always on her turf, often in her office, and they always endured a few minutes of small talk and awkwardness, rifling through a series of topics — family, weather, politics, health — like gymnasts required to perform a program of mandatory exercises before getting on with the heart of the competition.

This time, though, the movements felt especially stale, her refuge especially safe and stifling and distant. She was a political affairs officer now, the third highest embassy official, single again; they were getting older. Czesich asked about President Bush's recent visit — she and the rest of the embassy staff had worked sixteen-hour days — then he stood and wandered the room, making a show of studying the rugged portraits, standing at the window watching the rain, fingering a small glass decoration on Julie's desk. "Congratulations, by the way," he said to her back.

"Thank you."

"It's a real achievement, battling the men in white shirts all those years and ending up here."

"From this vantage point the men in white shirts take on a completely different aspect, Chesi."

"Do they?" He was preparing himself to be disappointed, to hear her say that all of it was, in the final analysis, not only necessary, but admirable, that the men in white shirts fondling their forms and security regulations and titles, were, in fact, the true defenders of freedom.

"I see them as part of a great spiritual pollution."

He could have hugged her.

"Which is how you *always* saw them," she added graciously.

Czesich watched the blurry traffic on the Ring Road. "There's hope," he said, resuming his seat. "People change."

Julie smiled skeptically. "I remember you telling me once that the foreign service was the suburbia of the spiritual world."

"I was famous for comments like that. All my foreign service friends hate me now."

"You said if we stayed in we'd end up high priests of compromise, fat and sexless and safe."

He shrugged. She was rubbing his forty-nine-year-old face in his twenty-six-year-old words. He'd forgotten how much she liked to win, and how much old hurt still hung between them.

"And look how it turned out," he said, humoring her. "You're the one who stayed in, and you're thin and sexy."

"What about the safe part, and the compromise part?"

"You're batting .500."

They smiled, broke eye contact, and went some time without speaking — an entitlement of old intimacy. Czesich was caught up in a vapor of memories, scenes from a dozen exotic postings in which he and Julia Stirvin had played out their curious mix of sexual tension and a fascination with the workings of the world. Both of them had been nurtured on the milk of a Russian grandparent's embittered nostalgia, both had been haunted all their lives by this country's sorry history. It was a blood bond Julie could not have shared with her golf-playing Ted, and one he had never shared with Marie DeMarco. He wanted to revive it now, he'd come eight thousand miles to revive it, but he felt suddenly awkward and full of doubt. "Things were looking up here for a while," he said.

She nodded. Politics was their safest common language. "Did you read Puchkov's speech?"

"Of course. Filson posted it on the office bulletin board under my name. He's a big joker, Filson. When he's wired on coffee, he likes to come over to my cubicle and tell me I'm in all the KGB files and they're going to arrest me this time, throw me in the Lubyanka and yank my fingernails out. The day after Puchkov made that speech, Filson took his shoe off and pounded it on my desk. 'Shpie!' he yelled. 'Ve vill bury you!' "

"Amusing," Julie said, but she didn't seem amused.

"The secretaries liked it. See the boss. See the boss make Anton nervous. See Anton give the boss the finger when he turns his back." Out of habit, Czesich massaged his bad knee: he associated Filson with chronic pain. "He still can't pronounce my name. 'Not Sez-ik, Myron,' I keep telling him. 'Chez-ik, like in Czechoslovakia.' He's starting to get it, finally. I've been there twenty-three years."

Julie smiled, but did not meet his eyes, and Czesich saw a thin fissure open in her Great Wall of formality. For some reason, it frightened him.

"If you want to back out of this," she said after a moment, "I can arrange it."

"You're kidding."

"Not really."

"You *must* be kidding. I begged for this assignment. I love coming back here, you know that. Another week in that plastic office cubicle and I would have been institutionalized."

"There's trouble in Vostok, Chesi. Demonstrations. Talk of a miners' strike. Other things. There hasn't been food in their state markets for a month."

"War and rumor of war, what else is new? Vostok is famous for it. That's part of the reason I wanted this assignment. Somebody has to straighten the place out. Somebody has to feed the Vostokians."

"There was a murder there last night."

"So?"

She frowned. "An assassination."

"Of who?"

"A church worker."

"A church worker? So what? Someone was out to steal icons. Jule, we were in San Salvador together, remember? I ran exhibits in Uganda. In the off-season I live in D.C., remember? There's a murder there every few hours."

Julie was watching him closely now, and Czesich had the queasy sensation she was seeing beyond this resume of courage and down into a secret place that hid something quite different. The truth was, he'd had a bulletproof embassy car in San Salvador, and the truth was, there hadn't been a murder in his Washington neighborhood for several years.

"Some people think the fuse has been lit."

"Oh, Christ. Come on, Julie. People have been saying that here since the day Gorbachev moved into the Kremlin. Someone is always coming up with rumors of a right-wing conspiracy. It goes with the territory."

"Puchkov's told the whole country you're a spy."

"It's been said of me before."

She squinted at him. "You're not trying to be a hero, are you?"

"What hero?" he said, and to his amazement, to his shock, the words came out coated with an old East Boston inflection. Tony

Czesich speaking. He was standing on the corner in Maverick Square, nineteen years old, talking with his hands to show his friends he hadn't changed since starting college. Whattaya mean, hero? Whattaya talkin'? But Julie had him figured.

She smiled at the eruption of this other self, and what had been hovering beneath her official mask finally broke free. Czesich watched her jaw relax and her eyes lose a layer of caution. "Still trying to be the macho man," she said with a lovely smile. "I love your Italian half."

"Macho has nothing to do with it," he said. "If there's anyplace on earth I can handle myself it's here. It's in my blood, for Chrissakes, you should understand that. I grew up with my grandfather teaching me how to shoot hockey pucks in the backyard and lecturing me about the Bolshevik devils." Czesich was on the verge of slicing himself open and revealing the ruptures and tumors of masculine middle age — office humiliations and a cauterized marriage and sad one-night stands and a son who'd just about disowned him, all of it — when he caught a flicker of something new in her eyes. The beautiful face assumed a very subtle shading of treachery, the trademark of lifelong bureaucrats, the very thing he'd warned her about in his quixotic twenties. It suddenly seemed to him that even the small amount of nakedness he'd allowed himself so far had been a mistake. Led by an old telepathy, he said: "You're thinking of cutting the program."

Julie's eyes followed the pattern of the sofa for a few seconds before she looked up. "Only the program personnel. The ships have already docked and been unloaded. The trucks have just crossed the Soviet border at Brest. Too late to stop them."

"Why get me all the way over here, then?"

"I told you. Circumstances have changed in the last twenty-four hours."

It rang false. In the first place, Julie would not have heard about the death of a church watchman in Vostok, not this fast. The Vostok press — still under the thumb of Mikhail Kabanov, the city's fascist First Secretary — was not known for reporting provincial scandals that might or might not have a political dimension. And in the second place, it wasn't as though Czesich was leading a group of Cub Scouts into the provinces. He was alone. This was a pilot program. Both the well-fed and hungry halves of the world would be watching to see how it played out. "Are the Germans and French singing this tune?"

"We've spoken."

"Have you talked to Filson?"

"An hour ago."

"And?"

"He's going on vacation today, so he left the final decision up to Ambassador Haydock and the Secretary of State."

"Nice," Czesich said. "Cut bait and run. Leave three million dollars' worth of food to Kabanov and his KGB sharks. Hang Gorby out to dry. It's wimp diplomacy, Julie."

"Bad choice of words."

There was no change in her expression, and for a moment Czesich thought the case was already closed, that she'd let him fly across the ocean only because she'd wanted to have him see her like this, subject for a *Ms.* magazine profile, a PAO squeezing him in for thirty minutes at the end of her busy week. This would be some kind of ultimate gold medal in their twenty-three-year Olympics of affection and desertion.

"You realize the message you'll be sending Puchkov and his KGB friends, don't you?"

"We've taken that into consideration."

"So it's already decided?"

"No. We wanted to talk with you, Filson, Embassy Security. It's Washington's program, though we have a lot of say in the field implementation, as Filson acknowledged. You know the embassy has a policy of not sending government employees out into the provinces alone, which means we'd have to assign one of our own people to go with you, which means we have to take their well-being into consideration as well."

"Send me alone," he said.

"It would be tantamount to illegal."

Tantamount to illegal. Czesich shook his head. "Where's the fight, Jule?"

She closed her eyes for a few seconds in a pantomime of impatience. "Why does it matter so much? You've done this sort of thing all over the world."

"Not this sort of thing," Czesich corrected her. "And this isn't all over the world. This is the Soviet Union. This is their one shot. We cut Gorby loose now and Puchkov takes over and they'll sink back into oblivion for another few centuries."

"It's not the same country we were so fond of a few years ago, Chesi."

He was watching her, trying to see through the act. "I was here a year and a half ago. Just after I saw you and Ted in Sofia, remember?"

"Things change faster than that now." Julie tried to peek at her watch without letting him see. "We don't have to decide this today," she said, not kindly and not unkindly. Professionally. Diplomatically. In the vernacular of Foggy Bottom. "Let's go forward as planned for the time being — your tickets and visa are in order, I assume?"

He nodded.

"You're scheduled for a briefing on Wednesday with Embassy Security and then a face-to-face with Ambassador Haydock, the Large One himself."

"But my train leaves Wednesday morning."

She handed him a sheet of paper with his typed schedule. "We'll change the tickets to Thursday, if we decide to send you."

Czesich glanced at the paper, scrambling. Julie, he told himself, was just not ready to let down her guard, not here, at least. The great advantage of having fought the white-shirted men all these years, the great reward for a lifetime of shrinking ideals, was that she'd finally ascended to a place where deference would be automatic, respect institutionalized. Marines would salute, and, in the smaller cities especially, the Soviets would turn cartwheels trying to impress her. He told himself that some part of her needed to hold on to a little of that, even with him, perhaps especially with him. It was her own kind of armor, and at the moment he wanted nothing more than to pierce it and see if there was still something warm and real below. "There's an appointment missing," he said, tapping the new schedule with one finger.

"What?"

"Dinner with the political affairs officer on Saturday night."

She looked away, then back. "The political affairs officer is tied up until Tuesday. With the business delegation."

Czesich made himself smile. "Tuesday night then, since everything's being put forward."

"Fine."

He knew she wanted him to leave now, that she was resisting the impulse to stand and signal his dismissal. There was a way he wanted this conversation to end, a way he'd imagined it ending, but the proper words eluded him. "I still think about you," he blurted out, standing. "I carry you around the globe with me."

Julie stood, too, and he saw the disguise slip. Her eyebrows quivered once. She tried a frown and could not quite pull it off. She appeared to be wondering where the words had come from, which negotiating position, which compartment of the diplomat's arsenal. It did not seem to occur to her that he had spoken in haste and from the heart.

When she opened the door for him, the knuckle-jawed foreign service officer was in the waiting area, watching, and there was something about his plain gray suit, and the bare painted walls, and the government-issue furniture, that made it almost impossible to do, but Czesich kissed the PAO anyway, lips to lips. Julie pulled back slightly, embarrassed.

He gave himself into the custody of his escort, and they squeezed into the elevator and made the jerky, silent drop to ground level.

"Plans for the weekend?" Czesich's companion asked as they walked down the long, narrow corridor toward the front door. The tone was falsely casual, expatriate friendly, something of the interrogator in it, something of Embassy Security.

Czesich glanced into the man's face, then away. Spying on our own people now, he thought. Catching the Soviet infection. "A drink at the British Embassy," he lied. "Church. The Izmailovo flea market."

"Careful out there," the man said. It sounded like a warning.

Czesich made himself smile and shake a clammy hand, and he went past the Marine and out into the street.

The rain had abated. The briefcase knocked against his thigh, rattling the box of candy. He wandered along in the general direction of the metro station, the pavement glistening now, bus tires hissing, the spacious and shadowy Moscow evening rising up around him in a way that reminded him more of Nevada than of Washington. It was that kind of place, Russia. There was something illogical in the air, a warm mysterious hope that flew in the face of centuries of bad history. He told himself it was the place of his heart, the place to be if the heart needed mending.

// CHAPTER 6

PROPENKO stood in front of his apartment building, looking down October Avenue toward the river. He could not see the Don itself — only the gray crest of the avenue pavement, and, on the far bank, two kilometers south, the tops of slag heaps and factory smokestacks — but he could see that a heavy fog was already filling the valley between. At dusk the fog would spill over the banks and spread south across the industrial plain and north over the city, swaddling the buildings on October Avenue and soothing Vostok in a damp, white peace. At the dacha, fifty kilometers north, the night would be clear and mild.

Lydia banged out the front door carrying a basket of towels and sheets. Propenko helped her squeeze the basket into the Lada's trunk and tried to start a conversation. "No rain this weekend."

"Good," she said distractedly, and then over her shoulder as she turned back toward the building: "Grandmother's waiting for the lift. One more load."

Propenko watched her bare, sturdy calves — so like his own — as she went up the walkway, watched her toss her hair and yank open the sticking metal door and start up the stairs at a run. When his little celebration in the parking lot had ended, and when his colleagues at the Council had finished stopping by with their congratulations, sincere and otherwise, he'd sat alone in his office for half an hour, mulling over the conversation with Bessarovich. It irritated him to think Lydia might be flirting with politics and not mentioning it at home. It did not fit the image he had of her, of their family, and in some way he could not yet understand, it frightened him. The murder frightened him, the shortages, the talk of a miners' strike. A thin, persistent fear slid through his arteries and veins, haunting his sleep and sullying his waking hours.

It was a typical Friday evening in August: half the people who lived in the building were packing up and heading off, by car and *elektrichka*, to their dachas, so the elevator was excruciatingly slow. By the time Raisa and Marya Petrovna finally appeared at the door, Lydia — who'd gone down and up and down by the stairs — was right behind them. They had to rearrange things in order to get the trunk to close. Propenko helped Marya Petrovna into the back seat, squeezed himself in behind the wheel, and they started off, the Lada coughing and sputtering as it warmed up.

"You remembered to lock the door, Lydochka?" Raisa said, half-turning.

In the mirror, Propenko watched Lydia frown. There were no tears now, but she was uncharacteristically sullen, and he decided she was working her way through the idea of death. Though it had been almost fifteen years, he could still remember this process, this wrestling with absence. There had been no warning then, either. His parents had flown to Lvov for a cousin's funeral and perished on the way home when their jet dropped into the river, a hundred meters short of the airport. They were with him one day, eating and laughing and arguing, and nonexistent the next. Part of him puzzled over it still.

October Avenue was slow in both directions, people coming home from work, people heading off to their dachas. Raisa stretched her arm along the top of his seat and rested two fingers on his shoulder. "Traffic doesn't matter," she said. "Nothing matters when you're going to the dacha."

"Whether you remembered to bring toilet paper matters," Marya Petrovna said.

"I remembered."

Propenko sneaked another glance in the mirror. Tikhonovich's funeral would be delayed until Father Alexei's return — Friday, he thought Lydia had said. She was staring out the side window now, traveling another road. It had taken Raisa and Marya Petrovna half an hour to talk her into coming to the dacha instead of staying home all weekend and mourning alone, or weeping with the old women at the church.

Propenko turned right onto Kaminskaya Street, traversed a shortcut cratered with potholes, and merged into heavy traffic on the Prospekt of the Revolution. He drove past his office without mentioning the new assignment.

Prospekt Revoliutsii was a wide, six-lane boulevard that ran east-west through Vostok's heart. It was split by trolley tracks, flanked, near the Center, by a few blocks of four-story granite buildings that had survived the war and now contained luxurious apartments where the First Secretary and the rest of the important criminals lived. Metal grillwork in the stair rails, curving balconies, guards at the door, limousines. Propenko had driven past them so many times he was no longer surprised by the luxury, alien as it was on the bland Vostok landscape. Marya Petrovna reminded him. This was the point in the trip where she always had a foul word for the men who'd broken up her life, and today was no exception. "Sons of bastards," Propenko heard her mutter. It was a ritual.

The Lada stalled once, and he made a mental note to have Anatoly find him new spark plug wires. They crept from stoplight to stoplight, sunset showing red in the rearview mirror and in a few of the higher windows. Soon, the homes of the Party bosses gave way to a row of nine-story shoeboxes like the one the Propenkos lived in. These buildings looked as though they'd been assembled by drunken cosmonauts and dropped from orbit onto their treeless, grassless lots — a thousand identical rust-stained balconies; ten thousand concrete slabs, cracked and broken around the edges and pasted to each other with toothpaste stripes of gray mortar. The exterior corners weren't straight. The roofs leaked from the day they were set. Pipes rattled, toilets groaned, fissures ran like lightning bolts across the ceilings and walls. He was sure the people who lived here had bribed and flattered and worked overtime for years in order to be placed on the list for one of these apartments. He remembered his own years of waiting. He remembered the time Malov had called him at midnight and asked him to come help push his car out of a ditch in Lepinskoe, a dirt village where Malov's mistress kept a dacha. Malov had paid him back for it — with a dinner somewhere or other — had thanked him profusely, had cloaked the whole thing in the guise of Commerce and Industry camaraderie, but both of them understood the subtext. An hour's drive at midnight, and he had done it. Practically cut off one of his balls and handed it over in exchange for Malov's help procuring four rooms in a leaky concrete box next to a plant that made tin cans.

And what was the alternative? This was the alternative, what they were passing now, these two-room log cabins on the city's dirty cuff. Huts with cracked windows and a rusty coal stove, an outhouse in one corner of the backyard, a cold-water spigot down the block. These people might as well hang a sign on their front gates: Here live those with no connections, the honest and the lazy and the unlucky, the true workers of the world.

Raisa moved her fingers back and forth on his shoulder, and Propenko realized he'd been clenching his teeth. It was an odd time for bitterness — there was a bottle of champagne hidden in the trunk; he was on the way to his sanctuary, his refuge.

They reached the city limits. To the left spread a vacant lot littered with broken concrete beams and truck skeletons. To the right was the airport and the brown loop of river into which his parents' flight had dived on a foggy summer evening like this. The memory flared and burned tonight, unusually so.

Directly in front of them, twelve o'clock on the traffic circle, stood the elevated glass booth of the Government Auto Inspectorate. A GAI officer was on the street there, gripping one end of his striped baton in each hand, his booted feet spread, a white whistle in his mouth. As soon as the Propenkos' Lada merged into the circle, the officer strode two steps into traffic and pointed his baton. They all heard the whistle.

"He means us, Seryozha."

Propenko cursed under his breath and pulled to the side of the road. Law-abiding citizen that he was, he kept his passport on his person at all times, and as the inspector sauntered toward them he slipped a ten-ruble note between the back pages. The inspector saluted and peered in at each passenger. He asked Propenko to get out. Propenko did so.

The inspector was about his own height, ruddy and cold-eyed, near thirty. He tucked his baton under one arm and opened the passport, pinching the back pages together as if to prevent red currency notes from falling out. He peered into Propenko's face, then at the photograph, and made a show of examining each line — name, city of residence, nationality — glancing at Propenko from time to time as if these facts could be verified by one's mouth or eyes.

Propenko waited stiffly, feeling the daylight waning, watching car after car slide off the traffic circle and head north, toward the dachas. The inspector was on the next page now, reading at the speed of an eight-year-old. Perhaps it was the arrogance in his cherry face, or the three women waiting in the car, that made Propenko say, after he'd been standing there several minutes: "I'm friends with Chief Vzyatin."

It was a mistake. The inspector turned down the corners of his lips. He flipped a page, stalling, dragging out the interview, considering a fine. Though he was no doubt familiar with Vzyatin's name, he answered only indirectly to the militia chief, and seemed unimpressed by the alleged friendship. Here on the road, he was the real authority, and he knew it. "We had a report of a rapist leaving the city in a red Lada," he said in a flat Ukrainian accent.

"Not me," Propenko said. He was ashamed for having brought Vzyatin into it. He wondered if Lydia had heard.

"A red Lada," the inspector repeated, while over the uniformed shoulder Propenko watched half a dozen red Ladas slip past.

At last, the inspector pressed the passport closed and returned it with a snap of his wrist. He made a final, cursory inspection of the car and its passengers, saluted, spun on a bootheel, and strode away.

Behind the wheel again, Propenko felt a hot prickling in his cheeks. The Lada did not start on the first two tries, and when the engine did turn over, and when he'd headed out onto the open highway, he made a point of bringing the needle well up over the speed limit and holding it there.

"Odd," Raisa said.

Propenko squeezed the wheel. Something in her voice told him she was going to start in where she'd left off at breakfast, that she'd imagined a link between Lydia's involvement in the church and the Government Auto Inspectorate, that she believed the Propenko family had been singled out for persecution, that the *chekisti* were beginning a campaign of harassment. "They're chasing someone in a red Lada," he said. "A rapist."

Raisa gave him a look.

"All swine, all of them," Marya Petrovna muttered.

Lydia seemed to have been summoned back from her mourning. "Did he take the bribe, Pa?"

Propenko shook his head.

"Because you mentioned your friend, maybe."

"Odd," Raisa repeated in the same suspicious tone, and Propenko bit the inside of his cheek to keep from shouting at her. He could feel a black mood overtaking him, rising out of its deep, invisible valley and spreading behind his eyes. He did battle with it. He reminded himself he had just been appointed Director of an important project — by Bessarovich herself — promoted over several more likely candidates. When that failed, he brought to mind his boxing days, but the boxing memories were of another era, as fine and faded as the socialist dream. What saved him, finally, was simply the landscape, Vostok's flat outskirts giving way to wheat field, wheat field to lush pastureland. As the highway turned northwest, away from the river, the terrain lifted and rolled, and took on, in patches, a beard of forest. Propenko admitted to a certain sentimentality about country life. Never having lived outside a city for more than a few weeks at a time, he harbored a notion that people who looked at woods and fields every day did not suffer from depression. He was never depressed at the dacha, and neither, from what he could tell, was Raisa or Marya Petrovna or Lydia. He could not remember his parents arguing there, or his sister weeping drunk, or the neighbors shouting at each other as they so often did in the concrete corridors of October Avenue. The countryside was medicine for him, and he took it gratefully. By the time they turned off the highway and started down the dusty road that led to the colony of dachas, he was almost at peace.

The dacha community had been built on a hundred hectares of rolling land that had belonged to one of Vostok's prerevolutionary mayors. It was a choice spot, bordered by a clean river, surrounded by woods, and, even divided up into a checkerboard of thirty-meter parcels, it somehow retained the magical feeling of unfenced Russian soil. After decades of obedient service as a correspondent for the newspaper *Soviet Labor*, Propenko's father had been granted a plot here in the early sixties. At first, he and his family had used the land only for growing vegetables, but, little by little, making use of his extensive connections in the building trades and his son's strong back, the elder Propenko had constructed a dacha — four square rooms with a loft that could sleep six.

The dacha came into view now, first in a line of eleven, a cinderblock temple with a peaked metal roof, and small wooden porches front and rear. Propenko parked, the family unpacked the car like a practiced team and assembled on the front porch in the very last of the light. He could hear the sound of hurried hammering a few lots away. He could smell meat being roasted nearby. Across the picket fence he and his father had built, and he and his daughter had recently repainted, he could see a light in the neighboring kitchen. "Lydia," he said, "go next door and get Vladimir Victo-rovich. I have a surprise."

He retrieved the bottle from the trunk — he'd packed it in ice in a towel, and it was wet and still cool. Raisa dragged the heavy wooden coffee table out from the living room and pushed it near the heavy wooden porch chairs. Marya Petrovna brought out glasses and plates and the fresh bread they'd brought from the city. When Lydia returned, their Bolshevik-hating neighbor was with her, smil-ing and tipsy and holding a block of cheese in the crook of one elbow.

"Sons of bitches are murdering people now."

Vladimir Tolkachev had been Propenko's father's oldest friend. They'd grown up together on Engels Street, been drafted into the army at the same time, attended the university together after the war. Propenko loved him like an uncle.

"The son of a bitch Kabanov is behind it," Tolkachev said.

"Behind everything," Marya Petrovna agreed. "The hidden hand."

Propenko watched Lydia out of the tops of his eyes. She was not eating, not listening.

"The other son of a bitch, Puchkov, is his good friend."

Marya Petrovna grunted. Raisa's shoulders were hunched, her mood going flat. Propenko felt himself stalked by a pessimistic demon: he had a few moments of peace, then the demon tapped him on the shoulder; a bit of good news, and the demon weighed in with some bad.

"The miners will fix them," Marya Petrovna said. She had been saying it since Lydia was in diapers. She followed the miners' strikes like a soccer fan following league games.

Propenko popped the cork into the front yard and filled the glasses. "I have an announcement," he said, and he paused, unable to resist a bit of melodrama. "An American food distribution program will be coming to the city next week, and this morning I was appointed Director."

To his astonishment, Raisa, Tolkachev, and Marya Petrovna let out with loud cheers. The women got up and hugged him where he sat, their fleshy arms around his neck and their breath against his cheeks. His friends at the office had made a big fuss, too, kidding him about trips to New York and hard-currency accounts, but he had not expected this kind of reaction at home. This was something right out of his pineapple dream, and he didn't understand it until

Raisa pressed their faces together and said, "Some *good* news, finally."

He felt Lydia squeeze in against him and lean down with her congratulations. "God bless you, Pa," she said, draping an arm around his neck, dripping tears. He put a hand on her shoulder and felt her trembling beneath it.

The fine August night fell. They drank the champagne slowly, adjusting themselves to a country pace. Over a dinner of fresh vegetables, fresh bread, and sour cream, Tolkachev ranted on about Mikhail Lvovich Kabanov, Vostok's son-of-a-bitch First Secretary, and his fellow sons of bitches in Moscow — Pavlov and Puchkov and Alksnis. Marya Petrovna nodded on her wrinkled neck, added an occasional word, crushed an occasional mosquito against her knee. They spiced this gray-headed duet with questions about the food program: How many Americans would be coming to Vostok? Would the Soviet Director's family and friends get an introduction? Would the Soviet Director's daughter get to practice her English with a native speaker? What kind of food would be distributed? To whom?

Propenko meted out his small store of information gladly, but he was playing everything down now, feeling a small serpent of concern slithering through the rooms of his mind. They talked and joked and complained for more than an hour, but he was watching Lydia the whole time, unable to celebrate without her. When Tolkachev left, and Marya Petrovna and Raisa went inside to make up the beds, he asked her to join him in a walk.

They went slowly along the dark road, picking their way past stones and potholes, not talking. Crickets trilled and whistled. On one of the back lots someone bleated out a Ukrainian folk song to the accompaniment of a strummed guitar.

"My father's mother was a believer, you know," Propenko said, hoping an old family secret might open her up. "When you said 'God bless you' a little while ago it reminded me of her. She said that all the time."

A shadow passed on the path and greeted them by name.

"Before the war it was a big risk to go to church," Propenko went on, telling her everything she already knew. "My father was an obedient communist, and here was his own mother, going to church services, blessing people around the house, crossing herself. It made for a lot of trouble."

"Obedient communists always make for a lot of trouble," Lydia said, and Propenko felt vaguely offended.

To their right and behind them, the moon cleared the tops of the trees, one day past full. The church watchman, Propenko remembered Vzyatin saying, had been lured outside and shot in the churchyard, a fine target this time of month.

"I wanted to tell you this morning," he said, when they'd walked almost to the end of the road. "Your mother and I both wanted to tell you . . . how sorry we are about your friend."

"More than a friend."

"Of course."

Beyond the last dacha, the road deteriorated, ending in a patch of weeds and a small pile of construction debris. A breeze chased off most of the mosquitoes. Propenko sat on a twisted wooden beam and motioned Lydia down beside him. What he wanted was to strip away the awkwardness that had somehow built up between them over the past few months. It had become clear to him in that time that Lydia wanted to step away from him and from Raisa, that she was attempting to shed an old skin they had fitted her with when she enrolled in the university, that she was trying to take her place among them not as an adolescent or a student, but as an adult. He was not opposed to it. He'd seen the damage done to his sister by parents who insisted on retaining control over her well into her thirties. His father, especially, had been unable to loosen his grip, and Sonya had exacted her revenge with drink and prolonged dependence and a hasty, miserable marriage that ended badly. Upon her parents' sudden death she was cast out into the world like a waif, a kite whipping, held to earth by one somber younger brother. Emotionally, she was half Lydia's age, and Propenko was wary of repeating that particular family tragedy.

Even so, he could not quite break the pattern. When he spoke to Lydia these days he heard only a father's voice, not a friend's. And she paid him back with occasional outbursts at the dinner table, allusions to "cowardly Moscow bureaucrats" and "Gorbachevian puppets," hurting him without intending to. Their differences were mostly generational. He was an obedient communist, had always been, had always believed in the principles of the Party — volunteerism, egalitarianism, modesty — even in the face of their profound and repeated corruption. Like their battered president, he still clung to the rusty old structure and hoped someday to see it reformed, while all Lydia wanted was to tear it down and start fresh.

After her periodic outbursts, he retreated, by reflex, into a semi-formal paternal authority. Fine, invisible curtains dropped into place between them.

Tonight he wanted to pull them all down. "It's not exactly the same thing," he said, "but when your grandmother and grandfather died, I couldn't do anything for weeks. I sat in my office looking out the window, or I stayed home and slept, or just walked, or worked out at the gym for three or four hours at a time. You were too small to remember."

At first, Lydia did not look at him or speak, and Propenko worried that the reference to childhood had wounded her.

"I'm just the opposite," she said at last, staring back down the road. "I *want* to work."

"Well, that's fine." Why was this so difficult? "You can work around here with me tomorrow. Classes will be starting soon, you can —"

"I'm taking over Tikhonovich's duties at the church."

"What? What duties?"

"All the duties. Caretaking the church." Lydia tucked her hair back over one ear and looked at him defiantly, her face all shadows, and moonlight, and innocent sexuality. She'd inherited her mother's big bosom and wide-set warm eyes and his own athletic build — all the most dangerous traits for a woman, Propenko sometimes thought, all the things that would draw men to her like sharks to hot blood. It was a subject they had never broached.

And the political meetings? he wanted to ask, but before the sentence reached his lips it somehow transformed itself into, "And your studies?"

"Once school starts I'll work after classes and on weekends."

He started to object. He started to say, But you didn't ask us, or But it will be dangerous there now, or But your mother will be worried constantly, or But you're only twenty. He phrased a question about Father Alexei's return, then one about the funeral, but spoke neither of them.

Lydia's sadness was gone, supplanted by a low-burning fury. "There are two options in our country now," she said in a sure voice, an adult's voice. "Either you wait, or you do something."

Propenko waited.

// CHAPTER 7

CZESICH would have preferred to dine at one of Moscow's *kooperativi*, the small, privately owned places Gorbachev had legalized in the late eighties, but Julie told him the *kooperativi* had all fallen under the control of organized crime now, and she wouldn't feel right spending her money there.

"What's wrong with organized crime food?" he teased her over the phone. "Some of the best restaurants I've ever eaten at were owned by the mob, what's wrong with that? You don't stop putting your rubbish out on the sidewalk just because it's trucked away by organized crime, do you? A person has to eat."

But she said it would send the wrong message, so he'd ended up making reservations at the Ladoga, one of the huge state restaurants where the waiters and waitresses served you on a bribes-only basis.

When he arrived, Czesich said the magic words, "American Embassy," and the *administratr* led him through a crowd of couples pleading for a seat, through a set of ornate doors, across an enormous, chandeliered room spotted with empty tables, and pointed him toward an alcove off the dance floor.

Julie kissed him lightly on the mouth.

Though it did not seem so at first glance, there were two menus at these places, the menu-for-show and the actual menu. The menu-for-show was a large cardboard affair listing dozens of dishes — crab salad, pork chops, carrots in cream sauce — that had not been served here since Chekhov. These foods were available *v principye* — in principle — which meant *in your imagination*, or *in the afterlife*, or *in the years before Lenin*.

What was actually available consisted of those six or eight items in the huge menu-for-show that had prices typed beside them. And even these were subject to the mood swings of the chef and the whims of corrupt food-service *apparatchiki.*

"So are you over your jet lag yet, Anton Antonovich?" Julie wanted to know. She was free of the office now, and warmer.

"Just about." He searched the huge room for a waiter. "I've been walking all day. I could eat a cow."

"Do you still get snappish that way when you're hungry?"

"Worse," he said. "Positively menstrual."

He'd forgotten what a beautiful laugh she had.

A few more lucky diners straggled through the door. The scene reminded Czesich of the Dodgems at Revere Beach, the sadistic carny ticket taker flexing his tattooed triceps and letting kids one by one onto the black metal floor, the kids hurrying toward the newest cars, trying not to run, smiling as though they'd been admitted to heaven.

On the other side of the dance floor a wedding party was into the dessert course, and beyond them, half a football field away, two waiters stood at a large table lazily folding napkins. Czesich raised an arm. One of the waiters seemed on the verge of acknowledging him, then let his eyes float on up to the tattered velvet drapes.

"Not even bread and butter, for God's sake."

Julie watched him suffer, and he exaggerated it a bit for her entertainment. He felt hopeful tonight, capable of taming his recent inner commotion, capable of getting Julie to enjoy his company again. In the days since their embassy meeting, he'd twice visited an old dissident friend in the capital, and a bit of the woman's Russian resilience seemed to have worn off on him.

Another blue-coated waiter appeared in the middle distance. Czesich gave him a signal. "Right back, right back," the waiter called as he scurried toward the swinging kitchen doors.

As conspicuously as possible, Czesich took an unopened pack of cigarettes from his sport jacket and placed it between his forearm and Julie's, in plain view. Within thirty seconds a mustachioed waiter had stopped by with bread, two wet pats of butter, two bottles of mineral water, promising to return "in a tiny second" to take their order. He eyeballed, but did not touch, the cigarettes.

"Amazing how it has to be Marlboros," Julie observed.

Czesich was buttering two slices of bread at once. "I made the mistake of using Winstons for a cab ride one time. The driver nearly spit on me."

"It's the cowboy thing. Marlboro Man. The black marketeers really get into that."

"I haven't seen as many of them on the streets this time," Czesich said. The first bite of bread had calmed him. "When I was here on the Design-USA show they were stalking the hotels like vultures."

"Puchkov's on a crusade to clear out all vestiges of black market activity. The scourge of Western decadence and all that, you know."

He knew. It was not the right time to start talking about Puchkov. "Champagne, vodka, or wine?"

"Couldn't we go nonalcoholic just once?"

"Offensive to local community standards."

"Wine."

Czesich caught the waiter's eye and tapped a finger against the side of his throat. "A bottle of Tsinandali," he said, when the man approached.

Before Czesich could bring up the subject of food, the waiter smirked and made for the kitchen. Czesich nearly went after him, but restrained himself. The key thing tonight was to seem level-headed, responsible, the kind of man who could be dispatched to the provinces, alone, without risk.

"How did you spend your weekend?"

He gave the short answer. He'd visited some of his favorite places — the small working church across from the Park of Economic Achievements, Kholomenskoe Monastery, the neighborhood near the Canadian Embassy. He did not say he'd walked up and down the bending four-hundred-year-old streets there marveling at the pastel buildings and formulating a strategy. He did not say he'd spent most of Monday and Tuesday stocking up on food and gift items at the hard-currency stores and the embassy commissary, or that he'd inflated the Food Distribution Pilot Program into a vision of Russia's salvation, and his own.

"So you still go to church?"

"More and more, lately," he said. "For the singing, mostly, but not just for the singing. Yourself?"

"Not since Ted."

"How is Ted?"

"Ted golfs. Ted drives his Mercedes down to South Carolina

about this time of year and putts and bogeys and whatnots all winter. He sent me a postcard from somewhere in New Jersey last month saying he'd hit a hole in one. I was overjoyed."

"Bravo." Czesich went for another slice of bread. Across the way the wedding party was getting drunk and loud. The mustachioed waiter was in exile. "What was it like, living with Ted?" he said, trying to sound casual.

"Ted," Julie began, and Czesich cocked an ear for every nuance, followed every change in intonation, every flicker of the eye. "Ted was the eternal optimist. It was helpful for a few years, then it began to get boring. I kept wanting him to get sick or something, just once, just the flu even. He was such a bull."

"And how was Ted in bed?"

Julie pursed her lips in disapproval. "You've been drinking."

"Nothing."

She looked away, then back. "Magnificent," she said. Unconvincingly. "Notice I don't ask that about Marie."

"Bravo."

"You *have* been drinking."

"Only a quick one at the hotel before setting out."

Julie didn't ask about Marie because she already knew. Twenty-three years ago they'd lain naked and sweating in a Novosibirsk hotel room and she'd asked him to describe his fiancée's lovemaking. "Very Roman Catholic," he'd said, licking sweat off her shoulder. He had an excellent memory for that type of thing, for all his charming disloyalties.

A sound like metal barrels being smashed together echoed in the big room. Czesich looked up and saw that the band had taken the stage. *"Gospodi pomilui,"* he said. "Father have mercy." He stood, and holding a reasonable expression on his face until Julie could no longer see him, made for the swinging doors.

The kitchen walls were covered with white tiles, and the air was full of steam. Half a dozen waiters lounged about, smoking, unfazed by the presence of a well-dressed foreigner in their midst. They glanced up without expression and went back to their vacant staring or their laconic wiping of clean glasses with clean cloth napkins or their tapping of foreign cigarette ash into tinfoil ashtrays. Two chefs slammed things around behind a steamy, white-tiled counter.

Czesich surveyed this circus. Ordinarily it would have amused him — especially after the drinks at the hotel — but his stomach was crawling, his mouth moist, his blood chemistry turning frantic. It was in the genes. His father had always paced the kitchen like a tiger before dinner, had started a small fistfight one humid summer night in line at the Dairy Queen in Maverick Square. As a precaution, Czesich pushed his hands down into his pants pockets.

He made it a habit here to keep dollars in the right pocket, rubles and kopeks in the left. The embassy still had a strict policy against using dollars anywhere but in the hard-currency Beriozka stores or the hard-currency hotel bars, and, technically, it was against Soviet law. But he was beyond all that now.

He took the mustachioed waiter off to one side and put a hand on his shoulder to keep his attention. The other hand pinched a bill off the roll in his right pocket — it turned out to be a ten — and pressed it into the waiter's palm. The waiter glanced down and made the bill disappear.

"Listen," Czesich said, pushing his face close, Soviet-style. "I'm going to ask that woman to marry me tonight and I want the best you have — black caviar, lamb, tomatoes, a little cognac afterward."

"No tomatoes tonight," the waiter said. "Tomatoes finished."

"Nonsense. I just saw you bring some to the next table."

The waiter shrugged. "Maybe a few small ones in storage."

"Fine. Bring the wine and some kind of *zakuski* right away."

Czesich squeezed the waiter's shoulder in a brotherly fashion and went out into a deafening rendition of "I Just Called to Say 'I Love You.' "

Julie raised her eyebrows at him. She was wearing dangling gold earrings with malachite stones. "Man talk?" she shouted over the band.

"Of the purest variety. I told him I was going to propose to you tonight, so act as if."

She smiled, but there was a small trouble in her face he could not read.

Nearby, couples were dancing wildly out of rhythm.

"How did Ted propose?"

"Why the sudden fascination with Ted? You had seven years to ask about him."

"I couldn't ask these things while you were still married. It wouldn't have been right."

"Male code of honor?"

"Something like that."

Their waiter brought the wine and a small bowl of caviar surrounded by spears of cucumber and flowered radishes. Diners at
the neighboring tables stared.

"He took me to the Riviera — Bandol — and proposed on the
beach after an exquisite dinner."

"Very nice."

"I turned him down."

"Hard on Ted."

"I was about to leave for the posting in Morocco and he still had
his business in Baltimore. I wasn't interested in a long-distance
marriage, and I told him so."

"And he said he'd come golf Rabat for a few years, work on his
sand wedge." Czesich was smearing caviar on a piece of bread as if
it were peanut butter and experiencing a twinge of guilt. Outside
these privileged walls, people were standing an hour in line for
bread; caviar, once a middle-class delicacy, was as scarce as
Brezhnev's name on a street sign.

"Ted sold his business to his son and came to Morocco with me.
And he didn't golf, either. That's what's so intriguing about the
man. He's perpetually content. If his life consists of running a Mercedes dealership seven days a week, he's happy. If it's sitting by the
pool in Rabat and going to embassy functions at night, he's happy
with that, too."

"A man of principle."

"Not especially, but a good man."

"I liked him right away."

"Everybody does. It took me the longest time to understand
what was wrong." The band was playing Deep Purple, and Julie
was still having to shout, and as she said "wrong" a speck of moist
bread the size of a sesame seed flew out and stuck on her chin. "Ted
didn't know anything about suffering," she yelled. "He was kind
enough. If you were ill or having a bad time of things, he'd bring
you medicine or ask what he could do to help, say he was sorry. It
was sincere, but empty. He just couldn't relate."

"No Russian blood," Czesich said. "Go like this."

Julie used her napkin. "It came to me finally that we were never
really going to have anything beyond a pleasant sexual friendship,
and that wasn't enough for me. And there was nothing I could do
to change it."

"You could have tried talking to him."

"I did, several times. It was like —"

"Trying to describe lovemaking to a virgin."

"I was going to say like trying to describe the Soviet Union to someone who's never been here. What's the matter with you tonight? You're just wisecracks and sex. It's unlike you."

"I'm nervous for some reason."

"Why?"

"Things have gone empty on me," Czesich said, but it was not what he'd planned to say, and it came out halfway between facetious and self-pitying, all wrong.

"I'm sorry. I was going on about Ted. I didn't really ask."

"No matter," he said, but that came out wrong, too.

Now that the band noise had finally subsided for a minute, neither of them could find anything to say. They heard shouting in the kitchen. The waiter brought their food — cubes of lamb and onion and one small portion of tomatoes — and set out the plates with a flourish. "Fine?" he said to Czesich.

"Perfect." The waiter raised a brow at Julie and went off.

"Still writing?" Czesich asked her.

Julie shrugged. She'd once confessed to a desire to write novels, and every time he brought it up now she seemed to think he was poking fun. "A journal. A literary journal, half about the Soviets and the embassy, half about me. I started it after Ted and I split up. As a therapy substitute." She tried a smile.

"Do you regret not having children?"

"Sometimes." The trouble was back in her face. "What does that have to do with anything?"

"When do you regret it most?"

"When I hear other women talking about the birth. Why?"

"I don't know," Czesich said. "Something about Ted made me think . . . I had these very explicit fatherhood fantasies when Marie was pregnant. It was always a boy, and I always pictured him about eight or ten. We'd be skating together on a frozen pond or just sitting someplace having a lemonade and talking, but there would always be this perfect rapport."

She nodded, slicing off a small piece of lamb.

"And it was a little bit like that with Mike, for about seven years. We lived in this yolk of mutual respect and then the yolk broke and everything has been slightly sticky since then, never quite right."

"But there were moments."

"Of course. I was just wondering if Ted had somehow figured

out a way to stay in that state forever. So there's not such a big gap between what is and what you want."

"Money helps."

"It's more than money. Religion, maybe."

"Not with Ted." Julie smiled. "It's just his nature. He's even content with divorce." She made a movement with her hand as if to say, Enough of that. Her earrings shook and glittered, and Czesich wondered if they were a gift, and from whom. "How is Michael?"

"Michael's gay."

"You never told me," Julie said, as if Czesich had known it forever.

"He lives in Reno and I think he's dealing drugs or selling his body or both, because he has no visible means of employment and he sends Marie checks every month."

"Does she know?"

"No. He asked me not to tell her."

"Does it upset you?"

"For health reasons, of course it upsets me. Prostitution — if it is prostitution — upsets me first. Drugs upsets me second. What he does with his genitals, really, honestly, doesn't. After I got over the initial shock it seemed obviously right for him." Czesich sucked on a piece of lamb fat and sipped his wine. "I paid a visit in June, unannounced. I had the address and I waited out in front of the apartment building. He was polite, took me upstairs. I told him I'd been in Vegas gambling and had just decided to stop by."

"Did you go to find out if he was gay?"

"Of course not. I went on impulse, the way I do everything. My fatherly fantasies had been reduced to two phone calls a year and I went to revive them or something, to put them to rest."

"Imagine growing up gay in East Boston."

"Imagine."

"Back in one minute," Julie said. She took her purse and skirted the dancers in the direction of the bathrooms. When the waiter came to clear the plates, Czesich gave him the cigarettes, then sat sipping cognac and watching the gyrations on the floor, wondering if Julie and he might sleep together again now that she was single, and why it suddenly mattered so much, why helping the Soviets mattered so much, why there was such a desperateness to things all of a sudden, as if the ice were collapsing behind him as he skated toward the far shore.

"I believe," Julie said when she returned, "that the ruble will achieve convertibility before the Soviets grasp the concept of clean public washrooms."

"That bad?"

"Bad enough to make me wish I were a man."

Czesich looked at the check. The food cost less than the bribe.

"I'd like to sit for a while and then I'd like to dance," she told him.

"Fine."

"Are you in shape?"

Czesich patted his soft belly.

"How did you discover Mike was gay?"

"I went into the bathroom and there was a stack of *Blueboys* in the reading basket. It didn't quite mesh with my fatherly fantasies. I felt foolish for not having guessed."

"Did you tell him?"

"Of course. I came out and I said, 'Michael, you're gay.' And he said, '*That's* right, Dad,' sarcastically, as in, '*Now* you're getting it.' We went out for a fancy dinner and he insisted on paying. When I asked him what he did for a living he said, 'Part-time stuff.' When I asked him what kind of a career he envisioned for himself, he said he was thinking of government work."

"He has his father's wit."

Czesich had had enough to drink to say: "You know what I think about sometimes? I think about him having another man's penis in his mouth."

"Not so surprising."

"No?"

"If you had a daughter you might imagine her in bed with her husband. Those are just the secret things no one talks about, Chesi, no one but you."

"Sometimes I think the guy he's blowing is subconsciously *me*."

"Your subconscious or his?"

"His. Trying to break the barrier. When I talk to him on the phone that's all there is, barrier upon barrier."

"You did his mother wrong," Julie said.

For a moment, Czesich could not speak. If he could have spoken he would have said: With you.

"Did the visit help?"

He shrugged. The imaginary life could never quite be equaled in reality. He supposed Marx would have had something to say on the subject.

The band played a slow song and Julie asked him to dance.

At first she held herself away from him, but turn by turn he pulled her closer until he could feel her breathing and smell her skin. He tried to suck in his belly, and he closed his eyes and tried to feel, everywhere there was contact, if she trusted him enough to let him into her bed again. She had never liked being asked. "Ask without asking," she'd said to him once, in a hotel room six stories above a Central American war. He had asked without asking and she had consented without hesitation and the memory burned on undiminished. *That* was the place he should have proposed. She had not yet gotten involved with Ted at that point; he and Marie had their tacit divorce, had not slept together in years. He remembered waking up at first light the next morning and standing on the balcony in his boxer shorts, the air sweet with frangipani and rotting politics, the traffic-choked city spread out below. Julie was hugging a pillow in her sleep — he could see her through the sliding doors — hair down over her cheeks, bare-legged. He'd come close to waking her up and proposing right then, and again later in the afternoon, but some vague fear had held him back.

A fight broke out at the wedding table. Two drunken men shoved each other, shouted, spilled wine. Czesich glanced over, but he was more interested in feeling Julie move, in indulging his fantasy of a medicinal middle-aged love. A big Soviet fellow with the thin end of his necktie sticking down a foot below the thick end tapped his shoulder and asked politely if he could cut in. Czesich was feeling magnanimous. "When in Rome," he told Julie. He went back to his seat and watched from there, aroused.

When Julie returned to the table she was flushed and happy. For a moment, a feeling almost domestic was in the air between them, as though they were a long-married husband and wife enjoying a romantic renaissance. "Shall we go?" she said, and, full of hope, Czesich escorted her across the chandeliered room and through the persistent crowd at the door.

The city seemed strangely quiet after the decibel assault of the band, and they strolled arm in arm along the Old Arbat, past shuttered shops and solitary street musicians mimicking Vysotski. Since his last visit, the styles had changed. He saw shirtless boys in black leather jackets now, and girls with orange spiked hair, everything that had been in vogue in the West a decade ago.

"Imagine what Puchkov and the Iron Colonels think when they see this."

"It doesn't match their fantasies," Czesich said.

"Right. The question is, what does?"

"A unified communist Germany."

For once, it seemed wrong to be talking politics, but the loose ends of Friday's meeting were slapping in the breeze all around them, impossible to ignore. Somehow, without his noticing its departure, the tender, domestic moment had slipped away.

"They want to turn the clock back twenty years," he said, to keep the silence from hardening. "They want something nice and stable, no surprises, no demonstrations in Red Square, no environmental disasters allowed on the nightly news."

"A fair number of ordinary Soviets want the same thing."

"Twenty-five percent," he said.

"You've taken a poll?"

"Twenty-five percent of each person wants that. Each person and each country. A nice, dead, safe life with a minimum of upset, no matter what the cost."

"I'd say fifty percent. Seventy-five."

They were in the darkest part of the Arbat now and Julie was pinching her eyebrows together, turning pensive. Twenty-three years ago, Czesich had opted for the nice, safe life himself — for his local love, Marie DeMarco, and her kindly provincialisms — and he was wondering if a quarter century of regret was sufficient penance, if it would ever be possible for Julie to forgive him, for him to forgive himself, if they would ever be able to exchange the comfort of old friendship for love's chaos. They were both secretly terrified, he thought. They had both married decent, stable, loving people and been miserable. "It's how we screwed it up in Lithuania," he said, lecturing himself in code. "We went with what was safe, even though we knew it was wrong, and we ended up sanctioning tanks and murder and Puchkov rising like a second Stalin."

"We don't sanction Puchkov," she said defensively.

"We don't stand up to him either. We didn't stand up to Somoza or Duvalier. We have a history of not standing up. Look at our UN vote on Tibet. Look at Bush's speech the other day in Kiev. We're playing it safe again. The devil you know . . ."

"It's not quite that simple," Julie said. And then, after a moment: "Are you bringing us around to the food program?"

Czesich supposed that he was. It had to be gotten out of the way.

They reached the end of the pedestrian walkway and made a *raz* across a stream of adolescents coming in the other direction. Julie let go of his arm. In the distance they could hear strains of singing and a faint police klaxon. "Ambassador Haydock can't meet with you tomorrow, after all."

"Shit."

They left it there for a moment, though as far as Czesich was concerned nothing more needed to be said. Julie's timing and tone of voice told him everything he had not wanted to hear. The Food Distribution Pilot Program had been put on the back burner until it became clear whether Gorbachev or Puchkov or Yeltsin would emerge as the man to deal with. Ambassador Haydock didn't have the time, or the courage, to say this to Czesich's face, so he'd instructed Julie to do it for him. Which was perfectly foreign service of him. Filson would have left Washington on Friday afternoon for six days of fishing in Montana, which was why they had not broken the news on Friday. Also perfect. It was a masterful playing of the game, and he almost did not want to find out where Julie had positioned herself.

"I spoke in favor of going forward," she said. "I know how much you care about it."

"No," Czesich said. "You can't."

"Try me."

He gave a disgusted wave of his hand and sulked for a few minutes, doing battle with a wave of self-pity the likes of which he had not known in years. When he finally spoke, the words came out of old shadows. "In our house in East Boston, everything was a catastrophe — did I ever tell you this? You spilled a glass of milk at dinner, you broke a window playing stickball, or the sink got stopped up, or Grandpa Czesich had pains in his chest. It was always screaming, crying, weeping, wringing hands, my mother yelling in Italian, my father in Russian, the end of the goddamned world.

"So I wasn't going to be like that. Nothing was going to really get to me. I was philosophical. Marie was miserable in Washington? Fine, no problem. Just go back to East Boston, Marie, I'll come visit, the marriage will survive, no big deal. We have a son? I'll mail him baseball gloves. He'll be okay. Running Democracy First exhibits in Malaysia during the Vietnam War? No problem.

Kissing ass in China? Sitting in that gray plastic fucking office building on Sixth Street working out budget projections and calling the Brooklyn warehouse to make sure they're packing enough popcorn poppers to give away in Guatemala City . . . then in Guatemala City three blocks from our exhibition on the American Constitution, students are having their eyeballs put out by security police with U.S. Government screwdrivers!"

Czesich noticed people turning to look and he lowered his voice. Julie was staring at the ground.

"The night I came home from visiting Michael I walked down to Georgetown for dinner, then afterward I went and stood in the middle of Key Bridge and watched the planes going in and out of National. For some reason, from that hour on, my life has seemed perfectly worthless to me. My grandfather always used to take me down to watch the planes land at Logan — I think that was part of it. I felt like forty-five years had gone by and I hadn't made anything but mistakes. I got married and screwed it up. I raised a son and screwed it up. I have this job where I fly around the world mouthing American propaganda —"

"And doing good deeds," Julie interrupted. "USCA is in the aid business now."

"The very occasional good deed . . . for people I'll never see again. But mostly it's airports, hotel rooms, a nice, regular paycheck, but it's all *out there*." He thrust his hands out and up, then brought them back and thumped himself on the chest. "And *in here*, nothing, hollow. I haven't ever really taken a stand on anything. Nothing! Not one single thing, Jule. I had so much fighting as a kid I spent the rest of my life avoiding it — I even avoided it during Vietnam. I didn't even have to make a decision then."

"You mangled your knee in a hockey game, Chesi."

"I mangled my knee, but even inside myself I didn't decide. I'd watch my friends marching at BU during the day, and I'd think, 'They're right.' Then I'd come home and listen to my father, ranting and raving about the hippies, and I'd think, 'Maybe they're wrong.' I just glided through it all."

"You made a decision about me," she said, without a particle of self-pity, and Czesich felt she had sliced him neatly open and pulled his diseased organs out under the streetlights.

"I didn't, though," he said, taking her arm for a second. "You never understood that. Marie was just the path of least resistance for me. That's what I'm saying, that's what I saw on the bridge, that I've been this perfect moral coward. . . ." He stopped for a moment, hoping Julie might see it the way he saw it now, that she might let down her guard as he was letting down his, but she kept silent.

"But I finally saw it. I saw it that night. And two days later, like a miracle, Filson calls me into the corner office and tells me he's thinking of sending me on this food distribution thing. The Soviet Union, the one place I've ever done anything worthwhile . . . a chance to see you again, a chance to do one small bit of good, finally, for people who've been screwed their whole lives, my grandparents' people. One shot to prove to myself that the whole career hasn't been a complete waste. One chance to see if we —"

"You're making it too black and white," Julie said. "There were things you valued about USCA. I remember a talk in San Salvador about people getting an understanding of America's contradictions."

"Christ."

"You're just looking for some heroism in middle age, Chesi. That's not what middle age is about, that's what eighteen or twenty-two is about. You want the rush of the sixties again, you want to change the way the world works. It's not going to happen. Even the sixties didn't change anything, really, but for a little while we felt glorious."

"I want to change the way *I* work," Czesich said, but she was silent, not looking at him, stubbornly shaking her head. "So those are the options, Julie? Immaturity or bullshit? Viva Fidel or look the other way while Black Berets crack skulls in the Baltics and kids get crushed under tanks in Beijing?"

"We didn't look the other way."

"I know. We gave them MFN status."

They had reached the Ladoga again and Julie was moving toward the cab stand. Czesich took her arm and steered her in the other direction, down the street. "I didn't see it, that was the worst thing. For twenty-three years, I was numb, blind, a walking piece of wood."

"Maybe Michael showed it to you."

Czesich went along a few paces in a stunned silence, not aware until Julie said, "Hey!" that he was squeezing her arm tighter and tighter. *That's right, Dad,* he almost said aloud. *And what are you?*

"The program is only on hold," Julie told him, "not canceled. You still might get your chance to be a hero. We're telling the Soviets it's been delayed for logistical reasons, that it could start up again any day. And it could. You know how the bureaucracy works."

He knew exactly how it worked. Slow as geology. Cautious to a fault. Every original or gutsy idea filtered upward through layers and layers of glorified clerks, each more anxious than the next to avoid making a mistake. He had no time for that now.

"Maybe I'll go down to Vostok on my own," he said, half-seriously. "Just snoop around."

"Don't be absurd. They haven't heard of glasnost down there yet. The local KGB would eat you alive."

Taxis rushed past a few feet to their left, roof lights bouncing toward the center of the city. A tank truck rumbled along behind them, squirting a stream of water at the curb. As it drew near, Czesich maneuvered Julie into the safety of a doorway where only a few light drops touched them. The street and sidewalk were soaked, no cleaner.

"Spend the night with me, Jule."

She shook her head.

"I wasn't going for sympathy with all that, it just came out."

"I didn't think you were. There's just nothing I can do about your past, that's all."

"Of course there is," he said, but she slipped out of the doorway and started walking again.

He caught up and fell into step, not taking her arm.

"I can't get to this immediately . . . ," she said, when they'd gone a block. Her voice made Czesich think of Friday's stiff-armed handshake. She hesitated, fell silent, then started up again. "But if you wanted to stay in Moscow, there's a position open at the embassy. We had someone lined up for it, but the clearances took so long she decided no." Julie stopped again. "I can't hike any farther in these shoes. Can you try for a cab?"

Czesich stepped into the street and raised an arm at a succession of speeding, empty taxis, but his attention was all Julie's.

"Political analyst consultant," she went on, standing at the very edge of the curb. "If you can believe that title. It's one grade below yours, but there's an apartment and a per diem. It's made for you, Chesi, some wandering the streets, some travel, a lot of reading and watching the news and meeting with various groups to try and give us an idea what kinds of things we should be thinking about, long term."

Let me tell you what kinds of things I'm thinking about, long term, he almost said, but he was trying to see through her offer. Forget the salary, he didn't care about money anymore, he had more money than he knew what to do with, decades of hardship pay and per diem earning interest in a D.C. bank. What did the offer *really* mean? That she wanted him around? Around in what capacity? For how long? Until she was posted somewhere else? He glanced at her eyes, then away. She put a hand on his shoulder and shook a pebble out of one shoe.

A cab stopped. They got in, Julie gave her address, and, miracle of miracles, the driver turned on the meter and started off. No dickering, no demand for cigarettes or dollars, no clicking white numerals that read 27.60 before you even sat down.

Czesich put his hand over Julie's but could not look at her. He felt he'd arrived at the place where years of dreaming intersected a sharp black reality, and it suddenly terrified him. An embassy job and a pleasant, nonsexual friendship held no appeal for him tonight. He wanted something extreme, a radical change, a huge perestroika of the heart.

Julie was quiet, pursing her lips.

When the cabbie pulled up in front of her building, Czesich made himself say: "Invite me up."

She squeezed his hand and shook her head no, the trouble out in the open now, written plain. "I'm seeing someone, Chesi."

"Who?" he blurted out.

She frowned, hesitated. "Someone at the embassy. Peter McCauley. He's in cultural affairs."

"Love?" Czesich said, but his voice betrayed him, wobbling like an old man's.

She frowned again, her face still full of trouble, pinched tight. "Think about the job. I'll make dinner Thursday night. We'll talk some more."

"Why Thursday?" he said, but she was gone.

The hotel suite was extravagant, strictly czarist, four rooms furnished with everything from cutlery to a bidet. In any other country on earth it would have embarrassed him; here, it was just part of the game, just another Marxist-Leninist irony. He was a *Direktr* here, and in Soviet Russia the word still carried echoes of nobility. People expected a certain pomp and sureness.

Before leaving for the Ladoga, he'd set out the Italian candies she liked, a bottle of vodka in ice, and a vase of flowers on the chance Julie would come back with him, and now these statues of optimism perched on the coffee table, mocking him. Julie was better-looking, smarter, wealthier, more successful. State Department compromises aside, she'd led a life rich in commitment and personal honor, and he'd made a career of indecision and half-assed protest, shooting Filson the finger behind his back. "The thing is," she'd said to him once in the same hotel in El Salvador when they were arguing about the war, "you have to pick a side and hang on to it, with all its imperfections, for better or worse. Otherwise you're not a serious person."

On that night, too, the line between the political and the personal had been blurred. She'd been too kind to mention Marie, but the implication was clear: *For better or worse.* She saw him as merely an entertaining coward.

He took a quick shot of vodka, nibbled a cracker with cheese, and stared at the dining room phone, still unwilling to release the last strands of hope. He "saw" other people, too, professional Washington women in their forties and early fifties, lonely souls like himself, spinning through the void with their satellite children and dry, wounded eyes. There were good hours to be had with such women — intelligent conversation, affectionate sex, moments approaching intimacy — but there was no history, and history was what he wanted tonight, good or bad.

He ordered a call to Nevada but was told he'd have to wait.

"How long?"

"How would I know?" the Soviet operator snapped. "Hang up and wait."

He hung up and waited, picturing this Peter McCauley. There was no urge to sleep, no hope of re-creating himself in Vostok unless Puchkov dropped dead or Ambassador Haydock was overruled by the Secretary of State. He could not imagine what he might do between now and Thursday night to show Julie he'd finally picked a side, that Marie DeMarco no longer had any claim on him, that he'd changed. Perhaps Michael would enlighten him. Again.

Much farther into the bottle, the phone rang. Czesich lifted the receiver, heard the operator's voice, then his son's. "Am I interrupting?" he said, speaking as carefully as he could so that Michael would not know he'd been drinking.

"Never, Dad. You're drunk."

"I'm in Moscow."

"Your favorite part of the planet, right?"

"It reminds me of Nevada," he said, and through the shifting alcohol fog he listened to his son laugh. "Are you okay?"

"Couldn't be finer."

"Being careful?"

"Utterly careful. Too very careful."

Czesich imagined there was someone else in the room and Michael was making faces over his shoulder as he spoke. "We'll both be in East Boston at Christmas. At your mother's."

"Great."

"I want to see more of you."

Michael was silent, stunned into silence, Czesich thought. People did not like you to change in middle age, they did not trust it. "I'm going to buy a small farm up in Vermont," he blurted out to fill the awkward moment. A vodka vision had come to him, complete to the last detail. He could see the farm, he could smell woodsmoke from a neighbor's chimney, feel himself walking down a dirt road to the country store. "I'm already looking into it. You can come up there if you want and I'll give you a parcel of land for a house. How would that be?"

"Great, Dad," Michael said, without enthusiasm.

Czesich was sitting on the arm of the sofa, looking at a dull green wall. "This is not just another five-year plan, you know. I have a lot of per diem saved up, and a good pension. You can bring a friend. I'm not just talking this time."

"I know. I believe you."

"You do?"

"Of course. Why not?"

"Because I've been a bullshitter all these years, is why."

"Not true, Dad. Not true."

"You have your mother's kindness."

"If you say so."

"Stop sending her checks, Michael. I send her checks. She makes a decent salary now. She wants you to use the money for yourself."

"Okay." Michael covered the mouthpiece for a moment, and Czesich could hear nothing but a very faint hum. "Gotta go, Dad. Call when you're home, all right?"

"Be careful."

"Always."

Call when you're home. The room spun gently. Czesich had one more shot of vodka — the Medicine of Forget, his Soviet friends called it — then stood, went to the closet, and with a clumsy drunken efficiency began packing his bags.

// CHAPTER 8

August 6, 1991

Whenever a president visits, whenever there is a congressional delegation in town, or a secretary of state, or a group of big businessmen, the embassy takes on the aspect of a pile of fall leaves hit by a gust of wind. The building's resources — its people, its phones, its copying machines and security-cleared computer screens, even its cafeteria tables — are caught up in one sharp exhaled breath from America, lifted and spun in a frenzied eddy, then dropped all up and down Chaikovsky Street. We spend the next two weeks raking everything back into place, returning our attention to the thousand daily errands which, cumulatively, constitute the official American presence here. We write and clear and send off cables. We collect bits of secret and not-so-secret information, and invite refuseniks (a species not yet extinct) to film screenings at Spaso House. We process visa applications and monitor the local press and make sure the embassy swimming pool is properly filtered and the embassy motor pool properly staffed, and that there are enough different kinds of cereal in the commissary, and that everyone receives their mail. Those of us who have an interest in the "host country" go back to paying attention to each new scene in her unfolding drama: Prime Minister Pavlov's latest press conference; a session of the Congress of People's Deputies; a metalworkers strike in Perm; ethnic unraveling along the Caucasus' ragged edges.

The rest of the embassy employees count the days until they will be back in Washington or Houston or Milwaukee, drinking orange juice and eating barbecue and watching baseball on TV.

This week, for me, there were two gusts of wind on Chaikovsky Street — Chesi and the President — and in my private and public worlds I am now scrambling about, trying to restore order, to pull the errant bits of myself back into one more-or-less manageable heap. It was not so difficult with the President's visit (though there were the murders in Lithuania this time, and his flaccid speech in Kiev). With Chesi it was, and always has been, much more complicated. He came to my office late Friday afternoon looking wounded and eager. Wounded, I think, at being kept waiting — though he would never have guessed the reason. Wounded, as he's been wounded for so many years now, by his inability to ever make peace with the East Boston side of himself, with Marie and her family and the things — impossible things — that have always been expected of him there.

And eager in a way I've never seen him, almost desperate, as though this pilot food program of his were the defining project, not just of his career, but of his life. It made no sense to me at first.

The decision hadn't yet officially been made by Friday afternoon, but I could have told him how it was going to turn out. Gorbachev bears the scent of a doomed man these days, and even though we've grown comfortable with him, and would go to some lengths to help him stay in power, it is only prudent at this point to be looking beyond. If, as many suspect, Puchkov is gathering his pals together for an old-time power grab, then we don't want to be caught dancing toward the center while the new regime is marching right. It wouldn't do to commit to a high-profile program like food distribution if, a month down the road, we find we're suddenly delivering food to Puchkov, or Pavlov, or even Yeltsin — anyone other than the steady, sober, reliable Mr. Gorbachev, the first friend we've had in the Kremlin in eighty years.

At least that's the way the more pragmatic State Department types see it.

Chesi, of course, does not see it at all that way, and it was not easy to tell him — just an hour or so ago — that the first deliveries have been put on hold until we can get a better idea of how long Gorby will actually be among the politically living, and who is likely to replace him. Chesi reacted as if I'd told him he had a month to live. All sorts of pain came pouring out of him, pain I'd never seen, pain I think even he hadn't seen until recently.

I wanted to soothe him. In the worst way I wanted to offer him some small corner of comfort, but I've been down that road with

Chesi before. Many years ago I saw what he did not quite see in himself: that he was born in a place that did not suit him, among people who valued him for the wrong reasons, who praised what was incidental in him, and completely missed the sensitive core, the good, wise heart of him. Long ago I tried to tell him that he would have to turn his back on that place or be ruined by it. He lacked the courage to do that then, and now, at fifty, he has halfway broken free and is halfway ruined.

There was more to his visit than that, of course, and I've saved this part for last, saved my own pain for last. (A habit of mine, I've come to realize, since starting this elaborate and long-winded "journal." I'm comfortable going on and on about Soviet politics, about the embassy, about Chesi, but when it comes to turning my sharp analytical eye upon myself, I dally, I avoid opening myself to myself the way some of us avoid opening our mouths for the embassy dentist. We're afraid of what he might find there, of course, what creeping decay might be uncovered. And the longer we avoid him, the deeper the decay spreads. And the deeper the decay, the more we want to avoid discovering it. I wonder, sometimes, if people see the businesslike surface of me, the career woman, the PAO, and think that's all there is. I wonder if Ted thought that. Perhaps I began this journal to remind myself that there is, after all, a nonprofessional me beneath that polished steel skin.)

This is part of what lies beneath it: Twenty-three years have gone by, an entire career, almost half of my life, and still when I hear Chesi talk about Marie and Michael it's as if someone has tapped a tuning fork inside me and it's resonating with a sour note. The sound is fainter now, thankfully. I have my career and my friends, and I have memories of some good years with Ted, so it's a much fainter note. But it does not ever seem to go silent. That old bruise does not ever seem to heal. And Chesi is so completely, utterly, maddeningly oblivious to it.

He is an ordinary-looking man. Every time I see him he seems more ordinary: thinning brown hair; a plain, rather wide face with the beginnings of jowls; large, sad eyes. He has a boyish side to him that is not always endearing. The things he says sometimes seem to erupt from a place that was formed in his adolescence, on the street corners of East Boston, rough cut then and never sanded, never polished. He drinks a bit much — especially in this country —he eats too much and cares too much about his clothes.

But he is — and even alone, putting this on paper only for my own eyes, it sounds like a crude way of saying it — but he is decent. And the older I grow the more of an accomplishment that seems. Just to be a decent man or woman. Just to have, or to have cultivated, a heart that is kind, seems like a heroic work in this mottled world.

I have a theory that drink reveals a person's true character, and with Chesi that is certainly the case. He is a soft, kindly, funny drunk, capable of deceit perhaps, capable of stupidity, incapable of meanness.

I enjoyed our Ladoga dinner tonight in a way I don't enjoy my embassy life or my embassy friends. Chesi asked about me in a way they don't ask. In spite of the old dread that had made me keep him sitting outside my door on Friday, in spite of the old bruises, and in spite of his new obsession with saving the Russian nation, I enjoyed his company. More than enjoyed it, can I admit that to myself?

And what did I do in response to this enjoyment? What old demon took hold of me? He tried, in his own clumsy way, to talk about "us." He asked to sleep with me — asked almost like a nineteen-year-old would ask — and all I could do in response was to make a vague offer of a position at the embassy, and to fabricate another man in my life. Peter McCauley, of all people! And why Peter McCauley of all people? Peter the Guarded One, Peter the Controlled, Peter who must always know more about everyone than they know about him, who must always protect himself and his country from being wounded, deceived, defeated. I want to laugh and weep, now, seeing this. Peter McCauley's name just came to me in the back seat of a Moscow taxi. It just appeared, the idea of him just rose up, a sign from the subconscious, a mirror I do not want to look into.

How Soviet of me to protect myself that way, to hide behind a lie.

// CHAPTER 9

BEHIND and above Malov on his office's spotless green wall hung a portrait of Iron Felix Dzerzhinsky, father of the Soviet secret police. Propenko did not dirty his eyes with it. He knew what Dzerzhinsky looked like — foolish little cap over a pointed nose and narrow face. And he knew the stories — Lubyanka torture cells, the Gulag's ratmeat-and-maggot cuisine. More recently, he'd heard a rumor from Uzinsk, where, it was said, someone had sneaked into the main square after midnight and covered the hands on Iron Felix's monument with scarlet paint. The next day the authorities removed the paint, but within a week the hands were red again, and this scandal repeated itself until the bronze hands had been scoured so many times they shone in the Uzinsk sun and there was no need to paint them again or to pretend they would ever be clean.

The country had outgrown Dzerzhinsky and his monuments and his torture, Propenko thought. But Malov had not yet figured that out.

Malov reached across the corner of his desk, took the special glass coffeepot from the special electric coffee maker he'd brought back from Leipzig, and poured out two steaming cups. It was real coffee, precious as diamonds these days, and the smell of it brought back richer times. The two men sat almost as friends would sit, touching the hot cups to their lips, eyeing each other without seeming to. It was Malov's move. Among his other duties, apparent and secret, Malov was the political specialist for the Council of Commerce and Industry, and this was his weekly chat, his way of keeping the office ideology pure.

"First of all, Sergei, allow me to congratulate you on your pro-motion," he began, turning the cup between his thumb and middle finger, and doing his best to sound sincere. Around the office, Malov often spoke with this exaggerated formality, clipping off his words in the style of actors playing military men. Backed up by Iron Felix, he was somehow able to make the affectation seem less than absurd. "A Director now. Working with the Americans."

"It's only a month, Nikolai."

Malov cocked his head slightly, putting his good ear forward. "A month on *this* assignment. But I'm certain if all goes well, this assignment will lead to something more permanent. Perhaps Vol-kov's job — he's nearing retirement. That would be the position for you, eh Seryozha — travel, a hard-currency account, a larger apart-ment?"

Propenko shrugged and sipped his coffee. Malov was a master of insinuation. On the most obvious level, the expression on his face and his tone of voice seemed full of goodwill. But one centi-meter beneath that congenial surface, everything was soaked in a righteous hatred unsullied by even the smallest stain of doubt. Sus-picion sprayed out of him like lead shot, sparing only the extreme right edge of the target, yet Malov always fired from behind this smiling mask. He was always squeezing shoulders and slapping backs in the Council corridors. And his colleagues seemed per-fectly willing to let him pretend. It was a trick of some sort, this blunting of everyone else's resistance. It had something to do with the fear that had been planted in the belly of every man and woman Propenko knew, something to do with Stalin, and Dzerzhinsky, and places far to the east.

"How was your chat with *Madame* Bessarovich?"

"Straightforward," Propenko said. "The woman says what's on her mind."

Malov winked. "Watch her, Seryozha. I advise you as a friend. Her activities are being monitored closely by our Moscow com-rades."

Your Moscow comrades, Propenko thought. Your embittered fellow fanatics listening in on phone lines and poisoning reputa-tions. He felt a small anger stirring, and did what he could to tamp it back down. His strategy had always been to submit dutifully to these sessions, responding to Malov's gibes with good humor, tell-ing himself the bullying and prying were only part of Malov's job, a role, not to be taken personally.

But tonight something seemed to have changed. For the first time, this casual interrogation — with its cautious feeling out of the opponent, its feints and jabs, the high price paid for a moment's inattention — reminded him of a sport he'd mastered long ago. He was a Director now; he wanted to see if he could compete in this ring. "Lyudmila Ivanovna was very upset by the murder," he said casually. "I had the feeling it was personal. Maybe a family friend."

"If he was a family friend, so much the worse for her." Malov's eyes darted back and forth over Propenko's face. "The man was keeping bad company."

"Tikhonovich? He was a watchman, Nikolai, a religious fanatic. I heard he gave up an engineering career to sweep floors and dust icons."

Malov grunted as though he knew better, and they attended to their coffee for a moment. Propenko found himself staring at a photograph on Malov's side table, the young Nikolai in the ring. Though it pained him to admit it, he and Malov bore a certain biographical resemblance. They'd grown up in the years immediately following the defeat of the Nazis, Stalin's glory days, a time of triumph and hardship. Both of them had been reared by stern, conservative fathers, and by mothers devoted to the communist dream. Both had been drawn to boxing — one heavyweight, one middleweight. Both had been active in Komsomol at the Institute, and had ended up at the Council of Commerce and Industry, a quiet pasture for good communists. But somewhere along the way — driven by ambition, or a skewed, insulted patriotism — Malov had strayed off into associations with the Security organs, and the years had nourished in him a sadism of such magnitude that Propenko often found himself pretending Malov did not really mean something he had just said or done, that he could not really be the person he had become, that stories of him kicking handcuffed men in the mouth could not possibly be anything more than office gossip. It was a dangerous attitude, held in place by the last remaining shreds of adolescent naivete, and at times like this, Propenko wondered what it would take to fully mature him.

"You know, Sergei," Malov said after a while, turning his blue irises, like camera lenses, on Propenko. Malov's eyes had taken on a strange cast lately; he seemed to be able to stop blinking at will. "Something very disturbing happened to me over the weekend." He looked down into his cup, then back at Propenko's face, and grimaced as though he had not really wanted to raise the subject.

Propenko arched his eyebrows, displaying mild interest, good humor, sympathy, but he was as alert as a stalked animal.

Malov scratched the bridge of his nose. "It was Friday afternoon, actually. I left work early."

"Everyone did," Propenko said agreeably.

"I took out my boat and went fishing at the mouth of the Malenkaya."

"A good spot."

"Usually. But there had been rain the night before, and there was a wind. The boat was knocking back and forth."

Propenko remembered the afternoon as being still and warm, fog over the river. He said, "Rain the night before helps sometimes, makes them hungry."

Malov's cheeks seemed to harden. "I heard a sound," he said, "a strange sound, a cry. It was already getting foggy by then, you know, and I couldn't see the bank very well. I heard the sound again and started my motor and moved closer to investigate, and I saw two people there, a man and a woman. At first, I thought they were engaged in sexual relations."

Engaged in sexual relations — who talked like this? The last of the Council workers had gone home at five o'clock and the building was very quiet, Malov's Swiss desk clock ticking like a bomb. Propenko waited.

"My boat glided in closer. I was at the point of turning away and leaving them to their lovemaking when I heard the woman call for help." Malov reached for the coffeepot and poured each of them another dose. "I had my pistol. I fired into the air and headed the boat straight in and the assailant saw me and fled. The woman was bleeding from between her legs. Half-naked. Hysterical."

Ordinarily, Propenko would have waited and watched. Tonight, he decided to put a small jab in Malov's face. "A rapist deserves no mercy," he said. "I would have shot him."

For one second, Malov seemed to lose confidence. He recovered by laughing his terrible laugh, a drawn-out *huh-huh-huh-huh*, perfectly transparent. "Huh-huh-huh-huh, well, you're stricter than I am, Seryozha. I always allow the criminal an opportunity to explain."

Propenko wondered how many explanations there could be for a half-naked, bleeding woman crying out for help.

"Especially in sex cases. With the female of the species, who knows?" Malov's right hand fluttered toward the window in a gesture of unpredictability. "Being married, of course, happily married, you understand them better than a bachelor like me, but to me there is always an element of playacting. A something behind the something. Don't you agree?"

"I would have shot him," Propenko repeated, and, for once, he stared Malov down. "Did you bring her back to the city?"

"I brought her to the pier at Zima. She was badly shaken. At the pier I went to find a telephone and she ran off."

"Did she know the man?"

Malov shook his head. "He picked her up in front of the tractor factory, somehow convinced her to go to the river, and proceeded to force himself upon her in that way."

Propenko was still watching. The tale was absurd — Malov out in his boat in thick fog, the woman getting into a car with someone she didn't know — but it wasn't the tale that engaged him; it was the teller, the something behind the something. "Did you see what he looked like?"

"I did," Malov said sorrowfully. He leaned back in the chair, bringing the cup with him and eyeing Propenko over the rim. "He looked" — Malov took a sip and moved the coffee around in his mouth before swallowing — "like you."

Propenko forced a smile. He was cold now, and smiling. His hands wanted to move.

"I tell you this for your own protection, Seryozha," Malov said, after letting Propenko suffer for a few seconds. "*I* know it wasn't you, of course, but the woman's description matches you perfectly, and the man was driving a red Lada."

Propenko heard Raisa's voice. He heard Marya Petrovna saying *chekisti*. He saw red Ladas going by beyond the GAI officer's shoulder.

"I'm just trying to give you a bit of advance warning, should she be found, should anything come of this."

The telephone rang, but Malov made no move to answer it. Propenko finished his coffee and ran a finger across his lips. The anger was harder to hold down now; it was mixed with other things. The phone rang again, loud and annoying in the small office. Malov seemed intent on ignoring it, so Propenko ignored it, too. He tried to speak casually, between the jarring rings. "Unfortunately, Nikolai . . . I am not that unusual-looking."

"Not true," Malov said pleasantly. "Quite the contrary. A man two meters tall, built like an Olympic heavyweight. . . ." He turned to the phone with a disgusted expression and brought the receiver up to his good ear.

Propenko stared across the desk and felt a shift within himself, a small, murderous alteration of perspective. His interrogator's right ear had been beaten shapeless in the ring, and looking at it made him think of a younger Nikolai Malov, an aggressive, talented middleweight, somewhat insecure and ill at ease outside the gym. They had roomed together during the Alma Ata tournament in 1966. He'd ended up winning a silver medal in the heavyweight division, but Malov, Vostok's other potential Olympian, had been eliminated in the semifinals, beaten nearly to death in the last round by an Uzbeki farmboy who could not knock him down. After Malov's fight they walked back to their hotel. Propenko bought two bottles of beer and some bread and salami at the *bufyet* on their floor, and they sat side by side in the cramped, cold room, eating and drinking and saying nothing. Propenko's left eye was swollen and he was completely exhausted, but he'd reached the finals and was anxious to call Raisa — his sweetheart then — and give her the news. Something in Malov's mood held him in his seat. In the middle of the meal Malov had abruptly stopped eating, put his bottle down on the coffee table, and went to the window. There was a father waiting for him at home, Propenko knew, an egotist suffering mediocrity, pinning his own puffed-up dreams on his son's boxing career. Malov was staring west out the dark hotel window in the direction of home, gingerly touching the exploded ear, snapping his fingers there, checking to see if he could pull a few strands of hair down to cover it. Propenko heard him say something beneath his breath. He went up to Malov and saw one tear swell at the bottom of his left eye, stretch out and down, then break off and wend its way over the cheekbone and into the corner of Malov's mouth. Malov seemed unaware of his presence. "There's no future any longer," he was saying. "No future."

Propenko examined the ruined ear now, in what had become their future, and saw the jaw muscles working beneath it. Malov's small, angular, blue-eyed face had turned pink, and Propenko supposed it meant the world was disappointing him again, refusing to trim itself to his exceedingly narrow tastes.

"Unbelievable!" Malov spat into the phone. "Unbe*liev*able." His fingers were white against the receiver. He listened for a few more seconds, then asked a series of questions in a commanding voice: "What time? . . . How many? . . . On whose order?"

Propenko assumed it was just one of the seedy criminal cases Malov was sometimes consulted on — another imaginary rape, perhaps; another imaginary troublemaker murdered beside a church — but Malov snorted in a vicious way, cursed, slammed the receiver down, and when he looked up he appeared to have forgotten the rape story completely. His right cheek was twitching, the veneer of sophistication gone, a truer, cruder self out in plain view. "The fucking miners just voted to strike," he said, between his teeth.

When Propenko opened the apartment door, he found his women in a strangely festive mood. Raisa had cooked Siberian dumplings for dinner, and her mother had spent the day prowling the markets and shops and had somehow managed to find cabbage and cheese to the limit of her ration tickets. Lydia contributed a bar of chocolate — another coup — and seemed buoyed and defiant. On the way home, Propenko had stopped for vodka. They sat around the kitchen table with the television droning in the background, and Lydia started right in on the strike.

"This will be the end of Mikhail Lvovich," she announced.

Her grandmother nodded as if she would never stop. Propenko and Raisa looked at each other, neither of them able to imagine Lvovich's end. Gorbachev had been undermining Vostok's hardline First Secretary for years now, maneuvering, calculating, trying various strategies to discredit and embarrass him. Lvovich had not budged or softened.

"This strike will be the end of him."

It seemed to Propenko there was something desperate in his daughter's enthusiasm, as if a vanquished First Secretary was just what she required to cancel out Tikhonovich's death. As she went on, filling them in on the details (all of Vostok's eleven mines were closed; the miners — seven thousand of them — were supporting the hunger strikers, calling for an independent investigation into the murder, demanding the resignation of Lvovich and his henchmen), he could not stop himself from picturing her on a foggy riverbank, hysterical, bleeding between the legs. Such was the power of Malov's concoctions; they haunted his dinner table. They rendered him quiet and pensive in the midst of the domestic swirl. And they moved him, finally, to open the first bottle of the Medicine of Forget and pour out four healthy shots.

"What's the matter, Sergei?"

"Nothing."

"You're quiet."

"I'm thinking about the strike," he said, only half lying. "I'm thinking the miners are the only people left in this country with any courage, any strength."

Raisa frowned.

Lydia set her jaw triumphantly. The strike had wrought a physical change in her, in her eyes and cheeks, in the way she held herself. It reminded Propenko of the drunk standing behind him in the vodka line an hour earlier, cursing the Afghani army. It was the posture of a person in pain and wanting a fight.

She cleared the dishes and rejoined them. "Not the only ones," she said. "The People of the Third Path have courage."

"Who?" Propenko asked.

Lydia shook a finger in mock rebuke. "You're out of touch, Papa."

Propenko looked to his mother-in-law, and then to his wife for help. "The Peruvian group?"

"Soviet," Raisa said glumly. "Local."

Still trying to wrench himself free of Malov's insinuations, Propenko poured himself a second glass of vodka and held out the bottle, snout forward. There were no takers. "Officially recognized?"

"No," Lydia said, and he thought he heard a note of pride.

"Are you a member?"

"I go to the meetings. Everybody does. It doesn't mean you're a member."

Marya Petrovna made the sign of the cross, and Raisa nervously busied herself at the sink, but Propenko chose to put this information in a positive light. These, no doubt, were the political meetings Bessarovich had alluded to. Unofficial, but harmless, he told himself. Kids sitting around in a small room, flaunting cigarettes and letting off some of the anger they felt toward their parents for being older, toward the world for not acknowledging their wisdom. He tossed off the second shot, poured a third, lifted it to his lips. Meetings were only meetings.

"Tikhonovich used to organize them," Lydia said.

Propenko's drink stuck in his throat. He coughed, forced a swallow. "The caretaker?"

"When Father Alexei returns he'll choose someone else."

"Not you," Raisa snapped.

"Don't panic, Ma, not me."

Three glasses of vodka were not quite enough to soften this blow, so Propenko poured another. Raisa brought the teapot over and set it down too hard. From the living room came the sound of martial music announcing *Vremya,* the national news.

Propenko and Raisa went in and sat on the living room bed, Marya Petrovna in the only soft chair. Lydia stood behind her grandmother and massaged the old woman's shoulders as they watched.

The Vostok strike had not even been mentioned on the local news, which was still controlled by the people at Party Headquarters. On *Vremya,* it was the second story. Heavyset miners with hard hats and sooty faces were shown walking out the Nevsky Mine's front gate. Propenko noticed patches of snow on the slag heaps behind them and realized it was footage recycled from the last strike, in February. He wondered if the intent was mockery, as in: They just walked off the job a few months ago and here they go again. It was impossible to tell nowadays; the news wasn't as transparent as it had once been; perestroika had made it more difficult to ferret out the something behind the something.

Nor did the announcer give much indication of official reaction. The miners, he said matter-of-factly, were striking for better working conditions, better food supplies, and the resignation of Mikhail Lvovich Kabanov, Vostok's veteran first secretary.

"No mention of Tikhonovich at all!" Lydia complained. "That's the *main* reason they're striking."

Now Kabanov himself appeared on the screen — outdated footage again — smiling in a conceited way and swinging his big belly back and forth as he walked into a meeting in Moscow.

And that was it. The commentator moved on to international news, and first Raisa, then Marya Petrovna, then Lydia drifted back to the kitchen. Propenko could hear them there, arguing about the strike, covering the whole spectrum of opinion from Lydia's zeal to Raisa's disapproval. He sat through the sports report, tossing back two more small shots and wondering how much to say about his conversation with Malov.

When the announcer signed off, it was quarter to ten and the kitchen debate still hadn't ended. Propenko took his place at the table and allowed himself a final drink. The world had softened beautifully. Malov's face had disappeared.

"What do you think, Pa?"

He waved an arm and spoke uncensored: "Five strikes in two years. It loses its meaning. They'll never chase Kabanov out." The kitchen was tossing gently in a vodka sea, and he felt cushioned from danger, carelessly optimistic, invulnerable. But, even drunk, he could see that his commentary had dulled some of Lydia's defiant shine. Marya Petrovna started to say something, but he broke in. "Tell us about the Children of the Third Way, Lydochka."

"Third Path, Sergei."

"Third Way, Third Path."

"*People* of the Third Path, Pa. Not *Children*."

"Fine, tell us all about them."

Lydia told them. Teetering on the precipice of adulthood, she lectured her elders on the world's two great failing empires, pointed out that they represented the two extremes of social organization — mindless collectivism and mindless individualism — spoke of pollution, worker alienation, twin corrupt bureaucracies that had fueled an arms race at the expense of ordinary people. She spoke of Europe, east and west, as the best hope for mankind, a mix of socialist and capitalist, the Third Path.

To Propenko, it was a simplistic assessment, shot through with naive enthusiasm and cliches, yet ringing, undeniably, of truth. A truth, he thought, that would be crushed like a beetle beneath the bootheels of power. A truth that landed you in prison, or in the kitchen of a workers cafe, cleaning pots, university degree in your pocket. A truth that, even in this, the most lenient time they had ever known, had earned at least one man a bullet in the back of the head. It seemed important to warn Lydia again about the subtle differences between what could be said at home and what could be announced to the world. He decided that was part of a Soviet father's duty, but, hampered by the drink, he was not sure how to do it.

"Your grandfather spoke like you do," Raisa said. "And died in Camp Ninety-three. Fifty-two years old."

"Times change, Mother."

"People are people. Evil is evil."

"Today Malov accused me of rape," Propenko blurted out. It had seemed to fit properly into the conversation until the words were out of his mouth. Now Raisa was staring at him, horrified, and he tried to make light of it. "It's not true, of course, but true doesn't matter. It happened Friday afternoon on the banks of the Malenkaya. Malov says he was out fishing and saw a young couple on the bank. The rapist looked like me, supposedly. He ran off. Malov took the woman to the pier at Zima. She ran away, too." Propenko waved an arm.

Raisa had tears in her eyes. Her face seemed to be floating.

"Then there are no witnesses except Malov," Lydia said.

"Malov can create witnesses, Lydia. He can invent them." Propenko felt detached from it now, as if speaking of someone else's fate, but he was watching Raisa out of the corner of his eye. "That's one of his specialties."

"But why would he?"

"Because he doesn't believe in things like the People of the Third Path," her grandmother told her. "That's why."

"He'll believe in them," Lydia said. "Soon enough."

Propenko nodded and watched the table sway. At least she hadn't said, "Believe in *us*."

Pressed against his wife on the small bed on one side of the living room, Propenko concentrated on the noises from the street — bus brakes and automobile horns and the clacking of trackless-trolley quills against their overhead wires. He wasn't thinking in a completely sober fashion, and he wasn't sure what he expected to hear outside — militia sirens, announcements being broadcast over army loudspeakers, the chants of demonstrators marching on Party Headquarters. Tomorrow they might wake up and find miners and Black Berets fighting in the streets. Or things could go on more or less as they had been going on for the past four or five years: barely enough food, a place to go and work, a place to come home to, a completely fogbound future.

The vodka helped him think over the afternoon's interview with a calmer eye. It seemed at least possible that Bessarovich would be interested to hear what Malov was up to, that Vzyatin and Leonid and a few of the other Generals might band together and raise some kind of protest. This time, it seemed at least possible to resist Malov's manipulations.

The miners, apparently, had inspired him.

Raisa was lying on her side with her back to him, and he thought she was asleep until she said: "I feel like our home has been violated."

He did not know exactly what she meant, but he flexed his fingers once on her stomach to show he was awake. She turned poetic sometimes now when they were alone. It reminded him of the early years in Makeyevka when, with Marya Petrovna, they'd shared two rooms in a sooty house in the shadows of the slag heaps. Brezhnev had just ascended to the Kremlin throne, and was busy closing all the doors Khrushchev had pried open, and he and Raisa had fancied themselves young liberals — though their liberalism went no further than whispering stanzas of Tsvetayeva and Mandelshtam in their cold bed. Lydia had been born while they were living in that house, and soon afterward he'd begun his slow climb at the Council of Commerce and Industry. Even with his connections there, and even with a child, it had taken them several years to move up the list for apartments, several more years before they were able to buy a car. He saw those years in a clearer light now: He and Raisa had made the journey from imaginary radicals to obedient servants of the State without the slightest resistance. They'd grown comfortable and quiet, part of the problem.

"All the talk of perestroika and glasnost, it hasn't changed anything."

"Because of one meeting with Malov?"

"Not just that, Sergei, all of it. Kabanov. Nothing on the local news about a strike in our own city. The murder. Now Lydia is going to have to go through what I went through. I can feel it in my body."

This, Propenko thought, was the meat of the matter, the stone in the heart of their marriage. For a moment it seemed to him that his one duty as husband and father had always been to prevent Raisa's miserable family history from repeating itself, to protect her and Lydia from the oldest of Soviet fates. Raisa's words felt like a threat: if he failed in this, he failed utterly.

He tried to think of a way to calm her. "Nikolai is only trying to keep me in line," he said casually, as if Malov had accused him of using too many pencils or forgetting to lock his office door. "It always happens this way when someone at the Council starts to work with a Westerner. They always gang up on you and try to scare you a little bit. They even do it when you're working with people from socialist countries. Remember when I first worked with Bulgarians?"

"I don't think it's you, Sergei. It's Lydia. It's the church and this Father Alexei. He meets with the miners, he's involved with this Third Path group, he goes to Moscow on mysterious errands."

"He's seventy-five years old, Raisa. I saw him once. He looks like a sparrow."

"But Kabanov is frightened of him, and of the miners. The strike is going to make it worse. He already has hunger strikers on the lawn in front of his office; now he'll have miners and students and the foreign press. What if he calls in the Black Berets and Lydia's out there demonstrating? What if mines all over the country go on strike, and factories start to shut down, and the KGB thinks it started in Vostok, at the church?"

Propenko said nothing. Raisa had the ability to take his vaguest fears and make them concrete with a few words. She had the ability to imagine each situation's worst end. "You never could have been a boxer," he said drunkenly.

"Meaning what?"

"You defeat yourself before you start."

She turned and faced him. "I have *reasons* to defeat myself."

"I know."

"I didn't grow up with a father who had a dacha, who was a favorite of the Party big shots, who —"

He put a hand on her hip and stopped her. Raisa seemed to be crying inside her body. "It's not the 1950s," he said.

"It is in Vostok, Sergei. In Kabanov's mind it still is."

He pulled their chests together and let her shake against him, shake out some of the anger and fear, but he felt distant. Her father was in bed with them again. Malov and Mikhail Lvovich were in the next room. Stalin was somewhere down the hall. The walls of their home had in fact been violated — but long, long ago.

// CHAPTER 10

CZESICH opened his eyes on a sly, jeering, vengeful light that slipped between the blackout curtains like a blade. He turned his back on it and lay absolutely still, blinking and breathing and smelling the just-washed sheets.

Moving himself up into the world again was accomplished in stages, each stage separated from the next by a pause. He sat up and paused, stood with his fingertips to the wall for balance, shuffled to the dining room door and paused again, taking in the coffee table with its tired flowers and half-empty vodka bottle. He crossed the room to the small refrigerator, and when he tugged open the sticky door the hammering in his head seemed to reverberate there among the stores of food he'd bought for Vostok — salami, cheese, pickles, olives — things he could no longer imagine putting into his mouth. He took hold of a can of Heineken, pressed cold metal to the bridge of his nose for a minute, then snapped the top and made himself drink. He shuddered. His stomach heaved. He drank again, clamping his teeth together and pressing his tongue against the roof of his mouth.

All right, he thought, beer for breakfast. A true Russki now.

The tub was equipped with a hose and leaky nozzle, no shower. He sat in it, intending to douse himself with icy water, but when the first cold drops touched him, he quickly turned the nozzle aside and adjusted the temperature upward. He soaped and rinsed himself as if scrubbing away a half-shed skin, then knelt and turned the water cold for just a second, in penance.

The next station of the cross was the window where he'd stood before going to meet Julie on Friday afternoon. The day was inexcusably bright, but he could see the Kremlin, and Saint Basil's, and taxis hurtling across the bridge where Mathias Rust had landed his Cessna four years before. It had been an act of dementia, that flight, a victory of individual risk over collective caution. Czesich could not think of it without smiling.

Gradually, his eyes grew accustomed to the light and he could make out crowds of Soviet tourists filing out of their buses and up toward the Universal Department Store. This morning, everything he could see and imagine spoke to him of protection: the stony faces; the *babushki* guarding soft hearts with layer upon layer of fat, then covering the fat with coarse, heavy clothing, even in summer; infants swaddled and stiff in their carriages; Lenin's massive tomb; the Kremlin walls; the city's cathedral-dotted, four-hundred-year-old center surrounded by a rind of the blandest architecture imaginable; the whole country throwing up barrier after barrier — military, political, bureaucratic — as if to keep the outside world from reaching its hands into Russia's raw, delicate middle.

It never worked, of course. Sooner or later the walls fell and the Potemkin villages crumbled, and everything you'd tried to protect yourself against came rushing in. There was a lesson here for him, he supposed, and for Julie, but he did not feel up to pursuing it this morning. He'd gotten drunk to avoid considering his options, which had seemed to include only returning to the death of all hope on Sixth Street Southwest, or signing up in the role of neutered old friend at the Moscow embassy, Sixth Street's foreign service equivalent, a place that had always seemed to him damp with the bitterness of half-led lives.

But he shuffled back to the bedroom and discovered a third option standing before him in the woozy morning, as actual and obvious as a packed suitcase. He held still, thinking about it for a minute or two, then went to the closet, chose his most outlandish necktie, laid out a suit — lightweight, brown Italian wool — and began to dress.

Julie had always been attracted to his impulsive side.

At 9:43, exactly on schedule, the locomotive sounded its whistle. Metal doors banged shut all along the line. A loudspeaker beneath the station eaves blasted forth a few bars of Soviet marching music. The string of forest green cars lurched, hesitated as if having second thoughts, then lurched again and started slowly forward, clacking over the rail joints and squealing through the first turn, carrying southward its cargo of Moscow vacationers and Donbass miners, and one well-dressed, hung over, American bureaucrat, flushed with belated rebellion.

Czesich stowed his suitcase and suiter in the overhead compartment. When the conductress brought his linens, he made up one of the berths, pushed the curtains apart as far as they would go on the wide window and wrapped them around their thin plastic cord. He took off his shoes, hung his jacket and tie on the hook behind the door, nestled his Nikon safely in the blankets of the unused bed, and set out some of his food: the Italian candy, a wedge of cheese, thin Hungarian salami, two bottles of water, aspirin, pickles, crackers, one bruised apple, one bar of chocolate. By the time he'd completed this ritual, the train had escaped Moscow's concrete suburbs and a sourish vodka calm had settled over him. Coal smoke drifted in from the corridor samovar, a scent he would always associate with his first visit to the Soviet Union. That, too, had been a breaking away, tantamount — in the court of East Boston provincial opinion — to illegal.

After a few minutes, the conductress slid open the heavy door and brought him a glass of hot tea. Without benefit of invitation, she sat on the empty berth — just missing his camera — and joined him in watching the unharvested fields slip past. She was a large woman, pillowy breasts and thighs and belly, a sparkle of humor in kind blue eyes. Czesich offered her a coin of salami on a cracker and she accepted it and chewed thoughtfully. "You're American," she stated after a time.

Czesich agreed that he was.

"Beeznessmin?"

"Deeplamat," he said, though it was the last thing he felt like this morning.

He offered her another cracker and a slice of apple, glad for the company. "How goes perestroika?"

She shrugged, squeezing a roll of pink flesh up against her jaw, and said: "Almost completely dead." She waved one arm at a passing emerald pasture, and told him to drink his tea before it got cold.

The land here was undulant and unfenced, broken periodically by a cluster of log houses or a swatch of woods, and Czesich was soothed by it. The train whistled through a village, and he glimpsed a string of old buses and dusty trucks stopped at the crossing, a perfectly straight brown road stretching to the horizon behind them. Except for these vehicles, a few strands of electricity along the railroad line, and the rare tractor raising a rooster tail of dust, he might have been passing through the nineteenth century. Even this close to the capital, men still carried water buckets from the well with shoulder yokes. Kerchiefed, rotund women in quilted work jackets walked worn paths, hoes over their shoulders, sometimes a single tethered cow trailing disconsolately behind. The land here was great and abundant, the whole tableau bespeaking a humble, serene, completely genuine existence. He found himself caught up again in the vision of a house on twenty acres somewhere in central Vermont. Winters, he'd split firewood and ski to the general store for supplies. Summers, he'd cultivate a garden the size of a football field, sell cucumbers and strawberries from his roadside stand. He'd read all of Turgenev and Dostoevsky in the mother tongue, walk down the road after supper to have a cup of tea with Michael and his friends. Most important, all these activities would be clearly marked on a spacious and immaculate interior landscape. The simple facts of eating and breathing and working the dirt would link him, through some mystical chemistry, to a dimension beyond the State Department and the evening news. He would no longer feel compelled to flit around the world in search of the place where real life was being lived.

Czesich thought of the Indian chiefs on Julie's wall and tried to convince himself she harbored a similar dream. She had wanted him to stay in Moscow. He wondered, still in the grasp of this vivid sentimentality, how she would feel about a counteroffer of Vermont.

"You floated away," the conductress said when he looked at her. She had his Nikon in one puffy hand and was turning it back and forth.

"I do that."

"You were thinking about your wife. I can see it on your face." She smiled approvingly and nestled the camera back in the blankets. "You already miss sleeping with her."

"We haven't slept together in many years."

"Plokho," the woman said, shaking an admonitory finger, which shook, in turn, a pound or so of flesh behind her elbow. She leaned slightly forward, intrigued. "Are you a homosexual?"

Czesich hastened to say that he was not.

The Russian word was *gomoseksualist.* In the past it had always made him think of some kind of priapic political party, or a circus act of some sort. Now it put him in mind of his son, of a prim society's numberless humiliations.

"Are you a spy?"

"Of course not."

"Why 'of course not'? You're American, aren't you? Going to Vostok, where all the radicals live. You speak Russian like the Czar."

"There are no spies anymore," Czesich told her. "You have glasnost now, there's nothing we don't know about you."

She flapped a hand at him and laughed.

"I'm with the food distribution program."

"I live in Vostok," she said. "I haven't heard about any food program, any Americans."

"Puchkov's speech," he prompted.

"I haven't heard about any speech."

Czesich took this as a positive sign. "It's a secret program," he said. "No one knows I'm going. Even the Ambassador doesn't know." Especially the Ambassador, he thought.

She peered at him, and he felt as though he were undergoing an examination he'd have to pass before the conversation could go any further. "Did you hear the news?"

"Which?"

"They're striking in Vostok. Our miners."

"When?"

"Last night."

"Why?"

"Political reasons." The conductress squeezed up the flesh around her neck again, as though the whole matter was beyond her. She glanced at the open door. "You've heard of our Mikhail Kabanov?"

"Of course. The First Secretary. Everyone has heard of him."

"The miners despise him."

Czesich found this unsurprising. Since they'd realized, a few years back, that Gorbachev was going to allow them to strike without packing them off to psychiatric hospitals, the miners had acted as the Soviet Union's democratic conscience, striking and threatening to strike, holding the fragile economy hostage as they tried to push their president faster and faster in the direction of reform. If there were any real heroes in the present-day USSR, they worked underground.

"And what do you think of our Kabanov?" the woman said casually, but Czesich knew there was nothing casual about it. What she was really asking was: Which side are you on? What kind of person are you?

"I despise everything he stands for."

The conductress smiled and seemed content to let the conversation die there, as though her mission had been to ascertain that he was not a spy, not a homosexual, not a friend of Mikhail Lvovich Kabanov. She sat with him another few minutes, and when the train slowed to a stop at Tula — Tolstoy country — she slapped the tops of her thighs, thanked him for the snack, and disappeared. Not until weeks later did Czesich give the visit any thought.

He did his best to keep awake, drinking quarts of the sugary tea, pacing the narrow corridor past men in blue jogging suits and women with small children, stepping down onto the platform at each stop and doing a few stretching exercises, trying to cajole his body back toward sobriety. The decision to leave Moscow unaccompanied and unauthorized seemed to float along beside him at a comfortable distance, benign and half-real. It was a gesture, a statement, something he could reverse at any time. Years from now he and Julie might look back on it and laugh.

As the train moved south into the industrial heartland, the landscape changed from rolling fields and woods to flat expanses of steppe. There were the occasional small mountains of mine tailings now, and factories belching variously colored smoke, and two prisons with their guard towers and barbed wire. Until very recently, this had all been part of the secret Soviet Union, the land journalists and tourists and congressional delegations never saw. It was similar, in a shabby way, to the poorest factory towns of the Ohio Valley, only here your forty or fifty hours of toil did not buy even a five-year-old car and a mortgaged, peeling bungalow. There were no backyard pools and barbecued hamburgers to come home to, only a log shack with no plumbing, and a plot of tilled dirt, and one food store in the village that offered soggy canned fish and dusty jars of pickled cabbage. People walked, or rode clattering bicycles, or squeezed themselves into wheezing, mud-spattered buses. They had their teeth fixed without charge by dentists who had never used novocaine or X rays, never touched a meter of floss.

He had always been drawn to just such desolate worlds. It was what had brought him to the United States Communications Agency in the first place. He wanted to help if he could — bring a photography exhibit to the workers of Ufa or Novosibirsk, show the latest medical technology to doctors in Donetsk, hand out a few thousand tons of food in Vostok. And if he couldn't help, he wanted to come here anyway, just to keep things in perspective. Years ago, in a small, industrial ruin of a city in the southern Urals, he and Julie had sat in a *bufyet* on the top floor of their hotel — surrounded by corpulent men drinking warm Soviet champagne and filling their bellies with a breakfast of horsemeat goulash — and discovered their common cause. He could still see her sitting across from him in her summer dress and hoop earrings, all fire and revolution. "Anton," she'd boasted, "the one thing I will never be is a tame, nervous housewife worrying about the color of my refrigerator while babies are starving in Bangladesh."

Julie had been the loveliest girl on the exhibit staff, a creature of Chevy Chase and Radcliffe, two years older and as exotic to him as the Bashkirian countryside. She was everything he'd grown up without — money, sophistication, family prestige — and he'd wanted badly to impress her. "Chekhov wrote something about that," he said. "I don't remember the name of the story, but one of the characters says something like: 'Inside the head of every happy person there should be a little man with a hammer, tapping away as a reminder of the poor.'"

That conversation had been their strange beginning. After that, no waiting Marie DeMarco, no Chevy Chase boyfriend, no amount of guilt had been able to save them from their disastrous infatuation.

They had been part of USCA's flagship exhibition, something called Photography USA, a small traveling museum filled with Stieglitz portraits and camera equipment and staffed by twenty-five Russian-speaking Americans whose job it was to explain democracy and capitalism to the Soviet hordes. And hordes they had been. Even then, even in the days when things American were officially suspect, people had come to the exhibit at the rate of two thousand an hour, squeezing into the hot pavilion, standing mute before photographs of the New York City skyline as though it were Oz, surrounding each of the American exhibit guides in a circle four and five bodies deep and firing questions at them like Kalashnikov rounds: How much do you make in a month? How many square meters in your apartment? Why are there no blacks among you? What are your impressions of our country?

And, over and over again: Why are you in Vietnam? Why are you in Vietnam? Why are you in Vietnam?

It was exhausting work, six days a week for five weeks, and when the show ended, two more weeks of manual labor, wrapping and packing and loading the displays and support equipment into freight containers for shipment to the next city. Even after the workday ended, they were still on duty, representing their country. Often, one of the Soviet visitors would invite them home to dinner. In groups of two and three the guides would squeeze into tiny apartment kitchens and be treated to the finest the family could afford — tough beef, borscht, vodka by the liter. They'd talk until midnight, offer gifts of books and felt-tipped pens and exhibit lapel pins, and be escorted back to within a block of the Intourist hotel, where the hosts would take their leave so as not to be seen by watchful doormen and loitering KGB thugs.

The job had lasted eight months in all, two months each in Ufa, Novosibirsk, and Moscow, with time between for in-country vacations while the containers were being shipped. He and Julie had stood out immediately from the other twenty-three exhibit guides. Their Russian had been learned, not in college classrooms, but at home, from the time they were in diapers, and their fluency attracted the largest crowds and raised them to an unofficial team cocaptaincy.

They began to take meals together in the hotel restaurant, probing the language's finer points, sharing frustrations, telling Stateside stories. It was quickly established that they were both spoken for in the sexual sense — Czesich had given Marie a ring not long before his departure, and Julie had been dating a Harvard law student for a year and a half. But, by the end of the first showing, by the "end of Ufa," as the guides liked to put it, they were accompanying each other on visits to Soviet homes, riding commuter trains out into the countryside on their one day off, sitting together well into the night listening to Cream and Creedence Clearwater, and mapping out their idealistic futures. They'd each had a stint of mindless, useless office work and wanted something better. The Peace Corps was a possibility, Julie said. Her Oliver had only a year of school left; they were always looking for good lawyers in the third world. She wondered aloud about a writing career, about the foreign service.

After Ufa, they vacationed separately. Julie went to Pyatigorsk with a small group of female guides, and Czesich and Mark Freedman from Wisconsin flew to Khabarovsk and rode the Trans-Siberian back to Photography USA's second showing city, Novosibirsk, western Siberia's unofficial capital.

It was midsummer in western Siberia, hot and humid and light until midnight. On the eve of their first day off, the whole group was invited out into the countryside for dinner and a sleepover at a factory dacha complex. Czesich and Julie rode out on the chartered bus together, sat together during a vodka-lubricated dinner, and, afterward, stumbled out into the twilight together and sat by the lake. Julie babbled on about Oliver Whitney, his torts, his contracts, his family's summer house in Rehoboth. Czesich stared across the water toward a stand of arctic fir on the far bank, and at some point simply reached out, moved her hair aside, and touched the vein on her neck with the backs of two fingers. Julie fell quiet for a few seconds and would not look at him, and it seemed to him that both of them were weighing distant obligations against something very close and warm. They were very drunk and slightly homesick. The damp, sandy piece of Siberia on which they sat seemed separated from America by an immeasurable distance, seemed unconnected to the rest of the world. The consequences of anything they might do here could not possibly echo as far back as civilization.

Julie, as he remembered it — and he had enjoyed remembering it across a long span of years — had not even wanted to kiss. There was a wonderful leonine haughtiness about her. She took his head in both her hands and pushed it gently down against the zipper of her jeans. He could smell her through the cloth. He could smell her, and the wet sand under her, and his own sweat and sour breath. When they had their clothes off he tasted her — exotic of exotics — licked the gentle contours of her flat, salty chest, licked under her arms, finally found her mouth and nursed there, rolled her over and over in the sand until she was lying with the top of her head in the lapping edge of the lake, laughing. What a difference it was from Marie! Marie was furtive and modest and they did it half-dressed in his parents' car at Revere Beach, or, once, hurriedly, in her bed in the third-floor apartment on Orient Street. With Marie, the act was always coated in a film of sin and fear.

Julie was sinless and fearless. Drunk and uncaring and pungent. She wrapped her legs around him, spun him over so that *his* hair got wet in the apron of the lake. A wave washed his face and he spluttered. She laughed and spun him back on top and writhed in the mud like a snake. He came too soon for either of them, but she pressed him tight and twisted her hips and ran her fingers up under him and made him stay inside her until he could move again. Julie grunted so, he worried he might be hurting her. This was new to him, luxuriant and sweaty and rough. Somewhere off behind them a laugh sounded, but they worked on and on and she finally slowed and gave up trying and lay back with her arms up on the sand, gasping, fingers in the water.

He worried he had failed her but could not say it. Before she could reach for her underwear she started to bleed, and even the drink couldn't save him from a moment of panic. "You're hurt," he said, and she laughed.

"My purse, please, if you would, Anton Antonovich," she said, gesturing regally up the bank.

So much for Marie. So much for Oliver Whitney.

Novosibirsk was like that. Exhausting days of answering questions in a pavilion without air conditioning, and twilit, muggy nights in the plain hotel. Sometimes after work they rode the *elektrichka* out into the countryside and explored a dirt village. Sometimes they packed a picnic and took a commuter hydroplane up to one of the uninhabited islands that dotted the cold Ob and made love on the sand there before the sky went black, then rode back to the city under all the stars. Sometimes they visited Soviet homes, but Novosibirsk was a military and science center, and the KGB had done a thorough job of intimidating the local populace. Invitations were rare. When he and Julie did visit, they always brought along something exotic to honor their hosts' courage — American liqueurs from the embassy commissary, jars of peanut butter, snapshots of their families.

Letters arrived from home and they read them guiltily in their own rooms and went on fucking, drugged by it.

After Novosibirsk they took their two weeks of vacation together on the Black Sea, half a week each in Sukhumi, Sochi, Pitsunda, and Yalta, fifteen days without mail or questions about the war or the complaints and curiosity of their fellow guides. Czesich knew enough now to be suspicious of the sweet syrup nostalgia dribbled over such memories, but with those fifteen days no syrup was necessary. Those fifteen days were not subject to the ordinary rules of human life. They existed in another dimension entirely, jewels in a glass box.

Darkness fell outside the train window. Czesich found he did
not want to remember further. Moreso than any other Soviet city,
Moscow was connected to the outside world, and their last two
months in Moscow had been mottled, good days and bad, a slow,
lustful sinking toward their difficult end. Recalling that end would
only cast him down into an old depression. He'd listened to that
sad tune enough over the years, been ashamed enough for an or-
chestra of men. He was not going to think about it now.

He went out into the corridor and stood for a while at the large
windows. A few other soft-class passengers stood there as well,
peering out at the darkness, but most were having dinner in their
coupes, or standing between cars in swirls of tobacco smoke. He
could smell beer and salami and soiled diapers, and he could feel
the last remnants of the vodka in his chest and head, hear the flag of
rebellion snapping beside him, still somewhat less than real. He put
a hand in his pocket and fingered the return ticket.

At 9:08 P.M., three minutes behind schedule, the Donbass Express shrieked and huffed into the station at Skovorodila, a ten-
minute stop. Czesich disembarked into the smell of sulfur, and
wandered through the stone depot to see what might be seen. What
might be seen turned out to be dark kiosks, a dark, closed *bufyet*,
tired men and women hunched over bundles on the damp stone
floor, sitting and waiting for some dark metal shape in the night.
He walked all the way through the station and out its front entrance, his shoes and suit drawing stares. He stood on the sidewalk
among somnambulant traffic moving in and out the swinging
doors, and was flooded — until someone tapped him gently on the
left arm — with the sweetness of total anonymity.

He turned. Beside him stood a man only a few inches over five
feet tall, with a thin neck, a long, wispy white beard, sunken eyes
and cheeks. Czesich's fingers were already down in his pants
pocket feeling for change when the man said, in quiet, elegant Russian, "You are the American, yes?"

Czesich said that he was.

"May I speak with you in your coupe?"

Czesich didn't see why not.

// CHAPTER 11

WEDNESDAY afternoon was foggy and damp, typical of Vostok in August, and Propenko stood in front of the Central Exhibits Pavilion in his raincoat, watching his countrymen work and thinking about Nikolai Malov. That was the *komitet's* strategy: they occupied your attention, knocked you just slightly off balance so that everything you did — everything from crossing the street to making a presentation at the office — carried a slightly higher risk of failure. Malov did not have to actually *do* anything, he only had to make you realize he *would* do it, that no sense of shame bound him.

Propenko started to pace. He'd spent all morning in the office with customs forms and waybills, the first physical evidence that the food distribution program actually existed. After lunch, more evidence had materialized, and it stood not far from him now: a line of nineteen tractor-trailers, each trailer loaded with two red freight containers with UNITED STATES OF AMERICA printed in white block letters on all sides. The strange alphabet made him uneasy, as did the fact that one truck was missing. The head driver told him the trailer had snapped an axle just south of Minsk, and a replacement was on the way. But, buffeted with false stories as he was, Propenko had his suspicions.

The first rig pulled into position under the twenty-ton crane, and two laborers in canvas pants and canvas-colored work jackets put a ladder against the rear container and clambered up onto its roof. They took hold of the dangling metal crane hooks, slipped them through steel eyelets at the four corners of the container, and climbed down. With a delicate shifting of levers, the operator raised his crane boom until the cables drew taut, then he lifted the container free of the truck bed, slowly, slowly. The crane swiveled just so. Fifteen tons swung in a tight arc, swayed, hovered, and set down with a soft *boom* on the asphalt lot.

It was a beautiful piece of work. Propenko could see that the crane operator was trying to preserve an air of nonchalance for the benefit of his small audience of drivers and laborers, as if that weren't three hundred thousand rubles' worth of American food he'd off-loaded in one masterful stroke, but just another steel box, as if this were just another job.

But none of the workers seemed to be approaching it as just another job. Their faces were set in serious expressions, and they snapped to each task without the customary shuffling and grumbling. Maybe our country can't feed itself, they seemed to be saying, but we can off-load containers as well as anyone in the world. There were not yet any Americans present to say this to, of course, but that wasn't important. The job had taken on a symbolic air. It had become a matter of national pride.

As the laborers climbed onto the roof of the forward container and wrestled again with the big hooks, Leonid Fishkin crossed the lot and came up beside Propenko, smiling his tight smile. Propenko complimented him on the workers.

"No one wants to be embarrassed," Leonid said.

Though they were almost exactly the same age, Leonid had gone completely gray, and, as if to minimize the effect, wore his hair cropped short. Combined with his sharp features, the haircut gave him a military look, a severity that bore little resemblance to the actual man. The actual man — Propenko's oldest friend — was generous and honest and Jewish; that he had risen to the level of pavilion director in the city of Vostok was a miracle on all three counts.

The miners' strike had been the prelude to every conversation in the office that day, but Leonid had other priorities. "I talked to everyone, Seryozha, from the chef to the cleaning women. I made it clear. As long as this operation is being administered from my pavilion, nothing will be done to lay disgrace on this city or this country. Let me show you the hall."

Leonid took Propenko's arm and escorted him toward a ramp that led up to the front door. Propenko had no idea why Moscow had chosen the Central Exhibits Pavilion as the distribution site. A show of mildly erotic photographs had been hung there a week before, and every afternoon the main floor was crowded with gawkers. There were other buildings in town with large parking lots and empty office space, buildings on side streets or down by the mines, away from the public eye. It was almost as though someone wanted to exaggerate the government's failure to feed its people, write it in lights on the roof of Party Headquarters: CITIZENS! WE CANNOT FEED OURSELVES! GLORY TO THE WORKERS' STATE! It made no sense.

They climbed the concrete ramp and went past a drowsy guard at the front door. Propenko had seen Leonid's hall a thousand times. Boxish, plain, a large main floor with a narrow balcony running above, along all four sides, the pavilion was used by Polish manufacturers displaying coal hammers and industrial hoses, by Komsomol organizations for their fairs and conferences, by the Vostok Oblast Artists Collective for shows like this — daring exhibitions of paintings and posters and photographs. The photography show had opened to the public hours ago, but, in anticipation of the American's arrival, workers were scurrying about, getting in everyone's way — a team of women mopping the hallways, men carrying extra tables out of storage, an electrician on a ladder replacing fluorescent tubes.

Leonid took Propenko upstairs and showed him a small, very clean office. "Everything is ready, Sergei. Tables, telephone, paper, pens. The telex will be installed on Monday, a rush order. I closed off a section of the restaurant for the American Director and whatever other official guests we might have — correspondents, embassy people, and so on. He'll have access to a secretary if he needs one."

By nature, Leonid was a nervous man — nervous in a way that moved him to do three times what his job required — but today he seemed especially tense, almost grim. Relax, Leonidovich, Propenko wanted to say, this is an ordinary human being visiting us, not a king . . . but he felt the same tension in himself. As far as he knew, there had never been an official American visitor in Vostok. The United States of America, after years of energetic propaganda to the contrary, had turned out to be far ahead of them, a kingdom of almost unbelievable wealth and sophistication. The Americans had recently won a Middle Eastern war in a matter of hours — against Soviet tanks and Soviet-trained troops. Propenko worried Vostok would seem shabby to the Western eye.

"The door locks tight," Leonid said, demonstrating. "I'll give the American my only extra key." He took Propenko's arm again and led him past the main offices and back downstairs, where he pointed to a plain blue door. "He'll have his own toilet. The women are cleaning it now, throwing sand on the floor and sweeping it up. They're complaining there's no soap. There hasn't been any toilet paper for two weeks."

"We'll figure something out," Propenko said. "I'll talk to Malov about the paper. He has the toilet connections."

Leonid smiled nervously. "He was here this morning, asking a hundred questions with that smile of his. And I saw his new Volga in front of the hotel last night. I think he was with Bobin. The man just has to put his smell on everything. He's like a dog running here and there pissing on whatever he sees."

"I'll take care of him," Propenko said, and, to his own surprise, his voice sounded sure and unworried. He was beginning to feel the authority of his new position. The various teams of workers were casting sidelong glances at him as he and Leonid crossed the main foyer. He thought he heard one of the women whisper "*Direktr*," and he realized then that, though the food program had an element of shame to it, it had, too, in a perverse way, an element of prestige. He'd been anointed by the Moscow powers to work, not just with foreigners, but with an *American*. Bessarovich stood behind him. Leonid was as solid a friend as one could hope for. Chief Vzyatin, too. Let Malov do his dirty work, Malov was not the Director.

Leonid escorted him back out into the noise and diesel smoke. They walked very slowly along the concrete ramp, admiring a neat row of off-loaded containers, the proud red boxes looking like a raw wound against the gray of the pavilion and the gray city skies. Already the Americans were showing off, and already the color, activity, and strange alphabet were drawing almost as many spectators as the photo show. People were wandering down from the Prospekt of the Revolution, crowding the perimeter of the work site, asking questions of those who'd arrived on the scene a minute or two earlier. It was already a public event.

"We're going to have a crowd-control problem, Leonidovich."

"Tell me some news. I can't believe they're doing this to me. I have four thousand visitors here every day looking at pictures of nipples and miniskirts. I can't believe this. Everyone in Moscow knew we were having the exhibition this month — I spoke to Bessarovich about it not three weeks ago. She knew what kind of numbers it would draw. And now I'm going to have this container circus in my front yard. Right off the Prospekt. People will stop by after work to practice their English."

"Can't you put the line for the photo show in through the back door?"

"We're already setting that up. Vzyatin came by. He gave us extra militiamen, but even if they go in the back door, people have to walk by this. They're going to stop and look, ask for handouts. It's a nightmare."

Propenko put a hand on his friend's back and felt nothing but bone and cable-tight muscles. Leonid had worries he could only imagine. When there was an art exhibition in the Central Pavilion, the KGB colonels hit him up for tickets. When there was a tool show, the Party bosses hit him up for free samples. When foreigners rented the space, the First Secretary's office called and asked if Leonid had been given any German calendars or Swiss watches or Italian fountain pens. Now the joint-venture types, Russia's new capitalists, were after him for names of his Eastern European business contacts, and local Pamyat members were writing letters of protest about "this public display of decadent pornography." On top of everything else, Leonid had to listen to Voice of America every night, hear about another planeload of Soviet Jews disembarking in Tel Aviv, and wonder if he and his family should be among them.

"They're secure, I assume," Propenko said, gesturing over the concrete rail.

"Soviet customs seals. American padlocks. Twenty-four-hour militia guard."

"Should the militia guard worry us?"

Leonid smiled distractedly. "Vzyatin wouldn't steal five kopeks from his worst enemy," he said. "But the rest of them are a bunch of country boys. They like guns and uniforms and girls." He shrugged, stared past the corner of the pavilion and out across the foggy river toward the mines.

"What's wrong?"

Leonid shrugged again. "This killing at the church has changed everything," he said, after a moment. "I just sense it. We're in a new situation now all of a sudden."

"A new weight class," Propenko said. He looked across into the mine district, too, as though he might be able to see what the strikers were up to. He could recall a dozen or so murders in

Vostok in his lifetime, usually the result of a drunken knife fight in one of the rougher bars, or a family argument in the poor neighborhoods south of the river. It was impossible to fit Tikhonovich's death into the same category. "My mother-in-law is calling it the second crucifixion," he said.

"It doesn't worry you?"

"It worries me, Leonid. Everything worries me now."

"Vzyatin told me someone painted a slogan on the church the night of the murder. His men saw it when they arrived. 'The Party Is the Mind, Honor, and Conscience of Our Era.' In red letters."

"Hooligans," Propenko said, but he could feel the skin at the back of his neck. "The Party Is the Mind, Honor, and Conscience of Our Era" was the type of official nonsense that might have shone in lights on top of Party Headquarters not so many months ago.

"Of course," Leonid said bitterly. "Whenever something happens, it's always hooligans. I suppose it was hooligans who convinced the miners to strike. Or foreign agents. Or Jews."

Propenko shook his head as if to shake away a buzzing insect. Leonid was speaking so softly his words were being swallowed up by the noise of the truck engines. He'd thought the days of whispering were behind them.

"Have you ever heard of an organization called the Third Way?"

"Third Path," Propenko said. A small spasm pinched his chest, not quite pain. "Children of the Third Path."

"They hold their meetings at the church." Leonid looked down at the workers. "I thought you might have heard of them. My son is involved."

Propenko could smell his own sweat.

"They organized a demonstration in front of Party Headquarters last night. Five hundred people showed up."

"Five hundred!"

Leonid nodded. "I told you," he said. "The murder changed everything. People are fed up now. The miners are waiting for their beloved Alexei to come back and hold the funeral. After the funeral, there could be five *thousand* people in front of Party Headquarters."

Propenko massaged his forehead. A woman slammed open the pavilion doors and started enthusiastically sweeping the ramp, showing off for her boss and the new Director. Propenko and

Leonid pretended to concentrate on the work being done below. Ten containers had been off-loaded now, another twenty-eight stood waiting on fourteen huffing, smoking trucks. The crane operator and laborers and a few of the drivers had stopped for a smoke and were standing at the side of the crane, laughing with their heads thrown back. Propenko watched them with a twinge of envy.

"I walked by the Party building last night on my way home," Leonid said quietly, when the woman had gone past and was working at the bottom of the ramp. "To see for myself. Sometimes I think I should be standing there with those people."

"Pavilion director on a hunger strike?"

Leonid did not smile.

Both of them were leaning on their elbows, shoulder to shoulder on the concrete rail. Propenko moved his head enough to see Leonid's eyes. "Do you know Lydia is involved in the meetings?"

"My son told me."

"Know who told me?"

Leonid shook his head and grinned for the benefit of some unseen observer.

"Bessarovich."

The grin slipped from Leonid's face like snow from a roof. "Strange," he said.

"More than strange. How does Bessarovich know more about what my daughter is doing than I do?"

Leonid pinched his eyebrows together. He took a pack of Bulgarian cigarettes out of his inside pocket and offered it with a shake of the wrist. Propenko declined. Below them the laborers struggled to regain their rhythm. One of them slipped on the wet container roof and fell on his elbow. He got up, laughing and shaking his arm, tried a karate kick at the dangling cable, and fell again. Propenko wondered if the men had been drinking during their break.

"Are there suspects?"

Leonid blew a puff of smoke out the side of his mouth. "If you believe Malov. Fingerprints on the church wall. Footprints in the dirt."

"The man lies like he breathes," Propenko said. "The other night he just about accused me of rape."

Leonid said nothing for a few seconds. He let the cigarette dangle from his fingers, and a small twist of gray smoke rose up along one side of his face. Propenko realized he'd mentioned the rape only to get Leonid's reaction, to measure it against his own, against Raisa's.

Leonid's reaction did not soothe him. "If it's reached that level, my friend, I hope you have someone higher up than me you can talk to."

Propenko thought of Bessarovich, tried to imagine what she would say if he flew up to Moscow, walked into her office, and told her what he'd just told Leonid.

"I think he's just trying to keep me in line, with the American coming and all. He's worried I'm going to ask for political asylum, take the family to *Menkhettn*."

Leonid looked as if he were in pain. "Just watch him, Sergei, that's all. You saw him in the meeting. He's been a little bit crazy lately. His world is breaking apart like everyone else's. I hope you have someone you can turn to."

Again, Propenko made a show of not caring. He shook Leonid's hand and walked away from the pavilion, thinking of Raisa and Lydia and Marya Petrovna. In the final analysis, they would be the ones he would turn to, the only ones. He had not wanted to say that to Leonid.

Raisa had taken the car that morning to drive her mother to the polyclinic for tests. It was five kilometers to their apartment — fifteen minutes on a packed trolley or forty minutes on foot. Propenko elected to walk, but he'd gone only half a block when he made an about-face and headed west in a crowd of rush-hour pedestrians.

Party Headquarters was set well back from the street, behind a small park with a statue of Lenin in its center. When he was still two blocks away, Propenko started listening for chanting demonstrators and looking for people who fit his idea of political activists, but he saw and heard nothing out of the ordinary. The park's green face came into view — still no people, no unusual noises. He reached the corner and turned right, saw the roof of the imposing granite headquarters off behind the trees, saw the top of Vladimir Ilyich's gray head, one arm thrust out, directing the masses. But there were no masses to direct. He walked a few steps into the park and saw something, finally, at the far edge of the lawn: a wooden crucifix, a few clusters of people milling about next to eight or ten placards stuck in the dirt like street signs. Another handful of demonstrators sat on a tarpaulin, talking with each other — the hunger strikers, he supposed. In all, the protest consisted of not more than fifty people, and gave off about as much energy as a crowded bus stop.

He stood and watched for a moment, relieved. Even a paranoid Mikhail Lvovich wouldn't feel threatened by such a motley group.

Satisfied with his brief inspection and already late for dinner, he allowed himself the luxury of a taxi. The driver smoked and changed lanes without signaling, and swung his head back and forth to a tape of Western rock and roll. Propenko let the city slip past, and watched his sense of relief turn rotten.

The first thing he noticed when he opened the apartment door was that Raisa and Marya Petrovna were sitting too close together. Raisa had both hands on her mother's wrist and was rubbing them back and forth there as if to restart her circulation. "Something happened," he said, taking off his raincoat and joining them.

"Something," Raisa repeated bitterly. "Your Malov was here talking to Mama while I was at work."

Propenko slammed his fist down on the table, rattling the empty sugar bowl and spilling some of his mother-in-law's tea.

"I came home to take her to the clinic and she was staring out the window, cursing like a Cossack."

The old woman shrugged and smoothed the tablecloth with one hand.

"What did he want?"

"He said he wanted to ask you a question about the food deliveries," Raisa said, "but he ended up talking about Lydia. What is she studying at university, where does she want to work afterward, how does she spend her free time? Everything was casual. He acted like a cousin on a social visit, smiling all the time."

"What did you tell him, Mother?"

"I told him I'd light a candle for his soul at the Church of the Sacred Blood," Marya Petrovna said ferociously. "I told him my husband had been taken out of my own house and beaten in the cellar of State Security, that they'd had to tie his hands before they beat him because they were cowards. I told the spineless *chekist:* 'If you haven't left the apartment before my son-in-law comes home, he's going to send you through the window with one right hand. A Master of Sport in Boxing,' I told him. 'One right hand and you're lying in the gutter covered with glass and spit.' "

They heard the metal elevator gate slam open and shut. Lydia's footsteps tapped in the hall; the click of her key in the lock seemed to suck away some of the kitchen air. "Maybe you could have skipped that last line, Mother," Raisa said dryly, and they made themselves smile.

After supper, Propenko sat in the armchair with a copy of *Soviet Labor* in his lap, running his eyes back and forth across the front page, trying to make a connection between these spots of ink and real, living events. He could not seem to keep still. He looked across the room at Raisa, who was sitting on their bed, sewing, pinching the muscles of her face in concentration, then at Lydia, drinking tea at the kitchen table and immersed in a book of Akhmatova's poetry.

He tried again to make sense of the lead article, but quickly gave it up, went into the kitchen, and poured himself a glass of water. Lydia stopped reading and looked up. "Lydochka," he said, "I'm going down to the gym for a little while. Want some driving practice?"

The offer pleased her.

She drove nervously and carefully, both hands gripping the wheel, her forehead furrowed like her mother's when she sewed, her eyes darting back and forth from one side of the road to the other. It was only a kilometer to the sports hall, and when they reached it, Propenko let her practice parallel parking for a few minutes while he practiced his lines.

"You drive better than I do," he said, when she turned off the engine. "Why don't you take the car and go see your friends, or Aunt Anna. I don't mind walking home tonight. I need to think over a few things."

"Are you in trouble, Pa?"

He turned sideways on the seat so they were facing each other. Lydia had been feisty and full of argument even as a child, and he did not want to breed into her now what had been bred into him. He did not want to help create a woman who could walk away from Party Headquarters *relieved* at the small number of demonstrators there. "I liked what you said the other night. About the Children of the Third Path."

"*People* of the Third Path, Pa."

"Right. It made sense to me. The ideas are good." He stopped and looked out the front window, trying to guess the language she listened in. "But I think it leaves something out." He checked her face. She seemed ready to argue, at least, if not listen. "Things like Marxism, capitalism, the Third Path — they have to be worked out in the world of people, you know. And every person has flaws, so those flaws are going to become part of any system. Can you see that?"

She nodded, watching him somewhat suspiciously. At the end of the block a trolley went along its tracks, throwing sparks.

"I'm not saying you shouldn't try to change the system — some systems absorb flaws better than others — but you should remember you're not dealing with predictable things. You're dealing with people, and people don't behave according to reason. People — men especially — can be vicious, I don't have to tell you that —"

"Does this have something to do with the man who came to the house? Is he a *kagebeshnik*?"

"It was Nikolai Malov from the office," Propenko said, feeling the name again just below his ribs. "You know him."

"Your friend with the ear. I've seen him a lot lately."

"Where?"

"Around."

"Around where? Has he been following you?"

"Just around, Pa. I saw him downtown once or twice, that's all."

Propenko chewed the inside of his cheek and tried to filter the fear out of his voice. "My friend with the ear has been jealous of me for thirty years. Whether he's KGB or not isn't nearly as important as the jealousy. Do you see that?" He felt he was slipping off the track. He'd meant to caution, not instruct. He'd meant to talk about *her*, not himself, not Malov.

"Of course, Pa."

"The situation with him is complicated. I can't tell you everything about it because I don't understand it myself. If I understood it, I'd know what to do, and I don't know what to do yet."

Lydia considered this a moment. "My friends on the Strike Committee say it's just about power. Father Alexei says the same thing."

"You have friends on the Strike Committee?"

She pushed her hair back over one ear and looked away. "I mean, if this man is in power, and if he's jealous, then jealousy has the power. It's the lesson of Stalin, isn't it? If one person has the power, then his faults and strengths matter most. If the power is shared, then everything is better, isn't it?"

"The lesson of Stalin is fear," Propenko told her. "And whoever shot Tikhonovich is trying to teach us all over again. If you scare someone, you can control them. It's an old tactic, prehistoric."

"So this Nikolai is trying to frighten you?"

"Us," Propenko said. He tried to forget everything he'd ever heard about Malov's interrogation methods, to appear as fearless as possible, but Lydia wasn't looking at him. She'd turned her eyes out the windshield and was glaring at the dark street, arms crossed stubbornly in front of her, exactly like Marya Petrovna. Friday's weeping and the weekend's sad silences were over with. "Then what we have to do," she said, "is frighten him back, Pa, right?"

Propenko put on a show with the heavy bag. He circled it, driving his left hand into the leather, head-high — once, twice — following with a low, hard right. As his body warmed up, he fell into his rhythm and circled slightly faster, jabbing, feinting, pulling the power up from his feet and legs. He stepped in closer and went at the belly of his opponent with both fists, each punch making the bag jump up and back on its chain. Some of the other boxers and gymnasts and weightlifters stopped what they were doing and watched the big, middle-aged man. But the big, middle-aged man was blind to everything but the twisting, jumping bag and the sweaty workings of his own arms and legs. He punished the old bag until it started dribbling a pattern of sand down onto the concrete floor and the manager of the gym came over and asked him very politely to stop.

// CHAPTER 12

CZESICH did not know quite what to make of the fellow sitting on the opposite berth. He looked seventy or even seventy-five, but moved and sat like a younger man. His clothes belonged to the working class — plain black work boots, wrinkled trousers, a clean blue sweatshirt — but the eyes were an artist's — steady, somewhat dreamy. Sharp cheekbones stood out above a long, thin beard like the kind worn by Orthodox priests, but if this ragged fellow was a priest, Czesich was a McCarthyite, a teetotaler, a Langley spook. By the time the train cleared the station, Czesich — who prided himself on such quick assessments — decided he was hosting a slightly drunken poet who'd had a life-long interest in the United States and who was now going to keep him up half the night asking questions about Jack London and Marilyn Monroe. Which was fine. He had a history of meeting interesting characters on Soviet trains. On the ride from Yalta to Moscow in 1968, he and Julie had fallen in with a band of Georgian theater types and stayed up until dawn drinking Tsinandali and trading Brezhnev anecdotes.

"Do you mind if we close the door?" the old man asked. His voice resonated in the small coupe, though he'd spoken quietly.

A poet used to reading for an audience, Czesich decided. He slid the heavy door to and twisted the latch.

His guest smiled with closed lips, said "Alexei," and extended a frail hand.

"Anton Czesich."

"Chezik. Chez-ik — not a Russian name," the old man observed. "A Croat?"

"It's Russian. It used to be Chizhik." The old man did not seem to understand, and Czesich repeated "Chizhik" a bit louder, and flapped his hands in a crude imitation of a siskin. "The bird."

"Then why do you use Chezik, not Chizhik?"

"Because it was changed by the immigration officials in 1917. They wrote it down wrong."

"Ah," Alexei said, smiling. "And why haven't you changed it back?"

The question was pleasantly put; still, Czesich found it slightly irritating. The old man's steady, porcelain eyes were beginning to irritate him, too, though they reminded him of his father's father, another Alexei, another wiry, kindly, tough little Russian. Grandpa Czesich had, in fact, been fond of complaining about the mutilated name, which now began in Poland and ended in Yugoslavia. Both his country and his name had been taken away from him, he often said, and he thought it unlikely either would ever be returned.

The poet was waiting for an answer.

Czesich shrugged. "Just never thought to do it."

They rode along for a few seconds in a friendly silence. "You're going to Vostok, someone told me."

"That's right. I'm with the food distribution program." Saying it, Czesich experienced a small twinge of guilt, but he soldiered on. "It's a pilot program. We're trying to find out what's the best type of . . . assistance to offer right now."

"You're with the embassy?"

Czesich nodded. It crossed his mind that this was the type of question, and the type of superficially pleasant, directed conversation favored by the KGB snoops who had always been assigned to his USCA exhibits, but Alexei did not fit the mold. Too old, for one thing; too kindly, not quite sober.

The train was rocketing along a flat, straight stretch, and Czesich felt wisps of doubt flashing past outside the dark window. His escape from the bureaucratic cage was almost real now, and beginning to worry him.

"Do you know Peter McCauley at the embassy?"

Pyotr Meekawley. Czesich received the sound of this name, which he'd heard first on Julie's lips less than twenty-four hours ago, like a sort of mocking punch to his soft belly. He'd created a mental image of Julie's lover — tall, confident, handsome as a model — and now he looked at the old man and tried to chase it away: "McCauley and I share a close friend," he said.

Alexei seemed pleased. "He told us he'd try to send someone to Vostok, but I didn't expect it so soon. He's assisted us before."

Czesich smiled from habit, but he was somewhat confused. "You live in Vostok, then?"

"Of course. Our friend was just killed there, murdered. Bogdan Tikhonovich."

An automatic expression of sympathy came to Czesich's lips, and he spoke it. The old man gave him a puzzled look, still scrutinizing, and Czesich had an intuition they were talking at cross-purposes, that Alexei had mistaken him for someone else. He felt something more was expected of him but had no idea what it might be. The dull vodka headache had returned.

"Bogdan Tikhonovich Arkhipov," Alexei prompted. "At the church . . . Sacred Blood."

"The watchman," Czesich said. He remembered Julie mentioning it; he remembered thinking she'd been making it up to try to frighten him.

"Meekawley's friend."

"Of course." It made sense now. Quite often, Soviet artists and musicians not in good standing with the authorities would find work outside their field — as church watchmen or parking-lot attendants, no-show or half-show jobs that enabled them to retain a legally employed status while preserving the sanctity of their art. It was the Soviet equivalent of America's waitress-actresses and cabdriver-novelists. The late Tikhonovich and this Alexei must have been poet buddies, or abstract painters, or jazz musicians, and this McCauley character was in the embassy's cultural affairs section — hadn't Julie said that? — charged with pursuing contacts among a large, loose stable of dissident artists and intellectuals. No wonder she'd heard about the murder so quickly; her lover had had dealings with this Tikhonovich. Why hadn't she just come out and said so?

Alexei was going to ask a favor now, Czesich could feel it. He'd want the name of literary magazine editors in the States, or he'd offer to pay Czesich to send him painting supplies or guitar strings from America. After all the years of working here, Czesich was used to conversations like this, quick friendships that led quickly to the famous Russian line: *Oo minya yest ahdna prozba.* I have one favor to ask.

He would, as always, be happy to oblige.

"I didn't know Tikhonovich," he said in his best, kindly-American-abroad voice, "and I'm not in McCauley's line of work, but if I can do something for you, just say the word. We know things aren't easy in Vostok right now."

There occurred then one of the extraordinarily subtle shifts of mood he seemed always a step or two slow in noticing. Alexei hesitated, thanked him rather awkwardly; they spoke cordially for a time about the miners' strike, and the food situation, the weather in Vostok. But there was no request for a favor, and after a few minutes Czesich sensed that something had gone awry. Alexei seemed to have pulled a shade down over his eyes, changed course in midconversation. Czesich wondered if he was imagining it, or if he'd somehow offended the old poet, and he went back over the last few exchanges carefully. Why was this always happening to him? How many times in his youth had he been swinging along in conversation with a cousin or uncle or East Boston friend, and suddenly felt himself being looked at from behind a false face? As though what the person was thinking *about* him, and saying *to* him, had diverged without his noticing. As if he'd misspoken, and his sense of not being who he was supposed to be — not Italian enough, not loyal enough, too bookish — had been exposed like a shameful infection. He remembered feeling that way when his teammates at EB High first found out some of the colleges he'd applied to were not "hockey schools," when his father caught him in the bedroom at midnight reading *The Brothers Karamazov* instead of *Playboy*. It mystified and frustrated him. He redoubled his conversational efforts, but Alexei's porcelain eyes were in shadow.

"Would you care for some beer? Pickles?"

Alexei shook his head, and there was another silence, not so comfortable. "Well," the old man said, getting to his feet, snuffing out their acquaintance before it had started to throw any light. "I wish you all the success in your program."

They stood close together between berths, Czesich almost a foot taller and trying to maintain his balance while reaching into his pocket for a business card. "I'll most likely be staying at the Intourist Hotel," he said. "I hope you'll come see me. I'll be happy to do what I can."

Alexei studied the card a moment, then pocketed it in a careless way and made a show of shaking Czesich's hand. "All the best, all the best," he kept saying, until Czesich unlatched and slid open the door, releasing him, and watched the strange old fellow walk off in the direction of the hard-class cars.

Anton Antonovich Chizhik slept the sleep of the dead, a slumber metered by the knocking of metal wheels and the berth's rock-a-bye undulations. He dreamt he was witness to a car accident, all shattering glass and screams. He helped pull a skinless body out of a ditch by the side of the road and was proud of himself — even in sleep — for not being sickened by the sight and touch of it. He knelt beside the body and was about to administer CPR when he realized he had never been trained in CPR. He did not know the first thing about first aid. The dream shifted and he was in a hospital bed himself, twisting in pain, skinless, raw. He called for help, but the doctor asked him to wait, and began doing crazy tricks with his eyes, crossing them, widening them until they were the size of golf balls, turning one in one direction and one in the other, yanking an earlobe.

When he awoke, perplexed and dry-mouthed, it was morning, and the Donbass Express was traversing a freight yard the size of a small lake. He stared out the window at row upon row of empty sidings, then, in staggered formation, lengths of stalled, headless freights laden with coal and timber, then dripping tanker cars and sleek, silvery military transports. In the corridor his conductress friend sang: "Uzinsk. Uzinsk." Brakes squealed. She knocked twice on his door. "Wake up inside, Comrade American. Who's in there with you?"

"All alone and naked," he yelled, and her loud, heaving laughter faded down the corridor.

The train wheezed and banged and shuddered to a stop, and a man in oily black pants and a black quilted work jacket came down the line tapping the brake drums with a long-handled hammer. Czesich drank from one of his Evian bottles and watched the commotion on the platform, where skinheaded army recruits formed ragged lines, and a pair of reunited lovers kissed. There was very little alcohol left in his system, nothing in the cloudy morning to keep him from seeing the magnitude of his unsanctioned errand, the foolishness and the risk. For as long as it took the embassy to track him down — and it would not take very long — he would be a lone impersonator in a Stalinist backwater. They were assassinating church caretakers in Vostok now; did he really expect to change anything with a few boxes of food?

When the train was moving again, he took his shaving kit and squeezed past his fellow passengers, who stood gazing out at Uzinsk's ravaged exurbia. The face that greeted him in the small bathroom mirror was wan and puffy, not a hero's face. He wedged one foot against the door, spread shaving cream on his cheeks and chin, and considered his options. Unless he caught the next train north, Julie would be furious with him, and rightly so. Professionally and personally, he'd be stepping far over the line, pinching her between friendship and career, breaking every embassy and USCA rule. Personally, the reasonable thing would have been to stay around Moscow for a few weeks, reinforce their sagging friendship, see where things really stood with this handsome Mc-Cauley character.

He ran soap off the blade and started in on his throat, working carefully in the smelly, rocking cabin. Professionally, the reasonable thing would have been to draft a classified cable to Washington outlining his argument for wanting to go to Vostok, then wait for an audience with Ambassador Haydock and present his case there, too — dispassionate, bloodless, diplomatic. There was at least a chance the program was being delayed from the embassy's end of things, not the State Department's. "Fresh information from the field," as they put it in federal parlance. He should have worked those odds, spent some time with Julie, let the U.S. Government play its slow hand. That would have been the reasonable thing.

He finished scraping his chin, splashed and dried his face, and regarded his new self in the mirror. Thin brown hair, sad brown eyes, a certain unwholesome, desk-job flabbiness that seemed to surround a shrinking soul. He had been doing the reasonable thing for twenty-three years. Look what it had gotten him.

Back in the coupe he pulled down his heavy suitcase and suiter, wrapped his camera in a sweater and squeezed it in among his socks and underwear, then unzipped the suiter and dressed himself for battle: a fresh white shirt; a modest tie of black and lilac diagonals; his best suit — black wool and silk with a thin blue thread running through it. He ran a cloth over his shoes and filled his right coat pocket with lapel pins and Marine Corps lighters, peered into the small square of mirrored glass behind the door, adjusted his collar, brushed a speck of old skin from one eye. Outside, a small river village slipped slowly past, and at its edge he saw a peasant woman shuffling along the dirt street cradling a bottle of milk against her bosom as though it were a bar of gold. The woman put him in mind of Grandpa Czesich's sweet nostalgia, of the wreckage behind Russia's cold, proud facades, of Pushkin.

"From a land of somber exile," Czesich said to her through the window, "you summoned me to another land."

// CHAPTER 13

ON THE MORNING of the American Director's arrival, Propenko left the apartment twenty minutes early, carrying with him the encouragement of his wife, daughter, and mother-in-law, and a stomach full of tea. He had not been able to eat a proper breakfast; he had slept only four hours. His thoughts were shadowed by a shape he could not see.

At the corner of Makeyevka Street he made an illegal left turn, drove a block, and pulled up in front of a small shop with windows that had not been washed since Khrushchev. The Lada stalled before he had a chance to turn it off. Inside the shop, Vladimir Tolkachev sat at a table covered with alarm clocks and pocket watches and oily, lilliputian tools. Tolkachev glanced up when he heard the door, smiled, and went back to twirling a finger-sized screwdriver against the casing of a man's watch.

"Small Sergei," he said, eyes on his work. "How many winters, how many years."

Propenko let out a nervous laugh — it had been days, not years — and sat on a stool to watch the master finish his task.

Tolkachev was a physicist by training and, Propenko's father had often said, an exceptionally fine one. But, like a handful of other brilliant young scientists in the early sixties, he'd decided his country needed him so badly it would allow him to speak his mind at scientific forums attended by foreigners, in professional journals, in classrooms and laboratories. Worse, he'd made the mistake of assuming that his genius entitled him to literary license, and at one conference he'd passed around a sheaf of typed pages containing his blueprint for scientific cooperation and world peace. A few years earlier, under Stalin, such precociousness would have been fatal. But in the early sixties, it had earned Tolkachev only a year and a half in the camps — where he learned to keep his peaceful notions to himself — and a slight change in career which condemned him to this drafty shop for the last half of his life.

Propenko saw him on weekends at the dacha (which Tolkachev had obtained before his disgrace, and held on to thanks to political help from Big Sergei), but he made it a point to stop in at the watch repair shop three or four times a month as well. The shop gave off an air of defiance; it reminded Propenko of what he was not.

"Comrade Director," Tolkachev said, when he'd tightened the last screw and set the watch down carefully on his cloth-covered workbench. "Your look is a worried one this morning. What is the news of the hour?"

"The American arrives at noon."

To indicate that the subject interested him, Tolkachev grunted and wiped his long, thin hands. "Tea?"

Propenko declined.

"Now the sons of bitches will descend on you like vultures," Tolkachev said, tending to his pot and cup. He'd rigged some kind of metal shield around his hotplate, so the water came to a boil in half the usual time. "Have they embarked on their shameless begging yet?"

"Who?"

"The idiots you work with and their idiot superiors."

"Not yet."

Tolkachev removed his thick eyeglasses and began wiping them meticulously with the clean tails of his shirt. "Don't be surprised if you get a call from the Chief Idiot himself." Mikhail Lvovich, Second Secretary at the time of Tolkachev's troubles, had been among a large group of Party bosses eager to denounce the young scientist. Tolkachev, of course, had never forgotten.

"He's soiling his trousers now, the son of a bitch, with an American coming to his city and the miners walking out. He's watching the locomotive come at him down the dark tunnel." Tolkachev replaced his spectacles and made a soft sound like *choo choo*.

"I went by Party Headquarters last night, though," Propenko confessed. "There were hardly any demonstrators."

Tolkachev sipped his tea. "Because the strikers called a public meeting at the Nevsky Mine, Small Sergei. They say there were two or three thousand people."

Propenko swallowed.

"This is the end for Lvovich, the charging locomotive itself."

"That's what Lydia says."

"Lydochka knows more than you think she knows."

Propenko was sure of it. It was beginning to be clear to him that the Lydia he knew at home — with her Russian poetry and rock and roll posters and her friends whose idea of revolution was to buy a pair of Western jeans and smoke a Bulgarian cigarette now and then — was only a small piece of the actual person, that her life could no longer be encompassed by his imagination. She had certainly known about this meeting at the Nevsky Mine and not seen fit to tell him.

Tolkachev was studying him as if *he* needed repair. "I was *relieved* to see it was a small crowd," Propenko went on, driving his confession past the point of comfort. There was not another person in the city he could have admitted this to, not Leonid or Vzyatin, not even Raisa or Lydia or Marya Petrovna. Something in Tolkachev's manner gave the impression that he had witnessed or imagined every treacherous possibility of the human heart, every compromise fear could inspire.

The watchmaker shrugged. "That's normal, Seryozha, that's what the bastard counts on. No one wants any more chaos than we already have. The son of a bitch understands that. He *uses* it, don't you see?"

Propenko nodded and looked away, half-absolved.

"But this time he miscalculated. You can't go around having people shot in the back of the head for no reason. Not now. Twenty years ago you could have done it, even ten years ago. Now, no."

"I can't imagine him actually giving the order to kill a church caretaker."

"He didn't have to, Sergei. All he had to do was create the conditions. Understand? Stalin didn't kill all those people. He didn't even give the order in most cases. He *created the conditions.*" Tolkachev tapped his spectacles back up against the bridge of his nose, and, as he was sometimes known to do, assumed the tone of a mystic translating for the masses. "Certain physical reactions occur at certain temperatures and pressures. The universe is bound by laws. The laws are rigid. If you have A and B, you must, within a certain probability, always have C. And it is the same with human beings." He brought the fingers of each hand together in a point and pushed the points against each other over his teacup. "A certain temperature, a certain pressure, a certain result. This is what believers sometimes mistakenly refer to as God's will. It is not God's will, it is simply the way of the universe. God has nothing to say about it anymore."

It was impossible to tell whether Tolkachev was being serious or performing a rueful mimicry at his own expense. The man had been schooled in the fine art of shrouding his opinions. At times he played the old fool, other times the professor. Sometimes he seemed to believe in God, sometimes to be ridiculing believers. He had his modest salary — augmented by bonuses for special favors — and his one-room apartment filled with physics texts and French novels. Weekends, he rode the commuter train out to his dacha and made cranberry wine and put up vegetables and went from house to house telling stories from his camp days. There was no chauffeured Volga, no trips to Sweden for professional conferences, none of the privileges other scientists of his caliber enjoyed, but Tolkachev seemed beyond regret. Chastened and misemployed, his genius caged in this tiny shop, he'd nevertheless found a type of peace for himself. Propenko could not help but compare him to his own father — admired in his field, cautious, materially comfortable . . . and miserable until the day he died.

"You have risen to a new altitude now, Small Sergei. Different temperature there, different pressure. Things will happen at a different speed."

"A different weight class," Propenko said.

There was a cacophonous ringing and buzzing and sounding of chimes as every working timepiece in the shop announced the hour. Propenko was late for work. He stood and stole a sip of tea from the old man's cup. "I came for a word of advice," he said, in part to flatter his father's friend, in part because it was true.

Tolkachev made a serious face and pondered for a while, the room reverberating around him. "When they bear down on you, Seryozha," he said, looking up, "be the boxer."

Propenko promised to try. He left the shop and crossed the dreary sidewalk, more anxious than when he'd arrived.

At the Council Building, he tried to steady himself with routine. Lyuba Mikhailovna came in to tell him what had gone on in the office the afternoon before, but her words seemed to reach him through batts of cotton. She spoke ("The missing truck is still missing, Sergei Sergeievich") and he responded ("Contact the GAI and have the roads checked between here and Brest"), but their voices were whispers amidst the ticking and ringing of his thoughts.

When Lyuba returned to her desk, Propenko made a list of things to do before leaving for the station. He had to call Vzyatin and arrange an extra police brigade for Monday morning, when the actual food distribution was scheduled to begin. There were packing lists to check, customs forms to finish filling out. Bessarovich had called and left a message suggesting he give interviews to the local news media. He had to contact the director of the Intourist Hotel, Slava Bobin, and see if there were any last-minute problems. But as soon as he picked up the phone to make the first call, there was a noise at the door, and two strangers appeared on the threshold. They were an odd pair, one well past retirement age with a cluster of war decorations sewn onto his worn sport coat and wild white hair shooting out above his ears; the other tall, balding, younger, but just as poorly dressed and wearing a set of spectacles so thick his eyes looked as big as one of Tolkachev's watch faces. The older one gave a short bow and said, "Comrade Director?" He was completely toothless, a stubborn, tattered remnant of the generation that had saved the country from extinction. Out of some inbred sense of obligation, Propenko motioned them in.

The two men sat at attention, each holding a hat on his knees. In addition to his hat, the younger, balding one carried a paper bag, and Propenko assumed, at first, they'd come to bribe Ryshevsky about jobs in the customs warehouse and had stumbled into the wrong office.

But the older one repeated his formal salutation, "Comrade Director?" and seemed to be awaiting permission to speak.

Propenko nodded.

"Yesterday we were at the pavilion where the American food containers are being stored." He twisted his cap in both hands, and Propenko saw that he was missing, besides his teeth, half of one index finger. "We want to work as watchmen there. We have experience."

The younger, balding one made two exaggerated nods.

"I'd be happy to hire you," Propenko said politely, "but we already have a guard there. The militia is watching the containers night and day."

"The militia is shit," the balding one said suddenly. "Shit from the village barns."

Propenko could not keep himself from glancing down at the clock in front of him. It was five after ten. He had to leave for the station in an hour, and the list of things to do before then was as long as his forearm.

"Show him," the old one said, and the balding man unfolded and opened his bag and took out a brass padlock. The lock was open, swinging on its hinge. He reached forward, placed it upright on top of Propenko's forms, and said, *"Amerikanski."*

"We were there last night," the old one repeated. "One of the container locks was already gone, and we found this one here hanging open, just like it is now. The boys try every combination of numbers until they get the right one."

"What boys?"

"Juvenile delinquents. The mafia pays them."

"What about the militia?" Propenko asked, in a slight panic.

The toothless one waved a hand. "Militia, what? The lieutenant is inside sleeping. Every two hours he wakes up and walks around with his flashlight and pisses in the weeds. The boys sit up on the hill, laughing. When the lieutenant goes back inside they come down like wild dogs and start in on their numbers again, 0-0-0-1, 0-0-0-2, 0-0-0-3."

Propenko turned the lock upside down. The combination showed that the juvenile delinquents had had enough time to work their way through one thousand two hundred and sixty-three combinations. The telephone rang.

"Ready for the American invasion?" Vzyatin shouted over the electric din.

Propenko was holding the lock in one hand, the telephone in the other, looking at the two men across from him and imagining thirty-eight neatly parked, brightly painted, and completely empty American containers. "Victor," he yelled back, cupping his hand around the mouthpiece for amplification, "a serious problem. Can you stop by and see me before I leave?"

"No! I can meet you at the station, or afterward, for lunch!"

"At the station! I'll be with Anatoly!"

When Propenko hung up, the toothless man was pointing to his decorations. "I was wounded outside of Warsaw," he said, the word coming across his bare gums as "Wah-wah."

Propenko nodded.

"We'd need a booth," his partner said. "I'd work nights, he'd work days. Sometimes we'd overlap, for company."

Propenko wasn't listening. "Did they break the customs seals?"

"Nah." The bald one waved a hand. "They want the locks, not the food."

"But other people want the food," the older one said. "It's just a matter of time. Customs seals don't mean that much anymore."

The phone rang again.

"Good morning, Sergei Sergeievich," a voice boomed in his ear, and it was a second before Propenko could put a face to it.

"Mikhail Lvovich," he said, doing his best to sound respectful. At the name, both faces across the desk went into contortions. The younger man — whom Propenko now understood to be less than completely sane — pretended to vomit on the floor.

"Congratulations, my friend," the First Secretary was saying. "I had dinner at the Intourist last night and Bobin gave me the news. My warmest congratulations."

"Thank you, Mikhail Lvovich. The American is coming in to-day. We're hoping —"

"Listen." The First Secretary cut him off. "Nina and I want to have you to the house for dinner. You, Raisa Maximovna, and us. That's all, the four of us."

Propenko saw Volkov go past in the hallway. His boss went out of sight, came back, made a see-me-afterward-in-my-office ges-ture, and stumbled on. "Whatever night is good for you, Mikhail Lvovich," Propenko said into the phone, and immediately regret-ted it. What was he thinking? Raisa would be furious.

"When do you actually start handing out the food?"

"Monday."

"Sunday, then. Sunday night." The First Secretary made it sound as though dinner with the Propenkos was an event he and his wife had been looking forward to all summer. "Before you get too busy." There was a brief pause, as if Lvovich had been dis-tracted by something in his office, then another burst of sincerity over the crackling line. "They couldn't have picked a better man for the job. When exactly are you expecting the American ambas-sador?"

"We have no official —"

"Unofficially."

Propenko paused for only a second. He was learning fast.

"Unofficially" — he picked the date of his wedding anniversary — "September first. But that's a State secret."

"Safe with me," Mikhail Lvovich said over what had now become a comical clanging and whistling. "Sunday night, eight o'clock sharp!" he shouted, and abruptly hung up.

"The oblast's number-one criminal," the bald one said furiously.

His partner shushed him. "We need a booth and we'll take care of the rest."

Propenko required a moment to compose himself. Things were happening too fast — American-style. "You've done this before?"

They nodded in tandem. "We're at the parking lot next to the Central Market. Where the pinecones park. Mikhail Lvovich himself used to park there when he went to see his girlfriend on Matroskaya Street."

"I whizzed on his tire one night," the bald one put in.

The older man looked dismayed. "He's crazy," he explained to Propenko, "but nothing scares him. It was him who saw the lock hanging. He chased the kids away. By now, two or three of the other locks are probably gone."

Propenko had already made up his mind, but he leaned back in his chair and considered the ramifications. Leonid would be upset about it. Vzyatin would throw a fit. And these two would no doubt spend half their time pestering the American for food, gifts, dollars, whiskey. It complicated things, but it wouldn't do to have the containers stolen out from under their noses, piece by piece. "Start tomorrow," he said, and his two visitors sat up straight as soldiers. "I'll talk to Chief Vzyatin about it, but you report to me. Afternoons, you come to me at the pavilion and give your report."

He took their names — Matvey Bondolenko was the crazy one, Ivan Shyshkin the old, toothless veteran — and told them to see Lyuba Mikhailovna on their way out. He kept the lock.

Just as they were going out the door, Matvey turned back and announced, "I'm the King of Jazz, you know. I only do this on the side."

Propenko raised his eyebrows. Shyshkin grabbed his friend and pulled him down the hall.

Volkov, drunk and pitiful, his bags packed for Bucharest, spent ten minutes pretending to give Propenko advice about working with Westerners ("They're slick, Sergei. They'll make you feel like a fool at every turn"), then got around to the important stuff. "Seryozha," he said, "my wife is going to come see you when I'm away. She'll be alone for two months, you know, and I was hoping you'd find a way to save aside a little something for her. A box or two, no more."

Propenko promised to do what he could.

"Did Mikhail Lvovich call you?"

"Fifteen minutes ago."

Volkov smiled. "You'll have new friends now."

"And new enemies," Propenko said.

Volkov went on smiling.

In spite of his workload, the rest of the morning passed slowly. Propenko looked at his clock so many times he finally turned it around on the desk so he couldn't see it. At five minutes to eleven, he went downstairs to the men's room, washed and dried his face twice, combed his hair, and paced back and forth in front of the row of urinals repeating the phrases Lydia had taught him at breakfast. *"Khe-low,"* he said trying to twist his lips the way she had shown him. *"Velkum do Vostok. Velkimm. Vell-kum. Mai naim ees. Mai naim. Mai. . . . Vell-kimm."*

An impossible language.

He returned to his office, made a final check of his list, put on his jacket and went down the hall. Lyuba smiled and wished him luck.

"Vell-kimm do Vostok," he told her. She seemed impressed.

Petya Dolgovoy, another ally in the office wars, gave him a big smile and a handshake, and then Propenko was out the door, slipping into the peach-colored Council Volga beside Anatoly and bouncing off down the Prospekt of the Revolution to meet his first American.

"Nervous, Sergei?"

Propenko shook his head, then said, "Yes."

Anatoly smiled, and the large pink-and-purple birthmark slid up across his cheekbone.

"You should sit in back, you know. You're a Director now."

"Volkov is the kind who sits in back. Volkov and Mikhail Lvovich. I'll stay up front with you."

"The American will sit in back, though, eh?"

"The American will be wearing a cowboy hat and a pistol and smoking a big cigar," Propenko said. All the cold war caricatures were coming back to him. He saw a bloodthirsty Uncle Sam riding a cartoon missile bound for Moscow. He saw the American president, *Dzhonson*, stomping a huge bare foot on Vietnamese babies.

"And now they're giving us food," Anatoly said, as though he could not quite believe it.

"Poisoned, no doubt."

"No doubt."

Anatoly took the river road. The gray city perched on a rise to their left. To their right and below, beyond the Don's flat arc, spread the shallow river valley with its factories and mines. Soon the cupolas of the Church of the Sacred Blood came into view, shining gold against a swirling, tumbling sky. Propenko looked the other way.

"Puchkov is on television tonight," Anatoly said. He glanced across for Propenko's reaction.

"Speaking of poison."

Anatoly nodded. Having lost a father not far from Warsaw, and a son not far from Kabul, he felt no obligation to tailor his beliefs to the Council's conservative style. Lately, he'd taken to wearing a bronze crucifix around his neck and speaking of Lithuania as if it were a separate country.

Two small raindrops starred the windshield.

"He's going to talk about the miners," Anatoly went on. "He's going to say their strike is part of a NATO conspiracy."

"Which will make Mikhail Lvovich happy."

Anatoly grunted and brought the Volga gently to a stop at the light. Despite his banter, Propenko thought the Council driver looked rather somber today. Anatoly could usually be counted on for a ribald anecdote or two in times of stress, but today he seemed to be going through the motions, faking a good mood. Like Leonid, Propenko thought. Like me.

"Puchkov's impatient," Anatoly said. "He hears Gorbachev's heart beating in his sleep. In his dreams he's at the presidential dacha in the Crimea."

"Gorbachev is finished," Propenko heard himself say. The words seemed to have erupted from some subterranean source, a freshet of clean water bubbling up through stone, a squirt of unprotected opinion. He looked at the side of Anatoly's face. Anatoly knew it. Everyone knew it. And no one had any idea what came next. "I'm surprised someone hasn't shot *him* in the back of the head."

They rode a ways in silence. Propenko watched a jet slip out of the clouds and glide in toward the airport.

"I remember the day Kennedy was shot," Anatoly said. "It was November, after the holiday sometime." They had left the river road now and come back up into city traffic. Ahead, Propenko could see the congested roadway of the bridge. His stomach was a stormy ocean, tea and apprehension.

"The twenty-second," he said. "Marya Petrovna's birthday."

"I was twenty-nine," Anatoly said. "The last year I was single. I was with this Natasha in the apartment of a friend who'd taken his family to Pyatigorsk. It was freezing outside, but she opened the window onto the courtyard. The radio was on next to the bed and the room was dark. We could see into apartments across the way — women cleaning dishes, someone sitting at a table reading a newspaper, someone shaving — at ten o'clock at night. I remember it as if it were yesterday. 'Domestic happiness,' Natasha said. She was a sarcastic woman, Sergei. Wild and sarcastic. I was trying to maneuver her toward the bed, trying to unbutton her dress, but she pushed me away and went back to the window. At the window, she reached under her dress and pulled off her underwear and flung it out into the courtyard — as a protest against the domestic life, I think. Six floors up. I ran over to the window and saw her underwear hit the ground, and I tell you, nothing has ever affected me like that. I was like a stallion that night. We were thrashing around on the bed when the radio said Kennedy had been shot. I'll remember it as long as I live."

They'd crossed the river now, and Propenko could see the green concrete station house, and streams of people crossing the tracks carrying shopping bags. Anatoly pulled the Council's Volga right up in front and killed the engine.

"Meeting an American for the first time in my life," Propenko told him, "and there's a lump in my trousers."

"In America," the driver said, "that's a sign of respect."

They were fifteen minutes early. For a while they strolled up and down the platform, checking the angry sky and watching the commuter trains pull in and disgorge their cargoes of countryfolk. When Vzyatin came striding through the crowd in his pressed gray uniform, Anatoly went off to sit with the Chief's driver. Propenko and Vzyatin walked to the far end of the asphalt, where Propenko took the lock from his pocket and handed it over. "From one of the American containers."

"Well, fuck me," Vzyatin said.

Propenko told him about the other missing lock, and about the King of Jazz and his toothless partner, and he watched Vzyatin's black caterpillar eyebrows crawl together. "All right," the Chief said. He looked north along the tracks. "An embarrassment. I'll go straight over there after this and kick Lieutenant Erfimov's ass. He'll never —"

"We'll need a booth."

Vzyatin lit a cigarette and tossed the match onto the tracks. "There's one across the street at the stadium. I'll have Erfimov carry it over on his back." He puffed away angrily for a minute. "They're okay, though, Shyshkin and Bondolenko, not as cuckoo as they pretend to be. Shyshkin's grandson was in trouble a few years back — likes to light fires. I took him out behind the Central Precinct one night and put my cigarette out on his arm. No more fires. Shyshkin bought me a bottle."

A freight train trundled past, spilling bits of coal. Vzyatin picked a piece of lint from Propenko's lapel. "We have footprints from the graveyard at the church," he said beneath the noise of the train. "Shoe size forty-two. Too bad there's only a hundred thousand men in Vostok with that shoe."

"Anything else?"

"We had to send the bullet to Moscow. Who knows what will happen to it there? . . . Other than that, we're still chasing clues. Everyone within three blocks of the church thinks they saw someone suspicious that night. Thirty witnesses, thirty different descriptions. The Russian imagination."

Propenko felt Vzyatin studying him, looking straight into his mind. After a few seconds the Chief said, in a perfectly calm voice, "Don't worry about Lydia."

"I can't stop worrying. She's involved at the church."

"Why don't you go in and say it over the loudspeaker?"

"The Children of the Third Path," Propenko went on more quietly. "She goes to the meetings."

"We know, Sergei. A lot of people go to those meetings. Mikhail Lvovich's nephew, for example."

"Impossible."

Vzyatin let out an uncomfortable laugh. "Somewhere along the line, my friend, you stopped paying attention. Times have changed. You think Uncle Leonid is still sitting in the Kremlin. You think the country is still bursting with loyal communists like yourself."

"He invited Raisa and me to dinner."

"Brezhnev?"

That was Vzyatin's way, throwing a sheet of humor over everything. The more something worried him, the more he joked. Propenko could not even smile. "The First Secretary."

"He wants to find out if there are any *Makdohnlds khemburgrs* in those red containers. He and Nina went to Moscow last year for the official opening. Don't get him on the subject or he'll spend hours telling you about *khemburgrs* and the paper they wrap them in, and the service, and how clean the toilets are. And on and on."

"Maybe he wants to talk about Lydia."

Vzyatin took the cigarette out of his mouth and spat. "Bullshit, Sergei. What he wants is to see what you can get him from those containers. He's the First Secretary. If he didn't try to squeeze every last drop of blood from the city, he wouldn't be doing his job. Just get the American to give him a few bottles of booze or an inscribed picture book or something, and he'll leave you alone."

Propenko nodded. By the station house clock it was ten minutes past twelve. There was no sign of the Donbass Express, and he found himself wishing the train would arrive without any American passengers, that the whole program would be canceled because of some political maneuvering in Moscow, that he could return to his former life, which seemed, from this vantage point, wonderfully untroubled. Thinking this, he looked toward the center of the platform and saw Nikolai Malov standing alone there behind a group of army recruits with shaved heads and loud, nervous laughter. Malov, apparently, had not seen him. Propenko could feel the blood in his hands and fingers, and a vicious urge — something straight from his dreams — joining his waking body like a spirit. He made himself look away, and he made himself ask Vzyatin if there had, in fact, been a rape on the banks of the Malenkaya on Friday afternoon.

"Something like a rape," Vzyatin said. "Why?"

They heard a loud whistle. The green passenger train, its locomotive pouring smoke into the stony sky, rounded the corner and came toward them.

"Malov thinks I'm the rapist. He came to the apartment Tuesday afternoon and was asking Marya Petrovna about me, about Lydia."

They were walking shoulder to shoulder now, the train coming up on them from behind. Malov saw them and waved an arm in a congenial way. Vzyatin said nothing. His eyes were fixed straight ahead, narrowed slightly, his lips clamped around the last of the cigarette.

The train ground slowly to a stop. Malov walked up to them, and in a cheerful, insinuating tone, chirped: "What's this? Official militia business?"

Propenko could not look at him. If he looked at Malov now he would take a swing at him, and if he took a swing, if he let that part of himself out of its bottle, he would never get it back in.

"A conspiracy," Vzyatin said in a pleasant voice, unsmiling. "We're out to get you, Nikolai."

The soft wagon's door banged open. Propenko looked up and saw the conductress, and behind her a sturdy, brown-haired man smiling confidently out over the crowd, wearing the most magnificent suit he ever hoped to see.

// CHAPTER 14

CZESICH stepped down onto the platform and was met by a crew of six stone-faced men, true Soviets. Two were dressed in dark suits, one of them six four or five and unselfconsciously handsome, the other almost a foot shorter, thick-necked, and cocking his head in an attempt to hide a cauliflower ear. One wore a gray militia uniform with the large star of a major general on each epaulet. The other three, judging from their modest dress, were drivers or assistants of some sort. They took his bags and headed off without a word. The major general and both men in suits introduced themselves. Czesich shook hands and forgot their names immediately.

In front of the station house a loaded, off-to-one-side discussion transpired about who would take the American to the hotel, but it was quickly settled. Czesich climbed into the back seat of a peach-colored Volga, behind the driver with the purple birthmark and the taller of the suited men. The major general in his blue-and-yellow militia car led the way out of the parking lot, followed by the thick-necked fellow in a shining white Volga, with Czesich and his two taciturn companions bringing up the rear.

Three officials, he was thinking, three new Volgas, three chauffeurs; the signs of impoverishment were everywhere.

They crossed the Don, wide and sluggish here and bending west to east, and plowed straight ahead into city traffic. The roadway was flanked by humble wooden houses on tiny lots, the type of dwelling you saw everywhere in Russia — one story, metal or tar roof, carved blue or green shutters guarding the front windows. Here and there a painted wooden fence or outhouse brightened the neighborhood, but the homes themselves were weathered brown or black, the sidewalks muddy, the sky leaden and wrathful, as though about to spew forth a shower of soot.

Farther along stood a phalanx of tattered apartment buildings the color of cornmeal — another Soviet ubiquity. Czesich stared out at them, at their rust-stained balconies and first-floor storefronts with dilapidated, generic signs: Fabrics. Watch Repair. Bakery. A few *babushki* strode the sidewalks lugging shopping bags in both hands, and off to the left he caught a glimpse of two black, slag-heap pyramids — utterly surreal — and another curl of river. He'd done a bit of research in Washington prior to his departure, and knew that 80 percent of Vostok's buildings had been destroyed during the German retreat, that the city had been liberated in October 1943, at the cost of fifty-two thousand Soviet lives, that it was known for massive coal deposits and massive metallurgy plants, its Cossack history and fertile outskirts, its busy river port. But what he looked for now, what he always looked for upon entering a city for the first time, was the place's fingerprint, a sense of what made Vostok Vostok. The city seemed, at first glance, singularly gray and featureless and bereft of beauty, but he understood that to be just another mask. Buried beneath this dour facade ran rich veins of love and courage, a soul-ore, ballast of Soviet reality. He could feel it in his blood.

He rolled down the window and smelled sulfur and gas.

His companions sat face forward, silent as jailers, and in a moment of panic Czesich wondered if it was because the Vostok Council of Commerce and Industry already had his number. The precarious, ridiculous nature of his position caught up with him then. Once the Council received word from its Moscow people that the program had been put on hold, only an impossible combination of luck and magnificent fakery would save him. This was professional suicide, and he knew it.

But, shortly, he became aware of a wheezing police siren and of a blue light flashing two cars ahead. Their motorcade seemed to have entered the heart of the city now, and here things were older and less grim. Thin trees enlivened the curbs, and the buildings were small, narrow town houses painted in pastels, some with wrought-iron balcony railings and tall French-style windows. The handsome man in the passenger seat gestured self-consciously toward the flashing police light and turned halfway around. "In your honor."

"Very kind of you," Czesich said. If he was to have any chance at all of pulling this off, it was important to make himself the model of tact and authority in these opening minutes. He watched the driver glance at him in the mirror exactly the way people in East Boston might glance at a wealthy guest, watching for signs of snobbery, protecting themselves behind a stiff exterior. The flashing light and siren was a roundabout welcome, all his hosts dared risk right now, and Czesich understood that. He had grown up with it, and preferred it still to the more facile warmth of the sophisticated world. He nodded at the driver and thought he glimpsed a grin.

Another few blocks, and the tall man — whom Czesich now assumed was some kind of tongue-tied bodyguard — repeated his awkward gesture, this time toward the driver's side. "Your containers."

They sat in a red row in front of a two-story, flat-roofed structure. Czesich was very glad to see them, but he'd counted only twelve before the car swerved ninety degrees right, into the driveway of the Intourist Hotel, an L-shaped, eight-story building, plain as a paper bag. Yet another stocky, suited man was there to greet him, standing on the patio steps with his hands clasped in front of him, looking nervous.

For a moment, Czesich wondered if he would be given a police escort right to the threshold of his room. He did not have to touch his bags. The man on the steps turned out to be the hotel's director — Czesich caught the name this time: Slava Bobin. Bobin took Czesich's passport, handed it over to an associate, and said that the hotel registration — one of the Soviet Union's outer circles of hell — would be taken care of. Before they'd even set foot in the building, Bobin had grasped Czesich by the elbow, and he did not let go until they'd negotiated the dreary, carpetless lobby, climbed a curving sweep of stairs, squeezed side by side down a hallway, and opened the door on what Bobin assured him — twice — was the Intourist's finest suite. Bobin smelled faintly of salami, and door to door did not stop talking. . . . You must be tired from your trip, he said. We've been looking forward to your arrival for a month now. We're proud Vostok was chosen as one of the pilot cities. We have fine workers here, no worse, you'll find, than American workers. If there's any problem with the hotel, anything you need, contact me immediately. . . . And on and on, all of it said in a conspiratorial whisper, Bobin's mouth only a few inches from Czesich's ear. The thick-necked man, and the bodyguard, and the militia general had been left behind, unthanked.

Bobin handed Czesich his key. "I've instructed our chef to send up a selection of appetizers and a little something to drink," he said.

"You needn't have."

"And I would be honored if you'd be my guest at dinner. The table is arranged. Everything is arranged."

Czesich thanked him, expressed his satisfaction with the room, and asked Bobin to put in a call to the Moscow embassy as soon as a line was available.

"Of course." Bobin copied down the number, gave a quick bow, and backed across the threshold.

Two-oh-eight was a suite of two small rooms, nothing like his Moscow quarters, but, after the ride in from the station, better than Czesich had expected. The living room windows offered a view of a rusty trash bin and the back of a stadium grandstand. There was a cupboard with plates and glasses, a refrigerator, a clean bathroom with a large porcelain tub and a mirror framed in garish orange plastic. He was testing for hot water when a porter came through the hall door carrying his bags. Tipped with cigarettes, the porter stood in the center of the room, sweating, and turned the pack over gently in his hand as though it were a museum piece. Before going out the door he saluted.

Over his twenty-odd years of checking into foreign hotels, Czesich had established a strict regimen for his first hours in a new place — unpack, bathe, get out and see the town — and he tried to fall back on that routine now to soothe a sneaky, swelling anxiety, but the strategy failed him. He'd barely swung the first bag up onto the bed when an awareness seeped into the room through hidden vents. Unpacking turned into an act of faith, but faith in what? The good humor of the United States Communications Agency and the Council of Commerce and Industry? Julie's friendship? The drunken impulse that had led him to this shabby room in this sooty city?

It didn't matter, he decided. He was winging it now, beyond logic, listening to a whisper. He folded underwear into the sticky drawers, and prepared a defiant speech.

But the phone refused to ring. As Czesich was opening the second bag, he heard a noise in the living room and found a kitchen worker taking plates of food from a tray and arranging them on his dining table. Strips of smoked sturgeon, slices of fatty salami, a decanter of vodka, half a loaf of black bread. When he tried to press a gift upon the woman she held the tray up flat to her breast and backed out of the room, incorruptible.

He paced, unable to touch the food, and unable to hold on to his righteous defiance. Through the tattered Oriental carpet and yellowish light, and the sickly smell of shellac, insecticide, and stale cigarette smoke, Vostok was beginning to make itself known to him, and it felt not just poor, but abandoned, cut off from civilization's simplest kindnesses in a way that reminded him of Ceausescu's Romania and the poorest parts of Poland. The fact that it was taking over half an hour to put a call through to Moscow seemed appropriate: Moscow, connected to the outside world as it was, existed in another dimension.

The unpacking regimen was broken. He paced the living room and poked about in the desk, startling a corpulent roach. He snapped the television on and off. He tested the water in the bathroom again, checked for a dial tone, studied the misaligned bureau drawers and the new wallpaper and the painting of Lenin's mausoleum above his bed. He tried again to make himself unpack, but a wave of pessimism overtook him, and he sat on the sofa and pondered it. For the first time in numberless years he had turned against the flow of inertia, and he could feel it rushing over him now, cold as consequence.

He sat in the tub and ran a warm bath for comfort, but found comfort elusive, his Vermont fantasy laughable. Julie was going to hate him. Filson was certainly going to have him fired. He was going to end up at loose ends in the Washington apartment, living on his pension and sinking into a solitary old age.

The telephone buzzed in the next room. He reached it on the fourth ring and asked the Marine to put him through to Political Affairs Officer Stirvin. A full minute went by, Czesich wrapped in a coarse towel and dripping on the carpet and couch, before he heard Julie's voice.

"Let me remind you that this call is being tape-recorded by both sides," was the first thing out of his mouth, a little joke, another shield.

Julie laughed. *"Entonces hablemos en Español,"* she suggested.

"No puedo. I've forgotten everything."

"We're set for dinner," she told him. "Anytime after eight."

Czesich closed his eyes. It was a second or two before he could get the words out. "Can't make it, Jule."

She laughed again, and it was like a knife cutting him.

"I mean it. I can't make dinner. I'm sorry."

"But why?" she said. Her tone was almost playful, almost hurt.

He let the line crackle for a few seconds. "I'm in Vostok. Room 208 at the Intourist."

"You're not serious."

Trying to be, he thought. He opened his mouth to speak his truth, finally, but what came out was propaganda. "They've been wonderful so far, glad to see me. The containers all arrived okay, in good shape. Everything's in good shape. The locals are being very cooperative."

He babbled on, and she let him. He had the feeling his words were feeding an explosion on the silent end of the line, but that if he could just keep talking long enough, Julie would get past the anger and let her professional training take over. Insulted or not, furious or not, there were things one refrained from saying into a KGB tape recorder. At least that was what he was counting on. The other option was for her to throw him to the wolves, to make it perfectly clear to whoever might be listening that an American with a diplomatic passport and a top-secret security clearance was in Vostok on an errand of his own creation, against the wishes of the embassy, unaccompanied and unlikely to be accompanied.

She would be within her rights to do it and she was capable of doing it, so Czesich kept talking, bubbling forth. "What a beautiful train ride it is, too, and the city is really a lot nicer than I'd expected. They've given me two rooms, not in a class with Moscow, of course, but perfectly comfortable. I was in the bath when the call went through, plenty of hot water. Soap. Toilet paper. The hotel director invited me to dinner tonight. They're setting up a telex for me here. I can send you the number tomorrow."

She let him talk, and eventually he ran out of gas and plunged into a prickly silence. "This connection's not so great," he said, for the benefit of the imagined tape recorders, but the connection was adequate. The silence deepened.

At last she spoke: "How is the weather?"

"Say again?"

"How is the weather there?"

Befuddled, Czesich looked out the window, but before he had a chance to speak, she added: "Are the planes flying?"

"Socked in," he said, and she laughed caustically. "Pea soup. They say it sometimes stays like this for weeks at a time in August." In fact, the strange Alexei who'd visited him on the train had warned him about Vostok's legendary fogs. And it did seem, from what he could see through the gauzy curtains, that the steely overcast had settled in the past hour.

He could feel Julie's patience unraveling. This was no time to cling to the literal truth. "All the local hierarchy met me at the station, Jule. The First Secretary was there, the chief of police, people from the Council of Industry, newspaper people. Everyone is anxious to start handing out the food . . . to the children, especially. Everyone was talking about the kids. There's a certain feeling of desperation, you know, that if we don't help them this time, they'll fall back into the old —"

"Chesi," she said curtly, "you'll get a telex. Follow the instructions exactly, clear?"

He thought of resorting to the broken phone trick, but he'd gone far enough as it was. He was safe for a day or two. From there he'd take it step by step. "Perfectly," he said. He waited for her to break the connection, and when she didn't, he could not keep himself from saying, "It's time to take a risk for these people, Julie. You should see —"

"Chesi," she interrupted, the anger unclothed. "What is this, your response to what I told you in the cab?"

"No. I was afraid you'd think that. This is my response to twenty-three years of being a puppet."

"A bit adolescent, isn't it?"

"Not at all. I'm sorry you think so." He could see her pressing her lips together, making the muscles tight on either side of her mouth, breathing loudly through her nose. He reached for the anger in himself, long buried, but it skittered away.

"Do you remember our little scene on the bridge in Leningrad?" she said after another long, crackling pause.

"Of course."

"Do you remember the last thing I said to you?"

"One of those remarks you never forget."

"Well, assume I'm repeating it now," she told him, and the line went dead.

He slid down in the tub so that his mouth was almost even with the soapy surface, and let a stream of hot water run between his feet.

From Yalta, they'd ridden the train back to Moscow for the last city on Photography USA's tour. They were suntanned and inseparable then, singing all night with Georgian troubadours in the next coupe; and America, with its riots and assassinations and expectant, jilted lovers, could not have seemed farther away. On the first day of the exhibit they were befriended by a young poetess and her daughter — Nadya and Marina Shokhen — who invited them to their cold-water flat for dinner, and introduced them to a circle of dissident artists and activists. For the next six weeks they barely slept. They worked the exhibit floor from nine to six, then rode the subway out to various, far-flung Moscow neighborhoods for poetry readings and drunken dinners and marathon conversations with the Soviet equivalents of Abbie Hoffman and Lawrence Ferlinghetti. He remembered the silence of those streets at 4:00 A.M., the feeling of being alone with Julie, finally, after a day full of people, the pleasure of speeding down an empty Kalinin Prospekt in the back seat of a taxi, thigh to thigh. He remembered riding a chartered bus to work past Saint Basil's, reading *Izvestia* articles about Richard Nixon and never wanting to go home.

When the exhibition finally ended, he and Julie and the other guides worked for twelve straight days to dismantle the show and pack it into freight containers for the trip home. They packed most of their personal belongings as well, said good-bye to Nadya and Marina and their dissident friends, and avoided discussing the future. Weeks before, they'd had one blithe conversation about breaking the news to Marie and to Oliver, but day by day, that blitheness had slipped away. On his very last visit to the American Embassy before leaving Moscow, Czesich found a letter from Marie in the Photography USA post office box. Her mother and father were planning a welcome home party. It was supposed to be a surprise but she thought he'd want some warning. She wondered if he'd grown his hair long like the rest of the college boys. She missed him and loved him.

He'd carried the letter down to the Moscow River in a cold, driving rain, balled it up, and tossed it over the rail. A split opened in him: on one side, Marie, with her old-world fidelity and straightforward loves and hates; and on the other, Julie, educated, liberated, guarded in matters of the heart. He believed, on that afternoon, that the only two women he'd ever slept with matched the two very different halves of himself, and that he would have to choose one and completely forget the other or be torn into two pieces that would bleed for as long as he lived.

Before returning to America, he and Julie had planned to spend a few days in Helsinki together, eating steak and drinking orange juice, celebrating their liberation from the communist world. On the way north they stopped off in Leningrad for one night. It was only late October, but winter had come early, and they disembarked from the Moscow train to find Peter's city quilted in snow, the canals sparkling and black, the buildings along Nevsky Prospekt scrubbed clean. At the dormant monastery across from their hotel they walked the slick paths with kerchiefed, bowlegged *babushki*, and Czesich listened to the church bells and felt himself sinking back down into an old Catholic pity.

They located Dostoevsky's grave, and there was something about it, and about the monastery grounds with the helmets of fresh snow on dark tree limbs, and about Brezhnev's KGB goons lurking near the church steps, that submerged him in a sea of guilt. It was not a specific guilt, not directly connected to what he and Julie had been doing for the last six months while Marie and Oliver wrote loving letters from home, but something more existential and all-encompassing. Original guilt. He wondered if Julie felt it, too, but could not make himself ask.

He'd almost slain his old demons then, almost rid himself of the subtle melancholy that had been stalking him all his life. If he could have brought it out into the open and looked at it with Julie he might have beaten it. He might have been able to do then what Russians have never been able to do — claim a bit of joy for himself. But he opened his mouth and the words that came out were: "I can't do this to Marie."

Czesich drained the tub, rinsed himself off, and took a long time getting dry with the thin, coarse towel.

Julie had let out a peculiar sound, a cry, then turned away from him without asking what he meant, without arguing, and walked back to the street with short, fast steps. He'd followed at a distance of two paces, poisoning himself against himself, mute with confusion. Marching in formation that way, they turned in the direction of the Neva and climbed a bridge into the freezing wind, Julie snapping her feet forward and crying, Czesich to one side and slightly behind. He had the feeling that, even though *he* had spoken, it was a decision they'd taken *together*, that they'd combined the wrong parts of themselves and created disaster when they might have lifted each other away from it. He felt condemned; the sentence had been spoken and was beyond appeal.

A navy destroyer plied the gray chop below them, hammer and sickle rippling. At the middle of the bridge he took hold of Julie's arm, but she pried his fingers loose and turned on him.

"You're a *coward*," she screamed, her face taut and ghastly. The cold wind caught the words and carried them downstream. "Just a fucking *coward*! You're *afraid* of me, aren't you?"

Czesich dressed slowly and deliberately and sat at the table. How cleanly anger like that cut through all the fatty pretense and reached the bloody little truth. Julie hadn't even thought about what she was saying — he was sure of it. It had just leapt out of the shadows, out of her own cowardice, her own fear of him. They'd had that one chance to rescue each other and had not, and could not rescue each other still. Some dark Russian piece of them — accustomed to cold and suffering — did not dare hope for rescue.

// CHAPTER 15

August 8, 1991

I am sitting here in my plain Soviet apartment — too large for a single person, and too filled with relics from my other postings — staring into the living room at a table set with unlit candles and untouched wineglasses and three yellow gladioli in a Burmese vase. There is a capon in the oven, all cooked, surrounded by potatoes that sit, by now, in a paste of congealed butterfat. It is an act of will to make myself write.

An hour or so ago Chesi called — from Vostok. I am struggling to set that fact against the proper background. For the thousandth time in my life I am struggling to understand him, fighting off anger, the hem of hatred, trying to determine what portion of blame to assign myself, and what portion to assign him.

I went to work early this morning so I could leave earlier than usual and have time to shop for our meal. It was a warm, dry day, and walking along Bolshaya Ordinka toward the metro I noticed that many of the first-floor windows were open, and I peeked in as I passed: old women sitting at the breakfast table with their kasha and tea; pepper plants in one window, struggling in the dirty city air; linen curtains; sparrows on a sill twitching after crumbs of bread someone had left them; a father tucking his young son's shirt into his pants before school. Soviet apartments have a certain smell — the warm, sweaty, soapy smell of people living close together — and once or twice I caught that scent outside someone's window and was carried back to the times Chesi and I went on our visits after work when we were guides. I recalled one visit in particular. It was No-

vosibirsk, and we were befriended by a young couple. They'd spoken with me on the exhibit floor, then waited outside until we finished work and followed us through the park (Chesi and I were in love then, and wanted to be off by ourselves as much as possible, and did not ride on the bus with the other guides) and asked us to their home for dinner on the following evening.

Their apartment was far out from the center of town, all the way at the end of one of the trolley lines, in a cluster of nine-story cement boxes set in a weed-choked wasteland. We clanked up in the noisy elevator and walked down an empty corridor — plain concrete walls and floor and ceiling, with one bare light bulb dangling on a wire.

Our hosts lived with their infant son and a boxer puppy in two small, hot rooms. They had set up a meal on a coffee table in their living room — a strip of beef swaddled in fat, pickled mushrooms, potatoes with onions, bread, wine for the women and vodka for the men. I remember it so clearly. I remember their puppy peeing on the carpet near the door and everyone making a joke of it. I remember Chesi and I passing around pictures of our families and of our parents' houses — leaving the snapshots of Marie and Oliver back in our respective hotel rooms. I remember the obvious joy these people took in hosting two Americans about their own age, the way they could not stop smiling and looking at us and plying us with food and oohing and aahing over our little collection of snapshots.

We left close to midnight, after having exchanged addresses and arranging another meeting and talking about getting tickets to see Don Quixote at the Theater of Opera and Ballet. It was not yet dark, and Chesi and I walked for a long time, following the trolley line, before catching a cab back to the hotel. We were both somewhat high and full of ourselves that night and we decided we had just seen the true Russian character, and that the coldness and meanness we saw on the streets and in the shops and sometimes at the exhibit were only there for protection, an armor.

I thought of that conversation this morning, walking past all those warm apartments, then pushing through the heavy glass doors of the metro and riding down the escalator with the stiff hot wind pressing my dress against me, crowds of stony faces on the platform and in the rocking, speeding cars.

I sometimes think that, on some level, Gorbachev is an instrument of the gods, and that his role in human history is to break open this mean, dour crust, and show a bit of tender Russian soul to the world. I remember seeing him on TV in his first or second year in office, standing on the street bantering with the crowds, and how amazing that seemed after what had preceded him. Whatever his motivations and whatever the final judgement on this era, it will always be miraculous to me that he came out of the system he came out of, and did the things that he did.

I was thinking about those things today, all day, to the point of distraction, and I have been thinking about them constantly since Chesi's call. Even to myself, it seems, I couch everything in politics and history, see everything against that background. That, I suppose, is my armor. Tonight, I was almost ready to take that armor off, to be naked with Chesi — literally and figuratively — to see if we could move out of our rut of hurting and being hurt, and try something new for a change, our own perestroika and glasnost. And what happens? What little joke do the fates play? My Don Quixote phones from the Donbass an hour before we're supposed to eat and tells me he's taken United States foreign policy into his own hands. I am so furious at him now. . . . I have a stone of anger in my stomach. I have no urge to eat, no urge to do anything but march into the Ambassador's office tomorrow like a scared daughter of Stalin and turn Anton A. Czesich over to the authorities.

But it's not that simple. I have looked too far into myself these past few days to be able to be purely angry at him, to make myself that hard again. He is acting like a fool, a boy trying to play hero, but there is one speck of truth to what he is doing — a professional truth and a personal one, and I cannot pretend to myself that I don't see it.

In spite of the hard, hurt part of me that claims otherwise, I suppose it is a step forward not to be judging him too quickly, to choose a difficult patience over an easy anger, to wait a day or two.

Or perhaps I am simply being duped, again.

// CHAPTER 16

IT HAD BEEN three years since Marya Petrovna's heart began to waver and flutter, and in that time her daily routine had grown increasingly unpredictable. Some days she was strong enough to go to market, or ride the trolley to the Sacred Blood and tend her husband's grave, or meet Lydia after classes for a short walk through the flower gardens near the river. Other days she did not leave the apartment. Two or three nights a week she had no inclination to sleep, and would sit up until morning, knitting or praying or listening to Voice of America on the shortwave, then go to bed right after breakfast and drowse until dinner, or fall asleep without warning at the table. For a woman who'd spent her life as the hub around which the family wheel turned, this inconstancy was a kind of torture, and Propenko watched with a mixture of sorrow and guilty relief as her hard edge was slowly worn smooth. He and Raisa slept in the living room now. They'd given up the back bedroom so Marya Petrovna would not feel bound by the household routine, and, though their own matrimonial rhythm had been disrupted by it, they never complained, never gave voice to dreams of a larger apartment.

There was, between Propenko and his mother-in-law, a residue of tension from old battles, from living for so many years in the same cramped apartment, but it was not something either of them tried to hide, and so it mattered little.

Tonight, Lydia was cleaning the church for Saturday's funeral, and Raisa had gone to her sister's for eggs, so Propenko and Marya Petrovna were alone. He mixed them his special *kokteil* of vanilla ice cream, apple juice, and ice, and they sat in front of the television and waited for the start of the national news.

Vremya began, as it had for the past several months, with a report about food shortages in various republics, and scenes from the ongoing political ballet — now Gorbachev, now Pavlov, now Yeltsin pirouetting clumsily across the screen. After such an introduction, some encouragement was called for, and the next stories were always positive and patriotic. Tonight they included footage of a nuclear icebreaker sailing out of the Leningrad boat works on its maiden voyage, and a long piece about a factory collective in Tadzhikistan that had developed a more efficient system for the production of high-quality hoes and shovels. A man in black rubber boots and dark work clothes appeared on the screen, standing at the edge of a field and holding two shovels, one made under the old system, one under the new. The camera moved in close on the shellacked wooden handles.

Marya Petrovna yawned.

Propenko brought their glasses into the kitchen and refilled them, and when he took his seat again, the news had turned international. One of the Hollywood movie studios had been bought by a Japanese company (this was encouragement of a different sort, intended to assure the audience that theirs wasn't the only superpower leaking at the seams). As the camera panned the lot and the street outside the studio, Propenko scrutinized the passersby to see how they walked, how they dressed, whether they looked happy or miserable. From this distance it was difficult to tell.

"How was your American?" Marya Petrovna asked.

Propenko felt himself blush. "Solid." He listened to the commentator for a few seconds. "So solid, I was struck dumb as a schoolboy. I felt like someone had caked me in plaster. An American, I kept thinking. An *American*."

"Just another two-legged body, Sergei."

"I know it. But I was frozen. I had the feeling there were eyes all around me, watching every move I made, recording every word, criticizing."

"That's your own inner eye," Marya Petrovna informed him, "flying out and roosting in someone else's head. You have to reach out and take it back."

"It made me feel young. It made me think of my first date with Raisa."

Marya Petrovna grunted as though not wanting to be reminded.

They watched an investigative piece on drunken driving in Gorki. A reporter and his crew had set up an ambush in the parking lot of a roadside cafe, and the reporter was calling out questions to wobbly drivers as they climbed down from their rigs. One of the drivers walked straight up to the camera and, lids half-closed with the weight of the drug, started shaking his finger and berating the camera crew. Didn't they know they were interfering with work here? Didn't they know some of these *rebyata* had already been awake for eighteen or twenty hours? Driving unlined roads with trenches running across them and potholes the size of — he stopped suddenly, snapped his head toward the reporter and demanded to know when the broadcast would be shown ... so he could call his family.

Propenko wondered how best to tell the American about the missing truck, if it would ever be found, or if, at this very moment, mafia soldiers were unloading it in an alley somewhere south of Kiev.

"Someone must be after the government auto inspectors in Gorki," he said, but Marya Petrovna seemed to have drifted away.

"Maxim was just home from the camp then," she said after a moment. "And you came to the door looking like Lenin's lost son. So neat. Such a neat little Komsomol anxious to please."

"I wasn't little, even then."

"No. You were tall and good-looking and you'd just washed your face. But you were still a Komsomol, zealous son of Marxism."

"I was," Propenko admitted. "In some ways I still am."

"Such a shame. . . . Maxim went to the window after you and Raisa left, and stared out for a long time, shaking his head."

Propenko had not thought there was anything Marya Petrovna could say that could still sting him. He sipped his drink, but the muscles in his throat were tight.

At last, when the international scene had been dealt with and dismissed, and the GAI chief in Gorki thoroughly embarrassed, they heard the commentator start in on a long, fawning introduction. Tonight, he said, the minister of the interior, Boris Nikolaevich Puchkov, had consented to join the program and provide a report on the status of the current situation in regard to Public Order.

"In two words," Marya Petrovna said, "not good."

Propenko turned up the volume.

Puchkov appeared on the screen, and his shoulders and head seemed to fill the room. He was dressed in a plain blue suit, white shirt, and blue tie, and beneath his high forehead the eyes were very dark and direct. Propenko thought the whole set of the face was intended to imply paternal disapproval, as though this were a person absolutely certain what was right and what was wrong, absolutely entitled to instruct everyone else, absolutely sure his children required nothing more than a thorough scolding.

"Our new leader," Marya Petrovna said, using *vozhd'*, Stalin's word, and soaking it with acid.

"Think so?"

"No question. Listen."

"Respected comrades," Puchkov began somberly, trying, as he always did, to disguise his high, frail voice with something that sounded more virile. "Our country, as you know, has been experiencing some difficulties in the past few months."

"Years," Marya Petrovna said. "Decades."

"It disturbs me, and I am sure it disturbs you as well, that certain groups are trying to take advantage of this difficult situation. It saddens me, and I am sure it saddens you as well, that values have broken down in our country to the point where citizens are marching and carrying placards in our streets instead of working. That we have young men refusing to serve in our armed forces. Children brought up on a diet of narcotics. Fathers and mothers who spend their money on bottles of vodka instead of shoes and clothes for their sons and daughters. That small groups of extremists are trying to break up a union in defense of which so many millions of heroic Soviet men and women gave their lives."

The Interior Minister paused and glanced down at his papers, revealing a dark spot on the crown of his bald head. "Worst of all is the fact that the very workers we most depend on during such times of crisis are the ones who now insist on inflaming our wounds. Yesterday, in the city of Kuznoretsk in western Siberia there was an explosion which permanently reduced the capacity of the Kirov Mine to produce coal. Today, in connection with this sabotage, we brought into custody one Valentin Borisovich Zastupov." Puchkov held up a photograph and the camera drew in close on the face of a surly, dark-haired man with dull eyes. "Zastupov is a coal miner in the Kuzbass region. Under questioning, he has admitted to drafting plans for a series of such bombings, in various cities."

"And what type of questioning might that have been?" Marya Petrovna asked the screen.

"Under questioning, Zastupov has admitted that he was acting on behalf of a conspiracy of miners, not only from Siberia, but from the other mining regions as well, and that the catastrophe in Kuznoretsk and the recent strikes in Vostok are part of a strategy to disrupt the political and economic life of our country. At this moment, Interior Ministry forces and agents of the Committee of State Security are investigating Zastupov's assertions."

Hearing the name of his city on Puchkov's lips sent a tremor along the length of both Propenko's arms. He glanced at Marya Petrovna out of the corner of his eye, but her attention was fixed on the screen.

Puchkov put the photo aside and folded his hands on the table in front of him. "The President has asked me to assure you that we will never allow a minuscule minority of demonstrators and conspirators and strikers to disrupt the social order. Such people are parasites who wish to live off the work of the majority of lawful citizens. In some cases they are aided — financially and otherwise — by foreign provocateurs."

"Your American," Marya Petrovna joked bitterly. "Part of a conspiracy."

Propenko tried to smile, but now, along with the fear, he felt one droplet of suspicion. This was the evil genius of people like Puchkov and Malov. They could say something you knew to be a lie, yet the lie would stimulate some secret, paranoid gland, the gland would squirt a few drops of poison into your blood, and you would begin, like them, to hate.

"In other cases, these people are acting on their own, out of a misguided and individualistic urge to interfere with the progress of perestroika." Puchkov paused for emphasis and glared at the camera. "Be reassured, comrades, that the finest members of our Security organs are working to make certain, not only that this particular case is solved, but that the roots of disorder — whether they are in religious, political, scientific, or labor organizations — are plucked from our hallowed Soviet soil."

The Interior Minister ended his presentation with a curt nod. Propenko saw that the commentator had returned to the screen. He heard the carnival music that introduced the sports report, but the sports report held no interest for him tonight. Puchkov's words hung in the room, the kind of crude code everyone in his generation had learned to decipher, and hoped, after Brezhnev, to be able to forget. Puchkov understood perfectly well that the miners were the greatest obstacle to his right-wing reprise, and with this performance he had declared war on them. This war would be fought with rumor and false accusation and bits of twisted truth. Puchkov's agents and State Security thugs would arrest and harass and intimidate, haunt the members of church groups and strike committees, see to it that their older relatives were "accidentally" knocked down at the market, that prime vacation dates were changed "in the name of socialist evenhandedness," that parents were accused of rape, or given high-profile assignments prone to failure. Propenko knew how it worked; everyone knew how it worked. The knowledge, and the code words, and the deep, invisible fear had a place in the Russian chromosome. He hoped Raisa had not been watching.

Marya Petrovna was staring at the soccer players on the screen, not seeing them. "I'll pray for Valentin Zastupov," she said, but her thoughts seemed far away again, and when the weather report was announced, Propenko switched off the set.

"Maxim would tell me sometimes what the guards would do to people in the camps," she said, as though they'd been speaking about the camps and nothing else all night.

Propenko sat stiffly, not wanting to hear.

"He said if they caught someone trying to escape they'd put them in with the dogs when the dogs were eating. The dogs lived in very small cages. The guards would make the other prisoners watch."

"And still people tried to escape?"

"Not many. Not very many." She scratched absently at a mole on the back of her left hand. "Maxim tried one time."

"In a truck," Propenko said. It was part of the family mythology, Maxim Semyonich sneaking through the gates in the back of a bread truck, then nearly starving to death on the Kazakhi steppe. He'd heard it fifty times. Lydia had been nursed on these stories of heroic defiance, and it was obvious to him tonight that they had led her directly to Father Alexei and his radical miners; they had led her to stand on the opposite side of the battlefield from one of the two or three most powerful men in the country . . . while her father stood by and wrung his hands.

"In the back of a bread truck," Marya Petrovna said, "hiding on the floor with eight wooden pallets on top of him, crushing him.

Every time the truck went over a bump in the road the pallets would fly up in the air and crash down on him. . . . When it was dark he jumped out — his back and legs all bruised from the pallets, big bumps on the back of his head from where the pallets had hit him. . . . He jumped out and went on foot across the steppe, drinking from dirty pools where the animals drank, walking all night and hiding in the day. For four days he didn't eat anything. Finally he came to the edge of a village and knocked on the door of a hut to beg for food, and the peasant woman turned him in."

"And back in the camps they beat him," Propenko said.

"They broke his arms. They added two years to his sentence, and near the end of those extra two years he died."

"He was a brave man," Propenko said, but he was squeezing his crossed arms against his body, staring at a spot on the floor, wondering whether bravery was the word for it. What would Maxim Semyonich have done if he'd made it back to Vostok after escaping? Kissed his adoring wife and daughter and gone to live underground? Wouldn't it have been better to serve out his sentence and come home to them alive?

"Too brave," Marya Petrovna said, as though reading his mind.

"I think," Propenko said, not looking at her. "Sometimes I think . . . I wonder if . . . Lydia heard that story so many times growing up . . . I wonder if she's involved at the church now to try and be as heroic as her grandfather . . ." He stopped. Spoken aloud, the thought took on a shading he hadn't intended. Marya Petrovna was staring.

After a moment the old woman looked away and shrugged, as if she'd expected nothing more of him. She slid to the front of her chair and prepared to stand. "You worry about Lydia, Sergei, but there is nothing you can do."

"If I don't try to do something I am not a father."

"You're her father no matter what you do, that's the thing you don't see. You can't protect her as though you were God."

"A father has certain duties," Propenko said stubbornly. He felt bathed in shame, steeped in it. Puchkov, this conversation, the American — he felt like a frightened boy among heroes and stern fathers.

Emitting a small grunt, Marya Petrovna pushed herself to her feet and looked down at him. "Fine," she said. "Duties are fine. But you can't remake a daughter in your own image. Believe me, it's something I know about. Lydia is going to live the way she wants to live, no matter what you do." She touched his shoulder and walked past him toward the back bedroom.

Propenko went to the window and stared down at October Avenue. A bus came out of the fog, stopped just below him, and set loose a lone passenger who angled across the street and disappeared into a courtyard on the opposite side. He thought of Maxim Semyonich sitting gaunt and unshaven at Raisa's kitchen table, and of Volodya Tolkachev bent over his gears and springs in the dusty, ticking workshop on Makeyevka Street. You could smell the fear on those men. Just being in the room with them was a lesson in fear. Just seeing their faces was enough to make you understand that the ordinary serene world was an illusion, that it lay like a shroud over something absolutely without mercy, a black well. All pain and terror.

He felt unbearably alone in the dark living room. He could not imagine having to face what Raisa's father had faced, a bloodstained interrogation room, beatings, broken arms, years without his family. He would not let himself think of Lydia facing it.

The door opened. Raisa came into the apartment carrying a net bag filled with white eggs and a bottle of milk. Her face was pallid and tight as a shell. "Were you watching, Sergei?" was the first thing she said.

// CHAPTER 17

S O," BOBIN SAID, unfolding his napkin and smoothing it over both thighs. His face was fatty and uneven in color, vaguely unwholesome. "Tell me about the great American hotels in *Menkhettn*."

Czesich was no authority. He'd spent a total of four nights in Manhattan's great American hotels, two extravagant weekends spaced decades apart. In 1958, when he was sixteen, his father had won $750 at the dog track one night, and next morning whisked the family off to New York City. The only Manhattan hotel his father had ever heard of was a place called the Plaza, so they booked a suite at the Plaza and spent two days squandering the winnings. Carriage rides. New York City pennants and T-shirts. Bus tours through Harlem and Chinatown. Two lavish dinners in Little Italy, "to please your mother." What Czesich remembered most about that weekend was the waiters slicing peaches into red wine at La Grotta Azzurra, and his mother and father singing along with the radio somewhere in Connecticut, a rare harmony.

His second New York weekend, thirty years later almost to the day, had been spent at the Gramercy Park Hotel with Eudora Bestweather, a travel clerk at Voice of America. Eudora was plump and ribald, on sabbatical from an abusive boyfriend. They rode the Metroliner to Penn Station on Friday afternoon and spent two seamless August days eating, visiting museums, and making love.

Manhattan hotels were, to him, a mix of these memories, undiluted pleasure. "Well," he said, meeting Bobin's somewhat defensive gaze, "there is almost nothing the truly elegant hotels won't do for their guests."

"For example," Bobin prompted. The hotel director had reserved a window table in his second-floor restaurant, though the view was obscured by gathering fog; he'd ordered appetizers, though the selection was identical to what Czesich had seen in his room a few hours earlier; he'd taken care of everything from handpicking a waitress to choosing the main course and wine. The elaborate welcome and slippery smile made Czesich slightly uncomfortable, but he'd known from the beginning that this assignment would require a great number of hearty handshakes and drunken dinners and forced smiles. Those were his specialties, were they not? Talents he'd spent two decades perfecting. An undertaking like the Food Distribution Pilot Program, in a country like the Soviet Union, in a place like Vostok, was the ideal vehicle for those talents, the command performance in a career of consummate bullshitting.

"For example, you can get your laundry done right in the hotel."

Bobin smiled cockily. He watched his waitress work the cork out of the wine, then took the bottle from her, poured the first few drops into his own glass, and filled Czesich's. He studied his guest's face as the wine was sampled, grinned when Czesich seemed to approve, puffed out his barrel belly. "You can get the same service here," he boasted. "Talk to the maid. She'll iron your underpants if you ask her to."

Czesich nodded. He had no desire to press the comparison with America, but Bobin was urging him on.

"Well, in some hotels they put the morning paper outside your door at six A.M., so you'll know what the news is before facing the day."

Bobin nodded and made a gesture with his free hand. Keep coming.

"For an extra charge, you can order breakfast in your room. They leave you a menu the night before, and you just check off what you want and hang the menu on the doorknob — coffee, juice, eggs, pastries."

"For an *extra charge*," Bobin said, scoring. "Here, breakfast is free. It comes with the room. Not only tea and juice, but bread, cheese, meat if it's available. We had sheep's liver this morning. You weren't around."

Czesich felt a slight, scratching irritation. Something in his companion's face or voice or manner had spawned a vague and unpleasant association. After a moment, he understood it: Bobin, broadly smiling and secretly self-conscious, reminded him of himself. "You can call up at two A.M. and get food and drink delivered to your room."

"All right," Bobin admitted. "That we don't offer. We have respect for our workers here. No one should have to cook for someone else in the middle of the night."

"They have telephones in the bathroom."

"Bathroom duties are bathroom duties. The telephone should be kept out of it."

"The televisions have twenty or thirty channels."

Bobin squirmed a bit. He was called away from the debate for a moment to assist a squat pensioner manning a barricade of chairs near the entrance. The scene was reminiscent of the Ladoga in Moscow, but on a smaller, rougher scale. Upon the pensioner pressed a crowd of young men and women petitioning for admission. Some of the men had bandaged hands, or dark bruises under their eyes, and stood the way young toughs in East Boston stood, arms away from their bodies, ready to launch a jab or an uppercut at anyone who made eye contact for more than two seconds.

"*Mest nyet,*" Czesich could hear the pensioner telling the crowd. "No places." No matter how vehemently the young couples pointed out that there were twenty or twenty-five unoccupied tables in the room, the pensioner only repeated this mantra, *mest nyet, mest nyet,* sometimes punctuating it with the word *zabronirovan* — reserved — to indicate that the tables only *appeared* to be empty. Some would be occupied by guests later in the evening, others held as insurance, in case the mayor or First Secretary brought his girlfriend by. Czesich considered pointing out to Bobin that, in American restaurants, two or three shifts of diners would make use of a single table in a given night, but Bobin was walking back toward him with a proud, proprietary smile on his face, and some instinct counseled Czesich to hold his tongue. An ally might be required here a day or two down the road.

The main course was an acceptable piece of beef with oily fried potatoes and a garnish of shredded beets and pickled cabbage. As he and Bobin dined, the empty tables gradually filled, and the room took on an increasingly raucous ambience. People began drinking in earnest, littering their tablecloths with fat green champagne bottles and thin bluish vodka bottles, shooting corks against the ceiling, sucking through one cigarette after another. A rock and roll band mounted the stage and blasted out a set of Western pop tunes to which young and middle-aged couples danced ecstatically, throwing their arms and heaving their bodies about. At one point, a scuffle broke out near the door. Someone had gotten sick of waiting and had shoved the pensioner, who retaliated by grabbing a broomstick and waving it over his head like a billy club, but it seemed half-serious, part of the evening's entertainment. Bobin talked lovingly about his two daughters, about a basketball team the hotel sponsored which was scheduled to tour Czechoslovakia that winter, and which he hoped would someday play in America. Whenever the food or wine ran low, he'd raise two fingers like a lord, make a hooking motion, and the waitress would hurry over with another bottle, or a sample of marinated mushrooms, or another plate of dark bread.

Czesich gave his anxieties a liberal soaking in the house's best Georgian wine, but could not seem to drown out the conversation with Julie or the feeling that he was about to be unmasked.

Over dessert, Bobin, somewhat high himself, turned personal. "Married?" he inquired.

"My wife and I have been separated for nine years."

"Children?"

"A son, twenty-two."

"And you are, if it's not a secret?"

"Forty-nine," Czesich said. "Fifty next month." Saying this, actually putting the figure into words, he felt a little tap of understanding between his temples. Fifty. The enormous five-oh. The half-century mark ticking like a bomb a few short weeks down the pike. In the anticipated light of that blast, so many things made sense.

"I'm fifty-three," Bobin confided over the noise of the band, and a silvery, vinous concupiscence shone in his eyes. "Not too old for the females, are we, Anton?" He punched the heel of his right hand against his left palm three times in the Soviet gesture of love.

"By no means," Czesich said. Since before the first course was served he'd been aware of young women sitting with older men at some of the tables along the walls. The women were dressed in the garishly sexy costumes that passed for high fashion in the provinces — ruffled, low-cut dresses; tourniquet-tight jeans; high heels. They all smoked. Most of them looked around the room with their eyelids half-lowered, like fifties movie stars. He found it a rather sad tableau, bordering on pathetic, but arousing nevertheless.

The room swayed gently and a surge of self-pity overtook him amidst the din of rock and roll. He was going to be fifty in four weeks, and sleeping alone.

Bobin reached across the table and touched him on the arm. "You didn't abandon some girlfriend up in Moscow, did you?"

For one awful moment, Czesich wondered if Bobin himself had been listening in on the conversation with Julie. He offered his best fake smile. "Unfortunately, no."

Bobin sat back, brushed a few crumbs from his necktie, and surveyed the room. "I don't suppose," he said, swinging his eyes around slowly until he was looking Czesich in the face again, "many American hotels provide *that* service."

"What do you mean?"

Bobin laughed as though Czesich were teasing him, man to man. The waitress brought their tea and pastry, and without asking Czesich's preference, Bobin shoveled three spoonfuls of coarse sugar into each cup. "I'm your host," he said. "I'm responsible for your entertainment."

"That's kind of you, Slava, but I'm here to work."

"You don't understand," Bobin said kindly. "The Russian way of work is different. Russians combine work with other things — a little drink, a little food. Romance. Talk. Before the Revolution, the peasants used to sing when they worked. It's more natural that way. Not like the Americans and Germans and Japanese, so serious." He turned his face into a block of somber concentration. "Robots."

Made careless by the wine, Czesich came very close to suggesting that the reason the peasants used to sing while they worked was because they had not yet heard of Marxism-Leninism, but he caught himself. Bobin had what appeared to be an American cigarette in his mouth now, and its smoke was drifting across the small table, rendering the evening complete in its unhealthiness. Alcohol, caffeine, fatty red meat, sour cream, sugar, fried foods, smoke — it was the classic Russian diet, the classic Russian attitude.

He recalled a restaurant in Georgetown that decorated its menu with tiny pink hearts next to those entrees especially low in cholesterol and fat, and when Bobin offered him a cigarette he accepted and puffed away happily.

Bobin sucked in so hard the ash turned red as a berry, then he swiveled his head and shot a stream of smoke against the curtains. Outside, a lone streetlight stood in a halo of saffron droplets, and a bus passed in slow motion on the foggy street. The city seemed very still and quiet, forsaken.

"A rich place, Vostok," Czesich said. "The mines, I mean."

"Of course," Bobin told him. "We fuel half the country." He leaned forward again so that his belly was dented by the tabletop. "When our miners feel like working, that is."

Czesich maintained a diplomatic silence. It took him a moment to find the ashtray with the drooping tip of his ash.

"Before this president we never had strikes, you know," Bobin went on, flushed now, pissed and pissed-off.

"Or your papers never reported them."

"No, I'm telling you. We never had them. Strikes were something that occurred in capitalist countries where the workers are badly treated. Not here. We never had strikes here. We never had other countries giving us food."

Czesich did not take the remark personally. His host's eyes were floating.

"Last night I went up to Party Headquarters," Bobin offered, and Czesich watched what seemed to be a truer, meaner self emerge. "I walked right up to one of the so-called hunger strikers — they eat you know, they have water and a little bread — and I asked him what good he thought he was doing. 'Here you are,' I said, 'starving yourself instead of working, instead of feeding your family and helping your country, and what, exactly, is the reason? What do you want?' " Bobin stuck out his jaw. "Do you know what he said?"

"No idea."

"He said: 'In America the husband and wife each have a car.' " Bobin slapped his fingers down on the edge of the table. "That's what has become of the Revolution. Imagine?"

This bit of rightist disinformation turned Czesich mute. He twirled his cigarette against the edge of the ashtray and looked out the window.

Bobin reached across and tapped his arm again. "No discipline," he said, as if it were a conclusion he'd reached after much field research. "That's the whole problem. That's what this Gorbachev brought us."

Not being a man of much discipline himself, Czesich thought it best not to respond.

"Remember Andropov?" Bobin made a fat fist and bounced it

on the table, rattling saucers and teaspoons. "Andropov was a real president."

"Head of the KGB before that, wasn't he?"

Bobin smiled. "And your *Dzheordzh Boosh*?"

"Touché."

They let the subject die. After a last few luxurious drags on his cigarette, Bobin crushed it violently into the ashtray and lit another. "Now *this* is where America beats us," he admitted, holding the cigarette in front of his face. "*Marlbara*," he said, in a loving way.

Czesich took his cue. "I happen to have brought a few extra cartons with me, in one of the containers. I'll see that you get some."

Bobin acted surprised, as though this had been the last thing on his mind. He thanked Czesich profusely.

And that, Czesich thought, is how the whole country functions, how most of the world functions. A few packs of cigarettes in exchange for special hospitality, a pair of black market Western jeans for a new windshield, and on and on, all the way up the ladder. There would be no set price for the maid's laundry service. You worked something out, some lipstick, a couple copies of *Mademoiselle*. It was more interesting that way, more intimate, and it created the illusion of freedom.

For a few minutes, while Bobin left the table again to confer with the besieged pensioner, Czesich found himself envisioning a scene somewhere in the labyrinthine halls of the U.S. Department of State. He was sitting at a table, facing a tribunal of career bureaucrats who were trying to decide what percent of his pension to subtract as punishment for his Vostok fiasco. None of the bureaucrats had ever set foot inside the USSR, and he was struggling to explain to them that things were different there, that the written regulations and rules were merely a bland canvas on which the messy portrait of real life was painted, that his unauthorized jaunt to Vostok should be looked upon as a creative gesture, the only practical approach — wrong, perhaps, but well intentioned. The tribunal wasn't buying.

When Bobin returned, he did not sit down. "Have to take care of some trouble in the kitchen," he said sadly, standing beside the table and gripping Czesich's hand in both of his. "But please stay. Order champagne, cognac, whatever you want. It was a great pleasure learning about America."

Czesich watched him saunter around the room, stopping here and there to have a word with one of his guests. When Bobin pushed through the kitchen door, Czesich waited a polite interval, then got up and made his way somewhat unsteadily along the edge of the raucous dance floor, through the smoky lobby and up the stairway to the sanctuary of his rooms.

It was 10:00 P.M., too late for the news. He'd just turned on the television anyway, hoping to catch a recap of Puchkov's speech, when someone knocked at the door. He went across the carpet in his stocking feet, expecting Bobin, or the maid asking for his underwear, or some mobster looking for the previous tenant. Instead, he opened the door on a pointy-chested young woman in tight white jeans and high heels. For a few seconds he just stared across the threshold at her, still half-drunk, uncomprehending. She hooked a thumb in the waistband of her pants — a gesture right out of some Western fashion magazine — and glanced over his shoulder into the room.

There seemed to be something in Czesich's throat. "Yes?"

"You're Slava's friend," she said, moving an inch closer. "Slava says you're nice. I'm here to keep you company for a while."

"Oh, I don't think so ... I —"

"Why not?" the woman purred. She hooked one finger over the top of his belt and pulled to within kissing distance.

Czesich could not explain why not. He could smell strong perfume and see a spot of misplaced mascara under the woman's right eye, a stain of lipstick on one tooth. His body was a study in extremes, a warm thumping in the core, a change in his breathing; yet, closer to the surface, resistance. It became apparent that he was blocking the doorway.

The woman tilted her head sideways and pouted. The finger fished around behind Czesich's belt. He took hold of her hand and freed himself. "Really," he said. "No."

"You don't want a boy, do you?"

"Oh, no, of course not. You're very attractive to me, really. I just ... I'm married, you see."

Her nasty little laugh echoed down toward the *dezhurnaya*'s station, and she stood there, appraising him, figuring the game. Something in her gaze threatened to drag him back to his mocked and mixed-up teenage solitude. He felt split, heated, tempted; still, he resisted. She shrugged. "All right then, I'll just go tell Uncle Slava you put your underpants on backwards. Our mistake." She spun and strode off, and Czesich stared blankly across the corridor for a few seconds.

When he closed the door, the suite rang with her mocking tone. The living room table and chairs and worn sofa had about them a whore's defiance, unloved and uncaring, nobody's. Shoeless still, he swung the door open again and ventured a few steps down the corridor, thinking he might see her there and call her back for a talk, at least, a glass of wine. But there was only the *dezhurnaya*, keeper of the keys, holding an open book in both hands and eyeing him sternly.

Later, spinning under a smoky sheet, too wound up for sleep, too far out on his limb now to consider stepping back toward something safer, Czesich wondered what aberrant gene or quirk of fate it was that had cast him so far from the territory of his youth. On Orient Street tonight, a pretty, lonely, black-haired woman was getting ready for bed in a house her mother owned, in a neighborhood strewn with cousins and aunts and friends who'd known her since she was a child. What scent was it that had warned him away from that life?

// CHAPTER 18

PROPENKO was on his way to the pavilion, running a few minutes late, about to drop Raisa off at the Kirov District Polyclinic, where she would spend the day auditing their books. He intended to pick her up again at six o'clock and take her to dinner at the Intourist Hotel. At the hotel, when they'd eaten a nice meal and danced a bit, he planned to break the news about their Sunday-night dinner with the First Secretary.

August was fog season, and the streets were shrouded. The traffic light at the end of October Avenue resembled a kopek-sized red sun setting in an ocean mist, and it made him think of Sochi, the smooth beach stones and sweet air, the Council spa with its gardens and high-ceilinged rooms and fresh peaches at breakfast. Their vacation was scheduled for October this year, prime season, and he tried to fix his thoughts there, tried to hold on to a vision of himself and Raisa walking the promenade after dinner, Vostok and its gray troubles five hundred kilometers away.

"She has my father's blood," Raisa said.

Propenko did not answer. Lydia had stayed out until midnight the night before, and come home full of revolution. The entire Strike Committee had been to the church meeting, she told them. Father Alexei was back from Moscow; the miners and the Third Path were planning a grand funeral for Tikhonovich, and mass demonstrations afterward in response to Puchkov's speech. The immediate goal of the demonstrations, she boasted, standing at her parents' darkened bedside, was to convince Mikhail Lvovich to resign.

"She's not going to stop until they drag her into a cell."

"They'll have to drag me in with her," Propenko said. The light changed, and he nearly drove up over the trunk of the car in front of them.

Raisa didn't notice. Her face was squeezed into a wrinkled nut, and her eyes were wet again. "Men's words," she told him angrily. "What good is that? They drag her away, drag you away, and what? Mother and I standing in line at the prison bringing you under-wear?"

Without taking his eyes off the road, Propenko reached across the seat and put a hand on her shoulder.

"She doesn't see it." Raisa twisted a handkerchief on her lap and shrugged off his hand. "She thinks she's immune to being hurt."

"Everybody thinks that at her age."

"Everything Mother and I told her about my father — it's as if we were speaking a foreign language. She doesn't listen to anyone but the priest, and the priest fills her head with the idea that Jesus Christ is going to come down from heaven and protect her in front of the Party building. No one can save you from those people. Not Jesus Christ. Not your father the champion boxer. No one."

Propenko pressed his teeth together. Raisa had been an eight-year-old girl playing on the courtyard swings after dinner when the *komitet* had come for her father the first time, and the sight of him being led outside and thrown into the back seat like a sack of flour was cut into the flesh of her memory. The smallest thing — a man in a gray raincoat standing with his hands behind his back, a black Volga parked near the house — would cause the old wound to crack and bleed. In twenty years of trying, he had not found the word or touch to soothe her. "This is not 1951," he said. "Puchkov is not Stalin."

"It's the same mentality, Malov and that type, exactly the same, and you know it. Why do you keep talking like that?"

"I'll take care of Malov."

"Please, stop it!"

"*You* stop it, Raisa." The traffic had dammed up at another fogbound red light and Propenko turned his head and saw his wife shrinking away from him behind red-rimmed eyes. "You're breaking yourself in half because of this. It's not like you. I can't stand it."

He coaxed the stuttering Lada forward. Raisa had balled up the handkerchief in both hands and was staring straight ahead.

"Nothing has happened yet."

"People coming to my house is nothing, interrogating my mother? People accusing my husband of rape, stopping us at the GAI post? That's nothing? You're pretending you don't see it, Sergei, and it makes me crazy because I see it plain as plain. Lydia and my mother are talking like revolutionaries, you're pretending everything is normal. I'm the only one saying the truth. You're making me feel like I'm insane! Why?"

"Because so far it's only Malov, that's why! It's personal. The whole city government isn't after us the way they were after your father, it's just Malov. And I've done nothing. Nothing! That's why. And I am not going to let him —"

"You're the father of someone who's involved at the church," Raisa shot back. "With the miners now. Your daughter has friends on the Strike Committee. That's something. That's enough. You're working with foreigners."

"Those are not crimes, Raisa."

"What my father did wasn't a crime either. He spoke up. Speaking up is not a crime. He spoke up and he went to church, that's all he did. Is that a crime?"

Propenko pulled to the curb in front of the polyclinic and they sat there a moment not looking at each other. He was late for his first meeting with the American. At the pavilion, he would have to sit in a room with Nikolai Malov, and pretend, before the foreign eye, that they were colleagues, comrades. While Malov was splitting his family in half. "For the sake of Lydia," he said, as calmly as he could, "you have to let your father go. You have to let the past go or there's no future."

Raisa was shaking her head. "Just the opposite," she said. "Just exactly the opposite." She got out of the car without looking at him and without saying good-bye.

It was eighteen past nine when Propenko opened the door of the conference room. The first thing he heard was Malov's voice, and he knew immediately that the meeting had begun without him. The heavy door flew out of his hand and slammed shut. Everyone looked up. He took a seat at the end of the table and glowered.

"We, too, want to expedite the clearance process," Malov was telling the American Director, who was sitting alone on one side of the table, facing Malov, Ryshevsky, Leonid, and Chief Vzyatin. The obligatory bottles of mineral water had been placed in mid-table to signify the neutral zone, but no one had thought to open them. Leonid gave Propenko a nervous, pleading glance.

"But, as I'm sure you are aware," Malov went on in his absurdly officious way, "there are formalities that have to be endured in any country. What our customs chief is saying is simply that we have to be certain you have not accidentally imported any agricultural pests or contagious diseases along with your food."

"And that will take two weeks?" the American said.

Propenko noticed now that the American's Russian, excellent as it was, bore a slight accent, a Muscovite sharpness that reminded him of his father's mother, the ardent churchgoer. It seemed aggressive, coming from a foreigner, and the churchly association was salt in Propenko's worried wounds. Still, in his dark suit and smooth white shirt, with his hands folded one over the other in front of him, his good posture and neatly combed hair, his way of calmly looking right through Malov as Malov whined and fibbed, the foreigner cut a fine figure. Unworried, Propenko thought. Unmolested by office intrigue and family troubles. The Soviet side of the table looked like a team of hulking schoolboys in comparison.

"We can try to expedite it," Malov said with his fake sincerity. "But the nearest laboratories are in Donetsk, a two-hour drive."

"The food has already been inspected. Your own inspectors came to our warehouse in New York." The American allowed a touch of impatience into his voice. "It has the United States Communications Agency stamp. International grade dry goods. In every country on earth all that's required in such cases is a visual spot inspection."

"This is not 'every country on earth,' " Malov said.

Propenko felt as though his body were swelling, about to burst. Ryshevsky was thumbing through his customs regulations. Leonid was fidgeting. Vzyatin sat stiffly with his red hands clasped on the table, staring at the American Director as if trying to memorize his face. And the American, after hearing Malov out, was scratching his jaw and contemplating one of the mineral water bottles. He seemed amused.

Propenko moved his hand and saw that his palm had left a damp patch on the tabletop.

"Mister Malov," the American began calmly, "having worked in the Soviet Union on and off for the past twenty-three years, I can tell you that I have the greatest respect for both the border agents and the regular customs inspectors."

Propenko watched Ryshevsky's ears turn red with the compliment.

"I can tell you, too, that my respect is shared by the Government of the United States and by Ambassador Haydock personally." The American paused and swept a speck of grit from the table with the tip of his middle finger. "And I have to say," he went on deliberately, looking only at Malov now, "that I understand your concerns. Your points are very well taken, and if this food were being delivered to Americans, we might hear the same objections from certain quarters. In fact, I'm sure we would."

Malov was smiling. The American was caving in. Propenko wanted to strangle them both.

"But what puzzles me" — the American altered his tone again, so that it was no longer quite so pleasant — "is that this program has been under discussion for over a year now, at the highest levels, not only in the United States and Soviet Union, but in France and Germany as well. Your top customs officials were present, and yet not once in those detailed discussions was our standard of agricultural inspections disputed."

Malov started to interrupt, but the American politely lifted a hand. "Leading me to the conclusion that either the top customs officials of your country are ignorant of their own laws — in which case I shall have Ambassador Haydock enlighten them immediately —"

Ryshevsky swallowed and looked out the window as if watching a favorite possession drift away in the fog.

"— or, and this seems more likely to me, that what we have here is some type of effort on the part of local officials to interfere with an international relief program. Which, I believe, is a development that would be of interest to our Moscow news correspondents, and to the French and German press as well."

The American had been looking down at his hands as he spoke. Now he raised his brown eyebrows as if the idea he'd just mentioned was mildly surprising, something he'd never considered before this minute. He looked straight into Malov's face.

"Excuse me," Propenko said. Five heads turned. He looked at the American and said, shakily, but loudly, "Sergei Propenko, Council of Commerce and Industry. We met at the station yesterday. I am the Soviet Director."

The American seemed surprised. Propenko's head and eyes turned, of their own will, to Malov. It required his complete concentration to keep from shouting. "Nikolai," he said, squeezing the name out between his teeth, "can you tell me what, exactly, is your position on this project?"

"Director of Security," Malov answered smartly.

"And can you tell me what, precisely, the Director of Security has to do with customs inspections?"

"I was assisting Yevgeni Ivanovich. We —"

"Is Yevgeni Ivanovich mute?"

"Of course not," Malov said.

"I've been here twenty minutes and Yevgeni Ivanovich hasn't said a word. You've been the only one talking." Propenko's voice grew steadily louder, as though someone were turning the volume knob on a radio. "You've been leading us in this discussion, though you have absolutely no expertise in this area, and you've almost led us straight into the international headlines!" He squeezed his hands beneath the table and turned on Ryshevsky. "Yevgeni, do you have any documentation of this inspection rule?"

"I was just looking for it, Sergei."

"Fine. Tell me if you find it. Otherwise, we begin customs clearance Monday morning, nine A.M."

"I was hoping we could begin this afternoon," the American said.

"Monday morning is the best we can do. That was the original plan."

Leonid and Vzyatin were staring at Propenko as if they'd never seen him before. Ryshevsky was flipping through pages, making a show of searching for the nonexistent rule. After sitting very still for two minutes, jaw working, Malov pushed back his chair and slammed out of the room.

The meeting faltered. Leonid opened one of the bottles and poured some mineral water into the American's glass. The American took a polite sip. Chief Vzyatin coughed and seemed to wink. Propenko did not wink back.

Slowly, after a bit more coughing and sipping and shuffling of papers, the discussion regained its momentum. Using the stilted, overly formal style they all seemed to adopt in conference rooms, Vzyatin spoke about the difficulties of keeping curious passersby from crowding onto the worksite. He and the American discussed it, Leonid put in a few words, apologized for the timing of the photography show, promised the ticket line would be rerouted before the customs clearance began. It was agreed that the whole parking area in front of the pavilion would be cordoned off with metal fencing, that four officers, plus two watchmen, would guard the containers night and day.

Ryshevsky found his tongue. He said he wanted to be sure "the American side," as he put it, would be present whenever a container was opened. In the absence of a customs inspector, he reminded them, customs seals could not be touched.

Leonid apologized profusely for the lack of a telex, and promised one would be installed in the Director's office by ten o'clock Monday morning. In the meantime, the Director was welcome to use the one already on-line in the main office. He mentioned that a table had been set aside in the pavilion restaurant, that his secretary brewed tea every morning; he asked if there was anything else in the way of office equipment the Director required.

Propenko listened to all these details as if from a great distance. What he had said to Malov, what he had done, replayed itself in his mind like a scene from some fantastic opera.

The meeting was winding down, Ryshevsky and the American pushing their papers together and opening their briefcases on the table.

"Two more items," Propenko forced himself to say. "I'm sorry to tell you —" he realized he had forgotten the American's name. He tried to pretend and move on, but the American had sensed it.

"Anton Antonovich."

Propenko managed a tight smile. "I'm sorry to tell you, Anton Antonovich, that one of the trucks had mechanical problems on the way from the border checkpoint at Brest. We are tracking it down. A substitute truck is en route but it will be several days."

"Which containers?"

Propenko consulted his folder. "Containers 1024-9996 and 1023-9996."

"Nothing crucial."

Propenko nodded. As he turned to the second item, he noticed Vzyatin look out the window much the way Ryshevsky had a few minutes earlier. "And," he said, "one of your padlocks has been stolen."

"The customs seal was not broken," Ryshevsky hastened to add.

"It was hooligans," Vzyatin explained. "Boys playing near the containers who took advantage of a moment when my officer was inside using the toilet."

"We've taken precautions," Propenko said, embarrassed beyond measure. What must this American think, in his thousand-dollar suit? Day one, and they were acting like a team of fools — no telex, missing containers, stolen locks, internecine arguments. "Three more militiamen and the night and day watchman."

Anton Antonovich nodded, obviously displeased, and Propenko waited for the famous American haughtiness to show itself. He expected a scolding, unflattering comparisons with other countries, a supercilious frown at least, but the displeasure passed quickly, a fleeting shadow. "I have some spare locks in one of the containers," the American said. "Along with some gift items for all of you from the Washington office."

Vzyatin and Leonid stifled smiles. Ryshevsky made a face. Propenko thought: *Along with some gift items.* The man was smooth. He'd handled Malov like a puppy.

They stood, shook hands, and filed out into the corridor. Propenko looked for Malov and did not see him. He found himself walking a few steps behind the American, trying to think of a phrase that might soften the strictly businesslike air of the meeting, something to dilute the terrible first impression. Anton Antonovich was, after all, a guest in their city. He was, after all, bringing them food, free food. He was alone. He was the only official American visitor Vostok had received in Propenko's lifetime, and he was likely to hold that distinction for the rest of the century.

Propenko drew even. "Anton," he said, leaving off the patronymic in the hope it would make things more casual. "Have you seen your office?"

The American stopped and smiled. His teeth were perfect. "Leonid was kind enough to give me a tour. It's fine." They went on, side by side. "I didn't know you were the Director. I would have spoken to you yesterday at the hotel, but Mr. Bobin captured me. I didn't even have a chance to thank you for picking me up, for arranging everything."

To Propenko's surprise, there was not a drop of superiority anywhere in these words, no conceit at all, no sarcasm, no artificial politeness. "How were you treated at the hotel?"

"Very well. I spoke with the embassy yesterday and we're all anxious for the actual distribution to begin. Thank you for helping move things forward just now."

They'd come to the end of the corridor and were standing between the temporary walls of the photography show and the front entrance of the pavilion. Propenko apologized again for the stolen lock.

"It's nothing, Sergei. It's a padlock. A few dollars."

They went out the door together and started down the ramp. Below, Propenko could see the militia guard looking conspicuously alert, and the old watchman standing outside his little booth making an obscene gesture toward the hillside where a pack of teenaged boys smirked and sauntered.

Malov was standing at the base of the ramp with his back turned, smoking.

"Your Russian is excellent." Propenko stopped in the same place he and Leonid had stood two days before, looking down on the neatly parked containers. The fog was beginning to lift, and some of the river valley was visible, not an especially beautiful sight. "It is our custom to give visitors a tour when they arrive. If you have some time tomorrow, I'd like to have my driver show you the city. We have a beautiful new ballet theater, some flower gardens down by the river, a natural history museum that's the pride of the oblast."

"I'd be delighted," Czesich said. "But let your driver have his weekend free. We can do the tour some afternoon when things are slow."

"As you wish," Propenko said. "He'll drive you to work starting Monday morning. His name is Anatoly. He'll be waiting out in front of the hotel at ten to nine."

"Oh, I can make it on foot," Czesich said. "It's only across the street."

"We insist." Propenko glanced toward Malov, who had half-turned and was watching them over his shoulder. "Let me give you my card." He wrote his home telephone number on the back of his Council business card and handed it over. The American handed him a card in return.

They shook hands again and Propenko watched Anton Antonovich make his way happily onto the lot, check a few containers for damage, then go right up to the old watchman and shake his hand as if they were equals, old friends. Out of the corner of his eye he could see Malov coming up the ramp. "Not here, Nikolai," he said, when Malov was upon him. "We don't need to display our differences for the American."

"Too late for that," Malov said, but he turned and walked with Propenko to the bottom of the ramp, then along a path to the rear of the building. They stood there side by side, looking out on the foggy valley.

"You humiliated me," Malov said after a moment. There was no smile now, none of the usual cockiness. The smile and the cockiness had been scraped away, revealing Malov's true self, mean and tightly wound. Propenko said nothing.

"Are you listening?"

"Can I help but listen?"

Malov laughed bitterly. "How a small bit of power changes a person."

Propenko put his hands into his pockets as a precaution. He could not stop picturing Malov sitting across the table from Marya Petrovna, plying the old woman with questions. Behind that scene, like a background of loud, off-key music, ran a string of petty humiliations and ridiculous acquiescence, a sordid, twenty-year history of kissing Nikolai Malov's ass.

"I've always thought of you as solid," Malov said, whining now, insinuating, beginning his roundabout attack. "Stable. Lately, I'm not so sure. This outburst in front of the American. The incident on the river. I'm not so sure, anymore."

"Keep trying with the rape, Nikolai."

"What do you mean, keep trying? I've been doing exactly the opposite. We spoke about the case and I was satisfied with your explanation. I took you at your word." Malov paused and looked over his shoulder. "But the fact is, the victim has come forward. And the description of the rapist fits you almost exactly, Sergei. My colleagues are pressing me to bring you together with the woman so she can either identify you or rule you out as a suspect, but I've been stalling them. I wanted to spare you and your family the embarrassment."

"I suppose that's why you came to the house. To spare me the embarrassment." Anger filled Propenko's voice like a sail; he could not hold it down. "When you could have contacted me any day, any hour, at work."

"I was passing by."

It was Propenko's turn to laugh bitterly. "As a liar," he said, "you're losing your touch."

Malov pretended not to hear, another of his tricks. "The issue is your dependability, Sergei, your loyalty. I wonder sometimes which side you're actually on."

"Which side of what?"

"There is a war going on, in case you haven't realized. There are forces working to break the Union up into tiny pieces. There are people who would like nothing better than to see the Party torn to shreds and thrown on history's garbage heap."

"Foreign agents," Propenko said.

"In part, yes. In part, people in our own midst, our own people. Those closest to us."

Propenko moved his eyes to Malov and then back out to the gray valley. He thought of slimy prison cells and broken teeth. He took a breath. "I talked to Vzyatin about the rape," he said. "The rapist was driving a red Lada, it's true, but the woman's description has him much shorter than me, ten years younger at least, speaking with a southern accent. There are ten witnesses, family and neighbors, who'll testify that my Lada was parked in front of our apartment building at the time of the rape. There's no suspicion of me, Nikolai. It's an illusion. Your own creation. I don't think you were even out on the river that day. I'm afraid you might be suffering from some kind of delusional illness." He had begun, and now could not stop himself. "And when you say, 'Those closest to us,' you no doubt mean Lydia and her involvement at the church. I know about it. I approve of it. If you want to take that to your bosses and try to use it against me, feel free." Propenko turned so that he and Malov were face-to-face. "You and Puchkov and all your friends can try every one of the old tricks, but it doesn't mean anything anymore, Kolya. The country can't go back to what it was. You do to me what you have to do, but listen closely." Propenko removed his hands from his pockets and took hold of Malov's lapels. "If you ever come to my house again, if you involve my daughter, or my wife, or my mother-in-law in any of your squalid maneuvers, if any of them suffers so much as one sleepless hour because of you and your fucking 'colleagues,' I am going to kill you." Malov tried to push Propenko's hands off his lapel, but Propenko only gripped them more tightly, twisting the material and moving his face close. "Not a threat," he said. "I've never threatened anyone in my life. A fact. I will kill you with my own hands."

Propenko saw himself acting and heard himself speaking as if watching a film. The words pouring out of his mouth were the words of another man, Malov's face the face of someone half-real, a specter. Malov said nothing, but his breath was coming in short gulps. For a few seconds they stood in that position, Propenko a head taller, their noses less than half a meter apart. Malov looked down at the hands on his lapel, and Propenko looked there, too, as if at alien instruments, and let go.

He must have walked around the corner of the pavilion, back up the path to the Lada in the front lot, but that bit of time was lost to him. Now he was looking down at his hands on Malov's blue suit, an instant later he was pulling onto the Prospekt of the Revolution in a state of shock. He had no idea where he was headed. It was ten-thirty in the morning. He had no appointments, no inclination to return to the office and deal with the paperwork on his desk, no urge to go home. He was just driving, moving through traffic with the other cars, stopping on red, going forward on green. His mind was blank, and when he saw the light flashing in his rearview mirror it at first meant nothing to him. There was no siren. He must have driven several blocks with the militia car trailing him, spinning its slow blue beacon, before he pulled to the curb.

Automatically, he reached for his passport, but when he turned to his left, out the window, there was no militiaman. He was checking the side mirror to see if the blue lights were imaginary as well, when the passenger door opened and Chief Vzyatin climbed in with a huge grin on his face. He seemed to want to hug Propenko, but settled for squeezing his shoulder.

Propenko let his shoulder be squeezed.

"What, exactly, is your position on this project, Nikolai?" Vzyatin mimicked, beaming.

Propenko was still holding the passport. Vzyatin took it from him and pushed it into the suit coat's inside pocket. "What did he say outside?"

"That I'd humiliated him."

"And what did you say?"

"I said I'd kill him if he hurt the family."

"You didn't actually use the word *kill*."

"Twice."

The big grin drooped. Vzyatin sat back in his seat.

"I told him what you told me about the rape."

"And how did he react?"

"He called me 'undependable.' He wanted to know which side I was on. I told him I supported everything Lydia was doing at the church, but I have no idea what she's doing at the church, Victor. I just said it. I was possessed. From the moment I walked through that door and realized the meeting had started without me, I was possessed."

"Long before that, Sergei. Masha noticed it months ago."

Vzyatin's wife, Masha, was a professor of psychology at the university. Recently — to the disgust of the veterans of the force, whose idea of psychology was kicking a prisoner between his legs — the Chief had started incorporating some of her theories into his militia work.

"You've hated him for years," Vzyatin observed, with his customary certainty. "You were just afraid to do anything about it. Now, for some reason, you're not afraid anymore."

"I'm more afraid now than ever."

"Not subconsciously. Subconsciously, you're fed up. And I'm fed up." Vzyatin rolled down his window and spat. For a moment they stared out at the passing traffic.

"We got the ballistic test back from Moscow already."

It was not high on the list of Propenko's worries.

"The bullet was fired through a silencer."

"A silencer," Propenko repeated. It was something straight out of the CIA-KGB spy films they'd grown up on. He almost wanted to laugh.

"The militia in Vostok isn't issued silencers. Even I can't get one. Silencers are issued to four people high up in the *komitet*."

At this word, which had been slithering along the borders of Propenko's thoughts all morning, he turned and saw a shadow in Vzyatin's eyes. In his dreams, Vzyatin would not see men raping his daughter, he would see men raping everyone's daughters and sisters and wives, people sneaking through a fence in the night and carrying away half a construction site, hundreds of thousands of black market rubles changing hands in the unlit parking lot behind the steel mill. His dreams would be full of battered wives, and drunks frozen to death in alleys, and the KGB, parallel law enforcers, interfering at every turn.

"It could have been a criminal," Propenko said. "Criminals have silencers, don't they?"

"By definition, any one of the *komitet's* top four would be a criminal," Vzyatin said, trying to make light of it. But after a few seconds the shadow was back. "They won't release the four names, naturally, but Malov must be one of them. His shoe size matches the print in the churchyard, but that doesn't prove anything."

Propenko let out a pained grunt. He'd known Malov since they were fifteen years old, and in spite of everything he'd seen and heard in those years it seemed impossible — physically painful — to stretch his imagination to include Nikolai the murderer. Nikolai the boxer, yes. Nikolai the world-class philanderer, the office bully, the liar, the sniveling, conniving, envying KGB officer. Nikolai the ally of Mikhail Lvovich and Boris Puchkov. Even Nikolai the torturer. But until three seconds ago, not Nikolai standing in the churchyard shooting a forty-year-old caretaker in the back of the head. "And *I* threatened to kill *him*."

"It may not have been him," Vzyatin said. "He wouldn't have used his own gun if he did it and he might not have worn his own shoes, so we have nothing, really, but we should be careful now. This is a tender time." He watched the cars and trucks rush past. "I'll put a plainclothes detective opposite your house, just to be safe."

The idea floated across the seat, completely unreal.

"He'll stay there as long as he has to. Until we solve the case, or until things between you and Malov settle down."

"What about Lydia?"

"Someone will watch Lydia too. And Raisa. And Marya Petrovna."

"You'll need half the force."

"I'll worry about the force, you worry about yourself. This isn't the boxing ring now, this is real."

"The boxing ring was real," Propenko said, but he saw now that he was saying it only to protect himself, to make himself believe he'd been through something like this before. In fact, it was Raisa who'd been through something like this before; he was only pretending, playing a role, fooling himself as he'd fooled himself about Malov all these years. "Why not just assign someone to follow Malov?"

"Not yet. We don't want to show our hand."

"I can't picture it. I can't picture him murdering a church caretaker."

"Nikolai is going crazy, Sergei. You can see it in his eyes now, in the way he left the meeting this morning, in the way he's been scurrying all over the city. And the man was no ordinary caretaker."

"Meaning what? That he organized a few meetings?"

The Chief shrugged. "He was *Alexei's* caretaker. Alexei is close with the miners. The miners are trying to get rid of the First Secretary. Think about it."

"Lydia is Alexei's caretaker now, that's what I'm thinking about. That's *all* Raisa's thinking about."

Vzyatin brought his big black eyebrows together. "Not good," he said.

"Not good," Propenko repeated. "And what am I supposed to do, forbid her? She's twenty years old. Am I supposed to train her in the old ways, so she can end up cowed and ass-licking like her father?"

"Her father wasn't doing much ass-licking today, from what I could see." Vzyatin put a cigarette between his lips and left it there, unlit. "Maybe you should tell her to do something else for a little while, make a different kind of contribution."

"No."

"Why not? You said yourself you don't know what she's really doing there."

"I know *her*. And I'm not going to try to remake her in my own image."

Vzyatin opened his mouth as if to counter this, but he glanced at Propenko's eyes and shook his head. "You're the father," he said, and, after a pause: "Where are you going now?"

"To the office. Raisa and I are having dinner at the Intourist after work. We're invited to Lvovich's on Sunday night and I wanted to break the news there rather than at home."

"Talk to Bessarovich first," Vzyatin said. "Before you see Kabanov. She told you to call if you had any problems, didn't she?"

Propenko nodded. He did not remember mentioning that part of their conversation to Vzyatin.

"This would qualify as a problem, don't you think?"

Propenko nodded again.

"It's a delicate moment, Seryozha. Kabanov's scared, but he still runs the show. He still has hundreds of people — big people — who owe him. Three first secretaries resigned in the last week — Kuibishev, Khabarovsk, and Donetsk — did you know that?"

"No," Propenko said, distracted. For a few seconds he thought he understood what Tolkachev had been getting at — if you have A and B, then you must, within a certain probability, always have C.

For a few seconds, it seemed that C was about to make itself known to him, a shrouded Rule of the Universe emerging, but then old preconceptions overtook him.

His friend Victor Vzyatin, knower of secrets, slapped him on the thigh, hard, and told him not to worry.

// CHAPTER 19

ON SATURDAY MORNING, fog still clung to the hotel windows, a pillowy, yellow-gray flesh. Czesich awoke sober and lonesome and lay beneath the covers for a time, listening to the hum and bump of a vacuum cleaner in the hall. Four decades had passed, and the sound still brought him echoes of the sunless second-floor apartment on McKinley Street, its sense of gloomy mediocrity, his parents' Saturday-morning wars. There was something ritualistic about those weekend battles, the empty vodka bottle and the fusillades of insult, the same scenario year after year, as if his father and mother had locked each other into their adversarial cages and could scratch and roar but never quite crawl out. It sometimes seemed to him that those echoes alone had been enough to send him fleeing the domestic life, running all over the world in search of an arrangement that made more sense.

A timid knock sounded on the hall door and, except for the sobriety, he answered it Soviet-style — in his underwear, unshaven, suspicious. Vostok was already working its magic on him.

At the door stood a beautiful Uzbeki maid in a pale blue work dress. She refused to look him in the face. In her left hand was a folded sheet of telegraph paper, at her feet the Saturday edition of *Pravda* — Bobin's nod to Manhattan's great hotels. Czesich accepted the telegram and asked her to wait, but in the time it took him to rummage through his bureau drawer the woman had placed *Pravda* just inside the room and fled. He was left standing on the threshold, half-naked, holding a tube of lipstick and a telex: NO LONGER AMUSING. FIRST FLIGHT CLEAR WEATHER OR TRAIN. JS.

He drew a bath.

While the tub filled, he sat on its cool edge and watched a cock-roach scuttle along the white tile floor. He pictured himself pack-ing his bags and slipping downstairs, making up a story for Bobin if they happened to cross paths in the lobby, bribing his way onto the first train north, walking into Julie's office on Monday morn-ing, meeting her Peter McCauley.

On the other side of the scales was a chance to get food to a few thousand people who needed it; a chance to confound both bu-reaucracies, to make a spectacular funeral pyre beneath all the old failures and strike a match for his fiftieth birthday. Humiliation on the one side, a glorious martyrdom on the other: What kind of choice was that, Jule?

Still, when he'd bathed and breakfasted, a residue of doubt re-mained. The Moscow train left at 2:45. He decided to seek his an-swer in the city.

The early-morning fog was slowly transforming itself into a low overcast, and Vostok was bathed in an eerie amber light, the air spiced with diesel exhaust and sulfur. Czesich walked north out of the hotel parking lot and turned left onto a four-lane avenue that ran parallel to the Prospekt of the Revolution. The road led uphill past a string of storefronts — a photo studio, a grim cafeteria, a two-tiered bookstore offering posters and calendars, and, even now, the complete works of V. I. Lenin, bound and shining in hard red covers. Above the bland storefronts the buildings were pressed tightly together, three or four stories high, with tall windows of the style in favor before the war, and gargoyles staring down at him from the cornices. He saw an old man leaning on a cane in front of the *video zal*, and, on impulse, asked directions to the nearest church. The man seemed pleased to be of service. He grabbed Czesich's elbow and hobbled to the corner, turned south there, then changed his mind, turned west again and sighted along one arm. "Go up here two blocks the way you were going," he said. "Turn left and follow that street, straight straight straight, and you'll walk right into it. It's the only church we have left now. Gold cupolas. You'll see it."

Czesich thanked him and, turning toward the crosswalk, caught sight of an odd movement in the pedestrian traffic behind him. It was nothing, he told himself, a shadow, a flicker of cold war mem-ories. He did not venture a second look.

At the corner he made his turn and came upon a crowd in front of a long, featureless building. As he watched, the building's glass door was slowly pushed open, expelling a middle-aged woman who struggled out toward the street through a terrific jostling of heads and shoulders. Step by step she fought her way out, twisting from side to side and butting forward until she popped free on the sidewalk and half-sat, half-collapsed on a bench, breathing hard, clutching a new pair of shoes to her bosom. An argument broke out in the crowd behind her — two women snapping at each other, nose to nose, a tall young man trying to separate them, someone taking hold of the tall young man from behind, other people beginning to shout and wag fingers and push. The ruins of Russian civilization, Czesich thought. He could not bear to watch.

He cut down a residential side street, skirting another, smaller crowd that had gathered around a con artist shifting cards on an upturned wooden box. Czesich made a quick left into a weedy courtyard and walked a loop there, an old trick Julie and he had used in the 1960s, when even lowly exhibit workers warranted a shadow. But no one followed him into the courtyard or stood waiting when he rejoined the sidewalk, and he tried to make himself relax. The pedestrian traffic flowed glumly on, every single person carrying something — rolls of toilet paper on a string; an unplucked hen; net shopping bags bulging with eggs or canned fish; an empty box that said TELEVISION. He stood still in the middle of the sidewalk, letting the stream flow to either side of him, fingering the telegram in his pants pocket, checking his watch, wavering. After a minute, he went on.

The side street intersected the Prospekt of the Revolution a half mile west of the hotel, then dipped into true slum. Filson had instructed him to bring back pictures "that prove they're really hungry," but Czesich did not even consider raising his camera.

Two blocks south of the Prospekt the pavement abruptly ended, but he went doggedly forward, walking a slick skin of mud, wandering, in the eerie, filtered light, his landscape of desolation. The fences were unpainted, the houses ramshackle black wood, the yards cluttered and muddy, with lines of laundry drooping in sooty air. He could smell oil and coal smoke, see a yellow riverine fog lurking ahead. A muddy-legged mongrel gave him wide berth. A militia car splashed past. Opposite one particularly desperate vision, he could not keep himself from leaving the roadway, standing with his hands on the splintery fence pickets and looking at a house that leaned so far to one side it appeared ready to collapse in a pile of nails and sawdust and tinkling glass. A small mound of coal ash stood in the front yard as if mimicking the slag heaps in the near distance. A black cat curled on a railroad-tie step. Above it was the pitted wood of the door, and staring out from behind a dusty pane, a man's face. When Czesich raised a hand in greeting, the old face held still a long moment, then drew back into the shadows.

He glanced behind him, in the direction of the city, and saw his tail in plain view now, a man with straight yellow hair and a linebacker's build, pretending to be wiping mud from the top of one shoe. Czesich pointed his camera and snapped off three shots, but the blond only straightened up and stared at him, shameless.

The church was not where the old man said it would be. Jittery now, forcing himself not to look over his shoulder, Czesich walked a maze of low-lying streets for almost an hour before spotting the tip of a gold cupola high up on a knoll to his left. The ground underfoot turned drier as he climbed, and the houses were more solid here, though small and soot-dusted, with yards hidden behind painted plank fences and looking down on the muddy Don. Soon he could make out two more gilded cupolas, a bell tower, the pale blue siding of what appeared to be a rectory tacked on beside the main building. He peeked behind him once — the blond was not in sight — followed a dirt road toward the church's wrought-iron gates, and stopped to take a photo there. It was a typical Russian churchyard, spiked iron fences surrounding most of the headstones, glass-covered black-and-white portraits above the names. There was one open grave, just dug and surrounded by flowers, the gold-tipped church beyond.

The building itself was sagging and tattered, but it had some color to it, at least, some style; it promised something beyond Lenin's gray, neutered utility. Czesich heard strains of a funeral hymn seeping through the wooden walls and was drawn toward it.

He climbed a set of rickety steps and opened a door onto a dim foyer. The singing trailed off. At first, he saw exactly what he'd expected to see, what you always saw in Soviet churches — a few old *babushki* in kerchiefs, crossing themselves and bowing from the waist — but he had not expected to see, beyond them, a nave overflowing with people.

Someone was speaking at the front of the church now, the voice at once frail and expansive, and somewhat familiar. Czesich could not quite place it.

He heard: ". . . is what we should remember in our bereavement," then a pause punctuated by soft female sobbing, then: "Our deepest essence is like a small child's hand squeezed into a fist in our breast."

Czesich thought of the priests in East Boston, pictured them making this fist for effect, holding a hand over their chest, mimicking the mournful Jesus of their imagination. Even in his altar boy days, melodrama had never seemed particularly holy to him, and he would have turned back to the streets had he not suddenly understood who the voice belonged to, suddenly noticed that the people clogging the nave were not just old women in kerchiefs, but young people — teenagers, even — and men with big necks and shoulders and thick, heavy hands. He slipped forward between bowing *babushki* and reached the doorway, where his path was blocked by a tight row of backs.

"Around that tiny fist," the voice went on, "is another hand, somewhat larger and stronger, the hand of family and close friends. For those of us who are aged, whose husbands and wives and friends are no longer living, this hand is absent, and it sometimes seems to us that we inhabit an empty universe, that our souls are tiny, inconsequential specks lost in the shadows of our lost loved ones, as we feel lost today in the shadow of our beloved Bogdan Tikhonovich.

"But over that second hand — or its shadow — is a third hand, much larger and more powerful, so large and powerful, in fact, that as it folds over our soul and family, it sometimes blinds us to everything else. Sometimes it squeezes the other two fists painfully, trying to crush them into extinction, to ruin the rich inner life on which the whole of the surface world rests. That, my brothers and sisters, is the hand of the State, a bloodstained, spiritless hand, the hand that has been suffocating our inner lives for seventy-four years."

Czesich pushed up and through the back row of mourners, squirmed forward another few feet, slipped left so he'd have a view around a thick, icon-covered pillar, and saw Alexei, his visitor from the Donbass Express, standing in the pulpit wiping a handkerchief across his high, narrow forehead. His peculiar friend was dressed in white and gold vestments, with a wooden cross dangling around his neck, and there was no longer any chance of mistaking him for a dissident watercolorist or a retired worker of the world. Czesich abruptly recalled a two-paragraph newspaper article from his pre-trip reading: Alexei of Vostok and his incendiary sermons, KGB harassment, legions of fanatical followers. Only with some difficulty could he make the connection between that article and the sweating, birdlike figure at the front of the church.

"What the State does not understand," Alexei intoned, "is that there is another hand, the Fourth Hand, which contains, in its immeasurable grasp, the entirety of the universe. Think of this. The entirety of the universe! Look into a clear village sky at night and you can see other galaxies, other worlds. Has the State created those worlds?"

Czesich heard murmuring all around him, men and women saying, "*Nyet! Nyet!*" like Pentecostalists calling "Amen!" in a storefront chapel in Southeast D.C. He could feel trick currents of anger running through the crowd, tugging at his knees.

"The State can send sputnik up into the cosmos, but sputnik is like a melon seed spit at a cloud. It is nothing, a joke, the wail of an infant in the vast Siberian taiga."

Alexei seemed to be performing tricks with his voice, sending each word booming out of his small body and up against the ceiling. Czesich was sweating, clutching his camera with both hands, trying to stand his ground against a fleshy pressure from all sides. Grandpa Czesich had consoled himself with a dream of Russian popular resistance, and he felt he had stumbled into that dream now, by pure chance, caught a glimpse of the small Russian fist so long ago buried.

"Brothers and sisters, I say this to you: No government, no perestroika, can survive and flourish unless it is rooted in the mysteries of the inner life. The time has come to open the child's fist within us, to create a government of the soul — not of the Church or the *apparatchik*, not of the tank and rifle and missile — of the soul!"

Father Alexei had reached such an angry, sweating pitch that Czesich thought he would have to come to the end of the eulogy soon or pass out where he stood. The white tip of his beard was trembling; rivulets of perspiration sparkled on his forehead.

"We do not need to have our Tikhonoviches shot in the back of the head as they pray! We do not need silenced men and women in Russia any longer! In the name of our slain brother and friend and in the name of Christ, we must stand up now. We must choose the thing that frightens us, the path that frightens us. We must step out from the safety of the silent shadows and act. But our actions must remain grounded in the spirit, or we will throw off our yoke and run from the hell of silence straight into the hell of hatred and civil war."

The old priest paused a few seconds to catch his breath, then raised a hand and very slowly made the sign of the cross over his agitated flock. The congregation did not want the stream of words to end, Czesich could feel it. He went up on his toes and caught a glimpse of a draped casket near the altar, but the watchman's body seemed almost incidental after such an oration. Alexei stepped down from the pulpit and went through the motions of the funeral mass, genuflecting, shaking his censer, disappearing through the door behind the altar, reappearing, reading his sonorous prayers from a Bible held up by a weeping young woman. Czesich looked around at walls literally covered with magnificent icons — gold and silver and wood, saints with long faces, hundreds of thin brown candles with flames licking this way and that in tiny breezes — and tried to unhypnotize himself. This Alexei — friend of the embassy's Peter McCauley — was a radical priest, not a poet. His church smelled of revolution. It was filled with long-haired, bright-eyed youth who could have stepped out of 1960s America, and miners with coal dust ground into their necks.

What did revolution have to do with cultural affairs?

Father Alexei was blessing the casket now, and the choir loft directly above Czesich's head erupted in song, a plaintive rise and fall of unbearably sad notes, a perfect representation of the misery he'd walked through half an hour ago.

> Bo-orn to a mother clean of sin,
> Bo-orn in a sinful world,
> Bo-orn to a sinless life . . .

But it was somehow very personal as well, intimate, secret.

At the swelling panegyric, the skin over Czesich's spine and arms drew up. Who knew what it was? Fear? Inspiration? A fifty-year-old's sentimental hope of heaven? Listening to the voices, it seemed to him that he was being allowed a glimpse down past the surfaces and the armor, down into the dark, cracked vault in his center, and that the hand he saw there was clutching what everyone's secret hand clutched — a bit of the soil of infantile feeling, forever sprouting adultlike dreams between the fist's tight fingers. Maybe Alexei had been trying to describe just that.

The service was drawing to its end, pallbearers stepping forward, Alexei shaking his censer over the casket. With his expensive camera, his curiosity, and his bright American clothes, Czesich felt like an intruder, another rich McCauley meddling. He squeezed back through the crowd and out into the churchyard, followed all the way by an a capella echo. He had no idea how you set about looking for your deepest essence after so many years of running away from it, decades of making decisions from the outside in, marrying the woman other people wanted you to marry, saying the things other people wanted you to say. He strode across the churchyard, trying to imagine that essence, to see the correct route to it. Follow the path of fear, Father Alexei had said. That seemed simple enough. Even in his agitated state, the path of fear was apparent: it led past KGB shadows and embassy "friends" and straight straight straight through the ruins of Russian civilization. He'd already been walking that path for a day or two; it only made sense to follow it to its end.

He was a samurai of the diplomatic world now, and this final performance his righteous hara-kiri.

// CHAPTER 20

EIGHTEEN RUBLES a kilo for cucumbers! It's robbery! These people come up from the south, they spend a few days standing around the market cheating everyone they see, and go back home with enough money to . . ."

Nina Vasilievna left her complaint unfinished and ducked into the kitchen with a wave of one braceleted arm, leaving Propenko to imagine various endings. Enough money to live like us, she might have said, in a six-room apartment big enough for a track-and-field competition. Enough for a black market Japanese television and videocassette recorder like the one in our living room. Enough to buy a few ounces of the gold you see sparkling around my soft throat.

Of course, in the case of Mikhail Lvovich Kabanov and his wife, it wasn't really a matter of money. They lived this way not because they had money, but because the man of the house dwelt in the center of an unimaginably intricate web of debts, terror, and ill-gotten influence, a sticky net he'd clung to and been nourished by for almost thirty years.

And, of course, Nina Vasilievna didn't have any real reason to get upset about prices in the private markets, since most of what she ate came from the special stores, a little bonus for her husband's loyal Party service. Her outrage was just a social device, something to make the Kabanovs seem like ordinary people, something to soften the chill in the room.

"At least you can *find* cucumbers in the private markets," Raisa said coldly.

Mikhail Lvovich frowned.

Nina Vasilievna stayed in the kitchen and pretended not to hear.

When she reappeared, Propenko noted the careless way she served the meal, as if the plates and utensils bore some lower-class infection. He noted the elegant surfaces — lace tablecloth, oil paintings on the wall, Ashkhabadian carpet, the soft, pampered faces of his host and hostess — but it was all slightly out of focus. He felt half-present. The other half was at home, sitting on the living room bed with the telephone in his hand trying to sort out what Bessarovich had said and not said, what he'd asked and forgotten to ask, what had been decided. It seemed to him that the real sum of her confusing and cryptic sentences was very simple: You're on your own, Sergei.

"So," the First Secretary said, straightening his knife and fork with two fat fingers and looking straight into Propenko's thoughts. "Have you spoken with our friend from Moscow recently?"

"Which friend is that, Mikhail Lvovich?"

"The mighty Bessarovich."

"Not very recently," Propenko said. Raisa shot him a look. "We talked in the middle of the week."

"A powerful woman, our Lyudmila Ivanovna. Well connected."

Propenko nodded in a neutral way. "She said to give you her regards."

"She's treating you well?"

"Neither well nor badly, Mikhail Lvovich. She came down here to set things up, and now that things are set up, she calls from time to time and says hello. I get the impression American food is not something she lies awake nights worrying about."

The First Secretary gave one of his small, mocking smiles and ran his eyes over Propenko's shirt and plain sport coat. "So the program is on track?"

"On track. Tomorrow morning we start handing out food."

"Congratulations."

Lvovich had mastered his act: the smile, the mean eyes, exactly the right mix of sarcasm and sincerity so you couldn't be sure which was real and which imagined. Propenko nodded, and his neck muscles did a little twitching dance.

The meal was red caviar in buttered scrambled eggs, and a piece of succulent beef, as luxurious and elegant as everything else in the house. Propenko and his hosts ate slowly, with relish; Raisa pushed the food around on her plate. After struggling through various topics, they took refuge in talk of the university, where each couple had a child.

"Classes begin soon," Nina said cheerfully. "Lyosha says the professors are too demanding. He's always complaining about it."

"Lydia, too," Raisa said, and she swung her eyes to Propenko as if to say: If you can lie, I can lie. If we came here to spend our Sunday night lying and pretending to be friends with these people, I'll lie and pretend to be friends. "Especially English," she added. "She says English must be the most confusing tongue on earth."

"After Chinese," Mikhail Lvovich put in. He tugged at the outside corners of both eyes.

"After Chinese, naturally."

"But English is a much more important language," Nina said.

"Much more important," her husband said, importantly. "The language of business."

"Even the Japanese are learning English."

"Instead of Chinese," Mikhail Lvovich said.

Propenko decided they must have practiced this duet at countless official functions. He tried to simultaneously pay attention to his host and hostess and savor the taste of their food.

"In a few years," Nina said resignedly, "the Japanese are going to take over everything in the business world — banks, factories, raw materials. They already control the currency markets, you know."

"Don't be so sure of your predictions, my dear," Mikhail Lvovich told her. "Don't count out the Russian bear quite yet."

This statement was so preposterous it silenced all of them for a moment. Propenko was not surprised to hear his hosts talking about banks and currency markets. The Kabanovs were communists of convenience, and the communists of convenience were finding it was to their advantage now to master terms like "convertibility," "investment strategy," "interest rates," as they had once mastered terms like "bourgeois decadence" and "enemy of the people" and "means of production." With the unpredictable Gorbachev-Yeltsin-Puchkov-Pavlov dance going on in Moscow, they thought it only prudent to have a leg on each side of the fence.

"Of course, the Americans have an advantage in the arena of business. English comes naturally to them."

"It comes naturally to the English as well, Misha," Nina Vasilievna said, with an air of loving exasperation, rolling her eyes and reaching out to touch her husband's hand as if he'd just said something quite stupid but couldn't really be blamed for it. "That doesn't seem to help *them*."

"Americans speak a harsher, more aggressive dialect," Lvovich insisted. "More suitable to making deals." Propenko was trying to forget Bessarovich now, forget the food on his plate, and give the banter all his attention. Mikhail Lvovich had not invited them here to discuss linguistics.

"The English made the mistake of trying to spread their way of life all over the world," Nina said confidently.

"So did we," Raisa told her. "At least the English didn't produce a Stalin."

"No," Nina said, smiling, "they gave birth to America."

"Exactly."

Propenko cleaned the last drop of buttery egg from his plate with the last bite of beef. Raisa was too far away or he would have reached out and taken hold of her hand under the table. She'd eaten almost nothing.

"America has its own problems," Mikhail Lvovich said. "It's crumbling."

"A cucumber doesn't cost half a day's pay in America."

"You're right, Raisa Maximovna," the First Secretary admitted, making sure to use the patronymic so Raisa would know he remembered her father, "but our friends who've been there say whole sections of the cities are too dangerous to walk through after dark. Children in the streets with machine guns, and so on."

"They say you point this out to Americans and they shrug," Nina chimed in. "It doesn't bother them, can you imagine?"

"Maybe it bothers them and there's nothing they can do about it."

"There's always something you can do — go on a hunger strike, for example." Lvovich repeated his small, scornful smile. Nina let out a short bark that resembled a laugh, but Propenko and Raisa missed the joke. "What does your American say about all this, Sergei?"

Propenko shrugged. He did not need more enemies now. He'd be happy to leave here at the end of the evening with an awkward truce, still on his feet. "He doesn't have to worry about it," he said, "with his money." Raisa gave him another angry look. Mikhail Lvovich and Nina smiled.

"You should see his suits."

"They buy them from Mexico," Mikhail Lvovich said. "They pay the Mexicans almost nothing for them. The Mexicans are the new Negro slaves now in America." He seemed ready to expand on this theory, but looked at his wife and caught himself. "Our suits are in no respect inferior."

Nina cleared away the plates and served coffee with a bottle of five-star Armenian cognac.

"So what is he like, Sergei, your American? What's the inside story?"

"Competent. A decent man."

"Aggressive?"

"Not especially."

"Lyosha saw him walking on Prospekt Mira yesterday," Nina said. "Taking pictures of everything, like a spy."

"He's no spy," Propenko said. Raisa shot him another look. They'd bumped into Czesich at Bobin's restaurant on Friday, and after a few minutes of small talk she'd stopped looking at him like he was a specimen in a zoo and abruptly invited him to their home for dinner. Propenko had been shocked, then proud, glad to have his wife back again. Now, too late, they both sensed the trap.

"How do you know he isn't?" Mikhail Lvovich said, grinning.

Propenko was somehow able to make himself laugh — just a few soft syllables, but it changed the mood instantly. "Foreigners aren't going to knock us out anymore," he said. "We're doing a fine job of it ourselves, without any outside help."

Mikhail Lvovich leaned across the corner of the table and patted Raisa's forearm. "He knows more about knocking people out than we do, Raisa," he said, winking at her. "He's the specialist in that department, not us."

Propenko remembered a Ukrainian proverb his father had been fond of quoting: The snake flatters before it bites.

"The American ambassador is coming soon, you know," Lvovich said, as though it were a bit of privileged information he was sharing with close friends and not a piece of rumor Propenko himself had fed him. "We should organize a reception, Sergei, no?"

"Of course."

"Perhaps at the Intourist. Bobin has a hall. I'll speak with him tomorrow."

"When is the Ambassador coming?" Raisa said.

"You mean your husband doesn't tell you his secrets?" Mikhail Lvovich leaned back in his chair and slid the tips of his fingers beneath his belt. From elbow to wrist both forearms rested on belly. "I'm joking, Raisa. Don't look at Sergei like he's keeping a mistress. He isn't. We're watching him. We know. He's as faithful as the czar's guard."

Propenko tapped his spoon on his saucer and kept his eyes down.

"We find out the date this week," Lvovich went on. He glanced at his wife. "There's never been an American ambassador in Vostok. It's a first."

"It's wonderful, Misha," Nina said, as if to a king.

But your castle, Propenko thought, is built on other people's humiliation.

During the meal a Shostakovich symphony had been playing quietly on the Japanese stereo system, but when Nina brought four pieces of iced lemon cake to the table, Mikhail Lvovich raised himself from the chair and put on Vysotski. Propenko saw a bitter smile touch Raisa's mouth, and he thought for a moment this was going to be the thing that pushed her over the line into open warfare, that she was going to jump out of her chair and point a finger and yell: *You* are the kinds of people Vysotski was singing about, can't you see it? *You* are the ones who made him a folk hero, because everyone had hated you for years and could find no way to speak their hatred until Vysotski came along. Vysotski was the beginning of the end for you, can't you see it?

But she only sipped her coffee and picked at the cake with the tines of a silver fork. Propenko felt a change, though. The rough guitar and rough voice seemed to have altered the light in the room, exposing Kabanov's hidden self — vicious, unscrupulous, unfettered by even the thinnest strap of mercy. The elegant surfaces and wonderful food and the small talk and smiles had been like a pretty lace kerchief draped over the cage of a snake, and now the kerchief was slipping, the cage door swinging open. It was not possible for Mikhail Lvovich to get through an evening without showing his fangs, without resorting to power, and Propenko could feel that power filling the air around him now. He wondered if the music had been chosen as mockery.

> *The hunter goes after the wolves.*
> *The hunter goes. . . .*
> *Blood on the snow*
> *And the red spots of flags.*

When they'd had some time with the coffee and cake and listened to a few songs, the First Secretary stood and went over to an ornate chest of drawers. He opened the top drawer as carefully as a jeweler opening the diamond case and took out a small box. "A smoke, Sergei?" he said, turning, two fat cigars in his hand. He motioned Propenko out onto the balcony.

"And off go the men," Nina said cheerfully.

On the balcony, Mikhail Lvovich handed Propenko a Cuban cigar — unavailable in Vostok since Brezhnev's days — and lit it. They looked down on the natural history museum and the Party Hotel, and two streetlights blurred by fog. The night was cool.

Much to his own shame, Propenko found himself standing in a somewhat submissive posture, half-turned toward the First Secretary, an expression of respectful goodwill stuck on his face. Such was the magic of power. "A very fine meal, Mikhail Lvovich," he heard himself say.

The First Secretary waved a hand through sweet smoke. "Nina's the cook."

Three floors below, Propenko glimpsed a figure pacing the foggy sidewalk. When the man turned and walked back toward them, he passed beneath the streetlight, and Propenko saw the uniform.

"Imagine having to live with a militia guard night and day," Mikhail Lvovich said. "Imagine how that feels."

Propenko said nothing. Vzyatin's men couldn't guard unmoving containers of food; how were they supposed to watch him and Raisa and Lydia and Marya Petrovna? What good was one sleepy lieutenant on the street if someone wanted to shoot Mikhail Lvovich or throw a hand grenade through his window? It was all for show, like everything else. He felt bitter tonight, toward Bessarovich for abandoning him, toward Vzyatin for his supreme confidence and subtle manipulations. He felt vulnerable and foolish and abused. The joy of his appointment had long ago gone sour.

"You can't know what it feels like to spend your days trying to make people's lives better, and then to have to be protected from those same people."

Propenko was glad Raisa could not hear this.

"It's a time when a man learns to see through the disguises that pass for friendship, for loyalty."

Propenko watched the lieutenant turn and start back through

the brightest part of the lamplight again. He drew on his cigar and held the smoke in his mouth.

"Know what I'm saying, Sergei?"

Propenko exhaled quickly and said that he knew.

"I used to watch you at the Komsomol meetings years ago, you know. At the hall on Morskaya Street. You were what, sixteen?"

"Eighteen."

"Eighteen. A boxing champion."

"Oblast champion, Mikhail Lvovich. That's all. There were better boxers in the —"

"Still. A Master of Sport. On the Olympic team, weren't you?"

"No," Propenko said. Lvovich knew he had not been on the Olympic team, and was saying this, no doubt, to bump a tender memory. He'd tried out twice. The second time he'd had his nose broken by a freak punch in the third round of the semifinals, and had been able to do nothing but cover up until the bell.

"I knew you'd rise in the ranks," Lvovich said. He walked to the end of the balcony and back, a pensive six-step excursion. "I know quality when I see it, and I saw it in you long ago."

More flattery, Propenko thought. Now the snake strikes.

"I hear there is some trouble with the food program."

"From whom?" Propenko blurted out.

"Friends."

"There's no trouble. We're starting work tomorrow."

"I hear there's tension. Quarreling. Missing containers. I hear rumors from Moscow that the Americans have been thinking of canceling the whole show, that they may already have canceled it."

"We'd know," Propenko said.

"Would we?"

It suddenly occurred to Propenko that Mikhail Lvovich had invited him here to relieve him of his duties. They were going to cut him loose. That was the secret he'd sensed in Bessarovich's voice on the telephone. "Some problems have to be solved closer to the source," she'd said, meaning: Malov can play his dirty games because he's a friend of Mikhail Lvovich, and Mikhail Lvovich is about to fire you, and there's nothing I can do about it. Save yourself any way you can.

"There have been one or two small problems, Mikhail Lvovich.

But every project has its problems. The food will be handed out on schedule. I guarantee it."

Lvovich grunted, and made another slow, big-bellied excursion, exhaling a cloud of smoke. A very light rain began tapping in the tree to their right, and they moved in closer to the building. "What about Lydia?" Lvovich said.

Propenko went cold. "What about her?"

"How is she?"

"Fine. An excellent student, a fine daughter."

"Our Lyosha speaks highly of her, though he's been trouble-some himself lately. Students live in a simpler world. . . . They get an idea into their brains and there's no getting it out."

Propenko went through the motions of smoking. He glanced across and briefly met Mikhail Lvovich's eyes, trying to see the next move there. "It's about power, isn't it, Pa?" Lydia had said to him, and she'd been absolutely right. He was standing in a place now where it was about power and nothing else. But what, exactly, was this "power"? What was it made up of? Where did it reside — in the voice, in the title, in the number of debts? In pure physical terror? As with Malov, there were constant rumors about Lvovich, a mythology of viciousness. The First Secretary was said to have forced the wife of a disloyal newspaper editor to visit her husband in jail just after he'd been interrogated, the husband naked and broken in a cold cell. Propenko wondered if Lvovich himself made up the stories.

"You know about the demonstrations, don't you, Sergei?"

"You can't live in Vostok and not know about them."

"I won't ask you what you think, because I know what you think. I've known you all these years, I've watched you at meetings, my people have given me reports on you. I know you belong to a solid core of communists in this city who aren't going to bend with each passing breeze. But you have to understand my position on this. The demonstrations are a tremendous embarrassment to me, with the American ambassador coming and all, a tremendous em-barrassment. I could make a phone call right now and have the Black Berets come in and throw all of them in prison — the hunger strikers, the miners, the crazy priest, everyone." Lvovich swung an arm to encompass all his enemies. "In other places they do it that way. Look at Tbilisi. Look at Vilnius. They come in, they swing their truncheons, break a few ribs, throw a few troublemakers in the van, and it's over. But I don't hate these demonstrators, Seryozha,

I'm not that type of man. I'm a father. I understand young people, and I understand miners. My uncle was a miner, you know."

Propenko said he hadn't known.

"I realize the situation is difficult for them now. Nina and I have our difficulties, as well, though we don't go weeping to the world. It's a hard time for everyone."

Propenko didn't trust himself to make eye contact. He smoked and stared straight out over the roof of the museum, a wooden man in the kingdom of rage.

"I've never asked a favor of you, have I, Seryozha?"

"No," Propenko admitted. You've barely spoken to me in thirty years, he wanted to say. We shake hands at the parades on May First and November Seventh, and the rest of the time we fly at different altitudes. "Not once."

The First Secretary nodded. "Well," he said solemnly, "now I need to ask one. Father to father. Friend to friend."

"Fine." Propenko braced himself. Father to father. Now he was going to be required to tell Mikhail Lvovich about the Children of the Third Path. He was going to be asked to tell everything he knew about the rebellious Father Alexei and his assistants. What had been done with fists and chains and electricity in the cellar of State Security thirty years ago was now done with cigars and caviar and vague allusions to loyalty, fatherhood, and the Black Berets. That, in Vostok, was the extent of perestroika.

"Tell me about the food program," Lvovich said. "I mean, how it works, in actual practice."

"Bessarovich gave us a list of distribution sites. We have to clear the food through customs, then load it onto trucks and take it to those sites. Each site has a contact person, also on the list. We set a time and a day, and the contact person sees to it that the food goes to the people who need it most. If everything works the way it's supposed to, it should take two weeks to empty the containers. Three, maximum."

"And who was involved in the preparation of this list?"

"I don't know. Volkov, maybe."

Mikhail Lvovich chuckled sarcastically. The militia guard heard the noise and looked up. "You are naive, my friend."

Propenko did not deny it.

"What are the sites on the south side of the river?"

"Only the Nevsky Mine."

"And in the Lenin District?"

"In Belaya Rechka," Propenko said. He swallowed, seeing, suddenly, what he'd chosen not to see. "At the orphanage next door to the Church of the Sacred Blood."

The First Secretary paused and scratched at a flake of paint on the building. "And what would be required," he said, "to put those two sites at the bottom of the list?"

This was not the favor Propenko had expected. It seemed to him, at first, that it would cost no one anything. He felt a small surge of hope. "Both are at the top of the list," he said.

"That's not an answer to my question, Sergei. I need a week now, ten days at most. I need ten days of guarantee that the people here who are trying to ruin me won't be publicly blessed by the powers that be — in Moscow and abroad. It's a very small favor."

Propenko hesitated.

"I don't want to resort to my other options with these people, Seryozha. You know me well enough to know that. I need ten days to have my deputies work something out with them. Peaceably. No blood. It's no accident the Nevsky Mine and the church are at the top of the list. You bring food there now and it's the same as telling the whole oblast: America wants Kabanov out of office. Moscow wants him out of office. Do you see?"

Propenko nodded. He saw. He saw that he had, in fact, been a puppet in a theater of political treachery. He saw that the people working the strings were now saying to him: I'm too far away to help. And that both sides operated according to the same principles: intimidation, manipulation, flattery, bribery — while ordinary people went on dancing their frightened, hungry dance. He wondered how much his friend Victor Vzyatin knew.

"Understand, Sergei, I am not asking for a gift. I'm asking *what would be required of you* to do me this small favor."

It was half a minute before Propenko answered. In that time, several dozen replies came to his lips, a whole roulette wheel of options, and later it would seem to him that the reply that finally emerged was simply a matter of chance, one more click on the wheel at Monte Carlo. "My family has been threatened," he said, a man speaking in a smoky, rainy dream. "I've been harassed. I want it to stop."

No sooner had the words spilled out than Propenko had an urge to scoop them from the wet air and stuff them back into his mouth; but it was too late. He felt something nudge his right elbow, and he looked down at the First Secretary's hand. He shook it in a black, weightless spinning that reminded him of nothing he'd known, then followed Lvovich back into the living room like a sheep. And there, with Vysotski croaking his symphony of moral outrage in the background, he listened to the dwindling, useless strings of conversation being tied in neat bows, the hunter standing beside his prey, smiling.

On the ride home, Raisa kept her face turned away from him, out the side window. Waiting at the stoplights, or when there was a clear stretch of road, Propenko glanced over at the back of her head and her damp coat collar. He was squeezing his knuckles white on the wheel. The feeling of being torn in two, half-present, had not left him, but now his other half was standing on Mikhail Lvovich's balcony.

"Why did you lie to him about talking to Bessarovich, Sergei?"

"Because it was none of his business."

They pulled up to another red light and the engine stalled. Propenko restarted it with a furious snap of his wrist.

"What did you say to her?"

"I told you what I said, Raisa. We discussed problems with the customs clearance."

"You called from our house to discuss the customs clearance?"

Trapped in his lie, Propenko said nothing.

"Did you ask her about going to the embassy?"

"What embassy?"

"The American."

"What are you talking about?"

She turned. The traffic started forward. "I thought that was the point of the lie, to keep that from him."

"Why would I go to the American Embassy?"

"Why are you shouting? To get emigration papers, why else?"

"Emigration papers!"

"Other people are doing it." They were both shouting now.

"And what, move to America?"

"Of course, what else?"

"First Moscow, now America?"

"Leonid and Eva are putting in papers for Israel."

"Leonid Leonidovich?"

"He's a Jew," Raisa said.

"We grew up together, Raisa. You don't have to tell me he's a Jew."

"They're going. What's the matter with you tonight?"

"He'll lose the pavilion if he puts in his papers. What's the matter with *him*?"

"They put in papers Friday afternoon. They're going."

"I don't believe that."

They rode for a kilometer without speaking, the engine chuttering unevenly, the presence of Mikhail and Nina Kabanov sticking to them like the smell of spoiled fish. When they turned onto the Prospekt of the Revolution, Propenko could feel a black mood chasing him. Raisa waited, watching.

"I talked to Bessarovich about Malov." The Lada was sputtering badly now, and he was having to play with the gas pedal to keep it from stalling. On a downhill grade, he popped the shift into neutral and raced the engine. He had an urge to put his fist through the windshield. "We had an argument after the meeting Friday. I threatened him."

"*Threatened* him? Malov? Not physically."

"I told him if he hurt anyone in my family I'd kill him."

"Oh God of mine." Raisa pushed her arms down straight against her seat. "God of mine. Oh, Sergei."

"Vzyatin has a guard near the house and people following us. Bessarovich had offered to help so I called her."

"Oh my God," Raisa said. "I married my father."

"Your mother doesn't think so."

Raisa began to cry without making any noise.

Just beyond the exhibit pavilion the Lada died. Propenko steered it to the curb, turned the key off, then on, and listened as the starter growled and the battery slowly lost its charge. He smacked one palm against the side window and cracked a spiderweb on the glass.

"What is *wrong*?"

A trolley rumbled past. Propenko got out and looked under the hood, poked his fingers in against the black oily shapes, wires, hot metal, the greasy battery cap. It was a charade. He knew perfectly well the Lada would not start again until the wires dried, and the wires would not dry until the fog lifted. Every time there was a string of foggy or rainy days, it was the same story, and every time it happened he told himself he was going to speak to Anatoly about getting new wires, and he always procrastinated until the sun came out and saved him. He spat into the street. Now it would be new wires and a new side window. Standing out in the rain for a taxi on

Sunday night, or a cold walk. He took the wiper blades off, threw them under his seat and slammed the door. They started walking. He looked behind him once, as if for a taxi, hoping to see Vzyatin's men. Nothing. Blind, hissing traffic, streetlight globes, the wet trolley tracks, but no idiot militiaman. He considered walking over to the pavilion and using the phone there, but he was too angry, it would be too much of a humiliation tonight, and who would he call now, Mikhail Lvovich? They walked.

"I'm sorry," he said after a block or so.

Raisa didn't reply.

"I'm a fool." Propenko tried to look casually over his shoulder. Still nothing. Vzyatin's man was using the toilet, no doubt. "I keep trying to find the beginning of it. I've gone over and over everything a thousand times. Where did it begin? Did it begin at the meeting on Friday? Or did I turn right one day in the distant past instead of left, and become an idiot? Every decision I make now explodes in my face."

For a minute, he thought Raisa wasn't going to speak to him at all. He glanced over his shoulder again and saw that a car had stopped behind his stalled Lada. Fine, he thought. Take the wheels. Take the whole fucking thing.

"It began with Lydia," she said. "But you refuse to see it. You refuse to see it because you still think of her as a little girl who couldn't possibly be involved in anything important or dangerous. It makes you feel strong to think that."

Propenko considered this, then shook his head. "It began when I was made Director. Anyone in the office would want to work with Americans. Malov, Volkov, Zhigorin. I was promoted over all of them. It began there, with Bessarovich. She's using the food program to get at Mikhail Lvovich, to humiliate him, and she stuck me right in the middle of it."

He heard a trolley behind them and turned to check its number. On it came, dull yellow and maroon against the wet blackness, rocking and sparking and headed the wrong way. To its left and behind, a set of headlights crawled along the curb.

Propenko took Raisa's arm and turned onto Decembrist Street. "I've tried all my life to stay away from political intrigue, Raisa. You can't believe the things I've done to stay away from it."

"It began with Lydia," Raisa insisted. "At the church. None of this would have happened otherwise. When have we been invited to the First Secretary's? That's not our level. Those aren't our people."

Propenko looked behind them again. No headlights.

"Despicable people. Trash. Complaining about the market when she hasn't shopped in the market in years. Vysotski on the tape player. When Vysotski was alive he wouldn't have gone there even to use the toilet. I don't understand why they even bothered to invite us. So they could find out about the American?"

"Who knows?"

"What happened on the balcony?"

Propenko looked over his shoulder. "We smoked. He told me how painful it was to try and help people and have them turn against you. He talked about the 'disguise of friendship.' "

"That's all?"

"That's all," Propenko spat out.

They were at the end of Decembrist Street where it met October Avenue, a block from Tolkachev's shop. As they crossed the end of the street, Propenko looked to his right. One drunk staggering down the sidewalk. A dog sniffing in the gutter. No headlights. They were not coming to poison him now. They did not have to. He would poison himself.

// CHAPTER 21

MONDAY the fog broke, revealing Vostok. From the flagstone patio in front of the hotel, Czesich could see across Prospekt Revoliutsii to the far edge of what he'd come to think of as the Valley of Devastation. Columns of smoke — white, yellow, and metal blue — rose from the factories and flattened against a ceiling of colder air several thousand feet up. He could see high-tension wires looping, catching the light, and streaks of brown and gray on the black slag heaps, and a spattering of wooden shacks on a muddy slope. The absence of fog made him feel watched from all directions — people at the bus stop, the broom-wielding *babushki* in front of the hotel, a knot of bus drivers and chauffeurs standing nearby smoking. It was almost 1:00 A.M., Washington time. In eight hours, Myron R. Filson, Jr., would walk through the security checkpoint at USCA's front door, hang his suit jacket on the office coatrack, find someone willing to listen to the complete and unabridged account of his Montana fishing vacation, then make his way to the telex. As per his instructions, the weekend reports from overseas would still be on the machine. There would be word from Elliot Bridgeman about the poster show in Kinshasa; something from the Vienna warehouse about tools or electric supplies or panel dimensions; Elissa Thurston checking in from Belize City.

And, if the pavilion telex was working, from the capital of the Donbass coalfields there would be this:

TO: USCA OVERSEAS BRANCH, FILSON
FROM: USCA, RLF 2, CZESICH

SUBJECT: REPORT FROM PARADISE

CUSTOMS CLEARANCE PROCEEDING APACE.
ACCOMMODATIONS, ETC., IN ORDER. EXPECT FIRST FOOD
DELIVERIES TODAY. BADLY NEEDED. LOCAL COUNCIL
OFFICIALS COOPERATIVE AND WELCOMING. DIFFICULTIES
GETTING THROUGH BY PHONE. WILL TRY WEDNESDAY 10:00
A.M. WASH TIME.

REGARDS
AAC

END OF MESSAGE

Czesich paced back and forth on the flagstone, working out the
scenario for the twentieth time. The telex would keep Filson quiet
for now. By late this afternoon, Julie would have realized he had no
intention of returning to Moscow. She would be required, then, to
go to Ambassador Haydock. Haydock would turn red and stamp
about for half an hour or so — nothing Julie couldn't handle. She'd
go back to her office, vent her spleen over the long-distance line to
Vostok, but beneath all the official disapproval there would, he
hoped, boil a drop or two of rebellious Russian blood, a bit of old
affection. He'd return to Moscow in a few weeks having fed some
hungry people, having shaken up the political situation in Vostok,
having interred forever the warm ashes of his former self. Julie
would see him differently. He'd see himself differently. And the
only price would be to endure the wrath of the bureaucracy for the
time it took Filson to expel him from a job he'd long ago come to
despise.

At ten minutes to nine the peach-colored Volga pulled up in
front of the hotel and the gray-headed driver with the awful birthmark got out and held the rear door open. It took a moment, but
Czesich remembered the name. Anatoly. He thanked Anatoly just
the same, said he'd prefer to sit up front, and watched a ripple of
surprise cross the marred face. "The pavilion's just across the
street," he said. "It hardly seems worth the trouble to have you
pick me up and drive me there. It makes me feel like a spoiled
American."

Anatoly smiled. "That's your role," he said. "Spoiled American.
You'll disappoint us if you don't play it." He pulled out of the
parking lot and up to the light at Prospekt Revoliutsii. "My role is

driver." He looked from the light to Czesich's face. "And we are eight minutes early. How would it be if I took you once around the block every morning so we have a chance to talk politics? I've never driven an American before."

Czesich said it would be fine, and Anatoly pulled away from the light as carefully as if he were piloting a limousine. The Volga, official car of the Soviet *apparatchiki*, was a square, unstylish automobile, reminiscent of the Ramblers of Czesich's youth, with a rattling exhaust system and an interior plain as a government desk. But the seats and dashboard and windows were spotless, and Anatoly had left behind his earlier layer of suspicion, and Czesich decided to sit back and relax and learn what might be learned.

"I've been watching you," Anatoly said. "The way you walk, your clothes, the way you shook everyone's hand at the station — even the drivers', even the old watchman in front of the pavilion the other day."

"How do I walk?"

"Like a man who owns the street."

"It's an act. That's not what I feel like inside."

"*Ponyatna,*" Anatoly said. "Understood. It makes you look a little bit like a spy, though. It fooled me at first."

"Let's hope it doesn't fool anyone else."

Anatoly nodded in a serious way that made Czesich uneasy. "Let's hope."

Vostok's morning traffic was thick with delivery trucks, taxis, and buses, not so different from an American city's rush hour, Czesich thought, except that the trucks had PEOPLE or BREAD stenciled on them instead of company names, and they were painted in drab greens and browns instead of garish advertisements and inner-city graffiti. The block turned out to be half a mile square. When they reached the first corner, Anatoly tapped a copy of *Pravda* wedged between the bucket seats. "Did you see the paper?"

Czesich said that he had. That morning's *Pravda* had featured Valentin Pavlov, the prime minister, in a rather transparent speech, a power play aimed at usurping a large block of Gorbachev's authority. Everyone noticed. The kiosk in the hotel lobby had been surrounded by people holding out their five-kopek pieces, pushing and shoving and grabbing at the stack of papers. And it had seemed to Czesich that the men coming out through the hotel's front door, and the drivers standing on the front step smoking, and the women sweeping the damp gutters, had all been especially alert, watching for the wind to change. " 'Our recent diminution of social order and central authority,' " he quoted. "What's that the code for?"

"It's the code for this: President Puchkov."

"Not President Pavlov?"

Anatoly shook his head. "Puchkov is the hidden hand."

"And then what?"

"And then the same as before, only worse."

Czesich watched the drab storefronts slip past and studied the sidewalk faces. " 'Russia drowns in blood and tears,' Pushkin said, 'and takes my head upon her breast.' "

Anatoly said, *"Da,"* in the drawn-out way Soviets liked to say it, in the way Americans of Czesich's generation had once said: "There it is."

They made the third turn, and the pavilion came into view against the background of industrial blight. Anatoly peeked across the seat. "Do you like Soviet anecdotes?"

"I collect them," Czesich said.

The small smile wrinkled the driver's face again, but there was not much joy in it. "Gorbachev, Reagan, and Thatcher go up to heaven to speak with God," he began, eyes fixed on the road. "Reagan approaches God and says, 'Lord, how long till my people are happy?'

" 'Your people?' God looks down at America. 'Twenty years,' he says.

" 'Twenty years!' Reagan says. 'I won't live to see it.' He goes off in a corner and weeps.

"Next, Thatcher approaches God. 'Lord,' she says, 'how long till my people are happy?'

" 'Your people?' God looks down at Great Britain. 'Fifty years.'

" 'Fifty years!' Thatcher says. 'I won't live to see it.' She goes off in a corner and weeps.

"Finally, Gorbachev approaches God. 'Lord,' he says, 'tell me. How long till my people are happy?'

" 'Your people?' God glances down at the Soviet Union. 'I won't live to see it,' he says, and he goes off in a corner and weeps."

Czesich chuckled politely, but his new friend looked across the seat, straight-faced, and said, "Lesson number one."

At the pavilion it was apparent that, along with rumors of Gorbachev's demise, the weekend had spawned rumors of free American food. A crowd had gathered. The old watchman and half a dozen militiamen were pushing people back beyond the farthest container. Workmen were unloading a truck that had been sloppily packed with lengths of portable metal fencing, and setting up a kind of corral around what would be the work area. *Babushki* seemed to be everywhere with their knee-high brooms. Czesich caught sight of Propenko taking leave of a young woman, and when she kissed him good-bye he walked over.

"A change in the weather," Czesich said, as they shook hands.

Propenko nodded distractedly. He looked as though he hadn't slept since Friday afternoon.

The chief of militia joined them. "We're all going to take off our clothes and go down to the river and sunbathe," he said. "Forget work."

Czesich grinned but couldn't hold eye contact. He had never liked the outright lie. "The Ambassador has agreed to visit," he told them. "I spoke with his assistant last night and they're going to arrange a trip as soon as they can. Possibly by the end of the week."

"The sooner the better," Propenko said absently.

"All that's needed at this point, for protocol reasons, is an official invitation from Vostok. It can be done by telephone, but it should come from high up, the Mayor or First Secretary, if possible. Strictly a formality."

"I can arrange it," Propenko said. "I'll call the First Secretary this morning."

"They're personal friends," the Chief said, winking. Propenko seemed embarrassed.

They'd started toward the work area when the short, thick-necked man with the cauliflower ear came striding across the lot, smiling like a salesman. Czesich had forgotten the name, and so put extra enthusiasm into his greeting. They shook hands, and the short man, still smiling, excused himself and led Propenko by the elbow toward the pavilion ramp. Something about the encounter held Czesich's attention. A few paces from the ramp they stopped and faced each other. The short man was doing all the talking, smiling up at Propenko, holding him by both shoulders now, chatting away. Propenko seemed stiff and suspicious.

"What's his name again?" Czesich asked the Chief, who was also absorbed in the one-sided conversation.

"Malov," the Chief said without turning his eyes. "Nikolai Phillipovich."

"Director of Security, correct?"

"More or less."

"A busy day for him."

It was a hectic morning, one of those bright, cheerfully chaotic
Soviet mornings that reminded Czesich of so many of the exhibit
installations he'd supervised in the seventies and eighties. A carnival atmosphere prevailed, a joy in physical work and a natural lazi-
ness blended together into the unique Russian soup. The laborers
were a mixed lot — three muscular twenty-five-year-olds who did
most of the bullwork, plus an Armenian forklift driver and two
other men about Czesich's own age, who slunk around the perimeter of the activity, lending a shoulder when it was absolutely unavoidable, stopping every twenty minutes or so for a *perekur* —
cigarette break — eyeballing everything, fingering everything,
their churlishness reinforced by an air of righteous Marxist superiority.

Russia's vodka-soaked ball and chain, Czesich thought. A leth-
argy to outlive God.

He was tempted to break out his instruments of incentive, but
because of the trouble they'd had at the Friday meeting, he decided
to hold off on opening the gift container. He'd begin with the
straight foodstuffs, move on to pocket calculators and distilled
spirits later in the day.

The worksite was breezy and warm, and the workers gradually
achieved a steady, sluggish momentum. One by one the heavy
wooden crates were forklifted out onto the lot, pried open, system-
atically rifled by the customs inspector with his clipboard of packing lists. Czesich stood by and translated. The laborers gathered
around, and from behind the barricades, curious spectators craned
their necks. "What's there?" someone would shout.

And one of the lazy older workers would shout back: "Beets."

"Beets? In a can? We have beets of our own, send them back."
And after a moment, "What now?"

"Peaches in syrup."

"And in the sacks?"

"Wheat flour."

"Get to the vodka," someone yelled, and the crowd of idlers
guffawed.

Ryshevsky, the gray-headed customs inspector, was all business,
though, humorless as the Politburo, deliberate as a detective. At

this rate, Czesich figured, Gorbachev would be retired and finished with his memoirs by the time they cleared the last container and actually started giving out food, but he held his tongue. Soviet customs agents were a special breed. You did not bribe them. Except in very special circumstances, you did not raise your voice. If something needed changing, you arranged for the agent in question to be tapped on the shoulder from above. The problem was, Czesich was not yet sure which direction was up. He'd need another day or two to get a feel for the local hierarchy. In the meantime, he'd stand sweating in the smoggy sunlight, wondering what was taking place in Ambassador Haydock's office, and providing creative translations for things like "hydrogenated vegetable oil" and "BHT."

By lunch, only one container had been cleared, and its crates were standing wide open a few feet from the curious crowd. Before leaving to send his telex, Czesich called the old toothless watchman aside and slipped him a Marine Corps cigarette lighter. The old toothless watchman kissed him on both cheeks.

Leonid had reserved an entire corner of the pavilion restaurant for him, three tables with small cardboard signs reading: RESERVED FOR FOREIGN GUESTS. Czesich looked out on a sunlit corner of the Valley of Devastation and worked his way through an appetizer of cold ham and tomatoes, a fatty chicken and rice soup, a plate of hard beef and french fries, a cup of tea. It was, he suspected, the very best Vostok could offer, and he ate dutifully, far beyond his hunger.

When he was on his second cup of tea he saw Propenko approach the table.

"Pleasant appetite."

"Thank you." Czesich offered him a seat.

"The meal is satisfactory?"

"Fine."

"Everything in order at the hotel?"

"Couldn't be better. Bobin is a warm host."

Propenko seemed astounded by this statement. He squeezed his eyebrows together and peered, as if looking for sarcasm. Czesich had seen him at the Intourist restaurant on Friday night, and he thought Propenko looked as miserable now as he'd looked happy then, he and his wife sitting at their window table like an advertisement for marriage. "Some tea?"

"No, thank you. I called Mikhail Lvovich, the First Party Secretary of the oblast. He'll cable your ambassador this afternoon with an official invitation to visit Vostok over the weekend."

"Wonderful," Czesich said, though his counterpart's earnestness shamed him. He could not imagine Propenko carrying on the kind of charade he was carrying on now, could not imagine him lying, straight-faced, no matter how noble the cause. Propenko held himself like an athlete, with an athlete's natural dignity. It reminded Czesich of a much younger version of himself, a proud and honest hockey-playing Tony, precorruption.

"Everything in order at the hotel?"

"You asked me that already. It's fine."

Propenko rubbed his eyes. "I meant with the workers, the unloading. Everything all right?"

"I was hoping to have cleared five or six containers by this point, but it's no fault of the workers."

"Ryshevsky?"

Czesich shrugged.

"I'll have a word with him."

Propenko seemed to be having difficulty saying what he'd come to say. He glanced around the room again, stalling. "We talked about dinner when we saw you Friday night," he said at last, in a slightly quieter voice. "At our home. Are you still interested?"

"Absolutely."

"Well, my wife mentioned it again this morning. The whole household is excited. Our daughter. My mother-in-law. Would you be able to come Wednesday?"

"I'd be delighted."

Propenko had his back to the room. Malov and the customs inspector were dining together at another table a few yards away. Propenko had already written his address and telephone number on a scrap of graph paper, and in a way that was neither surreptitious nor obvious, he slid it across the table. "It's not far. We're on the fourth floor."

From behind one of his customary expressions of polite appreciation, Czesich watched, trying to determine what was wrong. For someone like Propenko, he supposed — a man who could have stepped right out of a propaganda poster, one size larger than life, one notch better-looking — nothing would be solid now. The iron skeleton of the Party had rusted and tilted and bent under its own weight, leaving its decent, gullible, ambitious Propenkos stranded on the fourth floor, not sure whether to hold on or jump. He wondered what that must feel like — that, added to everything else on the road to the enormous five-oh.

"I saw you talking with a young woman this morning. Was that your daughter?"

Propenko's face changed at the word and Czesich felt a pang of envy.

"Very beautiful."

"She's studying English."

"Maybe we'll have a chance to converse on Wednesday evening."

"She'd like that very much."

"I believe I saw her at the funeral on Saturday," Czesich said.

Propenko's face lost its light, and he tried to hide it by rubbing his fingers once across his lips. Public worship would still carry its risks in a place like Vostok. Czesich wanted to kick himself.

"Yes. She is . . . she helps out there now. Very devoted. She . . . it comes from her grandmother, I think." Propenko tried to smile.

"My grandfather sometimes took me to church with him," Czesich said. "Russian Orthodox services. But my mother was Roman Catholic. It caused a lot of trouble."

Propenko nodded. "I went when I was very young. That caused trouble, too. In a different way."

That was as far as they could take it. When Propenko left, Czesich put five rubles and a lapel pin on the table and wandered out the wrong door to the back side of the pavilion, where the line for the photography exhibit curled and doubled back upon itself. Beyond it, on the nearest mountain of mine tailings, he could see sparkles of reflected sunlight, and, farther off, black smoke billowing up in thick plumes as if to shield the valley from God's eye. He thought of Propenko's face brightening at the word "daughter," and of Anatoly looking at him across the seat, so sincere. He glanced once at the line of people inspecting his shoes and suit and posture. How strange it was to be rich and to envy the poor, in the midst of their envying you.

At this very hour, his only true friend was sitting in Ambassador Haydock's office, selling him down the river, and she had absolutely every right in the world to do it.

In spite of Propenko's assurances, Ryshevsky did not move any faster after lunch. He insisted on making the laborers count every last carton of food to see how the actual quantities compared with his packing list numbers; on getting an exact translation of all the ingredients; on putting back the crates in the exact order in which they'd been removed. When they unlocked the third container — the loading of which Czesich had supervised himself, two months before, in the Brooklyn warehouse — and came upon the booze and cigarettes and a crate of modest gifts listed under "Miscellaneous Items," Ryshevsky just about lifted into orbit. He strutted around the work area, spitting and muttering and rapping his clipboard with the backs of his fingers. The workers went off on a *perekur* to keep from laughing, and some wit in the crowd behind the metal fencing started crowing like a barnyard cock.

They adjourned to the pavilion meeting room, and wasted an hour and a half there, paging through a Bible-sized book of customs regulations, arguing tariffs and duties, hard currency, rubles. This time around, Propenko was of little help. He seemed tired and preoccupied, and sat in a neutral corner while Czesich and the inspector haggled and Leonid looked helplessly on. In the end, Czesich agreed to a small tariff on the gift items, to be paid in dollars by the U.S. Communications Agency within sixty days.

But the momentum was broken. By the time they got back to work, it was close to the end of the day, and the laborers had time only to repack and lock the third container. Czesich stalked off toward the hotel in a foul mood. His second homeland, for all its depth and soulfulness, could sometimes be a tremendous pain in the ass.

Malov caught up with him at the curb. "So," he said cheerily, "what are your impressions of our city?"

Czesich was almost angry enough to tell him. He produced a civil response and watched for a break in the traffic.

"I hear your ambassador is visiting this weekend. Does it make you nervous?"

Czesich thought it a strange question. The light turned and he and Malov crossed together as far as the trolley tracks. "Not at all. He may not be able to come anyway."

"And if he doesn't? What are your plans?"

Something in Malov's voice sounded a second alarm. Malov was smiling at him, but it was a sinister, professional thing, and the eyes were dull and mean. Czesich smiled back, surprised it had taken him two full days to figure this out. His instincts were rusty. "If the Ambassador doesn't come," he said, "I'll have to go to the church alone."

Malov laughed. "So you're a believer?"

"Absolutely," Czesich said. It gave him an almost sexual pleasure to mislead the world's information-gatherers. He'd rubbed shoulders with so many of them over the years, but it still astonished him how similar they were. Chilean, Iraqi, Bulgarian, they all wore this same skin of congeniality over a vicious, sadistic core. They were all pathologically patriotic, ambitious, aggressive, lacking even a particle of compassion. From the moment he'd opened his mouth in Friday's meeting, Malov had exhibited all the signs, and Czesich was angry at himself for not having noticed sooner.

A trolley rumbled past, shaking the ground at their feet. When it was beyond them, they crossed together through a fog of auto and truck exhaust.

"You seem upset," Malov said. "Am I intruding?"

Czesich smiled. The classic. "Yes," he said.

Malov's disguise slipped, exposing a thing Czesich had seen before, many times. The danger in this thing was that it was cloaked in clumsiness and seemed almost laughable. In the States it stayed, for the most part, in the animal kingdom of organized crime; here, it had been government-sanctioned for at least seventy-four years.

"I can see you don't understand American humor."

Malov seemed to be sulking. Czesich wondered if he'd gone too far. "The Chief told me you're working as Director of Security on this project."

"Correct."

"An important position."

"Not really," Malov said coolly. "We don't expect trouble."

"I hope not. Not this week, especially."

"Not any week."

"I understand some American correspondents will be traveling with the Ambassador," Czesich said. "Vostok will be famous."

"I hadn't heard."

"All the big ones. *Time, Newsweek, Washington Post.* This is a pilot program, after all. People in the rest of the world are anxious to know how it will be received."

"It will be received very well," Malov said. "We accomplished a great deal today."

"Is that Soviet humor? Three containers in eight hours is 'a great deal'? I was just thinking of calling the embassy to complain about it."

"Our customs chief is under some pressure," Malov explained, and Czesich recalled him fibbing and conniving and caving in at Friday's meeting. In his experience, provincial KGB agents fell into two categories: clumsy, rank-and-file tough guys who shadowed and harassed you and asked transparent questions; and the much more sophisticated officers, slick as a bloody blade, capable of anything. He checked Malov's eyes and could not be sure yet. Malov seemed to have regained his counterfeit good humor, but there was a mix of worry and venom in his voice. Czesich had made an enemy.

"I should mention that there was an incident in Donetsk not long ago," Malov went on. "They found narcotics in a shipment of construction supplies. I believe it was an American container."

Naturally, Czesich thought.

"I'll do what I can to speed things up if you'd like. Seeing as your ambassador is coming, and the press. We wouldn't want there to be any unpleasantries."

"I'd be most grateful." One of Czesich's cardinal rules was never to do a favor for these people and never to accept one, but it had to be broken this time. If Propenko wasn't going to tap the customs inspector on the shoulder, it would have to be Malov — whatever Malov's twisted motivations might be. The point was to get as much of the food as possible out into the city before the large, slow embassy gears began to turn, and then to have a story ready and his bags packed when the charade began to fall apart.

"We always try to make our foreign guests feel at home."

"Very kind of you," Czesich said, but he was unable to keep a note of sarcasm from his voice. They shook hands, Malov squeezing very hard; the battle was joined.

Czesich had told himself he wasn't going to drink after work, but he wanted to shake Malov, so he went downstairs to the hard-currency bar, where Soviets were not welcome.

The bar was too bright, the booths upholstered in garish red leatherette and dotted with other solitary drinkers. He nursed a lukewarm beer and let the day's frustration ebb. He bought a second beer, a third, a seven-dollar can of German cashews, then realized he was sitting there only to avoid climbing up to his room and placing the call to Moscow. Somewhere in midafternoon, his faith in Julie's fiery Russian blood seemed to have evaporated. It was after five-thirty; he would have to call her at home now, where she would not be restrained by office decorum.

In his room, he ordered the call and had a drop of vodka to clean away the beer's fuzziness. Twenty minutes later the phone rang. He picked it up and heard a whistling and clicking, then Julie's voice, sentiment unmistakable.

"Does the fact that it's a just cause make any difference?" he said.

"I spoke with Haydock, Chesi."

"Do what you have to do."

"I did."

There were a few seconds of buzzing during which Czesich watched twenty-three years of faithful government service pass before his eyes. He could not bring himself to mourn. "That's it, then," he said.

Julie didn't respond.

"Did the Large One get the invite?"

"He got it. The first thing he did was call me upstairs, and the first thing I did was tell him what was going on. You left me no option."

"Could he grasp the concept?"

"It's still a joke to you, isn't it."

"Not really." Czesich considered this a moment. "The last thing it is to me is a joke."

"I feel like you did it just to slap me in the face."

"Absolutely just the opposite," he said. "You know why I did it. Think back to our old conversations and you'll know why."

"There are procedures for everything, Chesi. Including phone calls."

"What's the procedure for being hungry?"

She was silent for a time, then said, "The Moscow job is out. You've seen to that."

Czesich was looking through the gauzy curtains, imagining Malov or Bobin listening in. There were subjects that were never supposed to be mentioned over unsecured lines, but it seemed important to make a clean break from the rules of his cautious former world. He wanted to tell Julie he loved her — as a friend, at least, no matter who she was "seeing" — but it sounded too syrupy in his inner ear. So he proclaimed his affection this way: "I had a prostitute up in the room the other night."

There was another pause. "What am I supposed to say? Congratulations?"

"I didn't do anything. I didn't let her in the door, actually. I just wanted to tell you that. I didn't —"

"Anything else to confess to the microphones?"

"Nothing I can mention. Impure thoughts, that type of thing."
He was straining now, worried she might hang up, that she might
already have hung up. The static made it impossible to know.
"Things are changing," he said, "with me, I mean."

"I'm glad. Think about someone other than yourself."

"That's what I thought I was doing."

"Think again."

"There are different levels."

"Filson wants you to call him right away. That's one level."

"I'm not operating on that level anymore, that's what I'm trying
to tell you, Jule. I don't care about Filson anymore, and Filson's
rules, and Filson's —"

"I have to go," Julie said. "Someone's here."

"McCauley?"

"Don't be childish, Chesi."

"They seem to know him down here. I was just wondering —"

"Another subject," she said, "or I'll hang up. I mean it."

"Why?" he said. The line was not bad enough to keep him from
hearing the discomfort in her voice at the mention of McCauley's
name, and — perhaps it was the frustration of the day, or the little
bit he'd drunk, or plain jealousy — he had a quick and overwhelm-
ing urge to find out what it signified. There were procedures for
everything. The existence of certain types of embassy employees
was not supposed to be acknowledged over the telephone. "It was
strange the way it happened," he said. "I was chatting with a member of the local clergy on the train coming down here —"

The line clicked once, the static turned into a steady hum, and
Czesich had his answer.

// CHAPTER 22

PROPENKO watched Ryshevsky shuffle off toward his car with the thick customs notebook under one arm, and Malov follow Czesich toward the hotel, and the disappointed crowd of onlookers break apart and drift off in the direction of the bus stop, empty-handed. At the western end of the valley, two bands of lavender cloud were sliding up over the horizon. He watched them for a moment, but the black mood would not leave him.

When the work area was abandoned and quiet, Shyshkin, the older of the two watchmen, made a tour of its perimeter, checking behind and between containers, kicking pieces of broken pallet off into a corner, eyeing the surrounding terrain for teenaged guerrillas. His territory secured, he came and stood beside Propenko. "No driver tonight, Sergei Sergeievich?"

"Anatoly's wife is flying to Murmansk. I let him go early so he could see her off."

"You're a generous boss."

Propenko nodded. "Everyone says you and your partner are doing a fine job, Ivan. I'm glad I hired you."

The old man sucked his gums to keep from smiling. His partner, the King of Jazz, had taken to washing the containers at night to stay awake. Leonid said he borrowed a bucket and brush from the pavilion restaurant after dinner, and, without benefit of soap, scrubbed and wiped the containers until they were as clean as a fresh plate.

"The American gave you a nice compliment today. He said he wanted to take you and Bondolenko home with him so you could teach American watchmen your trade."

Ivan pulled open one side of his threadbare sport coat and tapped the neck of a bottle bulging the pocket there. "Our reward," he said. "American whiskey. The wife will be pleased."

"We all got some. Everyone but Ryshevsky."

"Stupid ass," Ivan said.

Propenko had wanted to have a word with Ryshevsky after lunch, and then again after work, but he believed Bessarovich had forsaken him now, that he had no one behind him, no power, nothing to threaten with. Leonid had been busy with the photography exhibit all afternoon. Vzyatin had shown up for a minute at the start of the day, then disappeared. Propenko had been left with the strange feeling of being a disloyal crew member on a jet with no pilot.

"Going home now, Sergei Sergeievich?"

"My car's broken. I'm going out hunting for parts."

"Where is it parked?"

"They towed it to the lot on Chernyshevsky Street."

Ivan grunted. "Safe enough." He glanced at the street as though working up his courage, and Propenko worried he was getting ready to ask for a raise, or for a few boxes of food to be diverted to his sister's house. He'd stopped by the office before lunch and found his desk littered with messages from acquaintances and friends of acquaintances, people he hadn't spoken to in months. Everyone from his barber to the janitor at the gym seemed to expect a can of American peaches or a bag of powdered milk. Volkov had been right: He had new friends now. Some of them in high places.

"I have something important to tell you, Sergei Sergeievich," the watchman said.

Propenko nodded, waiting.

"You know this afternoon when there was the trouble?"

"Yes."

"Whiskey, cigarettes, that trouble?"

"I was there," Propenko said.

"You know when you and the American and Ryshevsky went inside?"

"I remember."

"And I stayed with the open container?"

"Right."

"You know the fellow with the bad ear?"

"Malov."

"A case of whiskey."

"What do you mean?"

"A case of the American whiskey," Shyshkin repeated softly. "The one with the ear."

"He *stole* it?"

"*Took* it," Ivan corrected.

Propenko squeezed his hands into fists in his pockets. "Why didn't you stop him?"

Ivan didn't answer, and the question, floating unanswered, rang foolish. Watchmen did not go around telling *chekisti* what they could and could not do, and everyone knew it. "All right," Propenko said. "I'll straighten it out."

"You said you wanted a report. That's why I told you."

"You did the right thing, Ivan. I didn't mean it when I said you should have stopped him. You couldn't have stopped him. You did the right thing."

"First he carried it around behind the container, on the side where there are no people. After a while he took it from there and put it in the trunk of his car, the white car. He thinks I don't see."

Propenko put a hand on the old man's shoulder to calm him. "Chief Vzyatin's coming to pick me up now. We'll take care of him. We'll figure something out."

The old watchman nodded unhappily.

"Maybe you and Bondolenko can give him a flat tire some night, or something. Take your revenge that way."

Ivan almost smiled. The King of Jazz came walking down from the bus stop, swinging his arms in an exaggerated way, looking left and right to check for the wolves in Western running shoes who descended upon the containers after dark. Shyshkin bade Propenko good-night and went to meet his partner.

As militia chief, Vzyatin thought it best to be unpredictable, keep his opponents off balance. He came to work before dawn some mornings, worked until midnight, took a weekday off and showed up on Sunday, spent his time wherever he felt it was important — at the exhibits pavilion, at the demonstrations, in his office at the Central Precinct, cruising the streets. He loved to appear on the scene unexpectedly, and in different vehicles: the blue-and-yellow chief's car with his faithful driver, Oleg, behind the wheel; or driving himself in an ordinary sergeant's jeep; or using one of his detectives' unmarked Ladas or Zhigulis. Tonight he turned off Prospekt

Revoliutsii in a plain black Volga with a dent in the driver's door, and glided down the driveway very slowly, looking from side to side, inspecting his kingdom, filing everything away in his policeman's brain. He pulled up in front of Propenko and smiled out the open window. "Climb in, longlegs."

Propenko sat in back.

The Chief turned around and looked at him over the top of the seat. "Do I smell?"

"I want to stretch out."

"Are you having one of your depressions?"

Propenko looked out the side window.

"Do you know what the psychological definition of depression is?"

Propenko said he didn't know.

"Suppressed anger."

"Then I've had suppressed anger since I was fourteen years old, Victor."

The Chief reached between the seats, squeezed Propenko's knee, and turned around. "You need something new in your life," he said over his shoulder. "A fling."

"I'm not the fling type."

"Too pure, eh?"

"Pure as snow."

Propenko watched the King of Jazz make the same rounds Ivan Ivanich had just made, tugging on the American padlocks, peering into corners, under the pavilion ramp, between and behind containers, surveying the surrounding terrain like a general mapping out strategy on the eve of battle. The man was sane, Propenko decided, quite sane. He'd simply figured out that the best way to survive in Soviet society was to pretend to be crazy. The KGB left you alone that way, the militia left you alone; you could get away with almost anything on the streets, and go home to your jazz music and your two or three close friends, your family if you were lucky enough to have one. This was the way almost everybody he knew survived now. They narrowed their lives down to a very small playing field on which they had at least a chance of winning — a job they didn't take home at night, a few people they could trust, a favorite hobby, or favorite place. It seemed to him that his mistake had been in doing just the opposite, in trying to make his life wider, bigger.

"I went by the office this morning," he said to the back of

Vzyatin's head, "and Lyuba showed me two telexes. The first one came at ten o'clock: 'Western food aid project temporarily halted due to logistical considerations. Information to follow.' The second an hour later: 'Previous message in error. Vostok project to go forward as planned.' "

The Chief pondered this news for a moment. Propenko looked into the rearview mirror but could not see enough of his face to know what he was thinking. "Were they signed?"

"The second one."

"Whose name?"

"Bessarovich."

Vzyatin thought about it for another few seconds. "The first one must have been a mistake, that's all. You know how the Moscow offices are — one person bangs in a nail, the next person yanks it out, the next person bangs it in again. It keeps them busy."

Propenko nodded, a bit disappointed. He'd been hoping the first telex might be accurate, that Vzyatin would tell him the whole program had been called off, and that he was about to be returned to a smaller field of play.

"Call her up if you're worried about it, but if it's something important, use the phone at the precinct. You never know who's listening in at your office."

"What about my house?"

"Your house is worse. I'm telling you, call from the precinct if it's something you don't want everyone in the world to know."

"I called her from my house Saturday night."

"She was evasive then, I bet, right?"

"Very evasive."

"That's what I'm telling you."

Propenko shut his eyes. When he opened them, Leonid was coming out the front door and down the ramp. Leonid sat in front, greeted his friends without really looking at them, and they started slowly up the driveway.

"Ryshevsky is a pain in the ass, isn't he though?" Leonid said.

Propenko could tell from the first word that he'd been drinking. Drink was the second best method of survival, after craziness.

"All the fool has to do is keep his mouth shut and accept a bottle as a gift, but no, of course no, he has to uphold his sacred regulations. The sanctity of his borders."

Vzyatin came to a stop at Prospekt Revoliutsii and watched for an opening in the traffic. "Meanwhile," he said, "a thousand kilos of hashish cross his sanctified borders from the Afghani side every week."

"Anton Antonovich handled it well," Propenko said, trying to pull himself up out of his mood.

"Handles everything well. A good man. Though I thought I saw him walking into the hotel with Malov just now."

"Malov followed him."

"Still . . ." Vzyatin glanced at Propenko in the mirror and winked. "Judge a man by the company he keeps."

Propenko didn't answer. They were headed for a friend of Oleg's, someone with an auto-parts connection, semilegal, but it was mainly an excuse for the three of them to spend an hour together away from everyone else. Leonid had a confession to make — they all knew it — and it seemed easier to have him make it in the car, on a contrived errand, than in some cafe or office, or in his own home in front of his wife and children. What Propenko and Vzyatin were supposed to do now was to make small talk until Leonid was ready to say he was leaving them.

"Any news on the investigation?"

Vzyatin shrugged.

"Our Chief is at the point of not talking about it," Leonid said over the seat. He still could not quite meet his friends' eyes. Propenko knew the feeling.

"We're waiting," the Chief said. He pulled out into traffic and headed the unmarked Volga east, toward the railroad station. "There are facts and there is politics. Interrogating the members of certain organizations is a matter of politics. You have to go through channels. You don't just walk into State Security Headquarters and say, 'Excuse me, Major General Gavkov, we'd like to ask your men a few questions about silencers.' You have to do it through Moscow. You have to go over Lvovich's head and over Gavkov's head without letting them know it. That's the trick."

At the mention of the First Secretary, Propenko sank back a bit into the shadows. They were headed straight up Prospekt Revoliutsii, straight toward Lvovich's house.

"Victor's waiting for the miners to storm the palace," Leonid said, too loudly.

"Everyone's waiting for that," Vzyatin said.

"I'm not." Leonid smiled sadly, but could not seem to take it any further.

"What's the latest on the strike?" Propenko said, to give him time.

"The Siberian mines went down today," Vzyatin said. "Kolyma went down. Gold, salt, coal — the miners are all banding together. They wanted Puchkov out long ago, but that little speech he gave on TV made them want to cut off his balls."

"A friend of my son's is a taxi driver," Leonid said. "He was sitting at the train station last night, late, and saw a wagon full of Interior Ministry troops arrive. He thinks they went to the army base. A hundred or more."

"Lvovich wants to have them ready," Vzyatin said.

Propenko sank down further in the seat. They were in the neighborhood of fine pastel homes now, survivors of the war, symbols of communist equality. Leonid said: "Eva and I put in papers."

In spite of the fact that they'd both known about it in advance, neither Propenko nor Vzyatin could think of anything to say at first, and Leonid was left hanging for a moment in the vines of old friendship. "Because of Mark and Sara," he said. He turned halfway around in his seat and met Propenko's eyes. Propenko could not get any words up through his throat.

"It's a mistake, my friend," Vzyatin said. "Too soon."

Leonid shook his head, held Propenko's gaze for another two seconds, then turned around again.

"You'll lose the pavilion within a week. It will be months, maybe a year, before they let you go. What happens in the meantime?"

Liquor turned Leonid cheerful and loose, but, even drunk, he could not manage to smile at this. "Eva says they're murdering people at the church. Our son is involved at the church, it's time to go. She's right." He tried a joke. "Jews should never get involved in churches is the lesson here."

"Lydia's involved," Propenko made himself say. Both Vzyatin and Leonid had been told this, but separately.

"Your Lydia is involved. Leonid's Mark is involved. Only my Andrei is the fine Komsomol," Vzyatin said. "He'd kiss Puchkov's prick if he could reach it. Which is not how we brought him up, I promise you."

"We were fine Komsomols."

"We never kissed anyone's prick, Sergei." The Chief chased a cabdriver out of his lane. "Speaking of pricks, how was your dinner with Mikhail Lvovich? Did the subject of *Makdohnlds khemburgrs* come up?"

"Uneventful," Propenko said. They were only a block from Lvovich's house now, creeping along. He wondered if Vzyatin had somehow found out about his conversation on the balcony, and was taking this route just to torture him.

"You called Bessarovich first?"

"I told you," Propenko said. "Saturday night. From my house."

There was a black Chaika parked in front of the First Secretary's, a militia guard at the door. Vzyatin glanced over at the guard as he drove past. Propenko looked the other way. "The man is finished," the Chief said, as if he knew things no one else knew. It was part of why they'd made him chief: first, because he spoke as if he knew secrets; second, because he knew them.

Neither Propenko nor Leonid tried to contradict him.

Vzyatin turned off the main road just before the bridge and followed the river as it curled southward. The houses were uglier here, six-story concrete monstrosities set down in the middle of stony lots. Trees had been planted along the front edge of the lots, and they offered a spot of green in the desert, but the overall impression was arid and tattered and poor. "How can you leave us alone to fight these bastards?" Vzyatin said across the front seat.

He'd meant it as a friendly joke, but Propenko could tell by the tilt of Leonid's head that it hadn't been taken that way. Leonid lit a cigarette and held it out the window, and a bad silence floated among them. Vzyatin tried to push it away. "Everyone pictures two options," he said. "Either it's Stalin all over again, or it's America. The 1930s, or sex shops on the corner and policemen in big houses. There are other possibilities."

"The Third Path," Leonid said drunkenly.

The Chief shook his head. "Civil war."

They fell silent again. Propenko felt his depression deepen. The words "civil war" were connected, in his mind, in all of their minds, with starvation and despair and Bolshevik triumph. It was not a subject they spoke of lightly.

"You should all come with me, in that case," Leonid said. "We should all leave together."

Vzyatin was still shaking his head. "I'm staying." He peeked at Propenko in the mirror. "I'm going to stay and give my friends guns and teach them to shoot."

Propenko wondered if he was serious. He'd heard that, in

America, almost everyone carried guns, especially in the cities. "Malov came up and shook my hand this morning," he said, just to be saying something. " 'I know you didn't mean anything by it, Sergei,' he told me. 'No hard feelings. We all say things like that from time to time. We all lose our tempers.' "

"A snake," Leonid said.

"He's setting you up so he can ask for some food," Vzyatin said. But Propenko suspected something much simpler: Malov had gotten a message from Mikhail Lvovich overnight. The dogs had been called off.

"What did you answer?"

"I told him I was under a lot of pressure with the new job. He said he understood."

"Good," Vzyatin said. "No more talk about the rape, I take it."

Propenko shook his head. He felt dizzy.

"He's a snake," Leonid said again. "I'd worry now more than before."

"Your house is watched," Vzyatin said. "We have plainclothes detectives watching your family. The entire department hates Malov with a passion."

"The old watchman came up to me just now. He says Malov took a case of whiskey from the container when we were inside arguing with Ryshevsky."

"In front of my men?"

"You know Nikolai," Propenko said. "He could have made it look like he was helping with the unloading. Who'd try to stop him? Old Ivan was shaking in his boots just telling me about it, and Malov was nowhere in sight."

Vzyatin let out a string of curses. His men had disappointed him again. Propenko thought he must be the only person left in the city who could still be disappointed by the Vostok militia.

They turned left onto a side street and Vzyatin slowed down, looking for a number. He found it, pulled off onto the shoulder, and pointed. "It's a long shot," he said. "If they don't have the wires, take whatever you can and we'll trade it for wires someplace else."

"Anatoly can usually get them," Propenko said, "but it takes longer these days."

"I can usually get them, too," Vzyatin said. " 'Usually' doesn't apply now. You two go in without me. If they see me they'll think it's a raid. Number 112, fifth floor. Tell them Oleg sent you."

Propenko and Leonid got out and went carefully up the broken walkway. The front door had been propped open with a block of wood, and a pair of eight-or-nine-year-old boys had set up a make-shift soccer game in the lobby and were kicking a taped ball of newspaper back and forth.

"Reminds me of us," Leonid said.

Propenko nodded. He'd known Leonid since they were in kindergarten and was trying to imagine life without him now, someone else sitting in the big pavilion office, someone else at the Council meetings. He could feel the familiar depression working him over, pushing him down into himself, painting the future in various shades of hopelessness.

A cardboard sign hung on the elevator door: UNDER REPAIR. They located the stairway and started up.

"Well," Leonid said at the first landing, "I'm running out on you."

"You're not running, Leonid."

Leonid was shaking his head. "I tell myself I'm doing it for my children. Then my children talk about staying and fighting and I'm exposed for what I am."

"Which is what?" Propenko said sharply. The remark had landed too close to home. "A man who wants to live a normal life? That's a crime? We haven't had a normal life for so long we forget what it is. First we have enough to eat and we can't say anything. Then not enough to eat but we can say anything we want. Now, no one knows what we have or what we can say. Our insides are twisted up. The water comes out of the faucet looking like milk, and we think, 'Oh, wonderful, the water is not brown this morning. It will be a good day.'" Propenko finished this speech and avoided Leonid's eyes. They climbed on.

"Still, there's something to be said for fighting."

In this, Propenko detected a note he'd often heard. He did not know about women, but there was a place in men, a secret eye that looked at other men and built them up into something bigger, better, more courageous, more manly. He'd had the feeling himself, looking at war veterans, imagining their courage, comparing it to his own fears. It was ridiculous. Less than twenty-four hours ago he'd committed the most cowardly act of his life, and here was Leonid, looking at him as though he were a fighter.

They were on the fourth floor now, Leonid, the smoker, badly out of breath. Propenko let him rest a moment on the landing. He thought, perhaps, with Vzyatin absent, he might be able to force out his confession, cancel Leonid's small betrayal by admitting a small betrayal of his own. He went as far as saying, "I should never have had dinner with Lvovich last night. I shouldn't have gone there."

But Leonid said, between breaths, "Mark thinks Lvovich was behind the murder . . . at the church." And Propenko went spinning back down into his dark mood.

On the fifth floor they stepped from the shadowy landing into a shadowy hallway and saw the number 112 scrawled in chalk on a metal door right in front of them.

A frail woman in a bathrobe answered Propenko's knock. He mentioned Oleg's name and she admitted them to a two-room flat with lights burning everywhere and some kind of sweet soup simmering on a stove in a cramped kitchen. Near the stove was a couch and on the couch an even frailer old man, a sack of bones beneath a blanket, whiskered white cheeks and sunken eyes that watched the visitors, unblinking. Propenko looked away.

The man on the couch groaned. The woman went on stirring her soup, ignoring the two visitors standing in her hallway. After a minute she turned off the gas and poured the liquid into two blue plastic dishes. She carried one dish over and put it on the end of the couch near the old man's head and motioned for him to eat. He kept his eyes on Leonid. After a minute, Propenko thought he heard him say a word under his breath. "Jew," it sounded like.

The woman brought the second dish to the flimsy metal table and sat. She spooned some of the soup into her mouth, swallowed, and raised her eyes. "Lyosha!" she shouted crazily, glaring at the wall.

Propenko heard the toilet flush. A door opened behind him, and he and Leonid turned and saw a young man about Lydia's age come out into the hall stuffing his shirttails into the front of his pants with one hand and wiping his nose with the other.

The young man smiled at them and came and stood very close. "Good evening, comrades."

Propenko could see the tobacco stains on his teeth, and smell beer on his breath. He suppressed an urge to turn and walk out the door. "I have a Lada," he said. "Nineteen eighty-seven. It needs wires."

"They all do. Fog gets them. Needs a distributor cap, too, I'll bet."

There was another groan from the couch, but Lyosha seemed not to hear. He moved his eyes from Propenko to Leonid and back, flicked a bit of lint from his right sleeve. It was hot and airless in the apartment, and a film of perspiration coated his pimpled forehead. Propenko waited. "I can get wires for an '87 Lada," Lyosha said, meeting his eyes again. "It'll take about two weeks. Ninety rubles each."

"What!"

Lyosha shrugged and looked bored.

"The state price is a hundred and ninety-five rubles for the set," Propenko said.

Lyosha smiled down at the floor. "Right. In the parts store. Go ahead and go to the store and put your name in, and see what you get. When the wires are delivered, the people who work in the store buy them up right away. The people in the store sell them to friends. If I'm lucky, the friends sell them to me. By the time the store gets its money, and the people in the store get their money, and their friends get their money, and I get my money, you have three hundred and sixty instead of a hundred ninety-five. The set."

"Oleg gave us your name," Leonid put in, over Propenko's shoulder.

"I know that. Mother wouldn't have let you in otherwise."

"Do you know what Oleg does?"

Lyosha smiled his flat smile. "Drives for the Chief?"

"And do you know who's waiting for us downstairs, waiting to drive us home?"

"The Chief?" Lyosha guessed, his smile widening. "Victor Akakievich himself?"

The old woman had finished slurping her soup in the living room and was rinsing the bowl under the tap. Her husband belched loudly.

Propenko had heard of people like Lyosha, of course, though he'd always imagined them living with a girlfriend in a flat south of the river, wearing leather jackets, smoking foreign cigarettes. He'd always thought of them and their families as sailing a different course than the Propenkos; but now it seemed some mysterious force, some error in navigation, had brought them close together. He leaned back slightly. Lyosha leaned slightly forward, still smiling, breathing on him, high as a drug addict.

"Three hundred sixty rubles is almost what I make in a month," Propenko told him.

The young man pretended to be sorry to hear this. "You should find a better job, uncle. Three-sixty is the regular price. Since you're good friends with the Chief, I could go to three forty-five, but you don't even have that much in your pocket, do you?"

"No," Propenko admitted.

"You don't have three hundred even, I'd bet." Lyosha ran his shiny eyes over Propenko's clothing and smirked.

"Let's go, Sergei," Leonid said. He had his hand on the back of Propenko's elbow. Propenko was dizzy. Lyosha's eyes seemed artificially lit, bottomless. Part of him wanted to pick the boy up and throw him out the window, part of him wanted to agree to the price and get his car back on the road, part of him felt as though he'd stepped in glue and the glue was hardening, sticking him to this floor forever. He could not believe Vzyatin's driver had friends like this. The old woman walked by him and into the bathroom, and, as if to keep them from listening to her noises, Lyosha stepped to the hall door, opened it, and swept his arm outward in a grand gesture. Propenko did not look at him as he walked past.

In the first-floor lobby the boys were still at their soccer game, but Vzyatin had joined them now, and was blocking one goal with his body, egging them on. The boys took turns standing back and kicking the tape-wrapped ball of paper as hard as they could, Vzyatin blocking the shots easily, until finally the ball burst open and skittered crookedly across the floor. The Chief looked up, happy as a nine-year-old. "Any luck?"

Propenko shook his head.

"Your driver keeps strange company," Leonid said.

Vzyatin grinned and shrugged.

// CHAPTER 23

August 13, 1991

All embassies have their secrets, but the American Embassy, Moscow, has an especially rich secret life, layer upon layer of facts that some people know and others do not — everything from the name of the diplomat's son who has a drug habit at age fourteen, to the names of the Soviet scientists and army colonels who have been quietly slipping information to their American handlers for the past twenty years. There are days when you can feel these secrets slinking along the building's lopsided corridors, spinning in its messy courtyard and dusty offices, winding themselves around the eyes and tongues of the staff. Ours is a strange community, a collection of rootless women, men, and children, inveterate outsiders. Everyone from the temporary construction workers to the Ambassador has some level of security clearance, possesses some degree of knowledge that he or she must guard, and the cumulative effect of all this is, I believe, a certain spiritual spoilage, a subconscious tainting of relationships — personal and professional — and of people's interior worlds.

At the heart of this hive of secrets is the Security Office. The Security people specialize in suspicion — as, I suppose, they must. They see everyone, Soviets and Americans alike, as a potential source of treachery, a threat to America's good health and continued existence.

I do not mock them. There have been — in past years, especially, but even now — real threats to America's good health and continued existence — from without and within — and real dangers to individual Americans living here.

I do not mock the Security people, but, even after all these years of working with them in various places, I cannot bring myself to like them. If, as a community, our secrets corrupt us, then as individual souls their secrets and secretiveness corrupt them. And since their secrets are more significant, so, too, is their corruption. They live behind thick screens. They worry incessantly, obsessively, about being deceived and defeated. They hide their own weaknesses and actively seek out others' — a condition that seems to me the polar opposite of love.

It was no accident, then, that when I thought of protecting myself from Chesi and his reckless, unpredictable affections, I thought of Peter McCauley, no accident that his name leapt to my lips in my moment of terror. When I am around Peter I feel as though I am being palpated for psychological frailty, emotional instability, small cancerous lumps on my loyalty. Peter looks into me and seems to see every shadow and fault. He watches from behind his genial mask, too sure and rigid in his beliefs. And so, of course, part of me envies him.

After work today, Ambassador Haydock held one of his morale-building parties. We barbecued hamburgers and hot dogs on the lawn of the new compound, we ate brownies and watermelon surrounded by our ten-foot brick wall, and pretended we were in America. I dislike these events, but I put in an appearance. People talked shop and complained about the "Sovs," as we call them. There was a touch football game and Frisbees and children racing about and crying and the usual spectacle of women hovering around their husbands as if I might snatch them off to my divorcée's bed. It was all so tame and — beneath our self-conscious American joviality — so sad. So many people who want to be somewhere else.

I was talking with one of my favorite colleagues — Richard Gibbons, the feisty and white-headed IO — when Peter McCauley found me. He had a Coke in one hand and was dressed in an utterly plain sport coat and chinos, as if to make himself as inconspicuous and normal-seeming as possible. After a minute or two, Richard drifted off — something people tend to do when Peter arrives — and the pleasant, meandering conversation headed straight to Vostok.

"So," he said, "your friend decided to jump ship."

"That's hardly true, Peter."

He wiggled his eyebrows and smiled in what he must have

thought was a charming way. He took a sip of his Coke and for a moment I thought he was going to leave it at that and deal with Chesi alone, exact his own, secret revenge without another word to me. There were beads of sweat along the top of his high forehead — though it was six P.M. and the day was not especially hot — and he ran his gray eyes toward the touch football game and the bugged and mostly empty new embassy building.

"You passed on to him what I told you about Vostok?" he said quietly. "The murder, the unrest, and so forth?"

I said that I had. Just as he'd asked me to: without revealing my source.

"Weird that he'd still want to go there after hearing all that, isn't it?"

"Not for him."

McCauley shrugged and let his eyes roam. In the background I heard Marylyn Michlain's hacking, drunken laugh.

"He could be in some danger, you know," McCauley said in a casual way, pretending not to look at me, though I knew he was watching out of the corner of his eye. "We really ought to send someone after him and drag him back here, but I'm reluctant to put one of my people at risk for a joker like this."

He was trying, of course, to get me to reveal some emotion, to see which side I was on, trying — rather crudely, I thought — to trick me into doing what I'd half made up my mind to do anyway. I could feel the weight of his Stateside bosses pressing down on him. I could feel him sweating, worrying that Chesi would really do something outrageous and land all of us in the stew. But before I could volunteer to go south, Marylyn weaved and stumbled over to us and slipped an arm around Peter's waist, and I used that as my excuse to slip away and think about things a bit more.

So I've been home almost two hours now, sitting out on my shaky balcony and watching our militiaman watch our parking lot full of expensive foreign cars with diplomatic plates. Night has fallen, a cool, sweet, Moscow summer night. It has begun to seem possible that Chesi went to Vostok, not as a slap in my face, but as a slap in the face of the "men in white shirts," as he calls them, McCauley included. Sitting here in the dark, recalling McCauley's smug mask, it does not seem like such a childish thing to have done. I am angry, of course, but the anger is mostly stale, having more to do with Chesi's past than with his present.

Chesi knows who McCauley is now — or, rather, what he is — and I picture him down there in the bespoiled and desperate hinterlands laboring under a jealous illusion. It seems to me a not unreasonable idea to ask Haydock to let me fly down there and straighten out several messes at once, but I will sleep on it and see how it seems tomorrow.

// CHAPTER 24

ON TUESDAY — sensing, perhaps, the imminent arrival of the American press corps — the customs rooster discovered spot-checking. Stiff-lipped and sullen, he inspected eighteen containers in the time it had taken him to inspect three the day before. But, for Czesich, even this wasn't fast enough. He could feel his luck draining away, feel Embassy Security and the Council of Commerce and Industry closing in on him.

By Wednesday noon, Ryshevsky was clearing container number thirty-three and Czesich had taken to sneaking up to his private office every hour or so to check the telex. Every time Propenko or Leonid or Ryshevsky went inside to use the phone or the toilet, he expected them to come back out to the work area waving a fist and a cable from Moscow. One courageous reporter from an independent newspaper arrived to do a story on the food aid, and Czesich gave the interview swaddled in guilt, looking over his shoulder, hoping against reason that he could just get the food through customs and out into the city by the time the bureaucracies caught up with him. At five o'clock Wednesday afternoon, with a foul fog lurking once again on the horizon, Ryshevsky checked the last of the wooden crates and signed a document giving the United States Communications Agency the right to begin distribution of said imported items, packing lists attached. Czesich fought back a little fit of giddiness, the temptation to crack a joke. Thank God you missed the heroin, Ryshevsky, he almost said, in front of the workers and the crowd. Ten thousand Donbass addicts thank you.

Malov caught his eye and winked, and Czesich turned away, indebted.

The missing truck had supposedly been located and was supposedly on the way from Rostov-on-Don, but he did not expect to see it in this lifetime. Two containers. A five percent loss for him and a 600,000-ruble bonus for the Soviet mafia. It was the price of doing business here now, part of the new capitalism.

At the hotel, he changed into a sport coat, slacks, and running shoes, then sat by the phone taking slow breaths. It was 10:00 A.M. in D.C. Filson, already wired on caffeine, would be pacing his corner office like a Doberman on a chain. He could be a very crude man, Filson; this would not be pretty.

When the connection came through, Czesich said, "Myron Filson, please," and closed his eyes.

"Filson."

"Myron, this is —"

"Czesich!" Filson shouted into the phone. "What . . . the . . . *Christ!*"

"Don't yell, Myron."

"Don't *yell?*"

Czesich's boss was among those who considered the idea of KGB phone tapping so much anticommunist hysteria. Was there proof? he wanted to know. Besides the thoroughly bugged new embassy building — a special case — had a single piece of evidence ever been unearthed? Those people haven't figured out how to make unleaded gas yet, do you actually believe they can tap every phone in every goddamned Intourist hotel in the whole goddamned country?

"Haydock reamed my ass for twenty minutes last night, and you say *don't yell!*"

"The containers are cleared. We start passing out food tomorrow."

"Who gives a *shit* about the containers," Filson shouted. "What's going on? Do you have some Russki babe down there or something?"

"There are hungry people here, Myron. I was sent to pass out food and that's what I'm going to do."

"And you don't give a sweet goddamn that it's not appropriate at the moment?"

Appropriate. It was one of Filson's favorite words. "You don't have any idea what's going on here, Myron."

"You've lost your mind is what's going on."

"I made a decision on my own for once. It's not the same thing."

"Do you know what your 'on your own for once' has done to USCA? No ambassador anywhere in the world will trust us to take out the fucking garbage after this. We'll be led around on a leash everywhere we go."

"That wasn't my intention."

"What was? What the Christ, Chesi? It's not like you. What the Christ is going on, will you please tell me?"

"I got sick of the bullshit."

"*What* bullshit? What *bullshit*? You've done this for twenty-five years, all of a sudden it's *bullshit*?"

"I had a few drinks and the next morning it came to seem like bullshit." Czesich still had his eyes closed. He was struggling to find the exact truth in himself and to speak it plainly. "Part of it was that. Part of it was history. Part of it is I'm in love with Julie Stirvin and I was trying to show her I'm not just another bureaucrat with a necktie, kissing the next-highest ass."

Filson fancied himself an honorable man. The next-highest-ass remark would strike a nerve. Czesich bit his tongue for a few seconds, then could not restrain himself: "No offense."

"You're gone!" Filson exploded. "You're history. It's rocking chair time for you, you —"

"I'd appreciate it if you'd see that my pension is protected."

"Sure." Filson was sputtering, roaring into the phone. "Any other last requests?"

"Could you call Marie? I haven't been able to get through. Tell her I'm fine. Tell her we're still on for Christmas dinner."

Eight thousand miles away, Czesich felt the impact of Filson's receiver being slammed down.

Anatoly had offered to stay around an extra hour and drive him to Propenko's, but Czesich wouldn't hear of it. He stood on the sidewalk near the hotel, watching the fog move majestically out of the valley, and waving his arm at a succession of speeding, empty taxis. A wonderful and unfamiliar mood had taken hold of him, a solitariness. For the first time in memory he felt alone with himself, no one watching.

After standing there for almost ten minutes he began to feel chilled, and he decided to walk up the road a few blocks and try his luck in a quieter spot. He'd made it only as far as the first corner when he thought he sensed someone behind him, keeping pace. In the middle of the next block he tried the courtyard trick again, and when he rejoined the sidewalk he was, for a moment, looking across Prospekt Revoliutsii toward the pavilion. A white Volga was parked at the top of the driveway there, and, from this distance, the man behind the wheel bore a distinct resemblance to Nikolai Malov. Czesich waved in an innocent, amiable way, but Malov pretended not to see. Czesich walked a bit farther, cupped a pack of Marlboros in his outstretched hand and caught a cab within half a minute. Before reaching October Avenue, he stopped at the hard-currency Beriozka store for two bottles of Soviet gold-label champagne and some chocolate, and held himself to one quick peek out the back window: fog, buses, the jumble of rush-hour taxis. A white Volga changing lanes behind them. So Malov knew he was going to the Propenkos for dinner? So what?

The Propenkos lived in the most typical of Soviet apartment complexes, a cluster of shabby beige boxes, all stained concrete slabs and flimsy balconies. A gang of teenagers sat outside on unused planters. They smoked, they wagged their heads to a boom box blasting Western rock and roll. When Czesich struggled for a moment with the sticky metal door, one of the boys made a remark and one of the girls laughed.

Among what must have been a hundred visits to Soviet homes — most of them with Julie — Czesich could not recall more than two or three evenings that had turned out badly. The smelly foyer and banging elevator, the unlit hallway, the graffiti, the door frame to apartment 25 that appeared to have been hammered together by drunken carpenters — none of it fooled him. He rang the bell and waited for the door to open on four rooms of light and goodwill, four smiling faces expecting the best of him.

He was right. Propenko filled the doorway, a king in his kingdom. There were handshakes and introductions, much exclaiming over his gifts, a perfectly unselfconscious warmth he'd seen duplicated only in East Boston, where the people were also poor, the apartments also too warm and smelling of food, the families also crowded together in buildings they would never have any hope of owning. In keeping with Soviet custom, he exchanged his street shoes for a pair of slippers. Propenko's charming daughter, Lydia, led him into the living room and sat him on a couch. The grandmother, Marya Petrovna, stood a few feet away with her hands clasped at her waist and stared at him as if he were from another planet. "Be at home," she said.

And he was.

They served the meal on a cloth-covered table that had been carried from kitchen to living room for his visit. A salad of tomatoes and sour cream, then pork and shredded cabbage. He had promised himself he would not drink, but as soon as the food was served, Propenko opened a bottle of vodka and there was no refusing.

"We were studying the atlas before you arrived," Propenko said affably. He seemed utterly comfortable here, his manner straightforward and simple and free of doubt, but there was something amiss in his inner world. Czesich had a sense for these things. "We were trying to guess the place of your birth."

"Massachusetts."

"Massachusetts," Marya Petrovna corrected him.

"Massachusetts."

Propenko squeezed up one corner of his lips. "It's in the south?"

"Northeast. Not far from New York."

"Menkhettn," Marya Petrovna said. "Uollstree."

"Wall Street. That's New York City. I was born in Massachusetts. Now I live in Washington."

"Wide Haus," Marya Petrovna said. "Kepetl Kheel."

"You know America well."

"From the news," the old woman said. "Every night Vasheengtone, Menkhettn. Sometimes Kahleefornya."

"I hope they say good things about us."

"Good and not so good."

Propenko's wife hastened to spoon more food onto Czesich's plate. Propenko popped the cork on the first bottle of champagne and Lydia poured everyone a glass of that, too, for good measure.

"Are you married?" Raisa asked.

Czesich told them he was divorced. Divorce was a concept Soviets understood. A Catholic wife who refused to sign the papers was not. "We have one grown son. He lives in Nevada."

"Lass Vekas," Marya Petrovna said. "Prasteetutsia."

Propenko coughed and gave his mother-in-law a hand signal. "Forgive her," he said. "We had a drink before you arrived — out of nervousness."

"Prasteetutsia," Marya Petrovna repeated loudly, looking right at Propenko. "The American knows what it is."

Czesich winced: she could not imagine.

"Were you all born in Vostok?"

"Mother was born in the countryside," Raisa said. "In the vil-

lage. The rest of us were born in a part of Vostok called Makeyevka. Where the mines are. We moved to this building nine years
ago."

"Lydochka speaks American," Marya Petrovna said, apropos of
nothing. She appeared to have been waiting all afternoon to say it.

"Grandmother!"

"Say something, girl."

Lydia's face had turned as red as the tablecloth checks. Her
mother and father were looking proudly on.

"How old are you?" Czesich said slowly, in English.

"Twenty."

"And where do you live?"

"Aye leave een Vostok."

"And what do you like about Vostok?"

"Aye laik" — she searched for words — "the poleetical struggle
for demacracy."

Czesich laughed.

"I made a mistake?"

"Not at all," he said, in Russian now. "You speak beautifully."

Shto ana skazala? Marya Petrovna wanted to know, and when
Czesich provided a translation, the old woman reached across the
corner of the table and gave her granddaughter a playful pinch on
the lobe of one ear. "Always politics," she said. "Everything with
you is politics."

"There's no living without politics now," the girl said. She was
looking directly at Czesich, and he was looking directly at a memory of her holding the Bible open for Father Alexei. "Don't you
think so?"

"In this country, yes."

"And in America?" Raisa said.

"In America, you can avoid politics if you want to."

"And do you avoid it?" Lydia asked.

"For the most part, yes."

"But why?"

He did not know why. Because he associated American politics
with baby-kissing and big money, maybe. Because it seemed distant and futile. Because things were more or less satisfactory as
they stood. "I'm overseas a lot. I get involved in politics there."

"You work for the CIA?"

"Lydia," Propenko said.

Raisa apologized for her daughter.

"No, I don't," Czesich told the girl. "I wouldn't. Politics are just more interesting to me overseas. There's a safe distance, I suppose."

"And what do you think of the situation here?"

"Lydia, let the man eat," Raisa said.

"I think it's interesting." Czesich swallowed a mouthful of the sweet champagne, checked Propenko's expression, and decided to leave it at that.

But the grandmother was staring. *"Deeplamat,"* she said. It did not sound like a compliment. Lydia was staring, too, the same eyes as her mother and grandmother, the same earnestness as her father. She was, in an innocent, earthy way, quite beautiful.

Czesich tried again. "I think the miners are an interesting political force, very disciplined, very well organized. Our miners don't play nearly such an important role in America."

"People say they're being helped by the CIA."

Ask your friend the priest, Czesich thought. Ask his pal Peter McCauley.

"Give our guest a chance to eat his food," Propenko told her. "You're interrogating him."

"He's interested," Lydia said, but for a few minutes they turned to safer subjects. Propenko inquired about the hotel yet again, as if he couldn't believe Czesich was comfortable there. Raisa asked where he'd learned to speak Russian so well, and when Czesich told them, Marya Petrovna wanted to know all about Grandpa Czesich — when he'd left Russia, how he'd earned his living in America, how the "real" Americans treated him, what he said about the Bolsheviks.

Through all this, everyone kept to a steady pace of eating and drinking, and Czesich felt as though he were being lowered very slowly into a warm, safe nest. Filson's vitriol faded to something distant and amusing, without consequence. The end of his USCA career was not real.

He inquired if there was anything of special interest he should see in his free time.

"Go to my village," Marya Petrovna suggested. She rested a hand on Czesich's bare wrist and the warmth of the gesture startled him. He did not live a life rich in physical contact. "If you don't see my village, you haven't seen Russia, that's all."

"I'd love to see your village."

"I'd take you, but I'm too old. My heart wobbles."

"I'll take you," Lydia volunteered.

Czesich thought her parents stiffened at the suggestion. An echo resonated in the room, but he had not heard the sound.

"We could take the boat to Leskovo and see the church where grandmother was christened," Lydia said. "We could bring a picnic, speak English all the way there and back."

Czesich smiled and nodded, but sensed he was crossing into slippery territory. He was no expert in the multifarious workings of family life. With Michael he had most often felt they were speaking different languages. On the surface, a polite English; underneath, a wordless primeval dialect full of screaming and blood. The word for his brand of fatherhood was "clumsy," and the last thing he wanted tonight was to mark another family — this family — with that dirty thumbprint.

"We'll see," Propenko said. "It's an unstable time now. Maybe you should wait a while for your trip to the village."

"It's not unstable in the village," Lydia said. "What could be safer than going to church?"

They were through with the main course. Raisa and Lydia cleared the table. Propenko poured another round of vodka and they drank to the success of the food distribution, and passed a bit of genial small talk back and forth. The missing containers were not mentioned. Czesich noticed a pair of tattered boxing gloves hanging by their laces on the wall, and asked about them.

"Sergei was a champion," Marya Petrovna boasted. She, too, was slightly drunk, and a decade younger because of it. "Everyone in Vostok remembers him."

Propenko looked as embarrassed as a boy.

"I played a bit of hockey in high school and college," Czesich said, to make another kind of connection with them, make himself seem less alien in their eyes. "But fighting's always frightened me. I wouldn't have the slightest idea what to do if I got into a fight. It's been thirty-five years or more."

"Very simple," Propenko said. "You hit them here." He indicated the tip of his nose. "As hard as you can. Once. You don't think about it, you just decide to do it, and do it. Not like in the cinema — dancing and getting up off the floor. Just here, one time. That's all."

Czesich promised to keep the advice in mind.

"It was kind of you to bring chocolate," Raisa said, setting a plate of it in the middle of the table. "We have trouble finding it now. It's *defitseit*."

Lydia brought bowls of vanilla ice cream. Propenko made sure everyone had a full glass of champagne.

"Nothing is ever *defitseit* in America, is it?" Raisa said.

"Money," Czesich quipped, but no one understood. The deadly combination of champagne and vodka had reached him. He was flipping Filson an imaginary finger. He was popping Peter McCauley in the nose with a straight right hand.

"And there aren't any lines, are there?"

"Not really. Sometimes for a concert, or a special museum show, or to get into a very popular restaurant on a weekend night."

"Free market system," Marya Petrovna said. "An old man was trampled to death buying boots on Saturday morning. Like cattle they trampled him."

"Near the hotel?"

"On the corner of Sinyavskaya Street, the long gray building."

"I saw the crowd," Czesich said.

"Trampled to death," Marya Petrovna repeated.

"For Bulgarian boots," Raisa said.

Without actually looking at him, Czesich was still trying to sound Propenko's mood. A conversation like this was tricky business for a Party man, even discounting the American presence. "Our system has its own problems," he said.

"*Deeplamat,*" said Marya Petrovna again, and Czesich felt a twinge.

"I'm half Russian," he said. "I need more alcohol to speak my heart."

Everyone laughed. Propenko shot the second cork up against the ceiling and refilled Czesich's glass. They watched him drink — *doh dnah,* to the bottom — then Marya Petrovna said, "Now. Talk."

"Be political," Lydia said gleefully. "Be American."

"All right." Czesich watched a warm little eddy spin past behind his eyes. "I have a friend, a kind-hearted man, who's had a very difficult life. He drinks too much. He's endured a lot of bad luck — some of his own making: bad marriage, unpleasant job, and so on. Now he's getting old and he wants to change, but he can't. Do you know why?"

"He has no model for change," Lydia suggested.

"No. He's grown accustomed to being miserable. There's a kind of familiar comfort in it. In some way, the idea of not being miserable frightens him."

"What's going to happen to him?" Lydia said.

"No one knows."

Czesich turned to his ice cream. Out of the tops of his eyes he could see Propenko sitting very still with one hand on the stem of his champagne glass. Raisa left the table and returned with tea.

"And your friend represents the Soviet Union," Propenko said at last.

"Of course, Sergei," Raisa said nervously.

Czesich shrugged to show he'd meant no offense. The man represented the Soviet Union, the man represented himself. Their sad histories seemed to have merged.

"No one likes to suffer," Propenko said.

"I didn't say likes to. I said is used to."

"Used to," Propenko repeated. "And overly proud of."

"We don't have much else to be proud of," Lydia put in.

"The war," Raisa said.

"More suffering," Propenko told her.

"Space," Lydia said, contradicting herself. "Sports. Great writers."

"The writers are Russian," Marya Petrovna told her. "Not Soviet."

"You can be proud of the Russian family," Czesich said. "Russian friendship. The Russian soul." No one seemed to hear him.

"We are the champion sufferers," Propenko announced. He seemed quite tipsy himself, and looking at his shoulders and hands, and thinking of his boxing advice, Czesich was relieved to see he was a thoughtful and thoroughly amicable drunk. "If there were an Olympics of Suffering, Russia would take all the gold medals."

"With Ethiopia," Lydia said.

"We trained the Ethiopians. We sent special envoys there to teach them the most efficient ways to be miserable. The Ethiopians, the Cubans, the Poles, they're all hungry and miserable now, thanks to us."

"There's something I don't understand," Czesich said. "We've just eaten a fine meal. People I met in Moscow told me the government makes sure Vostok has plenty of food so the miners will stay peaceful."

"They're not staying peaceful, though," Lydia said proudly.

"Let him finish, Lydia."

"A man on the train asked me why Vostok was chosen as one of the places to hand out food and I didn't know what to tell him."

"There are hungry people in Vostok," Marya Petrovna said. "Have you seen the neighborhood near the church, Belaya Rechka? There are hungry people there. And on the south side of the river. And in the villages."

"Even so. You're better off than other places, aren't you? Than Ufa or Uzinsk?"

"Ufa," the old woman scoffed. "People were hungry in Ufa even before perestroika."

Lydia spoke knowingly, like someone twice her age. "Father Alexei says Vostok was chosen on purpose, to embarrass Mikhail Lvovich. Did he tell you that on the train?"

"No."

"He liked you very much," she went on. "He said you were a different breed from the other Americans he's met."

"When did he meet other Americans?" Raisa asked suspiciously.

"I don't know," she said, and Czesich hoped, for her sake, that she was telling the truth. "Maybe in Moscow."

"I liked him, too," Czesich told Lydia, hoping to sound pleasant and neutral, diplomatic.

"You should hear him preach. We could go to the village on Saturday and to his service on Sunday morning."

"The American ambassador may be here on Saturday and Sunday," Propenko said.

"We could introduce the Ambassador to Father Alexei."

"Mikhail Lvovich would never allow it."

"How could he stop us, Pa?"

"He can do things you don't know he can do."

"Lydia's friend was killed at the church," Marya Petrovna blurted out, as if to spite her cautious son-in-law.

Lydia fell silent, and the two older women looked at her, then at Czesich, as if for his opinion. Propenko studied his ice cream.

"I heard about that," Czesich said. "I'm very sorry."

The conversation stalled there. Czesich searched for something to say, for a way to smooth everything over, but the only things that came to mind were stale platitudes from his sterile career, and he resisted them. "What about Yeltsin?" he said, to try and draw Lydia out. "What's going to happen?"

"He's going to be president!" she said, defiantly. None of her elders agreed. Gorbachev, they admitted, was wounded, perhaps crippled, perhaps in his last days. But the consensus was he'd be displaced, not by Yeltsin, but by Puchkov, the army, and the KGB.

Some people, Raisa said disgustedly, thought it would be a change for the better.

"We look at history," Propenko said. "We remember Khrushchev, like Gorbachev, opening things up, taking risks. They crushed him like a squirrel on the highway."

"People remember it," Raisa agreed.

Czesich was drunk enough to wonder aloud if, maybe this time, the people themselves would rise up in the face of the army and the KGB. It was Grandpa Czesich's impossible dream, recycled.

"The ones who rose up in the old days were chopped down," Raisa told him. "You don't understand."

"But you can't surrender in advance, can you?" Czesich said, and Propenko gave him a strange look. Anger, surprise, offense — he could not quite read it.

Somehow — thanks to the alcohol, perhaps — the conversation shifted to less volatile subjects. They talked about President Bush's recent visit to Moscow and Kiev, about the magnificent Soviet hockey teams of the past, about Tolstoy and Dostoevsky and Akhmatova and Babel. For the next hour or so, Czesich sank himself in what, for him, was the exotic give and take of the family. Like something floating far from shore, the whole entangled mess of Moscow politics popped back into view from time to time, but as the air warmed, that began to feel like a secondary reality, a mirage shimmering in the misty distance. The more they drank and talked and laughed, the less possible it seemed that the ambitions of men so far away could have any effect on this home.

At eleven o'clock, Marya Petrovna announced that, American or no, she had stayed up as long as she could. She kissed Czesich on both cheeks, kissed her granddaughter, and went off to the back room. Czesich was comfortably high. He did not want to leave. They did not seem to want him to leave.

"I'm sorry about Ryshevsky and the rest of it," Propenko told him. "The padlocks. The meeting. It's embarrassing to me."

"I've seen it before," Czesich said. "In many different places." He told a short anecdote about a customs inspector in Kazan who'd once made him open eleven cases of toilet paper and count each roll.

"He was hoping you'd give him some," Raisa said. "That's all. He was tired of using *Pravda*."

Propenko nodded, but seemed unable to smile. "We'll start delivering the food tomorrow," he said seriously. "Three days behind schedule is not so bad. Ryshevsky went a lot faster these last two days."

"I think Malov had a word with him," Czesich said, and the air changed instantly. The echo returned. He thought, for a moment, the evening had been spoiled.

Propenko looked at his wife, then back at Czesich. "Malov is not a friend," he said quietly.

"I know who he is," Czesich said. "Sometimes you have to work with them, though."

"No," Lydia said. "Never. It would be like sleeping with the devil."

Something in Lydia's eyes reminded Czesich of a young Julie Stirvin, and he came within a millimeter of spilling his whole history at USCA, right up to and including his sudden, principled retirement. "You're right," he said, and a platitude slipped out. "You can only compromise yourself so many times before you forfeit your soul."

"Once," Lydia said. "Once is all it takes."

Czesich shrugged. She was young yet; the number would be revised as she aged. He sorted through a list of possible reasons why Malov might have suddenly turned cooperative and decided it had to be something more than fear of being exposed in the foreign press, or chastized by the American Embassy. There had to be a trick of some sort, a player to be named later. Men of Malov's type were not known for their spontaneous kindness. No one seemed to have any energy left for a debate. Propenko had fallen silent, and Czesich began looking for a comfortable exit. When Raisa went to the stove to make another pot of tea, he stopped her. "It's late," he said. "You've been very kind and it's been the nicest evening I've had in many years." For once, he sounded completely sincere, even to himself. The family had worked a kind of magic on him, and, saying good-bye, he tried to tell them so without sounding like a diplomat.

Lydia hugged him. Raisa smiled, took his hands in both of hers and wished him well. Propenko apologized for not being able to drive him home and insisted on walking him to the corner and helping him hail a cab.

"Fog again," he remarked, when they were out on the street. "August is the month for it."

A bit stiff-legged with drink, they walked to the end of the dark block and Propenko stood at the curb with his arm straight out. It turned out to be a bad night for catching taxis.

"Do you miss your son?" he said abruptly.

Not five minutes earlier, Czesich had been having an attack of missing, not Michael exactly, but the Michael he'd imagined when Marie was pregnant. He tried to locate the exact point in history where that vision had been extinguished, but the alcohol kept the memories mercifully vague. It was an amazing drug, really, God's way of compensating for the fact that He had endowed His children with such an enormous talent for screwing things up.

Even through the pleasant vodka haze, it seemed very clear to Czesich that what he'd expected from fatherhood was the thing he'd just witnessed in the Propenkos' cramped household — one bastion of intimacy in a life otherwise pocked with separation and falseness. What he wanted, the only thing he really wanted, was to be around people who knew him beneath the mask and loved him anyway.

"I do miss him," he said, "though he's not the son I had imagined." A cab finally stopped, but when Propenko gave the destination, the driver shook his head and sped away.

"Lydia is the daughter I imagined," he said. "The problem is, I'm not the father I imagined."

"*Tochna,*" Czesich said. "Exactly." He felt a real warmth for this man now, an unlikely psychic harmony. For a few minutes it was as if he were standing beside a very old friend, or a brother. Another of vodka's magic effects, this quick camaraderie. No wonder the Russians loved it so.

"What did you mean," Propenko asked hesitantly, "when you said 'forfeit your soul'?"

"It's just an expression. In America it's become a kind of meaningless cliche."

"But what did you mean by it?"

Czesich was momentarily at a loss. "It's biblical," he said at last.

"I'm not familiar with the Bible. What does the phrase mean to you, in your own life?" Propenko turned to the curb again and held out his arm, but he was looking straight at Czesich, his face the pattern for Lydia's now, open and utterly sincere, a seeker.

"It means you're living a lie."

"Ah."

"Not that you simply *told* a lie," Czesich hastened to add, as if to excuse himself to himself. "But that you're not living according to your principles."

A taxi braked to a stop a few yards beyond them. As they were walking toward it, Propenko said, "And what if your principles contradict each other?"

"Then the rule is: Choose the thing that frightens you most," Czesich said. He was not sure what, exactly, he meant by this; the words seemed to have emerged from some buried source, something he'd heard not long ago and almost forgotten.

Propenko appeared to understand, however. Over Czesich's objections he slipped the cabdriver ten rubles and told him not to pick up anyone else on the way to the hotel, then ducked down so that his face was framed in the open back window. "Anton Antonovich," he said, eyes wavering, his large jaw and lips working as if he were trying to say something affectionate and slightly embarrassing, *"vell-kim do Vostok."*

The driver pulled away, and Czesich watched the city slide past wrapped in scarves of fog. The drink and the warm company had turned him sentimental, made all his old Russian memories a degree sweeter. After a time, he leaned toward the front seat and regaled the cabbie with a bit of Blok:

> *And you are ever the same, my country,*
> *in your tear-stained ancient beauty.*

The cabbie smiled, tolerantly, and asked if Czesich had anything to sell.

// CHAPTER 25

THE LAMPPOSTS were still coated with dew and already *babushki* were assembling at the bus stop in front of Propenko's building, string shopping bags sticking out of their coat pockets, their lips and eyebrows set in hard lines, as if they were going, not to market, but into the trenches of an old women's civil war.

Propenko stood not far from them — not far from the spot where he'd had his brief conversation with Anton Antonovich the night before — in a sweater, a pair of stiff Hungarian jeans, and boots he used for gardening at the dacha. The same workaday world that had always buoyed him seemed an alien creature now, a sea shrinking away. He felt ashamed before the eye of morning.

A bus drew up to the curb and the *babushki* assaulted both doors. For distraction, for warmth, for the sake of burning off some of the storehouse of evil energy he'd spent the last four nights accumulating, Propenko began to pace. He went to the corner and back. He glanced up at his apartment windows. He went to the corner again and stopped, kicked a bottle top into the gutter, watched the women pressing frantically up the bus steps, and Vzyatin's plainclothes militiaman smoking in a car across the street, and trucks rumbling past, parking lights glowing in the mist, drivers hunched over their steering wheels like errand boys in the service of some terrible king.

He could not free his mind of the image of Anton Antonovich sitting at their dinner table the night before. With his wide forehead and jaw and hard Muscovite speech, the man might, at first glance, easily be mistaken for a Soviet. But there was something about the way he sat there, so calm and at ease in a foreign land, at a stranger's table; there was something in his eyes and clothes and in the way he joked with Marya Petrovna, even in the way he walked, something utterly *unconcerned*, that set him apart from any Soviet citizen Propenko had ever known. He could not imagine Czesich squeezed up against a bus window like that, or cutting a deal with a man like Mikhail Lvovich, or learning to shoot a pistol at 6:00 A.M. in order to protect himself and his family. Czesich did not need a pistol, or fists, or friends in the militia. He did not trot down the path on anyone's leash. In his country, there was law and dignity. Here, there were bribes, "arrangements," congenital shame.

A militia jeep swerved sharply to a stop in front of him and Propenko climbed in. Vzyatin slapped him on the leg and sped off, smiling as though they were setting out on a fishing trip. "What happened to waiting inside?"

Propenko shrugged. He had a small headache from last night's drinking.

Vzyatin was wearing a sharply creased new uniform, the gold stars on his epaulets standing out against the gray-blue cloth. As usual, his face was full of self-assurance, the bushy black brows happily twitching, eyes steady and alert, lips pulled tight in satisfaction. He drove as if he owned not just the road but the whole city, his hands twisting this way and that as he slipped the jeep carelessly from lane to lane, street to street, stopping for red lights only when it was absolutely unavoidable.

A prince, Propenko thought, on his early-morning canter through the kingdom.

At the Donskoy Boulevard light, Vzyatin reached into the webbed door pocket and brought out a pistol. Propenko supported the strange object on his fingers, keeping the muzzle pointed forward. The last time he'd held a gun in his hands was twenty-eight years ago, in his army days. The association was not especially pleasant.

"Nine-millimeter," Vzyatin said proudly. "Straight from the factory."

They leapt away from the light, crossed the river on the Tchaikovsky Bridge, and swept down onto a two-lane highway headed southeast, out of town. The sun rose to their left and flared bright for a few seconds before being gobbled up by a ceiling of clouds and smoke. The morning promised rain. "So what kind of impression does your American make in his private life?"

Propenko turned his face toward the window. "Honest," he said. "Decent. Lydia seemed to like him."

The Chief grunted. "It's only his clothes, Sergei. Young women always fall for an older man's clothes, for his style. Masha's psychology books say it's a *tranzferentz* of the girl's feeling for her father."

Propenko made a face at the foreign word, and at the mention of the American's fine clothes. Lydia hadn't fallen for anyone. Czesich's easy manner had simply brought a bit of light into the house, that was all. Lydia was young. She was susceptible to other people's moods. It wasn't any kind of *tranzferentz*. It wasn't a psychological event.

"Make sense?"

"Maybe."

A few bars of static crackled forth from Vzyatin's radio, and Propenko watched a convoy of six army trucks rolling toward the city. His inner ear was loud with Mikhail Lvovich's laughter.

"How is Raisa?"

"Afraid."

"She's smarter than all of us," Vzyatin said, but the comment sounded mechanical and insincere. Propenko peeked at the white needle on the dashboard. Vzyatin was almost doubling the speed limit.

"Did you watch the news last night?"

"We were having dinner."

"They interviewed two army colonels who'd been stationed in East Germany. Their men are back in Moscow now, living in tents because there's no other place to put them. And another fifty thousand are supposed to come home by the end of the year." Vzyatin took his eyes off the road for just a second and glanced across at his passenger. " 'Heroes' one of the colonels called them. He never thought he'd see the day when Soviet heroes would be living in tents in their own homeland. 'The army's patience,' he said, 'is not limitless.' "

To Propenko, this was just one more droplet added to the ominous cloud on a distant horizon. East Germany. Moscow. Vzyatin might as well have been speaking of another galaxy.

"God save us if those people come to power."

Propenko grunted and rubbed his eyes. There had been no aspirin in the house.

"But Gorbachev goes right on appointing them," the Chief

added, as though Propenko had encouraged him. "Shevardnadze warned him. Yeltsin keeps warning him. He goes right on appointing people who want to take us back to the old days."

Propenko felt as though Vzyatin was trying to sell him something. "Yeltsin is no better," he said.

"That's where you're wrong, Sergei. Yeltsin is a thousand times better. Bessarovich tells me he is a thousand times, ten thousand times better."

Propenko thought: One mystery solved. Add Bessarovich to the legions of *apparatchiki* abandoning the President in his hour of need. Now Yeltsin was the favorite. In a few years Yeltsin would be traded in for someone new, with every cabdriver and cook in the country spitting at the sound of *his* name. Russia was like a patient going from doctor to doctor, excited by the promise of each new miracle treatment, each new theory, each new cure for what was historically incurable.

The highway brought them through the ruins of a more familiar galaxy, past the mine buildings, past a forest of smokestacks sticking up from square factory blocks, across a small river covered with brushstrokes of fog, and out onto the edge of a plain that stretched as far as Central Asia. In the near distance, Propenko could see the wheat fields, almost gold in this light, gleaming like paradise. Well short of them, Vzyatin turned off.

"Have you ever thought of running for office yourself?"

"You've been drinking, Victor."

The Chief laughed. "You're intelligent, good-looking — a hero of Soviet sport. You'd be a natural."

They went past a closed gas station — a line of cars and trucks was already sprouting at the pumps — and through a village of twenty or thirty log houses, then more slowly down a dirt road that ended in an overgrown excavation site, three hundred meters across. All sand and rocks and weeds, the basin was one of the ugliest swatches of earth Propenko had ever seen. It looked like a place a murderer would dump a corpse.

Vzyatin parked the jeep and they kicked across the dirt to a weathered table that stood twenty-five meters in front of a set of wooden target frames. Vzyatin put a bag of ammunition and two paper targets on the table, and showed Propenko how to click the pistol's safety on and off, how to hold his arm straight and sight along it, how to distribute his weight, how to lock in a clip of bullets.

"Safety on," the Chief ordered. He carried one of his paper targets out to the wooden frame and began pinning it in place. Propenko stood by the table and listened to the pulse in his temples.

In a moment, the Chief was beside him again. "Safety off, Seryozha. Fire away. Excellent rating is twenty-five points or better with three shots. Score that, and you outshoot nine of my ten captains."

Robotlike, Propenko assumed the correct stance, moved the safety knob, raised his right arm, and sighted. His hand did not tremble. He saw the target clearly, concentric white rings on a light green field. He brought the bull's-eye up around the forward sight, held his breath, and pressed the trigger. The pistol gave a satisfying *pop*, and a second later, far far beyond the target, a puff of dust rose and kicked sideways on the sandy slope.

"Aim low."

Lips pressed together, forehead furrowed, he sighted a second time and fired. Another dust puff far off.

Vzyatin came up behind him and, holding one hand on either side of Propenko's rib cage, gently kicked his feet farther apart. "You're a giant," he said. "Aim at the ground."

His third shot went into the dirt to the right of the target base.

"Hold it as you'd hold Raisa's elbow."

Propenko drew a breath and fired, and a small dark tear appeared on the target's upper right edge.

"One point," Vzyatin said encouragingly.

In spite of his difficulties, the firing of a bullet struck Propenko as amazingly effortless. One flex of a finger and a quick, neat, invisible packet of rage went flying across creation. A bullet could change everything in one instant, make the world suit you better, make it disappear. He imagined Malov standing in the moonlit churchyard, sighting on Tikhonovich's skull, and in rapid succession sent four more shells into the dirt. He reached for the bag of ammunition, but Vzyatin stopped him. "Clear your mind, Sergei. Fill your mind with the target."

"My mind is filled with shit."

"Clear it out."

Some of the good humor had drained from Vzyatin's face, revealing a stern, chiefly presence. It was a magic thing. Long ago, someone must have seen this power beneath his jocular exterior. Someone in the highest reaches of the Vostok Party apparatus must have glimpsed a chief in the young sergeant, and begun the twenty-five-year process of moving him, step by step, up the militia's un-imaginably corrupt ladder, bribing, conniving, shunting rivals onto sidings like so many empty coal cars. Propenko could not stop himself from wondering — and it was a wondering soaked in var-ious flavors of guilt — if Vzyatin's patron might have been a man whose wife fancied caviar with her scrambled eggs, who liked Vysotski on the stereo, who had a balcony with a private militia guard below. Vzyatin would owe certain favors.

He sprayed the whole next clip into the dirt on either side of the target.

"Not my sport," he said.

"Not a sport, Sergei. Not a sport at all."

Propenko jammed another clip into the butt of the pistol, glared at the target, and sailed three more shots off toward the wheat fields.

Vzyatin was watching him intently now, and he leaned forward on the table, stiff-armed, and let out a breath. When he was boxing competitively, he had developed the ability to shut off his thoughts and the noise of the crowd and focus on his opponent as if nothing else existed. Sometimes, after a match, he would walk the streets for an hour or more locked in that clear bubble, sore and exhausted but sovereign of his own inner world. Each object, each person, stood sharp. Now he inhabited exactly the opposite state of mind. Voices buzzed around his ears. Something as simple as shaving, as firing a pistol, required an Olympian concentration he no longer owned.

"This is silly," he said.

"Is it?"

He laid down his weapon, walked to the front of the table, and sat there contemplating the depressing sky. Behind him he heard the safety click on. Vzyatin came and sat beside him. "Talk to me, Seryozha," he said, more like a kindly interrogator than a friend.

Propenko took a long breath and let it out. Confessions were complicated things, full of echoes and shadows. He remembered his sister calling from Leningrad to tell him that she and her hus-band were separating. Vadim had come home one night, drunk a bottle of wine, and told Sonia he'd been sleeping with one of his political philosophy students, that he was sorry, that it had ended, that he wanted her forgiveness. Sonia forgave him. They made love. And the next day when Vadim was at the university, she packed all her clothes and their daughter into a taxi and rode straight out of his life. "We're staying with a friend, Sergei," she said on the phone. "If the friend deceives me, we'll come stay with you. If you deceive me, I'll hang myself in your stairwell."

"Seryozha. Talk to me."

Propenko looked out past the target. "Things are not what they seem," he began.

Vzyatin laughed as if this were a great joke. "Never," he said. "Never."

A gust of wind blew across the sandy basin, and Propenko thought he felt a drop of rain touch the back of his neck. The words were still there, ready to spill forth, but Vzyatin's booming laugh had somehow dammed them up. He remembered standing on a street corner as a child, and hearing sirens and turning to see a pack of motorcycles and one black Chaika racing up the avenue toward him. It was an amazing sight, this speeding, screaming fleet of dark metal and flashing lights with a gray-headed first secretary lounging at its center. It was a thing you felt in your chest.

"You haven't been yourself since the meeting."

He said nothing.

"You came through that door as Sergei Propenko, and went out as someone else."

"No."

"What did Bessarovich say on the phone, Sergei? We never got into the details."

"Nothing." Propenko kept his eyes straight ahead. He could feel the truth collecting in his mouth like bile. He spat.

"That I cannot believe," Vzyatin said.

"Believe it. She has no power over Malov."

"Nonsense, Sergei. She could crush him with a phone call."

"Then she chooses not to."

Vzyatin crossed his arms over his chest and brought his bottom lip up over his top. "There's something you're not saying."

"I called her just as you told me to, Victor. I told her about Malov."

"And she had nothing to say?"

"She said she couldn't help me right now, that some things have to be solved close to home."

"Meaning what?"

"You tell me."

"That's it?"

"That's it. She said to give her regards to Mikhail Lvovich."

"Maybe she was just worried about your phone being tapped."
Propenko grunted.

"Maybe she's cooked something up with her friends on the
Strike Committee and they're going to take care of Malov on their
own. Maybe that's what she meant. She wouldn't be able to say
something like that over an open line."

"Maybe a lot of things."

Vzyatin stared at the side of Propenko's face for another few
seconds, then looked away. And with that looking away, Propenko
felt himself sink. Vzyatin knew. Bessarovich had known, before the
fact. She'd seen the disloyalty in him and held herself back, protected herself. He tried to spit again but there was a stone lodged in
his throat half-swallowed.

After a time, Vzyatin unsnapped his holster flap, took out his
pistol, and, still sitting, fired three shots. Propenko made out three
new smudges on the target. Nine. Nine. Ten.

The silence in which they returned to the city had nothing in
common with the silence in which they'd set out. Most of the way,
Vzyatin held an unlighted cigarette between his lips. When they
were crossing the river he took it between his thumb and middle
finger and snapped it out the window. Without turning his eyes he
said: "You're not looking to Kabanov for protection, are you?"

"Of course not."

"Good. Because he couldn't protect you even if he wanted to.
Politically, the man's on his deathbed."

Propenko made his face a blank mask.

"You don't believe me, do you?"

"No."

"You're living in the past," the Chief said, not very kindly. "You
and Leonid." He called in some kind of code on the radio, and
spent the next five minutes giving orders. When they drew up in
front of Propenko's apartment, Vzyatin handed him the pistol with
its holster and shoulder strap and three clips of ammunition. "Still
five rounds in it, remember."

"Malov will think he has me worried," Propenko said, aiming
for a facetious tone, for something to resurrect a good feeling, and
missing badly.

Vzyatin only nodded and offered to wait while Propenko
changed clothes.

Propenko climbed the four flights with the holstered pistol hidden beneath his sweater. The apartment was quiet. He took off his

boots inside the door and padded down the hallway to the back bedroom, where he found Marya Petrovna asleep on top of the blanket, her mouth hanging open and her legs spread, bare from the knee down, scribbled with veins. The room was filled with Lydia's things, the walls covered with a mix of religious objects — calendars and copies of icons and sketches of the church — and two posters of a young French singer in leather pants and hair like a horse's mane. Propenko watched Marya Petrovna's chest rise and fall. The men he'd promised to help today were the type of men — in some cases the very same men — who had given the order that this woman's husband be arrested and beaten and shipped off to some lice-infested "camp" where he would be beaten some more, starved to half his weight, and sent home for a few years as an example to his neighbors, then arrested again and brought back to the camp to die.

These were the people he was going to accommodate this morning. These were his new associates.

Marya Petrovna snorted and stirred and Propenko backed out of the room.

He placed the holster gingerly on the living room sofa and changed into suit and tie. His hands shook. It took several minutes to arrange the holster beneath his left arm, and when it was in place, and when he'd checked himself in the mirror to be sure nothing showed, he had an urge to take out the pistol and simply look at it. The thing was so light, its metal purple-brown and unblemished, the handle's small plastic pyramids streaked with sweat. He flicked the safety off, then on, then off again, held the weapon flat on his fingers as he had in the jeep, then curled his hand around it, raised it, and pressed the muzzle to the bone beneath his right eye, just to see how it fit there. He felt hidden from the life of the city, invisible; he could do anything he wanted in this room and it would not be recorded by the city's eye.

There was a shuffle of slippers on the kitchen floor. "Sergei?"

Using his back as a shield, Propenko slid the pistol into its holster and buttoned the middle button of his coat before turning around.

"Sorry I woke you," he said, in a voice that belonged to someone else.

Marya Petrovna peered at him sleepily. "You're not at work."

"On my way."

"You weren't at breakfast."

"I was out with Victor Vzyatin. We drove. We took a drive."

She looked at him for two or three seconds, mumbled something about tea, and shuffled back toward the stove.

On the second-floor landing, Propenko took off his suit jacket and wrestled free of the holster. Sweating beside the damp walls, he wrapped holster and pistol into a tight ball and draped his jacket over it. In the jeep, he gave Vzyatin back his gun.

"What's this?"

"I decided I don't want it."

Vzyatin laughed as he'd laughed at the shooting range, too loud, an aggressive sound, completely false. "Even if you can't shoot, it doesn't hurt to be seen with it on."

"Not me," Propenko mumbled. "That's all." He handed Vzyatin the three ammunition clips. "Let's go."

Vzyatin started the jeep and pulled out into traffic, driving more slowly now, pensive, ignoring the spitting radio. After a time he said, "You used to be a warrior."

Propenko did not respond. Vzyatin had an utterly skewed vision of him. He had never been a warrior. What he had been was what everyone else at the Council had been — a sheep bleating and trotting with the pack, thinking only of the next sweet tuft of pasture.

When they came in sight of the parked containers, Vzyatin spoke without turning his eyes. "I didn't want to say this in front of Leonid the other night, in his situation, but tell him now if you want." He pulled the jeep into the lot and parked with the engine running. A frown crossed his mouth, but it was a peculiar thing, and Propenko, in his agitation, could make no sense of it. "Something strange, Sergei. Beyond the usual logistical stupidities." Vzyatin's brows wiggled and his voice wavered slightly in what Propenko took to be genuine discomfort. "We received a shipment of handcuffs from Moscow Tuesday. From the Interior Ministry."

Propenko shrugged.

"Twenty-five thousand pair," Vzyatin said, and before the alarm on his face had a chance to make its slow impression, Propenko actually laughed.

// CHAPTER 26

CZESICH awoke in a state of grace. Some of last night's vodka and champagne still swirled in his blood, and his tongue and lips were dry, but he felt buoyant in a way not usually associated with mornings after. Standing up out of bed required less than no effort. He reached toward the ceiling in a kind of grateful yoga, then, to his own amazement, got down on the living room carpet and did a few wobbly push-ups and half of some long-abandoned stretching routine from his hockey-playing days. He was no longer bound to Sixth Street Southwest. He no longer answered to Myron R. Filson, Jr., and the United States Communications Agency. The sentence had been served in full.

Even the petty indignities of Soviet life could not tarnish such a mood. The bathwater was the color of milk this morning, ice-cold from both faucets. For breakfast there was bread, a brown jamlike glue, and tea. And as a kind of crown on the hotel's clumsy hospitality, when he was on his way out through the lobby, swinging his leather briefcase and humming an old Everly Brothers tune, Slava Bobin accosted him. Bobin was holding a folded sheet of paper in both hands and rolling a fretful bubble of air from cheek to cheek. "Good morning, Anton Antonovich," he said, strictly as a preliminary. "How was your sleep?"

Czesich was radiant, oblivious to the signs. "Wonderful," he said.

Bobin's small brown eyes squirted left, toward the stairwell, lingered there, then reluctantly traveled back to his American. He unfolded the piece of paper in front of his breastbone and looked up into Czesich's eyes. "Came this morning."

When he'd made out the meaning of the crooked lines of type, Czesich squeezed his lips tight. A small hand of fear took hold of him, but he was able to look straight into Bobin's face and smile. "Slava Timofeich," he said, resting a hand on Bobin's shoulder, "bureaucracies are pitiful creatures, are they not?"

Bobin's jowls quivered. He seemed to nod.

With a chuckle and a sad shake of the head, Czesich took hold of the sheet of paper and examined it more closely. The word SROCHNA — URGENT — was stamped all across the top margin, and it bore yesterday's date, 14 August 1991, and the phrase VOUCHER REMUNERATION TO BE DENIED. Filson must have slammed down the phone and spent the rest of the day writing this order and pushing it up the signature totem pole at USCA. He must have hand-carried it from one office to the next, explaining as he went, happy to inform a succession of political appointees what a traitor to the cause Anton Czesich had turned out to be, an undisciplined renegade, an insult to team players everywhere. The last signature would have been Walter Woroff's. Woroff, with his fetish for career-wrecking innuendo. Woroff, the name-dropper, the President's good buddy. The two of them must have been positively erect with vengeance.

He imagined Filson sending off this telex in a fever, then rushing home, half-hard, in search of his curly-haired Alicia.

Swine.

"My bill isn't supposed to be paid by Washington anyway," he said into Bobin's worried face. "It's always taken care of by the embassy." His poise wavered, just slightly, just for part of one second. "You haven't heard from the embassy, have you?"

Bobin shook his head.

"A clerical error," Czesich explained. "Everything in Washington is computerized nowadays. It's a mess. The same mixup happened to me a few years ago in Dushanbe, and you know the Tadzhikis, don't you? Can you imagine the fuss?"

Bobin smiled weakly, imagining it, but his features remained filmed with doubt.

Czesich was holding the telex in his left hand and, as he talked, he refolded it and thrust both hands down into his pants pockets. A moment later the left came up empty, the right clasping a small roll of green bills. He peeled off two twenties and a ten and tucked them into Bobin's palm. "My personal guarantee," he said, and Bobin, barely above a whisper and even as his fingers closed over the treasure, bubbled on for thirty seconds about how this wasn't necessary, wasn't what he'd had in mind at all; how he, too, had been sure the telegram was a mistake, but he'd felt he had to show it to Czesich just to get his opinion. Was everything in order with the room, by the way? Too much noise from the neighbors?

Czesich gave his assurances. They stood there a minute, beaming counterfeit smiles at each other, not so different men, Czesich thought, wincing, not so very different at all. "I'll have the embassy cable you with a guarantee by the end of the week," he lied, but Bobin, clutching the hard-currency equivalent of four months' room charges — off the books — waved an arm expansively. *"Nye nada, nye nada,"* he said, quite loudly now. "No need, Anton Antonovich."

"Are we prepared for the Ambassador?"

"Of course, Anton Antonovich. When will we be certain that he's coming?"

"A day. Two days at most."

"Ready," Bobin said. "Absolutely all ready." He squared his shoulders, pushed out his chest, and they shook hands warmly.

The front door was held open by Yefrem Alexandrovich, a sixty-year-old ex-wrestler in a brown uniform, the same chap who, on Bobin's instructions, took nightly bribes from the hookers and young couples hoping for a table in the restaurant, then passed most of these earnings on to his boss. Czesich had an inherited understanding of the way such things worked. The doorman heaped abuse on his poor compatriots, took their money, refused admittance to some, reported others to the KGB. For the American he smiled, gave a little bow, a little phony show of deference. Czesich smiled back, and walked through the door, feeling fine. He was going to take a small measure of revenge today, in the name of the abused masses.

Anatoly was crouching in front of his peach-colored Volga, running a rag over its spotless chrome grill. Czesich was happy to see him, but something in the driver's "Good morning" rang slightly sour. At first, he worried that Julie had contacted the Council of Commerce and Industry offices in Moscow and they'd gotten word to their Vostok colleagues. But Anatoly did not seem angry at *him*, just angry in general. Trouble with the wife, Czesich supposed, and he let it pass. He let pass, too, the fact that there was no edifying anecdote this morning as they made their tour around the block. Constancy was the Soviet short suit. Today there would be eleven thousand tubes of toothpaste in the *univermag*. Tomorrow, and for the next four months, no toothpaste anywhere. No hot water, no clean water, no water at all, and then, one fine vodka morning, all the water you needed flooding over the tipped basin, hot as Tegucigalpa.

Still, he'd come to think of Anatoly as a friend, and he had to bite down hard on an urge to probe the driver's mood or spill his own. He tried Bobin's gambit and asked Anatoly how he'd slept.

"I slept well, Anton Antonovich."

"Is your neighborhood quiet?"

"Fairly quiet."

"Is it far from the center of town?"

"Not so far."

"Does your wife work?"

"Yes. At the airport."

"And she likes it?"

"Well enough."

Czesich gave up and sat back in his seat. Anatoly had the radio tuned to a station that spat forth an uninterrupted string of peppy pop music. It was there purely for distraction, a mild narcotic against the nation's slow descent into ruin. It reminded Czesich of home.

A crowd of a hundred or so onlookers had gathered at the pavilion. Both the King of Jazz and his partner, Ivan Ivanich, were on duty, along with an extra unit of militia — twenty boyish patrolmen spaced every few yards along the portable fencing. Czesich was out of the car and walking past saluting lieutenants almost before Anatoly had brought the Volga to a full stop. This was, after all, what he'd come for — the actual handing out of food. But, to his surprise, Propenko seemed withdrawn and miserable. He was smoking, awkwardly, and much of last night's brotherly feeling had vanished; something vulgar was in the air.

All right, Czesich told himself. Whatever it was would eventually make itself known. He'd deal with it then. Nothing was going to spoil his mood today.

"I had a wonderful evening, Sergei," he said. "I could still feel the warmth of your family around me when I woke up this morning."

Propenko coughed on a mouthful of smoke and thanked him.

"Lydia is a fine young woman."

Propenko nodded.

"It's a joy to be surrounded by such people."

Propenko said that he knew.

With the two Directors and the customs inspector presiding, the first container was unlocked and opened. Crates were forklifted out and broken down into hundreds of small cardboard boxes that workers began loading into the beds of two farm trucks. Wheat flour. Canned peaches. Tins of dried beef and kidney beans and beets. Sugar. Several thousand pounds of powdered eggs. Czesich snapped a few pictures — for his own files now, not USCA's. As the loading progressed — young laborers perspiring in the mild, sunless air, bare-armed, tossing boxes up to the older men who stacked them tight in the bed — Propenko went off by himself, smoking one cigarette after another. Leonid Fishkin, the pavilion director, stood like a sentry on the concrete ramp. Ryshevsky fretted over his packing lists, checked things off, scurried about, made a nuisance of himself, though, technically, his work was finished here. Czesich moved from station to station, trading quips with the older watchman ("Have you heard the joke about Lenin and syphilis?" Ivan whispered. "Which one?" Czesich asked, winking, and the old man doubled over in great heaves of laughter), complimenting Leonid on the cleanliness of the pavilion lot, even standing for a few minutes at the elbow of the customs inspector, struggling to elicit one blink of human connection. By instinct, he stayed clear of Propenko and Anatoly. Perhaps they'd had words earlier in the morning. Malov appeared to have taken the day off.

At ten o'clock, when the loading was about halfway completed, Propenko's daughter came walking down from the bus stop on Prospekt Revoliutsii. Czesich saw her first and asked one of the militiamen to escort her through the crowd. They met just this side of the corral fence. "Goot merning," Lydia said. She was wearing a new pair of jeans and a white blouse, and she smiled at him as though he were a favorite uncle.

"The big day," Czesich said, warmed.

Lydia switched to Russian. "We've never seen my father so nervous."

"I noticed. Do we still have a date for Saturday?"

"If the Ambassador doesn't come."

"You're more important than the Ambassador," Czesich told her. "If the Ambassador comes, he'll just have to wait for us to get back from the village."

He'd meant it harmlessly enough, a spillover of his happy mood, an innocent flirtation. But Lydia blushed and skittered away. He watched her walk past the sweating workers and sputtering forklift, watched her father's face change when he saw her, watched Propenko put a hand on her back as naturally as if he were touching another half of himself, then turn and walk off with her to the far edge of the asphalt. They appeared to be having a disagreement — about the smoking, perhaps — but even so, Czesich could read some kind of marvelous mutual understanding in every nuance of posture and gesture. He observed it like an apprentice observing a pair of masters. So this was how it was done, father and child.

He was distracted by a minor disturbance among the workers, who were stretching their midmorning cigarette break past all reasonable limits. Leonid was scolding them, stamping a foot. They looked at him with their eyebrows up, comic strip characters, unapologetically lazy. What, they seemed to be saying, could possibly be in it for us?

And multiply this, Czesich thought, by a hundred million. He looked back and saw Lydia climbing the gentle rise toward the street.

When the last of the food had been loaded and the requisite six copies of forms signed and dated, Czesich slid into the back seat of the Volga, popped his briefcase open on his knees and took out the typed list of distribution sites. The plan was to visit one site in the morning and one in the afternoon. One of the loaded trucks would remain at the pavilion under police guard and Leonid's vigilant eye. The other truck, four laborers, Propenko, Anatoly, and Czesich would travel to the first site and begin the actual distribution of food.

Propenko finished with his smoking, flicked the cigarette away, and climbed in beside Anatoly.

"Nevsky Mine, it looks like," Czesich said enthusiastically, reading the first name on the list.

A strained silence fell across the front seat. Propenko cleared his throat. "There's been a change," he said. "A small change in sequence, if you don't mind, Anton. I've sent word to the miners not to expect us."

Czesich didn't mind — nothing could make him mind this morning — though the change struck him as peculiar. As they started off, he felt some of the gaiety slipping out from under him. He wanted everybody to be happy now. He wanted Propenko and

Anatoly and their families to be his guests at the big farmhouse in the Green Mountains. He was drugged with emancipation.

The new first distribution point was in a part of the city he hadn't seen, Vostok's western edge, a neighborhood of gray, six-story buildings with storefronts below, some of them obscured behind tight, snaking lines. The neighborhood reminded him of a part of D.C. not far from the office, a place he sometimes went for lunch when he was feeling courageous.

Anatoly followed the truck down a narrow street, then sharply left over the sidewalk and under a stone arch. Beyond the arch was a puddled courtyard onto which four apartment buildings backed. Each of the buildings had two rear doors at the top of two sets of crumbling concrete stairs, with a thin alley — tunnel, really — burrowing between the doors at the building's midpoint. As the Volga came to a stop, Czesich saw one of the eight doors swing open and a middle-aged woman with a basket of laundry on one hip step out onto the landing. She hesitated, stared at the truck, at the Volga, at the militia jeep pulling in behind, then did an about-face and disappeared back into the building.

When they got out, Propenko looked around as if for a landmark. "This is the right place," he said to Czesich over the roof of the car. "These four buildings are on the list."

Czesich did not doubt it.

"A very poor place," Anatoly added quietly, for Czesich's benefit. His great purple birthmark trembled and twitched, and for a moment Czesich thought he was about to reveal the morning's secret, but Anatoly only glanced at Propenko, then ran his eyes over the crumbling stairs and rusted railings. "Mostly old women living on their pensions." He glanced at Propenko again, then away.

"As long as they need food," Czesich said.

"They need it."

"They're on the list," Propenko repeated.

But, on the list or not, it was soon apparent that no one here was expecting a food delivery this morning. The fact struck Czesich as both queer and, for this country, almost predictable. The courtyard stood in shadow. He looked up and guessed there would be rain by midafternoon, though even the weather seemed reluctant to reveal itself today.

Propenko mounted the nearest staircase, disappeared behind the door for a few minutes, then came back out and ordered the laborers to begin unloading. Czesich stood apart and watched. There was little for him to do now except preside. He had played his role. Now the point was to see how the Soviets played theirs.

Things started out well enough. The workers threw down spare wooden pallets from the truck bed and reversed the procedure they'd completed half an hour earlier at the pavilion. Gradually, five blocks of packaged food, each the height of a man, formed in the center of the courtyard. Czesich took a few more photographs, but seeing it this way — his grand international rescue mission reduced to five piles of cardboard boxes in a damp, forgotten quadrangle — sucked some of the air from his sails. It seemed to him for a moment that he was witnessing the ridiculous, further-most extension of his own ego, a few thousand kidney beans in a gritty puddle.

Soon, though, faces appeared. The moment took on a human shape. First, a trio of cherubs materialized on one of the landings, standing shoulder to shoulder in dirty-faced wonder. They were joined presently by the woman who'd been carrying laundry, then five or six teenaged boys came sauntering down one of the alleys flinging karate kicks at one another. A second door opened and three more women stepped out, and Czesich thought he heard feet slapping in the stairwells behind them. He looked up and saw, among yellowed sheets of newspaper taped over cracked windows, a few faces staring, not at the food, but at him. A child cried, "Mama, Mama, the Germans!" and one of the laborers laughed.

Three minutes later, Propenko was standing in the center of a small mob, pointing his arms and giving instructions Czesich could not quite make out. The truck driver climbed down from his cab to help, and Anatoly pushed his way into the crowd and tried to clear a bit of room for the laborers. Czesich stood back, let people move past him toward Propenko and the pallets. This was not the plan. The plan was for the food to be delivered into the custody of or-phanages and hospitals and existing residence, factory, and miners' committees who would ensure its equitable distribution. But, he told himself, you had to allow for a certain deterioration of any plan in this nation of Plans. You had to allow for secrets, and fibs, and great countervailing undercurrents of motivation. You had to learn to go with the flow. Still, he'd expected better from his new friend Sergei Propenko, and he felt a wash of disappointment. He heard, above the clamor, a woman's scolding voice, and caught sight of a boy no more than ten wriggling out from under the far side of the truck and dashing off down an alley clutching a can of stolen food. It was all right. Propenko seemed to know what he was doing. In a minute the two militiamen got out of their jeep, strolled over to the crowd, and started shoving people. It was all right. It was fine.

Purely by virtue of his size and manner, Propenko commanded a certain amount of authority. Within half an hour he had managed to divide the still growing crowd into four ragged lines that approached the food from the four points of the compass. People were required to present their identity cards to prove they lived in one of the four buildings, and the truck driver copied down apartment numbers to make sure no one double-dipped. The crowd, and the pushing, and the shouted numbers, reminded Czesich, oddly, of a stock exchange trading floor. He tried to smile away a tentacle of alarm. He was, after all, a free man now. What could he possibly have to worry about?

In less than an hour, three of the five large stacks of food had been handed out. Propenko had set aside the last two piles for families who weren't at home, and a few dozen complainers hung around, badgering him, begging an extra share. A group of them made as if to approach Czesich, but Anatoly had taken up a position near the truck and he shooed them away. One wizened woman got through, though, a net bag holding two cans of American beets hooked over her forearm. She wanted, it turned out, to touch him, and when she had laid a gouty finger on his sleeve, she wanted to deliver a speech.

"You are truly an American, sir?" she said, the words so thoroughly slurred Czesich could barely understand them.

He nodded down at her. Her face, with its scars and striations, presented a history that stretched from the czars to perestroika, with Stalin and Brezhnev between. He imagined his grandmother and grandfather would have ended up like this woman, had they stayed. And he might have ended up like Sergei Propenko — with two decent suits, four small rooms, and a child who actually loved him.

"This is the second time I owe you my gratitude, sir."

"You don't have to thank me," Czesich said. *"Nye nada."* But the woman seemed not to hear, or not to comprehend. She cocked her head like a puppy, and he understood her to be slightly daft. He saw no route of escape. A policeman stood warily by, waiting to push her away, but Czesich could not bring himself to give the signal.

"In the woods outside Leningrad," the woman began, "we were starving and freezing to death. And my brigade was trying to work, sir. And my supervisor called me to her and said: 'Anna Grigorievna, these boxes are for your people.' Well, I looked inside. And there were gloves, sir, and warm underwear. Gloves and warm underwear." She reached out and grabbed Czesich's right forearm in both hands, trembling violently. "And I said, 'Marfa Andreyevna, where did you get them? Where?' And she said, 'The Americans.' The Americans, sir. . . . I've waited fifty years to thank you." She squeezed Czesich's arm tighter and pulled his face down within range of her toothless mouth, so that his camera swung out and knocked against her chest. He took a kiss on one side of his face then the other and heard her whisper, hoarse and too loud, what sounded like: "Drop all your bombs on these *bolsheviki!*" She pushed him to arm's length, blinked twice in an exaggerated way, then shuffled back to her anxious family.

Propenko was waving Czesich over toward the food. There was still a sizable crowd to push through, stragglers, complainers, latecomers. "Anton," Propenko said, barely meeting his eyes. "We have to wait here a little while longer. The chairwoman of the residents' committee is on her way from work. We can't leave until she gets here."

They were standing beside the truck, not far from the remaining full pallets. Many of the people were, as Anatoly had said, elderly women, but news had spread to the street, and Czesich could see teenagers and middle-aged men straggling in through the archway. A knot of young toughs stood off to one side, smoking, checking things out, and he wondered if his straw-headed shadow might be somewhere in the courtyard, eyeing him, or if Malov might be nearby, directing security.

"We should have more militia here, Sergei," Anatoly said uneasily.

Propenko frowned.

Czesich could hear, and then see, some kind of argument taking place at the base of one of the stairways. Two women were fighting over a box of food, tugging it back and forth like characters in a farce. The laborers were squatting in the truck bed, smoking and looking nervous. It seemed to him that those people holding boxes or cans were in a hurry to leave the courtyard and climb up their ill-lit stairwells to the safety of their apartments. He imagined them there, setting their bag of powdered eggs and six cans of peaches on the countertop, one spot of satiety surrounded by ten million hectares of rich, black earth.

"Why isn't Vzyatin here?" Anatoly said. His birthmark was twitching again. He ran a hand through his hair.

"Vzyatin can't follow us around like a baby-sitter," Propenko snapped, then quickly looked away. For a moment, Czesich thought he would apologize, but Propenko's attention was distracted by another petitioner, saying how her husband and brother and father and she all lived together in two small rooms, two children also. The men were away at work now and the children at camp. "Can't you let me take just three boxes from this big pile here? Only three boxes more? For the children? One of them is an epileptic. What would it hurt, Tovarisch Direktr?"

The population of the courtyard seemed to have doubled since the last time Czesich looked. At least a hundred people now, three-quarters of them men, more coming through the archway every few seconds.

One of the laborers hopped off the truck, sauntered up to Propenko and said that, if the boss didn't mind, the boys were going to trot down to the local *stolovaya* for a quick lunch before all the soup was eaten up. In a voice full of minding, Propenko said he didn't mind.

When the laborers were gone, Czesich detected a change in the courtyard air. Something — a sound in the loose, milling crowd, a movement off at its edges, a small nudging upward of the volume — triggered an odd sensation. Times Square.

Times Square in West Vostok. He must be getting homesick.

He watched a plump woman shaking her fist in Propenko's face and shouting. "Stop it now," Propenko shouted back. His cheeks were pink, the veins in his neck standing out. "We *all* have to wait now. Stop it!"

Anatoly was looking toward the archway with a miserable expression on his face.

Czesich tried to turn around and see what the trouble was, but a wave of bodies was suddenly there behind him, grunts, shuffling feet, a force. Almost imperceptibly, he was being moved toward the pallets. Only a few yards away, Propenko and the two militiamen were shoving back a small army of angry women. Anatoly, too, had been surrounded. Czesich pressed the Nikon against his chest, taking small, quick steps to keep from being knocked off balance. "*Perestantye!*" he yelled, and his own voice startled him.

Within a few more seconds, the remaining two piles of food were obscured, and he was being swept steadily toward them in a push of shoulders and tilted hats, men and women bumping him from all sides. He tried to dig in his heels, but it was like pushing against the tide.

"Forward to the triumph of communism! Forward! Forward!" some drunken idiot shouted, and the herd pressed forward obediently, a bit more quickly now. Czesich's arms were all but pinned at his sides. The man to his right panicked and tried to wriggle free, and an errant elbow flew up into Czesich's nose, his legs went rubbery, and he fell, hard, onto his hands and knees. The camera strap was up around his ears, and he grabbed the lens with one hand and held it off the ground. There was blood in his mouth, hot and salty, a slow wave of pain. There were boots and shins around him, gravel scraping through the knees of his trousers, thick venous legs near his face. A knee banged his ribs and he went over sideways, clutching the Nikon like a football. He quickly pushed himself onto his hands and knees again, but bodies were shuffling toward the food, dragging him along inch by inch, and he let go of the camera, grabbed for the nearest leg and felt a bony shin in his fingers for an instant before it kicked away.

He shouted and tried to push himself up, but the herd swept on, mindless, scraping him forward like a pebble in surf. The camera strap had broken and he was holding the ends against his body with one hand, trying to keep upright with the other, trying to lift one knee and set one foot flat on the tar and push himself to a standing position. The foot slipped and he fell forward. He felt hands on either side of his ribs, felt himself being lifted straight up, then the hands lost their grip and he pitched forward and down in a heap again. His palms were bleeding, bits of tar and grit being forced into the cuts. He spat blood and felt the hands on him again. He was rising up, and he kicked and struggled and had just gotten his feet under him when he was thrown to the side and down like a rag doll. His shoulder struck the truck tire, sending a line of pain down the inside of his arm. He rolled under the rusted chassis and came to rest in a puddle there, staring up at the corroded drive shaft, swallowing blood and gasping.

He turned his head and vomited his meager, smelly breakfast into the puddle, and tried to push himself a few inches in the other direction. His head throbbed like a clappered bell. The camera was gone, the person who'd rescued him huddled near his feet. He pulled out his handkerchief and pressed it to his nose until the bleeding stopped.

He saw shoes scraping past, a red kerchief entwined around the toe of a man's black boot, someone falling to one knee then getting up. He felt his stomach and the back of his throat seize up again, but there was no more food to expel. His rescuer was moving, and Czesich was not surprised to see Propenko's face. Propenko was holding himself up on his elbows, his head grazing the bottom of the truck. His neat black hair had fallen down over his forehead, and the muscles around his mouth and eyes seemed to be floating. He reached out with one hand and wiped blood from Czesich's cheek.

Czesich heard a girl scream. "Sergei," he croaked. "What happened?"

Propenko swung his eyes away.

"What's going on?" Czesich was trembling in fear and ashamed of it. A few yards away, the people he'd come to save were trampling each other for what amounted to one or two meals. He imagined women ripping cans and bags of flour from each other's arms. There seemed absolutely nothing human about it.

Propenko was shaking his head back and forth in tiny movements. He looked as though he were about to weep.

"Sergei," Czesich said sharply. "What happened?"

But Propenko wouldn't tell him, could not meet his eyes. He stared down straight in front of him as if trying to remember something, to solve a riddle; then, after a moment, he glanced at Czesich as though at a stranger, and slid out into the light.

The desperate scramble for food lasted only another three or four minutes. Czesich could feel the change in the crowd, he could feel the frenzy reach its peak then slowly wane. He saw a policeman's cuff and boot, people hurrying away, a scrap of brown paper drifting to earth near the truck tire.

He closed his eyes and tried to get his breathing back to normal. His heart still drummed. He tasted bile and blood. He could hear people blowing paper horns, people singing, people shouting about 1969. Marie was there, his wife of two months. The exhibit was over, both families glad their Anton had gotten all that traveling out of his system before the wedding. Julie Stirvin — he thought, he really believed — was out of his system as well, one brief sexual detour before the long, level, quiet road of marriage.

Times Square was to be a widening of Marie's horizons. It was the first part of a strategy to prove to her that a real, human world existed beyond the borders of East Boston, and that she was entitled to inhabit it. It had been, he saw now, another of his crusades. There had been that same small, horrifying change in the crowd, a second or two of stillness, of warning, then all hell.

They'd somehow gotten separated, his arm nearly torn from the socket trying to hold on to her, and he'd found her an hour and a half later, weeping beside a policeman on Forty-seventh Street, his case for the outside world lost forever.

"Are you hurt, Anton Antonovich?"

It was Anatoly on his hands and knees, peering under the truck. Czesich shook his head. He did not seem to have enough energy to move. His stomach still clutched and released, and, not so different from Marie now, he was reluctant to risk the outside world. Finally, after what seemed a very long time, he was aware of Anatoly and the driver helping him slowly out into the light. They sat him on an empty pallet, from which vantage he could see one-quarter of the blurry courtyard littered with cardboard and streaks of spilt flour, and a small knot of *babushki* with children at their sides.

Near his right ear, Czesich heard the word *bolnitza* — hospital. He imagined doctors probing him with World War II instruments and dirty syringes. He bleated out: *"Nye nada!"* Someone laughed.

Anatoly's face was in front of him again. "Your nose is not broken, Anton Antonovich," he was saying. "It's bleeding. You're scratched up. It's not broken."

From somewhere, of course, a bottle of vodka materialized, and Czesich pressed it to his lips. There were men all around, watching him. He was a Director, an American. He had a role to play. "The food," he said gallantly.

"Gone, Anton Antonovich. Evaporated. Swept off."

Someone was daubing a handkerchief soaked in vodka against his cheek, sending a smelling-salt sting up his nostrils. His vision cleared enough to bring into focus the remains of a dozen broken boxes. The *babushki* were staring at him. He turned slightly and saw a militiaman banging someone's head against the hood of the jeep. A second jeep, then an ambulance, rolled into the courtyard, blue lights twisting.

Eventually he could stand on his own, and then the pain came on with its full force. He kept a bottle of aspirin in his briefcase; he retrieved it and swallowed three pills with three bitter sips of vodka. His suit was ruined, wet and torn at every joint, his shirt-front streaked with blood. He balled up the jacket and tossed it into the back seat of the car. He and Anatoly made a brief, futile search for the camera.

"And now?" Anatoly said, when it was apparent they would not find it.

Czesich could not seem to put two coherent thoughts together. The truck was still there, empty except for the wooden pallets. A police wagon had been called, and three drunken men were trying to keep from being forced through its back door. The ambulance hurried away. With the exception of a few unaccompanied children and one crippled old man, everyone had fled the scene, leaving the courtyard as still as a soccer stadium after the riot.

"Where did Sergei go?"

"Walked away."

The laborers came strolling through the archway, back from lunch, and the truck driver started in on them. "You abandoned your post!" Czesich heard him shout. "You couldn't see what was happening? You couldn't have stayed?"

They yelled out their excuses, surrounding the older man and waving their arms until he was sufficiently intimidated. Czesich slid into the Volga, Anatoly got behind the wheel, and for a few seconds they watched the laborers and truck driver yell at each other, watched the lieutenant pry fingers loose from the door of the police wagon, watched the old man hobble to the center of the courtyard and poke through cardboard scraps with the tip of his cane.

Anatoly turned the key, revved the engine once, and snapped off the radio. "What happened?" Czesich asked him.

The driver lifted and dropped his shoulders one inch.

"Anatoly, what happened?"

"Our people have been turned into animals."

"I don't mean that."

The driver shrugged again and turned his face away. First the police wagon, then the two jeeps, then the truck with its squatting, scowling laborers, rolled out through the archway, leaving the Volga alone in the littered courtyard.

Czesich said the first thing that came to mind: "I'm not a spy."

"I know that, Anton."

"The cold war is over."

Anatoly nodded grimly, as if its end had come too late.

"Then tell me what was going on this morning. I want to know. For myself."

Anatoly fiddled with the radio dial as if threatening to turn it on. He kept his eyes averted.

"Listen, I'm not supposed to be here, do you understand?"

The driver shook his head.

"I volunteered for this assignment. I created it. The embassy put the program on hold and I came anyway. People are hungry here. I wanted to feed them."

Anatoly sat expressionless.

"Do you understand?"

The driver shook his head again. "What about your superiors?"

"My superiors are ten thousand miles away."

There was mostly suspicion in the look Anatoly turned on him, but beneath it was a spark, one twinge of trust. "This is my show," Czesich pressed. "The whole ridiculous thing."

"Not ridiculous," Anatoly said. The word had hurt him. "Humiliating, not ridiculous." Beneath the purple skin of his birthmark were ten or twenty small lumps the size of grape seeds. A dark mole sprouted just at the top of his left eyebrow. "Sergei changed the list," he said. "The Nevsky Mine was first on the list. Where the strikes started. Bringing food there means more than bringing food. It would be a sign."

Czesich turned his eyes forward and tried to concentrate. The windshield was spotted with drizzle. Just when it seemed he'd held the peeled, sweet fruit in his hands, he discovered another rind, something else to be gotten through, another layer of disguise. "Were these houses second on the list?"

"Last," Anatoly said. "Second on the list was an orphanage near the church."

"But why?"

Anatoly shrugged. "He told us only this morning. Leonid asked him why, and he walked away. I asked him why, and he told me to mind my business. He was not himself."

Finally, even through the pain, Czesich was able to mount a short stair of understanding, one stone fact upon the next. It was all a matter of symbols and signs now, gestures. He supposed he'd known that all along. He supposed that was what had brought him here.

// CHAPTER 27

PROPENKO walked from West Vostok to the center of the city, seven kilometers, without any destination in mind. He was not moving toward anything yet, just away from things, away from an old notion of himself. His suit was torn at the knees and elbows, his shirtfront and tie wet and spotted with blood, and he could sense people sneaking glances at him as he stood on the corners waiting to cross. He did not care now; a twisting internal world absorbed him.

Until two hours ago, the deal he had made with the First Secretary had been a secret thing, invisible, a few quiet words and a handshake. It had never seemed a good thing, but until two hours ago it had seemed at least defensible, and very small, and very private, the kind of compromise people made all the time. Even the lies supporting it had not seemed that important. He'd called the Nevsky Mine from his office before going to the pavilion, and told the secretary who answered the phone that the food delivery would be delayed a few days, and it hadn't seemed to matter to her at all.

Even when they started handing out food in the courtyard, it had still felt like the right decision. People, poor people, were being given something to soften the edge of their poverty. Anton Antonovich was taking note, and would pass the word to Washington that all was in order. Old women were thanking him, thanking America. It wasn't until the courtyard had started to fill up with men and women from the street that the hard crust of logic had cracked and broken open and all the hidden muck had come bubbling to the surface, all the anger, all the desperation, everything the old communist platitudes had masked for so long. It wasn't until one plump woman had started scolding him and shaking a finger in his face that he'd realized the crowd in the courtyard must see him as he saw Mikhail Lvovich, that he'd aligned himself with the forces that had been crushing people all these years, holding them down, suffocating them. He saw how quietly this suffocation had been accomplished, a slight twist of the thinking process, some tricks with the language, and a multitude of small, secret deals with men who lived in opulence and preached equality.

Now, walking the streets, he was stalked by a vision of himself in suit and tie and shined shoes, standing up against the ragged masses, defending the rules, maintaining order. But whose rules? An order that stood for what? Murder? Hunger? His whole adult life, twenty years at the Council, had the smell of a lie to it now.

He walked and walked, away from it, and when he looked up he was in front of the Theater of Opera and Ballet, not far from Raisa's office, two blocks west of Party Headquarters. He went the last two blocks and stood on the sidewalk there, peering through the trees at a small knot of hunger strikers sitting on a tarpaulin in Lenin's shadow, at the faces of the miners and the other demonstrators, at their placards and banners, one wooden cross leaning against a bench. He looked for his daughter and did not see her.

Galina, Raisa's assistant, stared at him as though he'd just climbed over the wall of Psychospital 39, then hurried into the back room to announce him. Raisa appeared in the reception area a minute later, and Propenko was aware of her hands shaking on his wrists, brushing his torn suit, touching his scratched palms as if the first order of business should be to remove any evidence of whatever it was that had happened. She sent an anxious look toward Galina — pretending to be busy off behind her desk — then into her husband's face, and whispered, "Seryozha, what? What is this?" but he was not yet ready to tell her.

They fled the office's eyes and ears and walked to a restaurant Propenko knew would be crowded and noisy even in midafternoon. On the way, he prepared her with a description of the courtyard riot — old women scratching at each other like animals, Anton Antonovich's bloodless face sinking beneath the crowd. And when they were seated at a small table in a corner, hemmed in by half-sober men and women who were supposed to be at work, he said: "I lied about what happened on Kabanov's balcony."

Raisa stared.

"I made a deal with him. I said I'd change the order of the deliveries so the food wouldn't go to the miners and the church for another week or two. He told me he needed time to negotiate with them. He promised to be sure no one threatened our family, that none of us would be hurt. It seemed like a small thing."

Raisa went on staring, and when Propenko couldn't bear the inspection any longer he shifted his eyes to the wall. He became aware of something, an idea, standing beside their table like a ghost: it occurred to him that part of what he'd really been trying to do on Mikhail Lvovich's balcony was to chase away the memory of Raisa's father, the man in whose large shadow so much of his married life had been lived. It seemed suddenly so obvious — not as the main motivation, but as a slinking minor character. His success at the Council had always been slightly tainted, because the Council was part of the system, and the system had killed Maxim Semyonich. Whatever strength or courage he showed in life could never match the myth of Maxim Semyonich's resistance in the camps. Even Lydia thought so. Look at the type of boys she went around with — always older, more political, more religious.

"I was thinking of Lydia," he said, looking at Raisa again. "Of the family." Which was true, but not a pure truth, and he knew it. The ghost refused to leave. From behind his talking mask, Propenko tried to determine if Raisa was aware of it, but her face showed nothing.

She shifted her eyes out into the room. He waited, thinking of Vzyatin's wife and her psychological theorems, her *tranzferentzes* and *komplexes* and *freuds*, things he'd never really believed in, foreign things. No wonder he'd resisted them all these years. Look what they revealed. Look what crouched beneath his communist respectability.

"What else did you lie about?"

"Nothing."

She was looking beyond him, remembering a gaunt, unshaven man taking a few breaths of air in the park behind her childhood home, the gregarious *babushki* there shunning him as though he carried the plague. By the time she was Lydia's age, her father was already an ex-convict, an Enemy of the People, socially, financially, and physically ruined.

The waiter graced them with his presence, and Propenko realized he'd eaten nothing since their dinner with Anton Antonovich the night before. He ordered what there was to order — meat and wine and bread — and when the greasy plates were set down in front of them, Raisa was still staring. Her face looked raw. He poured some wine into her glass and she ignored it. After a long time she turned her eyes to him. "And now?"

"I want you to take your mother and go to the dacha. Tonight. After work."

"For what? What are you going to do?"

"I don't know yet. Something."

"We have no car."

"Go on the *elektrichka.*"

"And what? Live at the dacha? Until what? Until the soldiers come? The miners blocked off part of Gorki Street this morning, did you know that? Galina saw three truckloads of Black Berets at the airport last night when she went to meet her husband."

At the word "husband," the first tears came into Raisa's eyes. She swiped at them with the back of a wrist. "What about *work*?"

A beet-faced man at the next table swiveled his head to look. Propenko stared at him until he turned away. "Only through the weekend," he told Raisa, though he was not sure why he said it, or what was supposed to have been resolved by Sunday night. He could see only as far as the next step. He emptied the whole glass of wine into the hollow inside him. "I'm going to find Vzyatin and Leonid now. I'm going to tell them what I just told you."

She frowned and wiped her face dry. "What can Vzyatin do?"

"He has connections in Moscow."

"Bessarovich? They set you up, Bessarovich and Vzyatin, can't you see it, Sergei? They tossed a hot coal in your lap."

Propenko shook his head. Bessarovich, maybe; Vzyatin, never.

"What if you just walked away?"

"And went where?"

"And asked for another assignment, asked to be transferred. She could transfer you. We could move."

He shook his head again. The meat tasted rancid.

"Why not?"

"A thousand reasons. You know —" he stopped. He'd started to say, You know I could never run away like that, but he could no longer boast in such a fashion.

"And what if Bessarovich and her patrons lose?" Raisa said quietly. "What if they're on the wrong side, Sergei? Vzyatin and the miners and Father Alexei? What if it's like it's always been? What if we wake up tomorrow and there are soldiers in the street and Bessarovich and her friends are all under arrest?"

Propenko would not let himself think of it. The civil war everyone called perestroika had finally reached Vostok — years late — and it seemed to him now that he could no longer hide out in his apartment, reading the papers to see what he should say in public, waiting to take a side until he knew which side would win. There was no more neutral ground. If you walked away from one thing now you had to walk toward something else.

"You and I were wrong," he said, and Raisa glared at him. "We kept quiet. That was the bargain. Keep quiet and we'll leave you alone to have your Lada, your dacha, your four hundred rubles a month. But you can't make deals with your life like that. Everything is spoiled if you do that. You rot from the inside out."

"Says the man who makes deals."

Propenko looked away, still haunted. "Your father was right."

"*Your* father was right. Your father and mother."

"They were right for Stalin. We don't have Stalin now," Propenko said, though not two days earlier he'd seen a picture of the mustachioed dictator propped up next to the woman who sold newspapers and calendars from a kiosk near the office. He'd told no one but Anatoly. Anatoly had made the sign of the cross.

"If your father were alive today he'd say the same things, and he'd still be right."

"Why do you talk like that?" Propenko said. "I know you don't believe it. Your mother knows it. Lydia knows it. Who is the disguise for?"

Raisa leaned forward, blood in her face. "The disguise is for the same thing your disguise is for," she said, too loudly. *"To get by."*

This loud truth fit itself nicely into a lapse in the restaurant's background noise, and Propenko held his eyes straight down in front of him.

"What are you thinking of doing? Tell me."

"I don't *know*," he said, but he was beginning to know. A vague notion was taking shape, a vengeance and a penance. "Whatever I do, it's easier for the militia to watch you at the dacha."

"And you trust them?"

"We have to trust them."

Raisa's face changed again, long wrinkles wavering along the length of her forehead, short lines running up from her top lip, a widening of the nostrils and narrowing of the eyes. Propenko was reminded of the expression on her face when she'd given him the news of Tikhonovich's murder. She looked away, then back, no tears now. "Sergei, he tried to get Lydia into bed with him."

"What? Who?"

"Vzyatin."

"What are you talking about? Victor's son?"

"Victor himself. Your friend. The Chief."

"When?"

"Last summer. In Sochi."

"What do you mean, Raisa? Victor's my age, Lydia's twenty, he's —"

"He was drunk. They bumped into each other on the path back from the beach and he talked to her for a while then kissed her. He tried to get her to come back to his room."

"Where was I?"

"In bed with me. It was midnight."

"Where was his wife?"

"Away."

"Why didn't you tell me?"

Raisa was twisting the stem of the wineglass into the tablecloth.

"Raisa."

She looked up. "I didn't tell you because I just found out. Last week. And because Lydia asked me not to tell you. He came to the church to talk to her about the murder and he apologized — a year late, he said. It would never happen again, he said."

"Lydia asked you not to tell me?"

"She said he'd just made a mistake. He was drunk. She didn't want you to hate your friend because of one mistake."

"Hate him? I'll break his arms."

Raisa was looking back at him like a mirror. "You don't have to talk that way for me anymore. And you don't have to talk that way for Lydia. And it would be better now if you stopped treating her as if she were still in grade school."

"You don't understand, Raisa. You don't know what men think when they look at her. I do. I know what Victor sees and I know what he thinks, and Lydia believes the world is one gigantic church where all the men are saints and all the women —"

"Tikhonovich and Lydia were lovers."

"What?"

"He was Lydia's lover."

"What are you talking about? The man was —"

"Forty-one."

Propenko put his face in his hands, pressed his fingertips into the skin of his forehead, and ran them from the roots of his hair down to his eyebrows and back again. With a loud scraping of chair legs, the beet-faced man and his drunken companion left their table and shuffled toward the door.

"They were listening to us."

"Let them listen."

Propenko looked up at Raisa and thought, for an instant, that she could be anyone's wife or no one's, that he knew no word or name that could contain her. He considered telling her that Malov was a suspect in Tikhonovich's murder, but what good would it do? Vzyatin was the person he had to talk to now, not Raisa.

They left a few bills on the table, pushed through a small crowd at the door and out onto the sidewalk. A soft mist hung in the air, and by the time they'd walked back to the steps of Raisa's building, their clothes were coated with a fine fur of droplets.

"Where are you going?" she asked him when they'd stopped.

"I told you. To find Vzyatin."

"And what, break his arms?"

"Forget that now. I'll come to the dacha tomorrow night. If Anatoly gets the wires, I'll come in the car. If not, I'll come on the train, or with one of Vzyatin's men. If you don't see Lydia right away, don't worry. I'll talk to her tonight. I'll convince her to come."

"She won't," Raisa said.

"I'll talk to her."

"She won't come, Sergei. She's made plans with the American. I asked her."

"I'll talk to her when she gets home."

Raisa gave up and turned her eyes away.

They stood close together for a moment, connected by nothing, Propenko decided, connected by what they thought they knew about each other. She turned, and he watched her climb the stairs and put on the mask she wore for the people she worked with.

// CHAPTER 28

"Y OUR FACE is not so white now," Anatoly said.
Czesich was glad to hear it. His hands and knees were
scraped and oozing blood, and his nose was swollen, but the
vodka and aspirin had pushed away most of the pain, leaving him
merely depressed. Anatoly was depressed, too, and his grim mood
was succeeding where anecdotes and terse commentary had failed:
Czesich, at long last, felt what it must feel like to live here.

They had left West Vostok behind and were cruising a wide
avenue in search of Sergei Propenko. An oily gray rain had begun
to fall, and in the lines snaking out from storefronts, men and
women covered themselves with whatever was at hand —
shopping bags, pieces of plastic, the occasional umbrella. The
Volga's windshield wipers squeaked. An army truck rolled past,
boys in brown uniforms staring glumly out the back. Czesich felt
stalked by deceit and desperation, a Marxist-Leninist melancholy.
"Sergei must have had a reason," he said.

Anatoly shrugged, pretending not to care, but Czesich could see
he was miserable. After another few minutes, a few more turns and
futile, side-street loops, the driver said, "We won't find him,
Anton," and Czesich gave in and let him steer the Volga back in the
direction of the hotel.

"You should rest now."

Czesich did not feel capable of resting, or of facing his suite
alone, or of accepting the idea that Sergei Propenko was involved
in some kind of double-dealing. Without enthusiasm, he suggested
they go by the pavilion and see about the second truck.

"You rest, Anton Antonovich. I'll tell Leonid you gave the

order to have the truck unloaded and the food put back in the container. I'll tell Sergei to call you if he's there, but for now you should rest. You've been hurt."

"I have some food in my room. Would you join me for lunch?"

The driver shook his head. "I'm too ashamed now, Anton. We're all ashamed in front of you."

Czesich wanted to tell him it was shame that had gotten the Soviet Union into trouble in the first place, that the solution did not lie in more shame, more covering up. But they had turned onto the far western end of Prospekt Revoliutsii now, and every dull facade and stoop-shouldered body seemed to argue for silence. When Anatoly swung the Volga to a stop in front of the hotel steps, Czesich invited him in again, just for tea.

Anatoly declined once more, and they sat looking at a busload of happy Finns who were crossing the parking lot and walking toward the hotel as if they owned it. Czesich was beset by evil possibilities, afraid to get out of the car. He wondered if Malov might have somehow engineered the courtyard riot, paid people to trample him. He wondered if Propenko had been in on it and changed his mind at the last minute. He wondered what Julie would say if she could see him now, bloodied and buried up to his neck in other people's business.

"What if they find out about you?" Anatoly said.

"Who?"

"Your superiors. What will they do if they find out?"

"They found out," Czesich said. "They fired me."

"When?"

"Yesterday."

Anatoly was terrified. "You'll be *bezrabotny*."

Czesich nodded. The word meant simply "unemployed," but it was linked, in the Soviet consciousness, with unspeakable horror and misery, with life outside the *kollektiv*.

"Why did you do it, then?"

Czesich said he didn't know, and they sat quietly for a minute.

"Someone in Moscow must know you're here. Someone must want you to be here or the Council would have stopped you."

Czesich had wondered about this himself. Now, true or not, it didn't seem to matter. He shrugged, touched his friend on the shoulder, and climbed out into the rain. Battered and bloodstained, he carried his briefcase and balled-up suit jacket across the patio to the front entrance. The door was opened by the same corrupt doorman who had served him earlier in the day, the bowing Yefrem Alexandrovich. Czesich had an urge to kick him in the balls.

The second-floor *dezhurnaya* took in Czesich's wet clothes and scratched skin with a glance, but did not risk comment. The circuit between face and feelings had long ago been broken. She slid open her drawer of keys and handed him number 208, then went back to her book of war poems.

Czesich soaked for an hour in the lukewarm tub, his wounds turning the soapy pool pink around him, his thoughts circling again and again toward surrender. Some stubborn gene resisted. He had believed he'd come here because he wanted the Malovs and Puchkovs of the world stamped out, because he wanted his grandparents' countrymen to be full and dignified and free again, even if they'd never been that way in the first place. But now it seemed at least within the realm of possibility that all that was allegorical, a dream-crusade, all *out there*. Maybe what he'd really wanted was to be free and full and dignified *in himself*, and the rest was just for show, a crude playing out of subtle inner dramas. Maybe all of history boiled down to that and nothing else.

He got out of the tub and into a bathrobe. He raided his dwindling stock of provisions and tried to calm himself by setting out an elegant lunch: canned crabmeat and black olives and a cold glass of beer, chocolate-covered Beriozka cookies for dessert. He went the whole route — tablecloth, cloth napkin, soft classical music on the radio — but had taken only a few bites when the phone rang, the extended first ring signaling long distance.

"I suppose there's no point in simply asking you to do the rational thing, Chesi," were the first words Julie said. Something in her voice made surrender impossible.

"If it were the rational thing, I'd do it," Czesich told her, and for a long moment there was the usual clanging of pipes, hums, whistles, staccato beeps. "Filson cut me loose," he said, when he could no longer stand it.

"I know."

"I'm unemployed. *Bezrabotny.*"

"I know that, too. I was wondering how you'd cope."

It sounded to Czesich as though they might still be friends, in spite of everything. He felt a small burst of courage. "I'm working around it," he said. "They love me in the Donbass."

"Have you been handing out the food?"

"Faster than you'd believe."

"No problems?" Julie asked, as though there should have been problems, as though she'd set certain problems in motion up there and was calling to find out if they'd reached Vostok yet.

Czesich wondered if she and McCauley had sat around after the last phone call and thought up some clever, CIA-type way of screwing him. He concentrated, pressing a hand over his free ear.

"What's the weather like down there?"

He looked through the curtains at the mess outside. "Sunny. I've been hearing planes." A single, diluted drop of blood fell from his nose onto his bare right ankle and he thought he heard footsteps in the corridor.

"You're in the doghouse in a big way, you know," she was saying now. It seemed to amuse her.

"Julie, I couldn't begin to tell you how little that means to me at this moment."

"What's the matter? Are we talking on an empty stomach?"

There was a little too much blade in the remark for Czesich's taste. He supposed he deserved no better — trying to blow her sweetheart's cover on an open line, going over her head with the invitation to Haydock. Still, she was kicking him when he was down, and he wondered, briefly, if Julie and he were condemned to a karmic eternity of injury and revenge and half-assed reconciliation. He looked out the window and was watching a young boy fish through the dripping trash bin when the line buzzed and crackled and spit this out: "Haydock can't make it, Chesi. I've been ordered to come down there and rescue you."

At first he thought he'd heard wrong, or that she was teasing him. He squeezed the phone so hard the scratches on his palm started to bleed again. "What?" he said. "When?"

"Sunday afternoon, five thirty-seven P.M. Aeroflot 1021."

He scribbled the time on a pad by the phone, and felt his bruised hopes rising like Lazarus. "We'll arrange an official reception."

"No tricks," she said. "I told them I vouched for your sanity, that you were a decent, patriotic American. That's the only reason Haydock's allowing it. That, and because there's some concern that things are about to turn ugly here and we want you out."

"I'll meet you at the airport," Czesich said, not really listening.

"Five thirty-seven P.M. If there's any jet fuel that day."

"I'll arrange for the jet fuel. I'll arrange a tour."

"It's not a picnic, Chesi, I have to tell you. There are going to be some very nasty questions."

"What can they do to me now?" he said.

"Things I shouldn't mention."

"What, really?" About the only thing they could do to him now was meddle with his pension, his guarantee of life after Washington. He'd heard of extreme cases in which USCA employees had been threatened with loss of pension, but he had never actually known it to happen. More likely, Haydock would subject him to an old-fashioned dressing-down, and the Embassy Security people would try to scare him, shake him up a bit to make sure he wasn't a spy, to make him realize the magnitude of his error. What if the KGB had decided to kidnap you, they'd say, or assassinate you? You were there alone, against regulations. You put our entire policy at risk.

It would be the same tiresome bullshit.

"Things," Julie said, as though to torment him. "A few nervous days."

"A few nervous days? Julie, a few nervous days would be like a picnic now."

"I thought everything was fine."

"More or less fine."

She didn't speak for five or ten seconds, and he worried their connection had been severed.

"Jule?"

"We'll talk when I get down there, Chesi. I have to go."

"Another date?"

"See you Sunday."

"Yes," Czesich said, but she was gone. He lay down on the hard hotel sofa, closed his eyes, and nurtured one small seed of possibility. The mind did these things.

// CHAPTER 29

PROPENKO went up the pavilion ramp, through the crowd spilling out of the photography exhibit, and climbed the stairs toward Leonid's office two at a time. Tanya, Leonid's secretary, smiled at him, pretended not to notice the torn suit, and gestured toward her boss's door. Propenko pushed through it and saw Vzyatin and Leonid sitting on either side of a coffee table with a bottle of American whiskey between them. Leonid pulled up a third chair and poured another glass, and they left him alone while he drank.

When he'd set the tumbler down, Propenko found he could not quite look into their faces. Vzyatin was looking at Leonid. Leonid was looking out the window. They could hear Tanya's typewriter tapping.

He'd gotten up at 5:00 A.M. for the shooting lesson. He'd had only tea for breakfast, a bite of bad meat and a glass of wine with Raisa, and now the whiskey and tiredness hit and sent him floating. He got to his feet and drifted over to Leonid's large window and stood there with his back to the room, staring down at the river and the smoking valley beyond it. He heard someone strike a match, and caught the first sharp smell of tobacco smoke. "Malov frightened me," he said.

There was silence for a moment, then Leonid's voice: "Come sit, Sergei."

Propenko shook his head. He was thinking very clearly now. Even exhausted and hungry and shaken, even drifting along on the whiskey, his thinking was hard-edged and clear. He remembered this feeling from boxing. Sometimes when the body was pushed beyond a certain point, the mind was forced to shut down all its secondary activities, its musings and mutterings and preoccupations, and focus on survival. Sometimes you concentrated so perfectly that the opponent's arms and hands and shoulders seemed to be moving in slow motion. You could sense the punch before it was thrown. You could sense his desperation and his fear, and you could feel his weariness as if it were your own. You could see him whole. If that happened, and if, at that moment, you could will your body to move correctly through its own pain and weariness and fear, then the fight was over.

"When they bear down on you, Seryozha," Tolkachev had said, "be the boxer."

He was the boxer now, again. Not the trappings of it, not the uniform and the trophies and the sounds of shoes on canvas and the things other people associated with it, the external things, the talking about it. Not that. What he was now, again, was what he had been *internally* in his boxing days, what he could convey to no one, a clarity, one focused point of intention, beyond fear. Malov had been set on frightening him from the first moment, he could see that now. He understood that everything had come out of Malov's own fear, Malov's sense of being *less*, of not having. Malov was afraid, and could not bear the shame of it, and so had to spend his life making other people afraid, too, so that he would not seem so loathsome in his own eyes. Malov and Lvovich had tapped him, and shuffled circles around him, and whipped up fear and confusion in front of him, but that was over now.

Then what we have to do is frighten him back, Pa, right?

Lydia had been correct, and Tolkachev had been correct, and Vzyatin had been correct, too: this was not the boxing ring. If you lost here you lost everything. "Where is Lydia now?" he said over his shoulder.

"At the church with the priest," Vzyatin told him, in a voice he might have used with a stranger on the street. "The priest was sent a message this morning, knocked down at the market. She's been with him since ten-twenty. I have two detectives in the churchyard."

"You know Lydia was . . . close with the watchman?"

"I knew that, Sergei. The priest told me."

Propenko turned around and made himself meet Vzyatin's eyes. "You have someone following Malov?"

"Every minute. Malov's not going to get within a hundred meters of her."

Leonid patted the chair. Propenko walked across the room and sat, checking each part of his plan one more time. Lydia was safe. Raisa and Marya Petrovna would be at the dacha, with a militia car out front. Malov was being shadowed. He could feel Leonid and Vzyatin watching him, and he could see the courtyard erupting around him, and Anton Antonovich's face slipping beneath the crowd, and Mikhail Lvovich laughing through cigar smoke. He took a breath and held a knee in each hand like a diver somersaulting ten meters above the pool. "I went past Party Headquarters an hour ago," he told them. "I was looking at the hunger strikers. I was wondering what would happen if we brought the food there tomorrow and handed it out."

Leonid stopped blinking and set down his cigarette.

Vzyatin stared at Propenko for a moment, stared into him, then clapped his hands together once, very loudly, and held his fists in front of him like a fighter.

Tanya poked her face into the room and said she'd be going home now and wished them all a good night.

It was dark by the time they'd talked everything out. Propenko remained locked in a hungry, dizzy dream state, but Vzyatin was full of fire, absolutely certain about what his men would do, or refrain from doing, at his command. The plan, Propenko suspected, would earn the Chief high marks in the capital.

After an initial moment of doubt, Leonid, too, seemed excited. His participation would go a long way toward easing the disgrace of emigration, his abandonment of the *kollektiv*. He would be able to write them letters from Israel now, and his old friends would be able to write back.

There were logistical problems, of course, but each time Propenko or Leonid raised one, Vzyatin would wave a hand as if it were nothing, a speck of grit beneath the locomotive's wheels. Propenko could not remember seeing him so happy.

They left Leonid's office not sober and not quite drunk, and shook hands solemnly at the front door, their conspiracy turning real now that they'd stepped out into Mikhail Lvovich's city. They'd divided the duties. Quietly, subtly, Leonid would arrange for extra transportation. Vzyatin would pay a visit to the home of the militia captain in charge of the demonstration detail. Propenko would have a chat with Anton Czesich in the morning.

Vzyatin offered to have one of his men drive Propenko home, and Propenko sat in the back seat of the militia car and watched the dark blocks slide past, planning his conversation with Anton Antonovich and feeling the comfort of the drink very slowly slip away.

By the time he was back in his apartment, safe behind the double-locked door, the whiskey comfort had been replaced by pure exhaustion. The plan was still only a plan, at once preposterous and perfect, not yet real enough to terrify him. He took off his torn suit and, sitting at the kitchen table in his underwear, ate four boiled potatoes with bread and tea. The house seemed empty and sorrowful without women in it, and, in spite of Vzyatin's cautions, if there had been a phone at the dacha he would have called and talked to Raisa for a little while, talked to Marya Petrovna, let some of her old anger infect him. He took his second cup of tea into the living room and sat in the dark with the silent television, vowing to stay awake until Lydia came home, and then to tell her everything.

An hour later, the phone woke him. He leaned sideways in his chair and fumbled for it, knocked the receiver off the table. When he held it up to his ear the line was dead. Vzyatin had warned him to be careful what he said over the wires tonight — even what he said in the militia car on the way home — but Propenko was worried about Lydia now, not himself. He tilted his watch until it caught the light from the street. Ten-twenty.

His mouth was dry from the whiskey. He looked at the top of the dark apartment building across the way and listened to the clock ticking in the kitchen. A door slammed down the hall. He heard shouting, a woman weeping. When the phone rang again, fifteen minutes later, he had it against his ear in less than a second.

"Pa?"

"Where are you?"

"At the church."

"You said you'd be home."

"Father Alexei was attacked. He's going to stay here tonight and I'm going to watch him."

"I want you home," Propenko said, too harshly. The plan had swollen while he slept. The morning seemed to be careening toward him.

"I'm tired, Pa, and he's alone."

"I'll come get you."

"What for? There's a room here. I've stayed here before. What's the matter?"

"Your mother —" he began, then caught himself. It would be a simple matter for Malov or one of Mikhail Lvovich's men to listen in, Vzyatin had said. He had to act as if it were an absolutely ordinary night. Even in the car on the way home, even on the way to work tomorrow morning — absolutely ordinary.

"What happened?"

"Nothing," he said quickly. "Your mother was worried, that's all."

"Is she there?"

"In the bathroom."

"You're all right?"

"Fine."

"I called earlier."

"A few minutes ago?"

"No, seven o'clock."

"I was out having a drink with Leonid. I'm sorry I yelled. I was asleep in the chair and the phone startled me."

"He's an amazing man," Lydia said proudly. "They can't crush him."

"Tell me tomorrow," Propenko said, again too sharp. "I'll come by the church, will you be there?"

"All day," she said, and there was something new in her voice. "You've never come here before."

"I'd like to see it. We'll have a talk."

Lydia hesitated, then said, "All right," as if he had threatened her.

We'll really talk, Propenko wanted to say. I didn't mean it that way. I have things to tell you. You have things to tell me. But he said none of it. They exchanged their usual good-nights, and he sat in the darkness for a while before taking off his clothes and lying down alone on his bed. There were no pineapple dreams tonight. He saw his tall, round-shouldered father digging in the dacha garden with his back turned. That was all.

// CHAPTER 30

A HORDE of flaxen-haired tourists filled the lobby, half of them drunk in the Scandinavian style, tottering amicably to and fro, smiling dazed smiles, dangling bottles from thumb and forefinger so that Czesich expected his morning to be punctuated at any moment by a wet shattering of glass. Their junket to the Soviet Union had something to do with the anti-alcohol campaign in Helsinki, he supposed, but he could not imagine what had brought them this far south, or how their Intourist guide planned to fill the day. The Lenin Museum would take care of the morning — Lenin's socks, Lenin's underwear, Lenin's wife's cigar. But what would they do to kill the long Vostokian afternoon, those interminable hours before the next vodka-soaked dinner? A trip to the hard-currency Beriozka, maybe, chance to drop a few hundred Finnmarks on shellacked wooden bears and other Marxist garbage.

He shouldered his way through the opiated masses and toward the front door. His wit was turning ugly now. It meant, he knew, that he was afraid. He'd breakfasted in his room — canned peach slices and the morning news — watched Puchkov waving his fist again, and it had made him wish he hadn't revealed himself to Anatoly, made him wonder if his house of cards was going to collapse just in time for Julie's arrival. She'd step off the plane, pretty and pissed off, and he'd have nothing to show her but a few empty containers and the dust of his pulverized ego. Or worse.

In the true spirit of Russian unpredictability, Anatoly and his peach-colored Volga were not to be seen. Czesich paced the patio, inspecting his sore palms and knuckles, bending his swollen right knee, composing an angry speech for Propenko about the previous day's delivery. This was supposed to be a pilot program, he would say. The whole idea was to see if Western aid could be distributed in an equitable way, without being mishandled by local authorities. And there was the matter of personal honor, as well . . .

It was the purest bullshit. Who was he to talk about personal honor? He'd been lying to Propenko from the first day. His very presence in Vostok was a lie — for a good cause, but a lie all the same.

He abandoned his speechmaking and sank into a funk. The Finns bumped happily out through the door and boarded their red-and-white Intourist bus, and the bus departed, bathing him in diesel exhaust. A minute later, the peach-colored Volga drew up to the base of the steps, but it was Sergei Propenko behind the wheel, not Anatoly. Czesich greeted him coolly and slipped into the front seat; they headed north out of the lot, away from the pavilion.

"Where's Anatoly this morning?"

"With the containers."

Czesich couldn't be sure what in Propenko's voice made him so suddenly uneasy. The brown eyes were cutting back and forth as though checking both sides of the street for an ambush, and Propenko was sitting up so straight the top of his head grazed the Volga's roof.

"I would like to have a private talk with you, if you don't mind, Anton."

"I don't mind," Czesich said, but the nervousness filled his chest now, a creeping premonition. He waited for the talk to begin, for Propenko to give *him* a lecture on personal honor, on deceit American-style, but Propenko drove on, lost to the world of words. Czesich wondered if Julie and McCauley had notified the Vostok Council of Industry, after all, if her visit was a fabrication, her way of humiliating him in return. When he could bear the uncertainty no longer, he resorted to patter. "I'm looking forward to getting out into the country, Sergei," he said. "It's very kind of Lydia to offer to take me."

Propenko was squeezing his lips together. "I don't think that would be a very good idea now, your outing."

"I see." Czesich looked out at the bland sidewalk. His window was open, the air was cool, and he was sweating. Propenko did not sound especially angry. Nervous, perhaps, very nervous, rather grim, but not angry. Maybe Julie or Anatoly *had* told him. Or maybe he'd gotten word through other channels that his new friend, Anton Antonovich, was a fraud. Maybe Malov and the Russian mob were hitting him up for food and he didn't know how to ask for help.

They turned right at the first main intersection, right again after half a dozen blocks, and descended a narrow street that ran between a row of apartment buildings and a large park. "I was too frightened to thank you for helping me yesterday," Czesich said, still trying to open the channels. "Most likely you saved my life."

Propenko pulled the Volga to the curb and nodded tersely. When he took his hands off the wheel Czesich saw sweat on the scalloped plastic. The air at the edge of the park felt coarse and cool against his face.

"Let's walk, Anton." A car had pulled to a stop thirty feet behind them; its driver got out and leaned on the hood with his arms crossed.

"Why the bodyguard?"

"I'll tell you in a moment."

Propenko took hold of Czesich's elbow and led him down one of the paths, footsteps tapping behind them. Men were playing chess on rusty iron tables. Ahead, above the treetops and a mantle of morning mist, Czesich could make out the suspension bridge's twin steel peaks sparking sunlight. His right knee twinged every time he put weight on it. He could smell the river, acrid sweat, the shit hitting the fan.

"Anton," Propenko said when they'd gone fifty yards, "what do you think of me, as a man?"

In other circumstances, Czesich might have smiled. Didn't Propenko know most people had a "what do you think of me?" swimming around somewhere behind their mask and that it was best left there, unuttered? Was the man that provincial, that unguarded? His attention focused on the pressure of Propenko's fingers on his left elbow. It was perfectly normal for Soviet men to walk arm in arm, perfectly normal; but there was something terribly abnormal about this moment, something hasty and illicit and odd.

"You . . . you're a family man," he said, and when that seemed less than what Propenko was after, he added the first thing that came to mind: "I have a great deal of respect for the way you work, the way you handle yourself."

"What would you think if I told you I had committed a great deceit?"

Czesich began to suspect some kind of setup. No one did this.

No one asked you what you thought of them, took you arm in arm for a walk in the park and confessed their private deceits. Not with a bodyguard trailing a few paces behind. Not when you were supposed to be at the pavilion half an hour ago, loading food. He cursed silently. Now his good and respected friend Sergei Sergeievich Propenko was going to hand him documents in a manila envelope, call over the lurking "bodyguard," and sign a statement saying that the American had offered hard currency in exchange for missile secrets.

Julie's self-righteous diatribes about the one-on-one rule came back to him in the loudest, most unpleasant tones.

Czesich made himself twist his neck and look up. The muscles along Propenko's jaw were flexing. If this man was a betrayer, then everything Czesich thought he knew about the Soviet Union, about human nature, would be erased in one stroke. Perhaps he was trying to defect, but even that seemed absolutely out of character. If Propenko defected, who would stay?

Propenko was waiting.

"A great deceit?"

"Yes."

"I'd say you were incapable of it."

Propenko winced. They went four or five steps in a raw silence. "What would you say if I told you my whole life had been lived beneath a film of deceit?"

Czesich felt a small shudder go through him. This was too close to home. "I'd say it was just a mood. Middle age. It will pass."

Propenko released Czesich's elbow, stopped, and faced him, blocking the path. In the handsome face Czesich saw no threat now. Propenko was not a KGB stooge. Nor was he about to ask for asylum in America. Some intuition told him that a man of conscience stood before him. A good man. He had tricked himself into thinking the species extinct.

"Anton, yesterday the food was not supposed to go to West Vostok. I changed the list without authorization."

Czesich stiffened. Confession elicited confession; he wasn't ready.

"My family is in danger. I made a deal with the First Party Secretary. He would see that we were kept safe, and I would try to delay any deliveries to the miners and the church district, to save him embarrassment, to make it look like the food wasn't being given to his enemies —"

"Your family is in danger?"

Propenko nodded.

"Because of the food program?"

"In part. There are other parts —"

But Czesich wasn't listening for the other parts. "Your family was threatened because of the food?"

"Malov came to the house. He accused me of rape. He tried to delay the distribution — you saw that yourself."

"Rape?" Czesich said, but he was only playing for time. He could imagine the scenario quite clearly. Dealing with Malov would be like dealing with the mob. These people had their own, unshakable, ruthless code, far outside the law. And one time-honored tactic: they found out what frightened you most, and smiled, and held it up before your eyes.

Czesich understood, finally. What for him had been a drunken, altruistic whim was for Sergei Propenko and his family quite literally a matter of life and death. The presence of the man trailing them made sense now. It was the devil come to claim the soul of the American meddler.

He knew what he should do and he could not do it. Somehow, he knew what Propenko would say next.

"Anton, I want to ask a favor."

"Anything," Czesich said, and he could not remember speaking a more sincere word.

When they arrived at the pavilion, Czesich unlocked the containers and work started immediately, the lot ringed by the usual on-lookers and crisscrossed by the forklift and by laborers in their canvas-colored clothes. It looked as though Propenko and his co-conspirators had requisitioned every unused delivery truck in the city, fourteen in all. In addition to the two farm vehicles they'd been using, there were canvas-canopied trucks with PEOPLE stenciled on the back, a dump truck, an assortment of delivery vans whose drivers smoked and hung about, pretending not to look at the food. Six extra workers had been hired, and the containers emptied quickly. Czesich and Propenko stood off to one side, sweating together.

"Who else knows?"

"Leonid and Vzyatin," Propenko said. "Anatoly. A few people on the Strike Committee — they provided the trucks. Father Alexei — he's providing prayers."

They were both smoking, awkwardly. The first sharp nervousness had been replaced by something heavier, half adrenaline, half numbness. Czesich's body kept sending him false summonses to the toilet, and he kept looking over his shoulder, uphill toward the Prospekt, expecting to see Black Berets charging.

Malov, Propenko said, had been diverted to the train station on news of a nonexistent shipment of hashish — Vzyatin's idea. The King of Jazz had sneaked down there to give him a flat tire.

The customs rooster had been told that the distribution was being accelerated due to the weekend arrival of American dignitaries — Czesich's idea. The house of cards was a skyscraper now, one lie balanced upon the next, and Czesich watched the boxes being loaded and waited for it all to come crashing down.

After a time, the chief of militia approached, nodded to Czesich, and put his hand on Propenko's arm. "Can I have a minute, Sergei?"

"He knows, Victor," Propenko said, and Czesich was the recipient of a surprised, not altogether pleasant inspection. From their first meeting, at the railway station, the Chief had fixed him with this interrogator's gaze, trying to see into him, trying to make him nervous. Czesich thought it a crude and unfriendly tactic, something from a faded era. It did not hearten him to see Vzyatin playing such a big role in things.

"There are more than three thousand demonstrators at Party Headquarters," the Chief said to Propenko, as if Czesich were not there. "The Strike Committee told their people it was just a mass meeting. The food was not mentioned. It will be a surprise." He checked Propenko's face. "Anatoly has the loudspeaker."

Propenko had seemed partially in shock all morning, and at this news he only nodded and looked up at the ramp, where Leonid Fishkin paced and smoked and shouted the occasional order.

"Lvovich called the precinct as soon as he saw the size of the crowd. The precinct called me. I told them to tell him I was temporarily unavailable but that some extra men were being sent over."

Propenko nodded again.

"We're going to have to stage an arrest, Sergei. Once things are under way, I'm going to have to come by and take you out of there."

"Why?"

"For appearances' sake, so it looks like I'm doing my job."

Czesich did not like the sound of this at all. Either the Chief was on their side or he wasn't. If he was on their side, what was the point of pretending he wasn't? And who was going to be left standing in front of Party Headquarters when Propenko was carted off?

But Propenko had other things on his mind. "You're watching Lydia?"

"Lydia's at the church with Alexei. I have three men there. I have a captain near the army barracks with his hand on the radio. Bessarovich made some calls to her military friends. She's pleased. She guarantees nothing."

"You called Bessarovich?"

"Of course. I was up all night calling people. This isn't the kind of thing you do alone." Vzyatin glanced at Czesich, then back into Propenko's eyes. "A few of the miners are armed, apparently."

Hearing this, Czesich tried to snap the butt of his cigarette into the weeds in a nonchalant fashion, a tough-guy maneuver, but his fingers failed him and the cigarette popped straight up in the air like a doomed sputnik shot and dropped onto the toe of his shoe. The Chief noticed.

"You have men with Malov?" Czesich said, trying to recoup.

Vzyatin stared two seconds before deciding to answer. "At the station," he said, smiling as though he knew more about Czesich than Czesich wanted him to know. "We have professional liars there, lying to him." He glanced at the trucks and turned his eyes back to Propenko. "Time to go," he said. "Anatoly will lead. Tell him not to dawdle. Lvovich hears a rustling in the bushes now and we don't want to give him a chance to shoot."

"I have to talk to the workers," Propenko said.

"No time for that now."

"Thirty seconds, Victor."

Czesich was sweating down the inside of both arms, imagining old age in the Gulag archipelago. Vzyatin shot him a look, as if this talking-to-the-workers nonsense had been his idea, sloppy American democracy, but they both stood by and watched as Propenko called together the laborers and drivers. The old watchman invited himself. They huddled around Propenko as if he were a basketball coach giving instructions in overtime. Czesich watched as Propenko's mouth and eyes underwent the slightest alteration, and every strand of wavering attention snapped tight around him. All doubt, all possibility of misinterpretation evaporated with the first words, leaving only the facts: "We are delivering this food to the demonstrators in front of Party Headquarters," Propenko said.

"Unauthorized." He looked at each man in turn. "Volunteers in the trucks. Everyone else is free to leave."

Czesich could feel the pulse in his face. For six or eight beats, the tight circle of men just stared in disbelief, and for another thump or two he felt the whole house of cards wobbling under the weight of Soviet history, Soviet inertia, the ultimate Soviet rule — never, never, stand out from the *kollektiv*. They are going to cave now, he told himself. Sons and grandsons of the Gulag, they are going to cave.

He was wrong.

One driver simply turned his back and walked off. Two of the laborers — brothers, it appeared — stepped to one side and engaged in a vicious whispered argument, then went off in a different direction, avoiding the curious crowd and the militia guard, and striding quickly away into the city. But the rest of the men climbed into their trucks, leaving one vehicle driverless and the toothless Ivan with his bemedaled chest thrust out. "Sergei Sergeich," he said, at attention. "I was a driver in the war."

And it was done.

Propenko and Czesich got into the back seat of the Volga. Anatoly turned the key, glanced once in the mirror, and led the procession out of the parking lot, up the short access road to Prospekt Revoliutsii, and west toward Mikhail Kabanov's front lawn.

Czesich had planned to make his confession at this moment, to clear the slate. He choked on it. How could he tell Propenko, after watching him and the noble Ivan Ivanich, and after seeing the joyous explosion of light behind Anatoly's eyes, that the United States Government had pulled out — *aidus interruptus* — and that he himself was a well-meaning phony?

It didn't matter, he told himself. The thing had a momentum of its own now. The dice were in the air.

In what seemed like seconds, Czesich could see ahead to where the storefronts were interrupted by a block of green foliage. It became somewhat difficult to breathe. Propenko was squeezing a knee in each hand. He looked across the seat at Czesich and raised his eyebrows once.

Both hands on the wheel, eyes steady, Anatoly drove to the far end of the park, made a right turn, went up the block a hundred yards and made another turn — too fast now, bumping straight over the curb and sidewalk and a corner of the grass, past a knot of demonstrators, and onto the asphalt drive marked Party Vehicles.

Half a battalion of militiamen stared at the Volga and the line of trucks pulling in behind it and, to Czesich's astonishment, did absolutely nothing.

Propenko and Anatoly climbed out. Czesich took a breath, wiped his hands on his pants, and joined them, his back to the Volga and the militiamen, his stomach making noises. Julie was going to crucify him for this.

In front of him spread a rectangle of park with the customary statue of Lenin surrounded by the customary linden trees, peeling benches, stone urns overflowing with cigarette butts. Thousands of people stood on the lawn. Some of them were holding placards and banners, some just milling about facing the wrong way, cigarettes drooping from their lips. In the front left corner, five sallow-faced men and one emaciated woman sat on a strip of black plastic as though sitting was what they did for exercise. There was a bottle of water next to each of them. They regarded the trucks with dull suspicion.

The arrival of the convoy stirred the assembly like a ladle in thick soup. At first, people turned their heads and glared, half-interested, wary, but when it became apparent that this was not just another KGB intimidation tactic — that these were not Interior Ministry troops jumping down onto the driveway, but ordinary workers — the demonstrators were drawn gradually forward. Czesich saw a boy of no more than six come toward the front edge of the park holding a sign that said simply в OTCTABKY — RESIGN — as if the order were aimed indiscriminately at every single person in the building, as if what was needed now in the CCCP was nothing more than mass resignation, twenty million corpulent bureaucrats sent to their pensions. The crowd seemed peaceful, sleepy even, slightly perplexed, but, facing them, Czesich had to fight down a flutter of yesterday's panic. His body remembered.

Propenko stepped through the militia fencing, advanced as far as the edge of the grass, and waited there, holding the loudspeaker in his right hand, and squeezing the left behind his back. More and more demonstrators moved forward. In a minute, the front half of the park was packed tight with people.

Anatoly and Czesich stepped between two sections of the portable fencing and joined Propenko in no-man's-land. "Sergei," Anatoly said, "up."

Propenko hesitated, glanced once at the militia ranks standing silently by, then climbed onto the nearest bench. The hand was working feverishly behind his back now, and for a moment Czesich worried he would lift the loudspeaker to his mouth and spit silence. Czesich turned his head slightly so he could see the Party building out of the corner of his right eye. In one of those fifth-floor windows stood the man all these в ОТСТАВКУ signs were aimed at, the venomous Mikhail Lvovich Kabanov, one of only a handful of Brezhnev's Party bosses Gorbachev had been unable to chase out of office. Kabanov would be watching this tall, dark-haired man on the bench, and running down a list of lethal options. The tall, dark-haired man and everyone else in the park would know it.

The crowd noise settled and Propenko found words: "This is food from America," he said in a wavering voice, then he paused and cleared his throat and said it louder: "This is American food."

Now almost all the protestors were squeezed into the two triangles of lawn nearest the Party building. Beyond Lenin's statue, at the rear of the crowd, Czesich could see people climbing onto benches for a better view, passersby coming into the back end of the park, attracted by the scent of free market abundance.

Propenko fidgeted a moment, sweat on his forehead, then raised the bullhorn once again: "The American representative and I have decided" — he gestured nervously toward the six people sitting on the piece of plastic — "in honor of the hunger strikers, and in honor of . . . all hungry Soviet people . . . we have decided to distribute the food here today."

Czesich watched Propenko swallow. He swallowed, too. It was taking some time for the real message to sink in. An uncertain cheer went up from the front of the crowd, and he saw a few people begin swinging their placards, and someone waving the old Russian tricolor. He and Anatoly moved a step closer to each other and a few feet closer to the bench.

"We ask our comrades in the militia not to intervene," Propenko said, waiting for the echo to fade. "And we ask members of the Strike Committee" — he pointed at a row of bullnecked men in front of him — "to ensure that the distribution takes place in an orderly fashion. Yesterday in West Vostok we had a riot when we tried to deliver this food. People were injured and arrested. We want to avoid that here."

Propenko paused again, as though he knew he should say something else but was not sure what. The dark eyes shifted from one side of the park to the other. People were joining the crowd faster now, and Czesich heard voices trying to get a chant going: "*V-otSTAVku! V-otSTAVku!* Re-SIGN! Re-SIGN!" Propenko waved one hand, but there seemed little chance of saying anything else. He hesitated, glanced about, then raised his left fist, awkwardly, as if he were a puppet and half the strings had been snapped.

In response to the gesture, a deafening cheer went up, a thunder of *V-otSTAVku! V-otSTAVku! V-otSTAVku! V-otSTAVku!* The plac-ards bounced as though it were a political convention and the nominee for president had just been introduced. Czesich watched the way people were moving, the sudden understanding in their faces, the rage and blood vengeance, and the Times Square fear stirred in his guts again. He looked toward the street, expecting armored personnel carriers. He glanced behind him at the militia-men and saw, beneath the gray visors and stern expressions, half a battalion of frightened Russian boys. And there was reason to be frightened now. If this worked, within an hour or two, half the oblast would be assembled here, massing for their free American food. All of Vostok's palpable, subterranean anger would be gath-ered in this park, focused on this brown granite building with the red star on its roof; and the man in the fifth-floor office would be looking out, not on two or three thousand protestors, but on ten thousand, perhaps tens of thousands. At this moment, Kabanov was surely on the telephone to the army barracks, and some hard-assed colonel in charge there was saying yes or no, thumbs up or thumbs down, not according to law, but according to what he thought of Mikhail Lvovich, or which answer would serve him best down the road, or where he and his superiors stood in Russia's undeclared civil war. Now, from the building's long corridors and plush Party offices, any communist with a remaining undamaged brain cell would be fleeing out the back door. With one gesture, Propenko had called down a lightning strike on this building. Czesich would not have thought him capable of it.

Propenko was not finished. He waved the arm above his head and tried to add something, but the crowd went on with its chant-ing and shouting, and drowned him out. The bench was sur-rounded by men and women reaching up and trying to shake his hand. Anatoly had hold of Czesich by the arm and was yelling something, but his message was swallowed whole by another series of tremendous *V-otSTAVku! V-otSTAVku! V-otSTAVku!* and the air was full of the energy of several thousand people thrusting out their fists and doing a little two-step of imagined power. "Be careful, Anton Antonovich! Be careful now!" Anatoly was yelling. Czesich's heart was drumming. He could not get the smile off his face, or stop wondering what Michael would think if he could see this. He saw Propenko step down into the crowd and felt himself pressed forward against a line of men with huge shoulders, necks, and arms. Thick paws of flesh enveloped his hand, and people were hugging him and thanking him and blessing him and saying things he did not catch but nodded at anyway. Ivan Ivanich had abandoned his vehicle and fought through the crowd, and he came up and grabbed Czesich's face in both hands the way Grandpa Czesich used to do, and kissed him straight on the mouth. One of the miners wrapped them in a bear hug and Czesich was embraced as well by a sense of righteousness he had not known in many years. He wanted very badly to trust it.

Somehow, in the confusion and euphoria, he was separated first from the toothless old watchman and then from Anatoly. He caught sight of Propenko, his dark head sticking up above the crowd, fifty feet away. At exactly that moment, Propenko looked over at him and made the same modest arcing gesture with his eyebrows, as if the speech had been an aberration and now he would be happy to step out of the spotlight and back into his quiet family life. Already, he seemed to be sliding off toward the edge of the park, letting the miners' attention shift from him to the logistics of crowd control and the unloading of the trucks' potent cargo. Czesich called out to him, but his "Sergei, wait," was a squeak in a thunderstorm. Propenko held a clenched fist over his head and Czesich sent the same triumphant gesture back.

The chanting settled into a rhythm, as if preparing to go on for hours, and Czesich pushed more intently through the crowd. He did not know what he was going to do — surely this was no time for a confession — but he had an urge to say something, anything, to make some deeper connection.

As the unloading of food continued, people pressed toward the food, and this slow tide of bodies separated the two directors. Czesich shouldered his way cross-current, trying to keep Propenko in view.

A miner was in front of him, enthusiastically shaking his hand. Czesich tried to see beyond him, but the miner's face was very close, soot permanently embedded in the wrinkles around his eyes and in the pores of his forehead. The man was thanking him, congratulating him. Czesich caught the word "Chernobyl." The miner was saying he'd been one of the first volunteers to tunnel beneath the exploded reactor and seal the rods in concrete. He didn't want any of the food, he claimed, let the others have it, he would die soon anyway. What mattered here was the gesture. "It's a great thing you've done," he said. "A wonderful thing. America heard us."

"Yes," Czesich told him. "Yes, of course."

People were chanting, *"V-otstavku, V-otstavku,"* all around them and pushing toward the trucks and grazing Czesich with their elbows as their signs moved up and down. He went up on his toes three times with several shuffling, shoving yards of progress between, and saw only that Propenko was not where he had been. The piles of food were growing tall in the driveway, and more and more people were coming in through the gates, and the front rank of demonstrators was jostling the corral fencing that separated them from the food and the steps of the Party building. In place of the paralyzed militia, the miners themselves had activated a guerrilla network of crowd controllers, heavyweights standing with their backs to the food and shoving people into formations that vaguely resembled orderly lines.

Czesich pushed and squeezed against the grain, making headway yard by yard. When he was two-thirds of the way across the park he looked up and saw a bus pull to the curb trailed by a blue-and-yellow Volga with MILITIA printed on its door. No one else seemed to notice, or care. Thirty men in gray uniforms poured out of the bus and formed a line at the edge of the park, and still no one but Czesich and a few sidewalk wallflowers seemed aware of them. The crowd had stalled now against the fencing; bunched tight, eyes forward. Marooned, Czesich stood on his toes again and finally caught sight of Propenko, almost on the sidewalk. Two of the newly arrived militiamen were talking with him. After a moment, the three of them turned and moved off toward the Volga, and Czesich hobbled after them on his gimpy knee, losing ground, ears ringing. Three heavy women formed a wall in front of him. He tried getting around them, but at that moment a gate was opened in the corral fencing and one whole sector of the mob surged forward, sweeping him along for a few steps before he was able to extricate himself and back away.

He climbed onto a bench and caught a final glimpse of Propenko. Two men and a woman were blocking the path to prevent his arrest, and Propenko seemed to be trying to reason with them.

He seemed, along with his police captors, to be politely trying to push past, toward the line of uniforms. Czesich could only watch. Propenko ducked past his defenders, disappeared behind the militia column, and a minute later Czesich saw the blue-and-yellow Volga turn onto the Prospekt and speed away. He looked down at the excited crowd, at the workers and miners and a few militiamen trying to force people to wait patiently for their allotment of food. He glanced up at the fifth-floor windows, then at the sidewalk that ran along the eastern edge of the park and saw Nikolai Malov standing alone there, looking straight at him. Czesich pretended he was a waiter at one of the huge state restaurants and let his eyes drift up, over Malov's head, then swing gradually back toward the piles of American food.

// CHAPTER 31

OLEG, the Chief's driver, cut the siren when they were out of earshot of Party Headquarters, but he kept the Volga headed in the direction of the Central Precinct — for appearances' sake, Propenko supposed.

Vzyatin was lounging on the driver's side of the back seat with a huge smug smile on his face. Thanks to Bessarovich's military friends, the Black Berets were staying in their barracks. Propenko's "arrest" had been timed perfectly to coincide with the first mad scramble for food. The militia, the miners, even the demonstrators — everyone had responded exactly as Vzyatin had said they would.

"Where to, Your Highness?"

Propenko laughed a laugh that was not his own. Vzyatin's glowing self-assurance was trying to stretch across the seat and take hold of him, but he felt himself resisting; he kept picturing the Chief in Sochi, drunk, slobbering over a nineteen-year-old girl. His wet shirt stuck to his chest. Raisa would think he'd gone mad. "Where's Lydia?"

"Still at the church."

"And you have someone with her?"

"Of course, Sergei. Not actually *in* the church, naturally — we're not sacrilegious — but there are plainclothes officers standing guard outside. My best people are with her and with Raisa at the dacha. I'm with you. How do you feel?"

"Numb."

"That's natural. We expected that. You did a fine job."

Propenko shrugged. He glanced at the dark back of Oleg's head, as though Vzyatin's trusted driver might suddenly pull to the curb, turn around in his seat, and transform himself into Mikhail Lvovich Kabanov, all huge ears and vicious smile. What he had done had been done in a speeding dream. What he needed now was a few slow hours to stand apart from it and think.

"I want to talk with Lydia."

"To the Sacred Blood, Oleg," Vzyatin said over the seat.

Oleg changed lanes.

"I should have stayed," Propenko said. "Anton Antonovich is there alone."

Vzyatin was vigorously shaking his head. "Generals don't fight in the trenches, Seryozha. Anything can happen with that many people in one place. Anything."

"Then why leave the American?"

Vzyatin didn't answer.

"He's a good man, Victor."

"Not as good as you think," Vzyatin said cryptically, but Propenko was not in a mood to indulge the Chief's omniscience, and he let the subject drop and turned his face out the side window. He supposed he should be grateful — nothing would have been possible without Vzyatin's experience and connections. Still, a vague unease tapped out its background tune. The mysterious allusions; Vzyatin's reluctance to warn the workers and Anton Antonovich where the trucks were headed; the "generals in the trenches" line; the fact that, from the moment the idea was mentioned, he'd taken charge, calling Bessarovich and the miners, giving orders, not really saying much about the possible consequences. If this was their new democracy, then the future would not be much different from the past.

"Lvovich is finished," the Chief said. "He called the barracks, and Colonel Kudrin turned him down flat, no explanation. Even the Berets are betting against him now."

Propenko faced him again. "How do you know all this?"

"I know," Vzyatin said, and when Propenko kept staring, he added: "We have people inside, Seryozha, in his office. I tried to tell you that this morning, but you were in dreamland."

"Who's 'we'?"

"We is us," Vzyatin said. "Bessarovich is with Yeltsin. I'm with Bessarovich. You're with me."

Out the Chief's window Propenko saw a schoolteacher leading a perfectly straight line of eight-year-olds down the sidewalk.

The radio crackled. Vzyatin leaned forward and listened for a few seconds, then sat back. "Lvovich is getting calls from Moscow now saying, 'Misha, time to step aside.' His deputies are quitting, one after the next. He has American food being handed out to his enemies, and the American ambassador coming to visit, and five thousand pissed-off people in the park. He's finished."

Propenko shook his head in very small movements. Mikhail Lvovich had been a mountain on the Vostok landscape for so long he found it impossible to imagine his actual disappearance. The city would be flooded with light.

"You and Leonid doubt me," Vzyatin said. "Lvovich is about to crack, I'm telling you. If I wasn't one hundred percent sure, I would never have let you take the risk you took today."

Propenko did not believe in being one hundred percent sure, about anything. He glanced at Oleg's flat eyes in the rearview mirror, then at his friend the Chief. Now, of all times, he felt as skeptical as Raisa. "So the Ambassador's really coming?"

"*You* told *me* he was coming."

"Anton Antonovich didn't mention it this morning, though."

"My sources tell me a request was made from the American Embassy, Moscow, for a diplomatic visa to Vostok. What do you think that means?"

Propenko relaxed a bit. If Lvovich did, in fact, resign. If the miners — his new allies — filled the city government with their own people. If Malov could somehow be controlled, or arrested. If Bessarovich's patrons did, in fact, gain more influence in the capital. . . .

"Oleg made a phone call very early this morning," Vzyatin went on slyly when they'd traveled another block. "From the precinct."

Propenko glanced in the mirror again. Oleg often acted mute; now he was acting deaf as well. Perhaps the phone call had to do with new wires for an '87 Lada.

"To one Mikhail Lvovich Kabanov," Vzyatin said. He seemed on the verge of laughing.

Propenko squeezed out three words. "And said what?"

"And said: 'Respected Comrade First Secretary, if harm comes to the American food, or to anyone involved in its delivery, or to the priest, or to the priest's friends, we will cut off your balls and hang them from the flagpole in Lenin Square.' " He reached forward and put a hand on the driver's shoulder. "Accurate quotation, Oleg?"

Oleg nodded.

Propenko felt Vzyatin's fingers squeezing the back of his neck, a gesture he had never liked. "We thought Oleg was the logical choice, since no one but his wife has ever heard him speak."

A drunk waiting to cross the street eyed the Chief's car as it went past, his true feelings revealed by the vodka, his face reflecting a century of contempt for the militia's beatings and bribe taking. Sober people looked the other way; drunks stared. None of them, Propenko thought, could imagine this.

"What did Lvovich say?"

"Nothing." Vzyatin chuckled. "Too sleepy. . . . And if you don't cheer up pretty soon I'm going to take you over to the gym and put the gloves on you and knock you down a few times. What's the matter?"

Propenko shook his head and tried to smile. He looked straight at Vzyatin finally, and saw nothing but goodwill on his friend's face. "I'm recovering," he said.

"Well, recover faster."

"What about Malov?"

Vzyatin's lamp dimmed a bit. "Malov is complicated, as it turns out. You were right. I talked to Bessarovich this morning, the minute you drove away from the pavilion with the food. She's calling people, she says she has some ideas, but Malov is a problem. He seems to operate . . . independently."

"Even the *komitet* is not what it seems," Propenko said.

"Especially the *komitet*. What's important now is to act as if you have friends in Moscow — which you do. Maintain your normal schedule. Go to the dacha for the weekend. We'll keep Malov away from you. For the time being, you and I have to act as if nothing can touch us. In a few days that will be the actual truth."

"I'm worried about Lydia."

"We're on Lydia like a shadow. We're on Alexei like two shadows — he tried to come to the park and we wouldn't let him."

"She wanted to take Anton Antonovich to Leskovo and show him the church."

"Fine."

"She wanted to go by commuter boat."

"Not a problem."

"I told him it wouldn't be a good idea."

Vzyatin patted him on the leg. "You're the father."

Oleg turned off onto the long side street that led to the churchyard gate, and the Volga bounced and rattled on the rougher road. "We're at the end of something now, Sergei," Vzyatin said. "All we have to do is hold on for a few days."

Oleg pulled the car up in front of the gate, got out, and scouted the churchyard to see that his colleagues were at their posts.

"I'm not made for this," Propenko said.

"Nonsense, Seryozha. You're a hero. When this chapter is finished, all kinds of things will open up for you. You should be celebrating your future."

Propenko had done that already, two weeks ago to the day. The memory kept him wary.

"There are elections next spring. Congress of People's Deputies. You should consider running. After today, you'll have the backing of every miner in the oblast, as well as some important Moscow types."

Propenko shook his head. "All these years and you still don't know me, Victor."

"You don't know yourself."

"I'm not political."

"Five hundred miners would argue otherwise."

They stared across the seat at each other for a few seconds. Propenko had new words in his throat now. He was wondering why Vzyatin didn't run for the Congress of People's Deputies, why *his* child and wife and mother-in-law didn't require protection. Why the Chief had worked behind the scenes with Bessarovich without telling his closest friends. How Vzyatin could have done what he'd done with Lydia and looked him in the face all these months as though nothing had happened.

"You always feel mixed after something like this, Sergei. It's understandable. If you didn't, you wouldn't be an adult. You'd be like one of the demonstrators in the park, waving flags and yelling."

"I thought we were on their side."

Vzyatin shrugged.

Oleg returned and signaled that everything was in order. Vzyatin escorted Propenko as far as the church gate, one hand on his elbow. Every message sent by the Chief's body, every gesture and cast of eye said the same thing: We're different from other people, Seryozha, you and I. We stand above. That's simply the way things are. Vzyatin stopped at the gate as if held there by a superstition, as if he were afraid Isus Khristos might usurp some of his extraordinariness if he got too close. "What did you do to convince the American to go along?" he said, grinning. "No strong-arm methods, I hope."

Propenko grinned back and lifted his eyebrows once, resisting.

"Really," Vzyatin said. "I want to know. For professional reasons."

"My secret, Victor."

The Chief laughed — approvingly, Propenko thought — and promised to wait and see that he got a ride to the dacha.

Propenko walked past the small graveyard where his father-in-law was buried, past the spot where Tikhonovich's body had been found, and up the three wooden steps. He rapped on the old door and waited. No one answered. He knocked again and ran his eyes over the churchyard until he spotted one of Lydia's bodyguards there, standing at a gravestone like a mourner. The man nodded at him. Propenko nodded back and the door opened.

"Pa!"

"Are you busy?"

Lydia reached up on her toes to kiss him. "Come in."

Propenko stepped into a dim vestibule. Beyond another open doorway he could see flickering candles and part of one icon-covered wall, and this sight and the smell of incense and candle wax awakened in him a herd of sleeping memories. It had been forty years since he'd set foot inside a church.

"What's wrong?"

"Nothing," he said quietly, the uneasy atheist.

"We heard about the food," Lydia whispered. Her face was lit from within in a way Propenko had never seen before. "Father Alexei has been praying for you and Anton Antonovich all day."

"Is he better?"

Lydia nodded, still shining.

Leonid had said to him once that the challenge of parenthood was to endure the gradual annihilation of your children's worship of you, and Propenko had remembered, and resisted, the idea all through Lydia's adolescence. Now it seemed absolutely correct, and he did his best not to snuff out her happiness and not to give himself too large a role in it. There had been altogether too much adulation in this country — the feudal lord, the czar, the State, Lenin, Stalin, tyrants of all shapes and sizes. It had turned Russia into a land of perpetual children.

"I just wanted to come by and see you for a minute, just to see the church, to say hello," he said, but it was not really true. He'd intended to come here and convince her to spend the weekend at the dacha, but something had happened at Party Headquarters and in Vzyatin's car. The serf in him had been freed at last, and, shackles broken, he found he had no need to chain anyone else. For one moment, he felt as though *he* were the child, letting go of the chair leg and risking a wobbly independence. He wondered if Lydia could sense it. She seemed different here, and at first he thought it was simply because they were meeting on her territory for once, away from the places where he had always been the father and she had always been the child. But it was something else. Lydia was Lydia; *he* had changed. A new space separated them, and he had to fight down an urge to reach across it and hug her, to close the distance again until she was once more a part of him, one of his reluctant republics.

He took a breath and tried to relinquish every bit of power. "It might not be such a good idea to take the American to Leskovo after what happened today."

She looked at him for a second, cocked her head, seemed to be trying to figure out this new voice.

"If you want to go, Victor said he can protect you, but it might not be the best thing this weekend. It's up to you."

Footsteps sounded inside the church. Lydia's lips stretched in the smallest of smiles. "You're not going to try to make me come to the dacha?"

"No," Propenko said, and he saw that, at last, they had broken the mold of their own private history, more important to him than a thousand *v-otstavkus*.

"Do you want to meet Alexei?" she said, and he fancied there was something novel in this "you" she'd aimed up at him. He nodded, and let her take his arm.

The nave swam in watery yellow light. A stooped old *babushka* stood at the back wall with a pair of men's glasses resting halfway down her nose. Near the altar, on the immaculate wooden floor, knelt Alexei, frail and white-haired, with a long, thin, uneven beard. The sight of him swept Propenko backwards. He was in a humble wooden church — long since destroyed — in the section of the city called Makeyevka, and the church was filled, as always on Sundays in those years, with women whose sons and husbands had died in the war. In the last months before she'd lost the ability to walk and had been forced to confine her religious impulses to quiet Bible reading and not-so-quiet lectures at the dinner table, his paternal grandmother had started bringing him with her to that church. He'd been five or six years old, and what he remembered most was the bearded priest, tall as a giant, who said everything in a very loud, deep voice and kept disappearing through a door behind the altar. There was a room beyond that door, his grandmother told him afterward, a room where Isus Khristos lived with all the people who had passed through the gate of death. The priest went back there to talk with Isus Khristos, who was God, and who was always watching over Sergei, night and day, and who would actually kiss him and hold him when he died, many many years in the future.

The young Sergei did not understand how Isus Khristos could watch over him night and day from that back room, or how his uncle and all the other people who had died in the war could fit in there behind the altar. But each time the priest opened the door to come in or go out, he'd strain forward for a glimpse of the crowded, mysterious place. Once, he even broke free of his grandmother's grasp and slipped off toward the side wall, hoping for a better angle, and one of the old *babushki* had caught him, wagged her finger in his face, and shaken his shoulder until he cried.

Lydia was tugging on his elbow, and he went forward bashfully, his shoes making too much noise on the spotless, painted boards. She knelt a meter or so to Alexei's right, and Propenko joined her there, casting one quick glance at the priest's face. The scratches on his knees hurt against the hard floor — a reminder of West Vostok — and he experienced a passing worry that, in kneeling here with his daughter, he might be playing yet another role for her, or propping up yet another edifice to take the place of the one he'd just abandoned. But he clasped his hands and bowed his head and offered up something much like a prayer — for Raisa and Lydia and Marya Petrovna. For himself. For Anton Antonovich. For the eventual liberation of Mother Russia.

// CHAPTER 32

CZESICH awoke sweating, and stared for several minutes at the backlit curtains and yellowed hotel ceiling before the echoes of the dream left him. There had been Black Berets with Kalashnikovs slung over their shoulders, and a woman who reminded him of Marie, buying fruit in a supermarket. There had been men with angry eyes, like Malov's, and the American Embassy's rat-warren hallways, without exit.

The telephone emitted a single, jarring ring, then went quiet. He could hear a television barking in the room above. His right knee and the middle of his back ached. The taut purse of his bladder and the film on his tongue and teeth were urging him out of bed, but he lay perfectly still beneath the sheet, listening, convinced that, outside in the gray city, Lvovich's deputies were stalking him.

He had stayed late at the demonstration — long after all the food had been handed out — talking to the miners, hoping some of their solid, quiet dignity would rub off on him. For a while, he'd squatted next to the female hunger striker and let her paint for him, in a daubing of hoarse sentences, the ugly portrait of Vostok city government. "Kabanov is a wounded lion now," she told him. "He could slink off into the jungle and die. He could lash out. You must be very careful."

Aside from staying in his room and staying sober, Czesich could not imagine what being careful meant under these circumstances. The bloom of righteousness he'd worn in front of Party Headquarters yesterday, the high of having his hand shaken by a hundred ordinary Soviets, of hearing people thank him and praise him and, in two cases, ask for his autograph — he had lost none of that overnight. Grandpa Czesich was smiling down at him from heaven, and, somewhere in his core, a portion of shame had been exchanged for a portion of satisfaction. But he was coming to understand that, by definition, there was a price to be paid for even the smallest heroism. In this country things had blood on them. You hurt people, and inevitably got hurt in return.

He climbed out of bed, finally, but a viscous, shifting fear hung around him as he bathed and shaved and dressed. Hungry as he was, he could not imagine actually unlocking the door and stepping out into the corridor. He pictured Malov waiting for him down the hall, or Bobin with some kind of official eviction notice, or the First Secretary leading a team of KGB thugs ready to beat him and drag him off to jail.

After pacing the suite for a few minutes, he took out Propenko's business card, dialed the scribbled home number and counted fifteen rings. It was Saturday morning. No doubt the family was at the dacha. He hung up and dialed again on the chance the lines had gotten crossed.

A bit more pacing and fretting and he tried Propenko a third time, then called the operator and asked for a line to Moscow. "No long-distance lines," she told him. "No long-distance lines since last night."

"What's the problem?" His imagination was going psychedelic. Coups d'état. Assassinations. Radical Ukrainian separatists blowing up bridges and power lines. He wondered if Propenko had been arrested overnight and was at this moment being interrogated in State Security headquarters.

"*Avaria,*" the operator said. "Emergency. A problem with the Vostok transfer station."

"When will it be fixed?"

"Who knows? Soon."

"Soon? An hour, a day?"

"Soon. Try back."

"But I'm calling the American Embassy. It's urgent."

She asked him to hold. After he'd held for fifteen seconds the line clicked and went dead.

In the clutches of a muscular paranoia now, Czesich tried Propenko one more time — no answer; then the operator — busy; then took his suitcase out from under the bed and began, rather hastily, to pack. He had a return train ticket, some money, plenty of *Marlbara*. . . . But, after a minute of folding T-shirts and boxer shorts into the suitcase, he made himself stop. It seemed wrong to run, and unnecessary. He was an American with a diplomatic passport, what was the worst they could do to him? The worst they could do was arrest him, try to intimidate him, and ship him up to the embassy, where other people would try to intimidate him — in his own language, at least — then ship him home. That was it.

Maybe the curse of the empty stomach was making him crazy again.

He put the suitcase away, found a bottle of mineral water in the refrigerator and drank it down. Vostok's only television station was broadcasting the Saturday-morning aerobics class. He clicked it off, roughly, and as if the two appliances were connected, the phone rang. He made himself answer it.

"Anton Antonovich?"

The voice was male and coarse and vaguely familiar. Czesich struggled to connect it to a face. "Listening to you," he said.

"This is Yefrem Alexandrovich at the front door, disturbing you. There is a young Lydia Sergeievna here. Excuse me, but I am not permitted to let her in."

And she is refusing to bribe you, Czesich thought, and you're hoping you can wring a pack of cigarettes out of me.

Stepping out into the quiet hallway, he was required to do battle with an overstimulated imagination. Scenarios from cheap spy novels tormented him — the doorman's call was a setup; the whole delivery had been a setup from the beginning; they were going to kidnap him now, torture him until he revealed the name of his CIA boss at the embassy.

But, aside from the lack of a newspaper outside his door, the corridor was no different than on any other morning. His *dezhurnaya* acknowledged him with a neutral nod — nothing suspicious, nothing unusual. Apparently she had not yet gotten word from Bobin to freeze out the American troublemaker. The curving stairs were lit by milky sunlight, the stone landing speckled with three stars of dried blood — badge of Friday night's drunken revelry, nothing unusual there either. The lobby stood empty except for the bulky Yefrem Alexandrovich in his dandruff-dusted uniform, who hurried over, all apologies. There were strict rules about allowing local people into the foreigners' hotel, he explained. We've been having problems with black marketeers preying on businessmen, making their stay in Vostok unpleasant. A few prostitutes, as well. This Lydia Sergeievna looked like a perfectly upstanding young woman, of course, but rules were rules. He was only trying to do his duty. He hoped Anton Antonovich understood.

Czesich thanked him and said he understood perfectly. Yefrem Alexandrovich seemed disappointed.

Lydia was standing outside, bare-legged in the patio sunlight. They shook hands cordially and walked a safe distance away from the door before speaking. "I thought our date was canceled."

"*Disinformatsia,*" she said, and Czesich could see that the doorman had not succeeded in dampening her spirits. She was wearing a pleated, knee-length blue skirt and a flowered white blouse, and she seemed especially happy this morning, at ease, at home on these streets. The mood was medicinal.

"Can we walk?" She gestured down the Prospekt.

Spurred on by a jolt of masculine pride — sponsor of many an unhappy venture — Czesich agreed without hesitation. What could they do to him, he asked himself once again. Suppose he bumped into Malov. What, actually, could Malov do? Shoot him?

The instant they were past the corner of the hotel, Lydia put her hands on his lapels and stopped him in his tracks. Her face was positively giving off light now, and Czesich assumed she was going to plant a kiss on his cheek and thank him for yesterday's delivery, but she blurted out: "Kabanov has resigned!"

He came close to wetting his pants. "How?" His hands were up on her shoulders, and he thought for a minute they were going to turn a dos-à-dos right there on the Prospekt sidewalk.

"He was seen leaving the city with his family before dawn!"

"By whom?"

"A member of the Strike Committee!"

"Maybe he was just heading off to his dacha for the weekend."

Lydia shook her head and laughed. "Someone else brought Father Alexei the same news from Party Headquarters. It's going to be on television tonight! He's gone! His office has been cleaned out!"

She embraced him in the completely innocent manner of young Soviet women, pressing her breasts and face against him and squeezing her arms round his ribs. Czesich squeezed back, then turned her in a slow, victorious waltz. Beneath the customary blank expressions of their fellow pedestrians, he was sure he detected some kind of collective jubilation. Not that anyone but the foolish foreigner and the overexcited girl was actually smiling. These people walking past were Soviets, after all, gold-medal pessimists, masters of the hidden emotion. But the secret grin was there; he was almost sure of it.

They released each other and drifted down the block, Lydia practically skipping, Czesich already imagining himself meeting Julie at the airport with a bouquet of flowers. Julie would love him for this. If she didn't love him for this, all was lost.

"We should go to the park, Anton. You'll be a hero there."

"Your father's the hero. He stood up on the bench in Lvovich's front yard and gave a speech. All I did was watch."

"*My* father did that?"

"Very capably."

She asked for a description of the events in the park, and Czesich was glad to oblige her. There was no need for embellishment, he said, her father was a man of genuine courage — moral and physical. By the time they'd gone three blocks she was blushing with pride, and Czesich, excited by the retelling, was being carried along on a little wave of self-esteem-by-association. His earlier panic seemed foolish here on the bright avenue with its trolleys rumbling back and forth. The day was mild, the streets calm. And, as though such things entered the visible spectrum only when evil first secretaries went *v-otstavku*, or as though Lydia's presence had somehow brought them into being, he noticed now that delicate trees stood at fifty-yard intervals along the curb, that there were potted flowers in many of the first-floor windows, and neatly dressed parents strolling by with young children — not shopping or queuing or making deals or arguing about the Party, just strolling — part of a sea of ordinary existence shifting lightly back and forth beneath the political storms.

"What if we just rode past the park on the bus instead of walking," he suggested. "I don't like big crowds before lunch."

Lydia laughed. "This is the market route. The buses are packed on Saturdays."

"How about a cab, then?"

"Robbers."

As they were discussing it, an impossibly crowded bus pulled up a few yards in front of them. They glanced at each other, then made a dash for it and squeezed up the steps. Just as the door snapped shut, Czesich sensed something on the sidewalk behind him. It was not even a thought, just a thought-shadow, an intuition, a scent of malice in the knot of waiting women. He wrote it off to paranoia.

Lydia was giggling. Czesich's right elbow was pressed into his neighbor's cleavage — the woman didn't seem to mind — his right leg entangled in an undergrowth of boots and bags, his chest heaving from their ten-yard sprint; his left arm was halfway around his pretty companion and clinging to the back of someone's seat. With each stop, each brutal exchange of bodies up and down the steps and up and down the aisle, he and Lydia were pressed, torsos twisting, further toward the rear window. Now they were pinched tight against each other, side to side, her handbag squeezed between their knees. She reached her mouth up close to his ear and said, "My chaperon."

He smiled, flattered back to his twenties, but she swung her eyes out the window at a militia car hugging tight to the bus's bumper. "My father arranged it."

"You're being followed?"

"Constantly," she whispered, as though it were a game. "Sometimes they're in uniform, sometimes not."

Czesich felt the fear drain out of him. "I sensed something. Back there on the sidewalk."

"They probably assigned someone to you, too, after yesterday."

He said he hoped so. The bus leaned and groaned and hauled its cargo westward. Opposite Party Headquarters, the driver slowed and switched lanes, and Czesich — pushed flat against the rear window — was treated to the sight of men and women singing and dancing drunkenly and waving their placards. The park was completely full, the mood approaching pandemonium. A few dozen people had spilled across the southern edge of the lawn onto the sidewalk, mixing there with curious passersby and a row of militiamen who were working to keep them out of the street. The scene struck him as astoundingly un-Soviet, so much exuberance, so much emotion right there in plain view, a happy anomaly he might never witness again. He grabbed Lydia's arm. "Let's go," he said. "I have to see it."

It took them two stops to work their way back to the door. The fighting was fiercest there, with newcomers crushed against each other on the narrow steps, reaching for a handful of rail, hanging on while one buttock or one elbow stuck out between the rubber door edges. There was not room enough for half another passenger, but when the bus squealed up to the next stop, a wave of hopefuls assaulted both doors. Czesich turned sideways, pushing against the tide, and made it as far as the top step. He ducked his head, leaned streetward, and took one giant stride into a sea of shoulders and chests. The mob cushioned him, but his foot struck just on the edge of the curb, and his bad knee twisted down and in, setting off a blaze of pain beneath the patella. Lydia was right behind him. She'd lost a button from the top of her blouse, but was otherwise whole. They rested a moment on the sill of a shopwindow.

"Do you have that in America, Anton?"

"Same sport. Different weight class."

With Czesich favoring his right leg, they backtracked three blocks and mingled with the other onlookers at the edge of the park. He needn't have worried about being singled out. There was no chanting or speeches, no organized activity of any kind save the row of militiamen along the curb. People were drinking from communal champagne bottles, singing, strutting about, and it seemed to him they wanted nothing more than what he wanted: just to be present at this. He had the feeling they'd all carried their private wounds and resentments here in order to set them free in a mass rite of public soul-cleansing. This cloud of collective bad history would rise over Party Headquarters, drift off in whatever direction the First Secretary had fled, and haunt him for the rest of his miserable life.

"I wonder if your father knows," he said to Lydia, who was holding his arm, still radiant.

"They're at the dacha. Someone will tell him."

"You don't want to go downriver still, do you?"

She shook her head.

"Let's go out to the dacha and all celebrate together."

The idea earned him another hug. It was nice, this being hugged by a pretty woman and not being sexually stirred. It was different, part of his new self, a gift from the liberated city of Vostok.

"One problem," he said when Lydia released him.

"What?"

"If I don't get something to eat within the next half hour, I'm going to turn into some kind of crazy, wild, vicious American monster that — "

She stopped him. "I have a plan, Anton. We'll go to the private market and buy something for lunch and something to bring to the dacha for dinner. We'll stop by the church and say a prayer . . . if you don't mind."

"Not at all. I'll light a candle to Saint Jude."

"We'll catch the four o'clock train and be at the dacha in time for dinner. Everybody will be happy."

Lydia was smiling, squeezing the spray of freckles across her nose. Two or three of the people standing nearby had overheard this schedule of celebration, and, beneath their masks, they seemed to Czesich to be smiling as well.

// CHAPTER 33

AT THEIR DACHA, the Propenko family had a Saturday-morning ritual: breakfast, a walk to the river, then an hour or two of work in the vegetable plot that occupied every square meter of the small backyard. Their garden — potatoes, tomatoes, carrots, radishes, onions, cabbages, cucumbers — was cultivated as a buffer against hard times, and helped feed the family well into winter. This morning, though, it was not the promise of carrots in January that sent them out into the hot sun, but the fact that it had become unbearable to sit in the house, alone or together, and wait for news from the city.

"The potatoes have bugs," Raisa said, slicing a spotted beetle in half with one thumbnail. It was the first thing she'd said since breakfast.

Marya Petrovna climbed the back steps and began washing onions in a bucket of well water.

"The soil is dry," Propenko said. Raisa was crouching only a few meters away, and he wanted to keep the conversation going. "It rains in the city every day. Fifty kilometers away we have a desert."

She seemed not to have heard.

"The smoke from the factories makes it rain in the city," Marya Petrovna said from the porch. "Years ago, when it rained in the city, it rained here. Not now."

"Chernobyl," Propenko suggested.

"All those sputniks puncturing the atmosphere," Marya Petrovna said. "All that coal smoke."

Raisa didn't look at them. After a minute, she stood, brushed dirt from her dress, and went past her mother and into the house.

When, after fifteen minutes, Raisa had not reappeared, Marya Petrovna sighed loudly, a signal. Propenko went up the steps and through the back door, and found his wife standing at the stove pretending to have something in her eye. He stood close behind her and put a hand on either side of her waist. They had argued late into the night, made peace, argued again, cursed Mikhail Lvovich and his corrupt friends, cursed the city of Vostok and the day they'd been born there, fought about the food delivery and what it might lead to, fought about Vzyatin, and Malov, worried about Anton Antonovich, superstitiously avoided mentioning Lydia's name. Now that a real concrete step had been taken, now that Propenko had so conspicuously chosen sides, even Marya Petrovna, family militant, seemed to be having second thoughts.

"You should make a big dinner anyway," Propenko said. "Maybe she'll surprise us."

Raisa nodded, clutching a potato in one hand like a talisman.

Propenko squeezed her hips. "I was thinking about getting out the last of Tolkachev's wine. I was thinking it would help us to drink something."

"All right, Sergei."

What he really had in mind was for all of them to spend the afternoon taking the classic Russian cure: drinking Tolkachev's bittersweet cranberry wine by the liter, sitting out on the dacha's front porch and handing themselves over to an alcoholic blur. He'd taken his hands from Raisa's waist and turned in the direction of the root cellar when the voice of the winemaker himself sounded out by the garden.

Tolkachev was babbling loudly to Marya Petrovna, but the only words Propenko caught were "holiday" and "unbelievable." He walked toward the screen door to see what all the commotion was about, and was presented with the spectacle of his seventy-one-year-old neighbor bounding up the stairs and across the porch like a teenager. The door was yanked open before Propenko could even say "Vladimir Victorovich," and the physicist stood there framed in worn wood, chest heaving, thick eyeglasses slipping down his nose, his small eyes bulging. "Small Sergei . . . ," he huffed, "Raisa Maximovna. . . . Satan has been . . . chased . . . from the garden!"

The reference touched only a faint chord in Propenko's memory. For a moment, he thought Tolkachev was referring to a neighbor's dog, or that he'd taken his medicine with vodka again and was raving. He glanced at Raisa, who seemed to have almost understood, to be one step ahead of him, flushed with some quick, hopeful fever.

Tolkachev was having trouble catching his breath. He'd stepped into the kitchen, and his arms were thrown wide as if anticipating a hug. "Kabanov," he said loudly, straight into Propenko's face, "has fled!"

"No!"

"Yes! . . . *V-otstavku!*"

Raisa shrieked.

Propenko wasted two seconds checking Tolkachev's eyes for madness, then grabbed the old man around the thighs, lifted him as though he'd just been declared featherweight champion, and paraded him back and forth in the kitchen with his head nearly scraping the ceiling. Tolkachev was thumping ecstatically on Propenko's shoulders. Raisa and Marya Petrovna were kissing each other's faces, then holding both hands and doing a Ukrainian dance step; then Propenko had his arms around Raisa, and Tolkachev, still puffing and gasping, was trying to get Marya Petrovna to let him kiss her on the mouth. Raisa turned on the radio and twisted the dial in search of news. Propenko climbed down into the root cellar, and, seeing that there was not one, but two big jars of Tolkachev's wine left, he crouched low in the dank cubicle, made his hands into fists, and dodging and weaving as much as the cramped space allowed, pummeled an imaginary midsection until the other fighter's legs gave out. He crouched a bit lower, dropped his right shoulder, shot out with a sneaky uppercut that snapped his opponent's head back, then continued up, up, and smashed into the beam that supported the kitchen floor.

Forget January. They ate the vegetables they'd spent the morning picking. Raisa boiled a potful of potatoes, sliced them into dishes of sour cream, mixed in some onion and a bit of radish, and served it with Tolkachev's wine and a loaf of dark bread.

Propenko sat with a dishcloth full of ice wrapped around his bruised right hand, drinking more than he ate, looking out at the road. Marya Petrovna was referring to him as the "dumb boxer" again. Raisa was smiling. The family was almost what it had been.

Tolkachev had moved a lap ahead of everyone else in the drinking. "More where this came from," he kept saying as Propenko refilled the glasses. "More where that came from." When the plates were cleared, he announced an anecdote.

"Mikhail Lvovich Kabanov," he began professorially, pulling his shoulders back and sticking his meager chest out as far as it would go, "in the spirit of the New Thinking, decides to go to America and talk with Dzheordzh Boosh and see if there's anything he can learn from the son-of-a-bitch capitalist connivers." Tolkachev pushed his glasses up against the bridge of his nose, leaned back in his chair for effect, and came within a centimeter of toppling over backwards. "He travels to America," he went on, when Marya Petrovna had helped him right himself, "to the White House on *Pinsalvahnya Ahvinyu*, and asks Boosh what is the secret. How should he test his ministers to make sure he is surrounded by the most intelligent people in the oblast?" Tolkachev took a sip of wine, eyed each member of his audience in turn, and punched the sliding spectacles back up against his eyebrows. "Boosh calls in his deputy, Den Kvail, and gives this demonstration: 'Den,' he says, holding up a finger like this, 'answer me one question. What is the name of the son of your mother who is not your brother?'

"Kvail hesitates only a moment and says, 'Den Kvail.'

" 'Correct,' Boosh says. Then he gives Kabanov a conceited look and adds, 'That's how it's done in America.'

"Fine. In front of Boosh, Kabanov pretends this is no big deal, but he thinks about it all the way back across the Atlantic. When he gets to his office he immediately calls in his assistant, Gannov, and says, 'Gennadi Pavlovich, answer me one question.'

" 'Anything, Mikhail Lvovich,' Gannov says, bowing.

" 'What is the name of the son of your mother who is not your brother?'

"Gannov thinks this is a trap. He rubs his jaw. He looks serious. After a minute he says, 'Well, Mikhail Lvovich, this is a complicated matter, not a simple thing. I'll need a bit of time. Perhaps I'll convene a committee and we'll discuss it and present you with our answer in — '

" 'I'll give you five minutes,' Lvovich says.

"Gannov leaves the office absolutely in a panic. Five minutes! He runs the question back and forth through his mind a dozen times but nothing comes! Nothing comes! Son of your mother, he thinks. Not your brother. Nothing makes sense! It's a trap, is what it is. Three minutes have gone by, four minutes. He sees Boris Yeltsin walking down the corridor as if in a dream, and he runs up to him and says, 'Comrade Yeltsin, tell me, please, what is the name of the son of your mother who is not your brother?'

"Yeltsin doesn't hesitate. 'Boris Yeltsin!' he booms out, swinging his fist as though leading a cheer.

"Aha. Gannov, all excited, bursts back into Kabanov's office just as time is running out. Kabanov is waiting. Gannov stands opposite him and says, 'Mikhail Lvovich, I have the answer.'

" 'Fine,' Kabanov says. 'Let's hear it.'

"Gannov draws himself up and says, sagely, with a flourish, 'Boris Yeltsin!'

"Kabanov gives him a pitying little smile and shakes his head. 'No, no, no, Gennadi Pavlovich,' he says sadly. 'Not right, not right.'

"Gannov is ready to faint. 'What, then?' he says, trembling.

"Kabanov looks out the window and sighs, as if it is actually painful for him to have to enlighten this collective farm donkey. Finally, he turns, looks Gannov straight in the eye, holds up one finger and says: 'Den Kvail!' "

They laughed a bit longer than the joke warranted, sat back, sighed, laughed a little more, complimented Tolkachev on the telling of it, on the wine, glanced around again in half-sober satisfaction. After a while, Raisa left the table, and Propenko watched her set out an array of vegetables on the counter and stand there looking at them, deciding which to eat today and which to save for winter. There seemed to be a future, after all. He supposed he owed a word of thanks to Victor Vzyatin.

// CHAPTER 34

VOSTOK'S CENTRAL MARKET occupied a long, two-story concrete warehouse with water stains like dirty lace beneath its windows, and a man selling *kvass* from a tank truck out front. Czesich and Lydia pushed through the heavy wooden doors, and were caught up instantly in the tumult of free enterprise: Georgians thrust cut flowers at them; stall upon stall of Russian and Ukrainian women in white aprons offered carrots and apples and sunflower seeds, tomatoes, honeycomb, walnuts, garlic, eggplant. Beyond them stood another phalanx of dark-haired southerners, this group hawking fruit in their coarse accents, winking at Lydia, holding out pieces of red melon on a knife blade, calling to Czesich to buy his young sweetheart a few roses, a kilo of oranges or apricots, one or two of the tastiest peaches on the planet. Czesich could not stop smiling. The earth smells, the bright colors, the energy — he wanted to buy everything, bargain with everyone, rub himself like a dog in the scent of the place. Next to this, forty containers of powdered eggs and tinned beef seemed like so much State Department sterility, an insult.

Lydia quickly set him straight. She pointed out how few of the shoppers were doing anything more than looking and shaking their heads. "Eighteen rubles for a kilo of cucumbers," she said. "Eighteen rubles is a day's pay. It's a quarter of my grandmother's monthly pension. At the state markets, cucumbers cost six rubles sixty."

Plus two hours' wait in line, Czesich thought, but he did not say it. He was not in a mood to disparage Soviet reality now. Soviet reality was blossoming bright yellows and greens from its dull gray shoot, and the only difficulty was to take that at face value, to keep from imagining an iron fist beneath the flowers.

A swarthy fellow with a cigarette stored over each ear was waving them toward his stall. On the counter in front of him stood a perfect pyramid of cherries on juice-stained newsprint. Czesich accepted a free sample, then bought two kilos at an inflated price, and gobbled up a fistful while the vendor shoveled the rest into a newspaper cone.

"You're the American," he said quietly, checking the foreigner out, eyeing the push of bosom beneath Lydia's flowered blouse.

Czesich nodded.

The vendor wrapped up another pound or so of cherries and fit it into Lydia's canvas shopping bag. "For what you did yesterday," he said, almost in a whisper. Czesich shook his hand and moved on, trying to brush away a tendril of worry. What was the matter with these people, still whispering and looking side to side? Didn't they know that was over now?

"Our Georgians," Lydia said in a tender way. She helped herself to a handful of fruit and asked Czesich the English word.

"Cherries," he said.

"Jeddeast."

"Cherries."

"Doo meny jeddies on our lanch," she said.

"Way too many," Czesich agreed. They were walking between noisy, busy rows of stalls. He looked up, taking in the light from a high window, and saw two men at the rail of the dry-goods balcony, watching. Neither was in uniform. Lydia saw them, too, and waved. The men pretended not to see.

She sighed. "How will I survive without my bodyguards?"

Czesich said he didn't know.

He went overboard on the food. They bought flat bread from a clan of Uzbekis, tomatoes and an onion from a woman who refused to speak to them in anything but Ukrainian, then white cheese, raisins, peaches, a large chunk of honeycomb for dessert, a couple of apricots, two bottles of mineral water, and some sunflower seeds for the train ride. They stopped to watch a man with a hatchet and a bloody apron chop a thousand-ruble lamb into sections, and then, shopping bag bulging, ran the gauntlet of flower sellers and back out into the noon air. In all, Czesich had spent 157 rubles, six dollars, half a month's pay in Vostok.

They ate on a bench beside the War Memorial, a Pioneer keeping vigil at its eternal flame, a granite soldier, partisan, and peasant standing guard above. The day had grown hazy and still, almost hot. Czesich filled his stomach, Lydia nibbled and sipped. From time to time, they indulged in speculation about Vostok's future — who would take Lvovich's place, would the strikers return to work now, what would become of the People of the Third Path — but mostly they were content to sit and eat and savor the afternoon. The Soviet Union was being liberated again, Czesich thought, precariously, city by city, and, just as in the late 1940s, it would require a period of repair and rebuilding — of hearts and minds, this time. Naive young radicals like Lydia Propenko would have to be left alone for a while to raise and abandon new heroes. The country would have to endure a certain amount of chaos and ethnic enmity, two or three reactionary relapses, and then, maybe, half a lifetime down the road, his Russia would finally find its peace — of a shape no one could predict now, or pack into orderly five-year plans, but a real peace all the same.

When they'd finished eating and cleaning up, and had packed everything back into her shopping bag, Lydia mentioned the church again. It was the proper thing to do, didn't he think so?

Absolutely, Czesich said.

"There's a beautiful path we can take there. It runs above the river. Is your knee all right?"

The knee had stiffened during the hour they'd been sitting, and was swollen and sore now, undeniably fifty years old. He told her it was fine.

They walked down Chernyshevsky Street, Czesich slowing the pace and trying to hide his limp, the bulging bag swinging between them, the blue-and-yellow militia car rolling along behind at a respectful distance.

"I wish Pa would call them off now," Lydia said, looking over her shoulder at her bodyguards. "I feel like I'm in nursery school again. A father's love can be overpowering sometimes."

Czesich said nothing.

Chernyshevsky Street fed straight onto a path that ran along the waist of a weedy hillside, parallel to and just downhill from a little-used two-lane road. Beyond a stand of white birch the view opened out, revealing a curl of wide brown river — the Don's surface speckled with solitary fishermen in small, silvery boats — and the smoking, smog-bound Valley of Devastation beyond. Down-stream, Czesich could see the suspension bridge touching a wingtip to either bank, and two coal barges pushing slowly beneath it.

They walked a ways in silence.

"May I ask you a personal question, Anton?"

"I thought we were going to speak English today."

"English on the train. There's too much I want to ask now."

"Fire away."

She turned serious. "How long has it been since you and your wife lived together?"

"Nine years."

"And why haven't you found another woman?"

"I have friends," Czesich said, somewhat defensively. "I have a friend at the embassy."

"A potential wife?"

He was superstitious about these things, wary, like any Russian, of asking too much of the Fates. "I lead a life rich in potential," he said, and Lydia pretended to understand.

They stopped for a moment to rearrange the food.

"There they are again," she said. She waved up at the militia car cruising the road above them, and this time two policemen — both in uniform — waved back.

"And you, potential husbands?"

"I had a lover," she informed him, the word — *liubovnik* — almost a boast. "Someone older. Forty-one."

"And what happened?"

"Politics interrupted."

There was something too flat in her voice, and for a moment Czesich endured an internal debate. The flatness seemed to be call-ing out, a chained sadness, and as a friend, as a father, as a friend of her father's, he wanted to set it free. But he could see the church's gold domes now, glinting above a screen of trees, not far at all, and he decided to leave Lydia's secrets undisturbed.

At the churchyard gate, he looked over his shoulder at their bodyguards. The man on the passenger side made a hand gesture as if to say: "Leave the bag, we'll watch it for you," and Czesich nod-ded his thanks.

They went through the gate and into the shaded graveyard. "This is where he was shot, then, the watchman," Czesich said.

Lydia nodded. Her face changed as though they'd stepped from light into shadow, and Czesich was thumped over the head with a notion. No, he thought, not possible. The only words he'd ever heard associated with the church watchman were "saintly" and "assassinated," and neither of them seemed to fit very well next to this pretty young girl with peach juice on her face. A tragedy of such dimensions did not square with his view of her, the cute little box he'd placed her in.

She led him to the new grave — no stone yet, just a large mound of wilted flowers — and Czesich stole glances at her as she said a silent prayer. She showed him her grandfather's stone and they stopped for a prayer there, too, then walked toward the church steps. The door was not locked and the entranceway was empty; Czesich felt another prickle of worry. It seemed too easy for Russia — no one there to scold, no pleading for admission with a hard-hearted caretaker, no crowds, no protection. Even Lydia seemed mildly surprised by it. The nave was dim and cool and quiet. They moved slowly along walls hung with icons enough for a museum wing, Lydia stopping occasionally to provide the hagiography — the Archangel Michael; Saint Nicholas the Wonder Worker; Elizabeth, Mary's mother, visited by an angel. She seemed at home in this building, not so sad, not so young as she'd seemed a few minutes before, and Czesich wished he could transplant her and the whole Propenko family to his fantasy house in the Vermont countryside, the first friends of his new existence.

"Is Father Alexei here?" he whispered.

She nodded. "There's a bed in the rectory. He must be resting. He must have forgotten to lock the door."

As they neared the altar, Czesich thought he heard a sound — quick, soft footsteps. It was nothing, he told himself, Alexei making his rounds. He looked into the corners, a tickle of fear on his skin, but the room was still, cut by dusty sunbeams angling down from the higher windows, steeped in the smell of candle wax and incense. Lydia lit a thin brown candle and placed it before an icon of the Virgin holding the body of her crucified son. There were halos hammered in gold around both their heads, and Czesich heard Marie's mother, Angelina: "No a *real* circle round they heads, Tony," she had told him once, in her beautiful hybrid English. "*You* know. *You* seen it in people. Itsa *shine*, no a real light."

There were no pews in the room, nothing soft or easy. In an utterly unpretentious way, Lydia knelt on the floor in front of the altar and bowed her head, and for a few minutes Czesich just watched her, trying, as he had with the miners in front of Party Headquarters, to absorb the teaching. It was not a halo he saw, but there was something alive in her that had perished in him long ago, and it had only secondarily to do with youth. Long ago he had traded away a tender part of himself in exchange for never being fooled, or frightened, or hurt, and he wanted the contract rewritten now. He wanted real, unfiltered pain and joy, and a real, mature love — and though he could not quite bring himself to get down on his knees, he did close his eyes and bow his head and offer up a petition to his God-who-might-exist.

Let me, he prayed, stop running.

He spoke a word or two for Julie and Marie and Angelina and Michael, and then something — a figure moving across the light, or a shoe hitting the floor a certain way — struck him as vaguely out of place. He looked up, and across that one cold second three bodies moved too fast. The speed itself had something professional about it, sinister, cynical. He saw Lydia turn her head to the right and get halfway to her feet before the first two men were upon her. For an instant, Czesich was frozen in place. Something about the men made it impossible to move or speak. He should have screamed, or made for the door and warned the militia, or grabbed the nearest candlestick, but for that instant his body insisted on turning in upon itself, clenching, shriveling. He saw a hand locked on Lydia's white throat, heard what sounded like a squeak come up from her, saw her back bent over at a terrible, impossible angle, the knees giving way. He forced himself forward through a soup of fear. One of his arms, impossibly heavy and slow, swung out and connected with the shoulder of one of Lydia's assailants. The man's eyes turned up at him with a spark of pain and surprise, and Czesich swung again and caught him near the mouth and then something very hard cracked against the side of his own head. The floor seemed to shoot up flat against his shoulder and cheek. A cry burst out of him. He pushed himself to one knee, to his feet, and staggered one more step toward Lydia — two men holding her down now, pale breast showing through a torn blouse, all wrong — before the stone fist cracked against the side of his head again and the world went black and still.

Timelessly after in some horrible half-vision he saw a spider making its way across the flat universe in a light that was pure pain. It seemed impossible that the creature could lift its limbs through agony like that, its joints bending loosely, its body high up and lit by this fiery torment.

He was aware of someone whimpering on the floor behind him. He heard church bells — beautiful — then nothing.

Later, another vision, the door moving, swinging into being a terrible sunlight, a burning box of it, pure pain once again. He tried to scream. He heard someone whimpering behind him, saw a man in a gray uniform crossing the room, coming toward him fast, boots banging, banging.

// CHAPTER 35

HAPPILY HALF-DRUNK, and sipping cranberry wine at a pace intended to keep him that way, Propenko sat alone on the dacha's front porch and stared across the rutted dirt road. Tolkachev was making the rounds of his other friends. Marya Petrovna and Raisa were in the kitchen, preparing a lavish dinner. Above the tips of the spruce trees on the opposite side of the road stood a late August sky, perfectly blue except for a plume of dust off low to the southeast, in the direction of the highway. The smell of roasting pork floated through the window behind him, and he heard the measured *tut . . . tut* of knife blade hitting cutting board, and wondered if the plume of dust meant Lydia was coming to join them for dinner.

The kitchen noises changed — rattling pot lids now, plates clanking as they were lifted out of a cupboard — and brought Propenko a memory of his mother. Even more than her faithful communist husband, Lyudmila Propenko had made a religion of Marxism-Leninism — leading the volunteer Saturday cleanup crews, attending Party meetings as though they were church services, suckling her children on the myths of World Revolution and the Loving Coexistence of Soviet Minorities. To her, Lenin really had been born to carry humanity out of the swamp of self-interest and subjugation. He was, to her, what Isus Khristos was to Lydia and Marya Petrovna, a point in history after which the everyday balance of misery and joy should have shifted. What would she say now, with the Azeris and Armenians slaughtering each other, and the International Socialist Revolution running full speed in reverse, and her granddaughter off with an American, celebrating the overthrow of the local communist pope? How sad would she be to see her pure Red paradise turn mottled, like everything else? What shape would her Russian requiem take?

He poured himself another glass of wine and checked the plume of dust again. Vzyatin's men remained at their post, parked off to the left not far from the front of the yard, and as the dust cloud curled closer, the man on the passenger side — a captain — opened his door and got out. The captain was looking intently down the road, beyond the point where Propenko's view was obstructed by trees, and after a moment he unsnapped his holster guard, peered into the shadows, and started dutifully forward.

The Council's peach-colored Volga bounced into view, Anatoly behind the wheel, his passenger obscured by the windshield reflection.

"Who's there?" Raisa called from inside.

"Anatoly," Propenko called back. "He's come to celebrate."

He stood, shook away a slight drunken dizziness, and watched the Volga skid to a stop in a pillow of dust. Anatoly got out, said a word to the militia captain, then glanced up at the porch, and Propenko thought it peculiar that he didn't smile or wave. The passenger door opened, Leonid's head and shoulders appeared above the roof, and there was something odd in his face, too. A greeting stuck in Propenko's throat. He could not seem to move his legs.

Anatoly and Leonid came up the path and up the steps as if in slow motion, walking through liquid. When Leonid was finally on the porch, standing close, he said, "Where's Raisa?" as though he'd meant, until the last instant, to say something else.

"Inside," Propenko told him, and for some reason added: "Cooking." He looked at Anatoly's eyes — slightly averted worlds of frozen blue — and thought he heard him say: "Sergei, Lydia was attacked."

Propenko was trying to force sobriety upon himself, but the gears were not quite engaging. Part of him refused to understand; part of him had understood at the first glimpse of Anatoly's face. Though he still could not seem to move them, his legs had begun to tremble, and he was aware of his hands closing tight and of Raisa's voice through the screen door: "Sergei?"

Leonid's chin was quivering. "They took her first to the hospital," he said. "By now they have taken her home."

Behind the screen, Raisa made a noise like someone being

kicked in the stomach. "She's alive?" Propenko heard her ask. He watched Leonid nod.

Half a head shorter than Propenko, Leonid now appeared to be sinking even further. His shoulders and the muscles of his cheeks sagged. Propenko was waiting for him to say what he had not said, and what was printed large on his sagging face, but Leonid seemed to have been emptied of energy. He seemed about to wither away completely. The door opened and the porch boards flexed under Raisa's step and Propenko felt her hand on his arm. Anatoly moved closer — as if to be ready to catch her if she fell — and Leonid managed "Sergei, Lydia . . ." before a very tiny, horrible, and completely inadvertent smile flickered across his face and something that sounded like "raped" slid out from between his lips.

On the way in to the city, Propenko sat in the middle of the back seat with his knees pushed up almost to his chest, Raisa's fingers in his left hand and Marya Petrovna's wrist in his right. The speedometer read 125 kilometers per hour, but Anatoly seemed to be driving at the pace a child could walk.

Raisa had tears on her face. Marya Petrovna was staring straight ahead, twisting a handkerchief in her lap. Leonid was smoking, but instead of using the ashtray, he would periodically push his cigarette out the window until the ash was torn away, then stick the filter back between his lips. Anatoly gripped the wheel like a wax figure.

Propenko's thoughts spun in tight circles around an image of Nikolai Malov looking at him over the top of his coffee cup. He could feel the blood in the muscles of his arms and hands, and he could see himself — actually see himself as though he were outside his body — holding Malov up off the ground by his lapels and breaking his head open against a black stone wall. It seemed very clear to him that his body was going to take its revenge for his daughter's body. It was simply a blood fact, inevitable.

"Sergei!" Marya Petrovna cried out, and he looked down and saw her rubbing her left wrist where he had been holding it.

The road passed beneath them in slow motion, colors washing by to either side — dark green forests, light green fields; now, slowly, the first brown buildings at the city's edge.

At the traffic circle, the government auto inspector saluted. Anatoly raised a hand in response, then wiped the thumb and second finger across his eyelids, as if to squeeze a different dream out from under them.

Leonid finished his cigarette and pushed the butt out the window. The militia car had followed them in from the dacha, and as soon as they crossed the city line it pulled out in front and turned on its siren and flashing light.

"Anton didn't *protect* her?" Propenko said bitterly. The words had flown out of him, addressed to no one. He had not even been thinking about Anton Antonovich.

Leonid turned halfway around in his seat. "He tried, Sergei. Vzyatin said he tried. He's in the hospital now. The priest, Alexei, is there, too. Both of them were beaten very badly."

Raisa put a hand up to her face and began to sob into it. "What about Vzyatin?" Propenko said, more bitterness. He'd sunk a pipe down into an unbearably bitter well, and the pipe was spitting out bits of air and syllables, sputtering before the eruption.

Leonid turned all the way around to face him. "Vzyatin has every militiaman in the city searching for them, Sergei. He's searching himself. He'll find them."

They turned onto October Avenue, cars drifting to a stop on either side. Anatoly pulled up in front of the apartment and they were suddenly in the dank lobby, pressed close together in front of the elevator cage. Raisa had stopped sobbing, but she was still holding Propenko's hand in her cold fingers, squeezing it every few seconds like a pulse. Leonid kept hitting the bottom of his fist against the plastic elevator button and peering up through the square of wired glass, but the elevator would not come. Propenko could hear cables groaning and the box bumping somewhere on the eighth or ninth floor, and someone laughing there, drunk. The smell of boiling cabbage seeped out from one of the nearby apartments. One second he felt Raisa's arm around his back, and the next he was sprinting up the stairwell, taking the steps two at a time, pulling himself around the landings, banging through a metal door, running down the corridor.

The apartment was open and people had spilled out into the hall. As Propenko approached, Yakov Davidovich from next door caught his hand and tried to look at his eyes, but Propenko pushed through the entranceway, past a few friends standing in the kitchen, straight back to Lydia and Marya Petrovna's bedroom. She was lying there as he'd imagined her, perfectly motionless, staring at the ceiling. Raisa's sister, Anna, sat next to the bed, biting her lip and holding Lydia's right hand and humming the same few bars of song over and over again. She did not look up when Propenko came into the room. He knelt beside the bed and leaned over so that he was looking down into Lydia's face. There were three long welts across her throat, a streak of blood near one ear, partially washed away. Both lips were fat and cut, and her cheeks were an unnatural white, like old linen. She was exhaling thin breaths that smelled of alcohol, and the pupils of her eyes were wide as buttons.

"Lydia."

Her eyes shifted a centimeter, and Propenko imagined he saw the faintest smile catch and lift the corners of her lips, then break apart. He leaned his face down so that her hair was in his eyes and mouth, and he choked out four words, the only coherent thought he'd been able to form during the endless ride in from the dacha. His heavy breaths had transformed themselves into sobs, and for a moment, with his face pressed into the pillow, he thought he and Lydia were sobbing in unison. He thought the hand on his shaking back was her hand until he lifted his head and saw that she had not moved or changed expression. She was consumed by a vision playing behind her drugged eyes, unreachable. It was Raisa's hand on his back. It was Marya Petrovna bulling her way forward, pushing her hip in his face, reaching down with Raisa and touching and kissing Lydia's eyes and hair and shoulders in a language he had no access to. He watched, sitting even with Lydia's knees, far away. He looked up at Anna, who was staring almost as blankly as Lydia, still humming her tune and rubbing the lifeless fingers, then he stood, sober finally, and backed out the door.

No doubt someone tried to talk to him as he pushed through the kitchen and down the short hall. No doubt Anatoly and Leonid were among the people there, and perhaps they tried to stop him. He must have gone down the three flights of stairs, but he remembered neither the corridor nor the stairwell nor the loud metal doors.

Two militia cars were parked at the curb in front of the house, and they alone sent some signal that pierced his cold universe, because he immediately cut across the ragged patch of lawn, away from them, and broke into a run.

He did not sprint, but ran along October Avenue at a measured pace, harnessing his strength, the heavy work boots clopping up and down on the sidewalk. Something — keys or coins — jumped out of one of his pockets and skidded along the pavement. Faces sailed past, bodies, buildings, side streets. He turned left onto the Prospekt of the Revolution, breathing harder but still holding the flame at a steady, even burn. His mind was clear. Two men came out of a doorway to his left; he saw them too late and knocked them against each other and felt their muttered curses bounce off his back and drop away. He was less than a kilometer from Nikolai Malov's apartment when he began to feel the fire spread to his thighs and lungs and he began having to work harder to push his heavy legs up and forward, to suck the breath in and force it out. What had been a clear, cold spot of intention when he left the apartment now became muddled and hot. His eyes wobbled a bit with his wobbling concentration. Rivulets of sweat trickled into his mouth, and just as he lifted his right boot off the curbstone of the next side street and slapped it down again, a militia jeep careened a skidding, ninety-degree corner off the Prospekt and he ran into it broadside, banging his forearms and knees against the gray metal door and falling back and down, hard. He'd pushed himself up and halfway to his feet before three militiamen jumped on him and held him on his side against the pavement. He slipped his left arm free and sent an elbow into the ribs of one of the men and heard a snapping noise, and tried to swing a fist, but they were sitting or standing on his back now, crushing the breath out of him. His face was pressed against the tar. They were bending his arms backwards so that sharp bands of pain went up each side of his neck. He felt handcuffs on one wrist, and then both hands were cuffed and the men were still sitting on him, all of them pumping for breath, Propenko weeping. A small crowd had gathered. After a minute, the militiamen lifted him, pushed him toward the jeep, and squeezed him into its cramped back seat like a sack of flour. The doors slammed. The jeep jerked forward. The radio squawked out Victor Vzyatin's voice.

// CHAPTER 36

IT WAS a narcotic sleep, a slow blue gliding through painless seas. In it, he and Julie were strolling across Red Square's cobblestones at midnight, slipping through crowds of tourists and Soviet pilgrims, arm in arm. Floodlights illuminated the mausoleum and the Kremlin wall, and the hammer and sickle snapped above the Council of Ministers Building.

"The guard is about to change," Julie whispered in his ear, and as they approached the mausoleum, the bells in Spassky Tower began to chime, seven minor notes on a descending scale, unbearably sad. They heard boots slapping pavement in a sharp rhythm, and saw the elite mausoleum guard emerge from the base of the tower and goosestep out into the night, a trio of perfect death angels. Julie squeezed up tight against him, and Czesich was about to say what he had been trying to say to her for so many years, when the drug released its grip, the dream dissolved, and he floated up away from her, into pain. The room into which he awakened was institutional and dark and without comfort. He thought, for a moment, he was in prison.

He began to feel his body again — the long bones of his arms and legs, his stomach and jaw and forehead. He belched, and a sprinkle of cherry bile touched the roof of his mouth. By turning his head very, very carefully left and right, he could make out shapes in the blackness, empty beds, the sill of a window, a pocked concrete wall. He knew where he was now, he knew what the reliving of lost time would reveal, and the pain of it spread behind his eyes, bone to tissue to bone. There had been the face of a militiaman, very close, begging him for a description of Lydia's assailants, and he remembered struggling to form the Russian words and push them out between his lips. Lydia and he had been loaded side by side into an antiquated ambulance, exhaust fumes seeping up through the floor. He'd tried to speak to her, but the pain was grinding the bones of his face and neck, and all he could do was grit his teeth tight and hold her cool wrist and wait for it to end.

He blinked, squeezing a tear out onto one cheek. More of his body came awake — calves, knees, hips — but the pain seemed to have reached its limit, a drumbeat in his temples and neck and behind the eyes, nearly bearable.

He faded, then returned. Sleepy, shuffling slippers sounded in the corridor, and it now seemed some internal authority had granted him permission to move. He flexed his toes. He drew his knees up very slowly, pulled himself to the edge of the bed and rested there on his side, coated in sweat. With his left palm on the mattress near his face, he hoisted himself up to a sitting position and closed his eyes against the hammering and the stars and the urge to vomit. When the world was still again, he locked his arms at the elbow, took a breath, and pushed himself to his feet.

His knees shook. He was nauseous, but thinking more or less clearly. The clearest thought was: *Get out.*

Someone had laid his clothes neatly in a cardboard box on the chair beside the bed. He could see them there, each fold catching a furry line of light from the street, and after a time he slipped free of the hospital gown and began, at the pace of a ninety-year-old, to dress. Visions assaulted him. Lydia on the church floor with her face contorted, one arm flailing. A man in a gray uniform shouting down at him, "Only one. Just one of them, for God's sake! Describe one of them!" Czesich tried to concentrate. They'd brought him here and drugged him, stuck him with a needle while he lay on a stretcher stained with someone else's blood. He had to reach down below the drug now, push away these visions, put his thoughts into one straight line that led out of this place.

He could see five other shadowy beds, all empty — a private room for the *Amerikanetz*. But there were no televisions, no beeping monitors, no nurses squeaking down bright, clean corridors. It was an infection prison, a place to be sick alone, a place to die. Every fiber in him wanted out.

Trembling, he found a glass jar on the bedside shelves and urinated into it as quietly as he could. His head hurt more now, and his right knee was swollen and throbbing, but, at the same time, there was a vagueness to everything, a buffer between him and the night's hard edges, a small pool of energy. He checked the sky outside his window — middle-of-the-night black. If this was anything like other Soviet hospitals he'd seen, he stood at least a chance of walking straight out the front door, unmolested. On the street he'd wave twenty-dollar bills at any vehicle that passed. He'd ride back to the hotel, call Propenko, call the embassy, hole up in his suite with the doors barricaded until Julie arrived.

The other option was to wait here for the militia or the KGB to come get him — which was no option at all. With the possible exception of the Propenko family, he trusted no one now. He could not risk custody of any sort.

His watch was missing, not on his wrist, not on the bedside shelves. He checked his pants pockets — the dollars and rubles had not been touched — then stood and began his passage across the ward.

Just outside the door, a militia sergeant slumped in a chair, sound asleep, hands folded beatifically on his belly. Czesich could hear the pulse thumping in his temples, and he stood there for a minute, debating, then made his decision and slid silently along the corridor in the opposite direction. He reached the exit sign undetected, took a left through a noisy tin door and into a stairwell, listened, then step by quiet step made his descent.

A bar of light shone beneath the door at the base of the stairs. Beyond it he heard a telephone ring and ring as if it would go on forever, then suddenly stop. Very gently, he pushed through the door and into a lobby where one yellow lamp lit patched walls and the night clerk sat snoring in a chair behind the desk. There was another chair next to the entrance, empty. A wooden cylinder was wedged through the door handles, and a huge expanse of linoleum lay between his feet and the black out-of-doors. What light there was wounded him. He looked at the sleeping clerk, drew a breath, and began. Squinting and sliding quietly, one foot after another, shoelaces dragging, he'd made it nine-tenths of the way across the lobby when he heard, behind him: "And *this* is what?"

The night clerk waddled over, squat, uniformed, a kind of dutiful rodent.

"And this is what?" he demanded a second time. He'd scurried into position between Czesich and the door and was standing very close, thrusting out his rat's chest.

Czesich was light-headed from the exertion, from the bestirred remnants of the drug, and for a moment he was not quite sure where nightmare ended and night began.

"Uh?" the clerk said.

Czesich searched for a strategy. The edges were vague, the reflexes muffled. All he could manage was: "I'm the *Amerikanetz*."

"You're the *Amerikanetz*," the clerk repeated sarcastically. "I have no eyes?"

No eggs, Czesich thought, no balls, no heart, nothing. He had somehow come to associate this man with the thugs who'd raped Lydia Propenko, the sadists who'd ruined Russia by following a very simple plan: kill the best, torture the best, rape the best; turn everyone else into sheep. He could feel a congenital anger uncoiling. "I have an important meeting. The Ambassador is coming."

The rodent smiled, all stretched lips and two sharp top teeth. "At two-thirty o'clock in the morning?"

Czesich squinted. The clerk's sleep-strewn face wavered like a television screen. "What can it mean to you?"

"Phillipovich will crucify me is what it means. They'll all crucify me."

"Maybe it would be for the best," Czesich said in English. He shut his eyes and tried to concentrate. Phillipovich. The floor beneath his feet was shifting in a sickening way, and the idea of walking out into the street and hailing a cab was coming to seem more and more like an opium fantasy. He took ten rubles from his pocket and forced the bill into the clerk's hand. "I'm going to the hotel. You can call me a taxi if you'd like, but I must go."

The man did not soften. He peered. He had seen the pain and it made him bolder.

Czesich tried a desperate bluff: "Call the doctor then."

"I call her at this hour," the clerk replied proudly, "and she crucifies me."

"Fine." Czesich reached into his other pocket, took out an American bill, and without checking the denomination, squeezed it in next to the rubles. It had no effect. The clerk stood there with his hand out, taking, mean, hard as metal.

"I *do* have official visitors arriving from the embassy this afternoon, and I *must* get ready. You can call Sergei Propenko if you don't believe me. You can talk to the militia guard upstairs. *He* let me go."

The rodent crumpled the bills and pushed them back into

Czesich's pocket. "You're trying to escape. You did something wrong."

"Nothing," Czesich said, but he could see that the face below him was not marked by even the smallest bruise of doubt. The clerk was a Stalinist, survivor of decimated gene pools, one piece of the spiteful granite from which the original Soviet monolith had been quarried. Czesich looked around, spied the chair by the door, took three steps and sat. "Call me a taxi," he said, in his Director's voice.

The clerk snorted.

Czesich was shivering very slightly now, his fingers twitching. He had reached the end of his small spurt of energy, and the ache in his right temple, softened all this while, had begun taking on a frightening edge. Thin ribbons of pain snaked back into his ear; he reached up and felt a lump there the size of a small plum.

"I know what you did, in front of Party Headquarters."

"You should thank me then."

The clerk snorted again, turned, and shuffled back to his desk. Czesich heard the high scratching of a telephone dial, a pause, a great deal of apologetic mumbling, then one faint, echoing *ding* as the receiver was put back in place. He was, for some reason, shoveling away a thin coat of snow in front of a house in Vermont. The storm had swept east over the mountains, leaving tongues of cold, clean wind, and he had a scarf wrapped around his neck, and gloves, and a hat, and was running the long-handled shovel down the driveway, watching a dimpled mound of snow build up in front of it and dribble away to either side. A neighbor was doing the same thing just across the road. Czesich called out hello, something about the storm. Inside the house, Julie was making a hot breakfast. The domestic scene he'd spent his whole life fleeing seemed perfect in this vision, a tame paradise. The urge to escape it had finally been beaten out of him.

The clerk hurried off down the hall without making any noise. To the toilet, Czesich supposed. Or to find the sleeping doctor and tattle.

He was sitting a pain meditation now, his mouth dry as dead leaves, his eyes at the level of the wooden cylinder wedged between the door handles. Why call a taxi first, and *then* go and wake the head doctor? Why call a taxi at all, if the rodent was so set against his leaving? Why all the apologetic mumbling into the telephone?

The lobby tilted and reeled. He thought he heard Lydia say

"jeddies." He thought he saw her waving to the men on the market balcony, and the men averting their eyes the way he'd averted his when he'd seen Malov on the sidewalk near Party Headquarters. Malov staring at him like . . . if looks. . . . Czesich felt himself embark on another slow glide, but a name sounded in his inner ear and brought him tumbling out of it. His eyes snapped open and he was staring across the lobby at the empty desk. Nikolai Phillipovich. There was energy now. He was on his feet, wobbling, listening. He turned 180 degrees, pulled out the wooden cylinder, banged his bad knee slipping between the doors and was out in the night air, bent double with pain, hands on his thighs, clutching the cylinder as if it were a relay baton. He willed himself to straighten up. One feeble light above his head illuminated a short walkway in front of him. There seemed to be a gray militia jeep parked there, at the end of the walkway. He took two steps toward it and almost fainted. He locked his left leg to keep himself upright and thought he saw a shadow moving in the jeep's front seat, a man waking, turning. "Ey!" Czesich yelled, once. It was a salutation from his youth. He dropped the baton, heard it rolling on stone, and he had his eyes closed, one hand in his pocket, feeling for bills as he fell.

// CHAPTER 37

THE CELL measured two meters by three, with a hole in the corner for a toilet, one iron bunk with a stained straw mattress, and a sliding panel at the base of the door, through which, hours ago, a bowl of cold soup had been offered, then removed. Propenko sat on the edge of the bed with his elbows on his knees, opening and closing his large hands. The air smelled of sweat and urine, the walls were cool as buried stones. It was almost four o'clock in the morning, but the noise from the other cells went on continuously — shouts and screams, drunken raving — a frenetic external universe that no longer claimed his attention.

"Then choose the thing that frightens you most," Anton Antonovich had said. The thing that frightened him most, it turned out, was himself.

Footsteps sounded amidst the clamor. The peephole slid open and snapped shut, but Propenko did not look up. They had been checking on him all night, waiting for him to offer a sign of surrender so that their chief could come in with his confidence and condolences and tell him what he was supposed to do next. But, even exhausted and hungry and half-mad, he could see no surrender in his future. He'd been granted a portion of understanding in the night hours, a glimpse of the wider stage: Bessarovich and Vzyatin deciding to send the food to Vostok; making lists of distribution sites; weeding out timid old-guard types like Volkov; *creating the conditions*, as Tolkachev had put it, for the removal of Mikhail Lvovich Kabanov. If you have A and B, you must, within a certain probability, always have C. He had been their C, their ambitious and obedient boxer. After a round or two on the ropes, staggering and bleeding and ready to quit, he had done the job for them, thrown a desperate right hand and knocked the champion out of the ring.

Which was fine. Except that, in the process, his daughter had been beaten and raped, and something had hardened inside him that his handlers hadn't counted on.

The peephole snapped open and shut again, but there was a click at the door latch this time, and two men appeared in the glaring light from the corridor. They were his own height, built like barrels, and Propenko thought for a moment they'd come to administer a beating.

The first man signaled him to stand, and patted him down very thoroughly while the other watched: boots, socks, pant legs, crotch, sweaty shirt, back and front and under both arms. He made Propenko open his mouth, ran fingers inside his collar and cuffs, inside the waistband of his trousers, checked his hands, roughly, silently, competently. They were not in uniform, unfamiliar, too good to be Vzyatin's men. Without a sound they motioned him out of the cell and led him down the corridor, one in front, one behind. Too much light. Dented doors on his right hand, barred windows high up to the left. The racket of his fellow prisoners echoing everywhere. A door, then down four short flights and Propenko found himself in a quieter, more familiar part of the Central Precinct — ground floor, rear, outside Vzyatin's office.

One of the guards knocked twice and pushed the door open. The chair behind the Chief's large desk stood empty. On the side wall was a painting of the changing of the guard at Lenin's tomb, and beneath it Vzyatin's Finnish sofa, and on the sofa Lyudmila Bessarovich with her hands folded calmly in her lap. Bessarovich gestured toward a chair opposite her and Propenko sat, his back to the door and the bodyguards. No greeting leapt to his lips this time. There was no submissive posture, no worry about what news she might be bringing down from Moscow. At last, in his bitterness, he was free of that.

Bessarovich had one of the men bring two glasses of tea, then dismissed him.

She stared at Propenko for a long time, and he stared back. She seemed smaller than he remembered her, more worn, but there was still the texture of power in her posture and eyes and voice, the hard polish of someone used to being obeyed. It was a trick Propenko understood now: you eliminated doubt and presumed authority and people followed you. That had been Vzyatin's secret all these years, the heart of his confidence and the heart of his error. He wanted nothing to do with it.

"First the facts, Sergei," Bessarovich said quietly, her eyes perfectly steady, tired, empty of emotion. "Lydia sat up and had tea and bread. She is speaking. She asked me to bring you home."

Propenko felt the words pierce him, and a prickling of tears behind his eyes. He looked over Vzyatin's desk and out the dark window.

"Her assailants were apprehended at the GAI post in West Vostok, forty minutes after the attack — one local man, two from Uzinsk. They are in Makeyevka Prison." Bessarovich took a sip from her glass and spent another few seconds inspecting him, and Propenko saw a small change in the eyes, a fleck of feeling he could not read. "While being questioned, I am told, the rapist tried to escape and was severely beaten."

Propenko squeezed his right hand to stop it from shaking. Revenge brought revenge, he knew that. Hatred gave birth to hatred. He tried to force himself back from that edge, to push himself in the direction of October Avenue, where he could hide out again under the guise of his fatherly duties, let someone else take his revenge and make his decisions for him. He tried as he had been trying all night, but the forces pushing the other way were too great. He did not know why he believed this, what trauma, what intuition was instructing him, but it was clear to him that if he did not plunge his arms into the blood he would never be able to talk to Lydia again the way they'd talked in the church. The only way to know her now was to go down and down, into the wretchedness in himself, to let go of everything he had held on to so tightly for so long.

He was not sure his voice would work. "Who questioned them?"

"Victor, at first. Then my men."

"And who ordered it . . . the attack . . . who gave the order?"

"Nikolai Malov."

"On whose . . . authority?"

"His own — as far as we have been able to —"

"Not Mikhail Lvovich's?"

"Not Lvovich's, not the *komitet's.*"

Outside the boxing ring, Propenko had not hit another human

being for thirty-five years, since childhood. Now he could imagine nothing but hitting. "Where is he?" he said.

"In a mine south of the river," Bessarovich told him. "In the custody of the Strike Committee."

"And the Strike Committee answers to whom? The priest? Vzyatin?"

"Father Alexei died thirty minutes ago, Sergei. The Strike Committee has always answered to me."

"Which mine?" he demanded.

"I could tell you," Bessarovich said calmly, gently, "but I'm concerned you would — "

"Which MINE!" Propenko brought both fists down on the flimsy wooden table between them, smashing the top into three splintered pieces and knocking his untouched glass onto the carpet. Immediately he folded his arms and pressed them against his chest and squeezed his eyes and lips closed. He heard the door handle bang the wall behind him, and Bessarovich's men rush into the room, and he opened his eyes to see her motioning them back out toward the hall. One of the bodyguards hesitated, stared at Propenko with his flat eyes, held his arms out away from his body. "Kostya," Bessarovich said, as though speaking to a dog. "Out."

When they were alone again, she fixed Propenko with the same, steady, green-eyed gaze he remembered from the conference room.

"He *raped* my *daughter*," Propenko said through his teeth. "He had my daughter *raped*!"

"And he will be punished. The point is, you are not the person to administer that punishment."

"Who decides that?"

Bessarovich stared at him without blinking. "I do."

Bessarovich's face was blurred. Propenko ground his teeth together, and felt a wave of tiredness catch him and try to drag him toward surrender.

"In the mine where Malov is being held there are hundreds of very small tunnels," she said. "Crawl spaces. Seams of coal that have been mined and must be allowed to collapse so the earth above them will remain stable. The miners will take Malov into one of these crawl spaces. A charge will be set off. That will be the end of it. There will be no body to discover, no problems with the *komitet*, or the procurator, no blood on your hands, my hands, or Victor's."

"I want to look into his face," Propenko blurted out.

Bessarovich frowned as though disappointed in him. "You'll kill him if you look into his face."

"I will *not!*" he shouted, but he was speaking for his body now, and the body would not be spoken for. He felt a muscle begin to twitch next to his left eye and he reached up and pressed his fingers against it until it went still. The ultimate, final curse of men like Malov was that they infected you with themselves. If you loved and trusted and hoped, they made you hate and suspect and despair. That, to them, was victory.

Bessarovich looked down at the wreckage of the table, at the tea bleeding into Vzyatin's expensive carpet, then up into Propenko's face.

Propenko was squeezing his hands between his knees as though they might fly up and out the window if he released them, as if one arm might be pulled one way, and the other arm the other, tearing him into two ragged, bleeding halves. "I have to see him," he said. "I cannot go home and face Lydia and Raisa and Marya Petrovna without seeing him."

"Nonsense," Bessarovich told him. "A man's nonsense. All they want is for you to come home. That's where you should be right now instead of screaming and kicking in a prison cell. You belong home now."

He closed his eyes for a moment and tried to return to the quiet center of himself, the place he had reached after half a lifetime of blind obedience, and an hour or two of screaming and kicking in the prison cell. If he could speak to Bessarovich from that place, he was sure she would not refuse him. "I have the rest of my life to be home, Lyudmila," he said, leaving off the patronymic, and feeling it cut through her. "I'm asking one thing of you: Before he dies, I want to see the face of the man who had my daughter raped. That's all."

Bessarovich stirred the hard cube of sugar at the bottom of her glass and took a small sip. Propenko could see her making her calculations, weighing risks and gains, trying to wriggle free of a sliver of doubt. He felt as he had felt with Mikhail Lvovich on the balcony, that the roulette wheel was spinning, that there were deals and possibilities moving round and round in front of him, too fast to see. After what seemed a very long time, minutes and minutes, Bessarovich looked up. "I didn't fly down to Vostok to say this, Sergei," she said. "You can believe that or not, as you like, but I'm going to say it anyway. Lvovich is gone now, for good. Victor is as

loyal as a puppy and clever in his own way, but Victor has made a terrible mess of things lately and he knows it and has lost some of my confidence because of it. With the exception of a few people on the Strike Committee — people who lack your education and experience — the city is completely without trustworthy leaders now. In Moscow, the guard is about to change. We need to make two or three key appointments in Vostok, and you are to be one of the two or three."

Propenko glared at her, all of the hatred up in his face, and for one instant Bessarovich's disguise seemed to slip. She might have been any other frightened Soviet woman for that instant, any other Vera or Lyuba huddled in line in front of the bakery on Vostochni Street, shopping bags weighing her down, thick legs planted as though she'd grown out of the sidewalk. "I'm not interested in your shit appointments," he said. "It's the last thing I'm interested in."

"Of course not. No one would be now. As I told you, I wasn't planning to say this tonight, but then, until a few seconds ago, I wasn't even considering letting you anywhere near Nikolai. I'm not talking about temporary positions with an American food program, Sergei. And I'm not talking about the Council of Commerce and Industry. These are appointments at the highest levels, the people who will remake this city. I'm willing to consider letting you see Malov, just *see* him, if you give me your word to simply consider what I'm offering here. I wouldn't want you climbing to those heights with blood on your hands, that's all."

"I'm not climbing anywhere," Propenko said, but Bessarovich seemed to be looking right into him, at a place he could not yet see.

After a moment, her face softened slightly. "I'm very sorry about Lydia," she said, "but from what the miners tell me, she is not the type to be defeated by this, and neither are you."

Propenko let the flattery fly up and over his head. In the powdered face opposite him, he saw nothing less than a reflection of his country. One shifting mirror after the next, mask upon mask, tricks and games and maneuverings. There were two options: you sat at home and fortified the walls around your domestic kremlin and tried to keep yourself pure; or you chose your side, for better or worse, and waded out into the blood and filth. He had tried the pure, domestic option. It had led him only to this small surrender.

He nodded. Bessarovich seemed to smile without moving her lips. "He's at the Nevsky Mine," she said. "Victor is waiting out

back to take you there, if that's where you decide to go. At the mine, ask for Yevgeni Vasilievich. I'll call them now and tell them to tell Nikolai you are coming, so he can spend half an hour or so expecting you."

Propenko went past the bodyguards, down the back hall, and out into the night.

There was a light above the building's rear door, and in the small dirt parking lot he could see Vzyatin sitting behind the wheel of an unmarked Volga, smoking. Vzyatin heard the door of the building slap closed, and he got out, shoulders sagging, his left arm hanging at his side as though he could not raise it, all the confidence bleached from his face. Propenko walked up to him and saw spots of blood on the front of his shirt, and a grave weariness in his eyes. Vzyatin looked as though all the air had been let out of him. "The assailants are in custody, Sergei," he said, and Propenko understood that this was as close as the Chief would ever be able to come to asking forgiveness.

"The American gave a description, and I had every single militiaman in the city on their trail within four minutes. Every detective, every informant and ex-convict, every drunk who owed me a favor from anywhere in the past twenty years, was called within half an hour. We alerted the GAI, the oblast militia, the Special Criminal Unit. By the time my men stopped you on Prospekt Revoliutsii, the assailants were already in custody. Caught in a van at the GAI post in West Vostok."

Propenko nodded his small absolution, but Vzyatin seemed inconsolable, in mourning for his tarnished reputation, perhaps, or for his lost kingdom.

"Oleg deceived me," he went on. "My driver for fourteen years. I've had him to my house a thousand times. I bring his daughter birthday presents. I sat with him all night at the hospital when his brother died."

Propenko nodded again. He did not need this information now. He did not even need to hear Vzyatin apologize. His body was not listening.

"Malov was behind it."

"I know."

"The American tried to protect her. They almost killed him in the church. Malov tried to find him at the hotel and finish the job, but we found Malov first."

Propenko had nothing to say.

"I'll take you home," Vzyatin said, flicking his cigarette into the weeds. The apology was apparently over; the old authority was creeping back into his voice.

Propenko shook his head. He was looking at Vzyatin and seeing a forty-five-year-old married man, drunk, kissing his friend's daughter on the dark path behind the hotel in Sochi.

"Get in, I'll take you home. I've been there half the night."

"I'm not going home. I'm going to see Malov. You're supposed to drive me."

"I can't do that, Sergei."

Propenko wondered for a moment if he had been tricked. "Bessarovich just called the mine and told them I was coming. She said you'd take me. Go in and ask her."

Vzyatin was shaking his head, sadly, resolutely. "It's not what you want," he said. "Believe me, Seryozha. I was at the prison earlier. I was with the men who . . . that's not an answer to anything, believe me."

Propenko just stared at him, barely breathing.

"He's gone now, Malov, a dead man. They're going to bury him."

Propenko kept staring.

"I have people in the camps who owe me, the worst kind of people. Every day Lydia's assailants spend there will be hell. Every time they —"

Propenko reached out and hit Vzyatin in the middle of the chest with his index finger, once, hard, and the small blow seemed to deflate the Chief a second time.

Vzyatin looked at him long enough for Propenko to see the surprise, then he opened his mouth, closed it, opened it again, shrugged, and slouched off toward the precinct's back steps. When Vzyatin had gone into the building, Propenko waited for the count of five, then climbed in behind the wheel. The key was in the ignition. He turned it, backed up in a neat half-circle, and was out of the lot and driving toward the river before the Chief had reached his office door.

It had been many years since Propenko was out in the city in the hours before dawn. The air was cool, still as death, and streaked with fog. Silence had taken the place of noise, and shadow the place of light, and the few vehicles moving along the street seemed bent

on solitary errands like his own. He rolled down his window and let the wet night air blow against his face.

Traveling a route that kept him as far as possible from October Avenue, he reached Donskoy Boulevard, turned left onto the Tchaikovsky Bridge, and climbed through a quilt of fog. At the crest of the bridge the air was clear, and he saw tremendous opal columns of smoke rising out of the valley ahead, and flecks of light marking the tops of the factory chimneys, and he could not keep himself from looking to the right and down, as if expecting to find four gold cupolas on the swaddled bank.

The fog was even thicker on the south side of the river, and, descending, he could see nothing but a few meters of roadway and the vertical railing pipes flashing past. The end of the bridge came with a loud thump beneath the wheels, and he took the first exit, then swung to the west and down, into the heart of the mining district. Sagging wooden homes and junk-strewn yards lined the road here, ghostlike in the fog, not a light in any window. He heard the high hum of an invisible factory and felt his heart beating steadily, twice its normal pace.

After a few minutes, he turned onto a crunching gravel drive and pulled up to a chain link gate with haloed spotlights behind. There were guards at the gate, smoking, their cigarette embers making tiny red eyes in the fog. One of the guards recognized him and let him through a smaller gate, into a large, dusty lot. On one side of the lot an office building hulked. Opposite it, dark and forlorn and weather-beaten, stood a two-story wooden structure with no windows and a gaping black entrance.

"Where is Yevgeni?"

"Below."

"Take me down, then."

In the weather-beaten shed, Propenko was required to put on a helmet and a black miner's jacket like any ordinary visitor, then was escorted into an elevator with chain link walls. The miner slammed the gate shut and punched a red button, and they dropped down the shaft, gaining speed as they descended, so that Propenko's empty stomach rose against his lungs. His hands had started to tremble violently. He could hear cables whirring and banging above his head, see a blur of ragged wall an arm's length away, taste soot in the cool, stale air, smell the miner's sweat. He felt as though he were being lowered away from the surface world forever.

The elevator slowed to a soft landing, and the miner clanged open the gate and motioned him out into a curving tunnel, its five-meter ceiling supported by a succession of steel arches. Bulbs along the wall cast a wavering light, and Propenko could hear water dripping and a distant drone of fans. "A hundred meters," the miner told him, holding the elevator door open with one leg and pointing. "You'll see a door. Yevgeni and the two guards will be waiting outside."

Propenko nodded, breathing hard now, beyond politeness. He started off along the tunnel, with railroad tracks and puddles at his feet, the ventilator fans blowing a warm, gritty wind in his face, telephone and electric wires strung along the walls and ceiling, and an old image of Nikolai Malov occupying his inner eye. It was the third round, the match already lost, and the Uzbeki middleweight was driving his fists into Malov as though he were a heavy-bag. Not one member of the team, not one boxer or coach or trainer, would have blamed him for falling to the canvas and saving himself sixty or eighty seconds of torture. But Malov had stood there with one hand up and his feet apart, absorbing it. When it was over he'd staggered stiff-legged toward his corner and vomited his mouthpiece and blood and mucus into the water bucket.

A string of coal cars — low and gray — stood on the tracks at the first turn, and when Propenko was beyond them, he saw three men standing near a doorway, looking small and befuddled in the massive, shadowed tunnel. He realized then that he had no idea what Bessarovich had said to these men. Perhaps he was just Tolkachev's C again, a cog in some larger apparatus, a provincial fool. Perhaps it was him they were going to bury here, along with his secrets and his bitterness.

It seemed to take a very long time to reach the doorway. When he finally drew close, one of the men stepped forward, held out his hand and said, "Yevgeni Vasilievich." Even in his agitation, Propenko could see the deceit on Yevgeni Vasilievich's face, a new type of Soviet deceit, cloaked in openness, cloaked in respect. "Your daughter is our finest," he said, and Propenko stared at him, trying to keep his breathing under control, to be ready. He pulled his hands out of his pockets. One of the men worked the padlock on the metal door, and when Yevgeni Vasilievich swung it open Propenko saw a black-walled room with a plain table at its center, and a true Soviet man — bruised inside, too proud, full of old humiliations — dangling from a ceiling timber with an electric cable around his throat. One of Malov's shoes had fallen off, his fingers were spread and rigid, his eyes bulging and white as eggs.

Propenko stood close to the body, alone in the room, and watched it swing back and forth very slightly in an invisible draft, a pendulum in the earth's center. He had been used again. Bessarovich had been a move ahead of him all along, but it didn't matter. He could go home now and tell Raisa and Lydia and Marya Petrovna that it was over, that Malov could no longer harm them, that the ghost of Dzerzhinsky's secret police — Russia's curse — was about to be buried beneath a million tons of earth.

He could go home and tell them that, and for a little while all of them could pretend to believe it.

// CHAPTER 38

August 18, 1991

I am writing this in a cramped seat on Aeroflot 1021, Moscow–Vostok–Minvodi, hence the wobbly handwriting. To my left, in the aisle seat, sits a middle-aged Central Asian man wearing a tibuteka on his bald head, clutching a muskmelon in his lap, and staring straight forward as though at an image of death moving toward him at five hundred miles per hour. Beyond him, two men — miners, I think — are standing in the aisle because there are not enough seats for them. They have been there since a few minutes before takeoff, facing each other, hands braced against the overhead compartments, smiling and joking and sneaking the occasional nip from a bottle one of them has hidden beneath his sweatshirt. Beyond them sits a large and fascinating assortment of paper-wrapped parcels and carry-ons piled up neatly against the emergency door. No one seems to care. The stewardess came by once — just after we reached our cruising altitude — with a tray of plastic cocktail glasses half-filled with rose-colored mineral water and glanced at the obstructed door and pushed the miners curtly to one side, but now she has disappeared. Anarchy reigns. Up ahead someone is holding a very small and quietly bleating goat.

It is a clear, hot, mid-August Sunday, and below us I can see green fields stretching toward a slightly blurred horizon. I am on route to the city of Vostok, capital of the Donbass coalfields, slipping southward into my own history. There is a small exhilaration at having been liberated, for two days, from the embassy community, but it floats on the surface of a brew of other feelings, a bubbling cauldron of anger and affection and self-pity and puzzlement, the same things I have felt about the Soviet Union and about Anton Czesich since I first encountered them, almost half a lifetime ago.

At this moment, poised here tens of thousands of feet above the earth, among strangers, the surprising news from Vostok and Ambassador Haydock's cautions ringing in my ears, I feel like a speck of soot in the enormous palm of Fate or God or History, or whatever. I feel that all my tiny tantrums of will, all my decisions and exertions, all my stretches of good and bad luck, have only brought me in an enormous circle, so that I am again just a single, somewhat spoiled American woman moving toward a man I am drawn to and infuriated by, in a place that each of us simultaneously loves and hates.

I have tried, many many times, to explain my feelings about this country to friends who haven't been here, and to explain my feelings about Chesi to myself. How can a people be, simultaneously, so maddening and so endearing? So sentimental and so heartless? So hurtful and so kind? Why do I request to be posted here, again and again? Why do I find myself flying toward Chesi now, instead of away from him, with all that he has done, with all the other men in the world? I look up from this page and see our fellow Slavs, crowded into this diving, lurching, smelly jet, crowded in like animals without so much as a smile from our stewardess, without so much as a hard roll and a piece of fruit to ease our passage . . . and the two miners in the aisle are laughing. If only I could do what they do. If only I could take all the old notes, sour and sublime, and blend them into a bittersweet Russian hymn, and go on. If only I could understand, really understand, what they seem to take for granted: that the people you suffer with are the people you love.

We've begun our descent now, already, at what seems much too sharp an angle. The plane is starting to shake in earnest, and even as these scrawled words grow less and less legible, the world below moves into sharper focus. No stewardess, still. No seat belt check. No comforting syllables from the captain. My neighbor — on his way to visit relatives who haven't been able to afford a melon in two years — squeezes his gift so hard I worry it will split open in his lap.

The miners in the aisle are rosy-cheeked and winking at each other, looking down at me and nodding, grinning, as if to say, Isn't this fine, isn't this just a fine joke on all of us, coming in for a landing like this, on our feet, holding on, shaking, smiling? Out the window

I can see slag heaps now, and two strip mines like eye sockets in the earth, and cars and buses on a straight gray highway. In a minute it will be time to tuck this book in my bag, brace myself for the landing, and for whatever it is that is waiting for me on the ground in Vostok. If I could pray for one blessing in these next hours, it would be for an end to our private little cold war — mine and Chesi's. It would be for the ability to see each other as we are, instead of clouding the image with the past, with so many years of protection and suspicion and embittered competition. Not that I expect — or even want — him to meet me at the airport with flowers and an apology. Not that I picture us setting up house together in an embassy apartment in Paris, or in some quaint cottage on the Maryland shore, and living happily ever after, as we should have lived in the first place. We have too much bad history between us now for something as simple as that, just as the Soviets have too much bad history for a painless, overnight cruise into the still waters of democracy and abundance.

What I ask for myself is only what I ask for them: a measure of forgetfulness, and a measure of memory, and the courage to live unprotected.

Our stewardess approaches, wagging an angry finger. Enough.

// CHAPTER 39

FROM dreams of torturers and church bells, Czesich woke to dust motes and misaligned drawers. He knew where he was and what had happened, but not what had awakened him. A sound, he thought, though the room was quiet now.

He was lying on his side with the hotel's fat pillow against his left cheek and a sheet of pain against his right. A clock ticked softly behind him, and after a moment he heard what sounded like knocking, muted by the dining room wall, then creaking hinges and footsteps. Clenching his teeth against the pain, expecting Malov or one of Malov's men, he raised his head off the pillow just far enough to see the figure of Slava Bobin clouding the doorway. Bobin came over to the bed and squatted down so that his face was only an arm's length away, warty and booze-softened, a mirror of Czesich's sleepy dread.

To Czesich's surprise, an old reflex seemed to have been broken during the horrible night: he felt no desire to pretend affection, no need to have it pretended back at him. He watched Bobin squeezing his hands together, fretting, playing his role, but it no longer inspired a response.

"Anton Antonovich," the hotel director said, "your Deputy Ambassador has arrived and is almost finished checking in."

Too fast, Czesich spun beneath the sheet and looked at the alarm clock on his night table: 6:10. It could not possibly be 6:10 P.M. Six-ten P.M. would mean he'd been back at the hotel for fourteen or fifteen hours, sleeping the sleep of the dead. He stared at the seam of light between the curtains — tired, yielding, afternoon light — then back at the clock.

"Which room?"

"Eight-eighteen."

He pushed himself to a sitting position and swung his feet over the side of the bed. The exertion sent something clanging up his spine and into his temples, and the world was starred for a moment, softly spinning, though the worst of the pain had subsided while he slept.

"I heard the difficult news about Lydia Sergeievna," Bobin murmured. "The men are in custody. It will go very badly for them now."

Czesich rubbed his eyes. He was in his hotel room, Bobin here, Julie upstairs. He could not yet bear to think about Lydia Sergeievna or the men who had assaulted her. He needed an hour or two free of pain and fear before he could think about them. He wanted Bobin to leave now, and let him shave and wash up and prepare to face Julie, but the hotel director seemed genuinely upset, in need of company. His customary exaggerated hospitality had given way to this peculiar drunkenness, all mewling and simpering and wringing of hands, and Czesich wasn't sure what to make of it until Bobin spoke again, in mourning: "Mikhail Lvovich has abandoned us."

Czesich patted him once on the shoulder, and kept his hand there to pull himself to his feet. He limped into the dining room and toward the bath, Bobin trailing, expecting sympathy. Czesich closed the bathroom door, sat, and supported his head gingerly in both hands, eyes closed. There was Lydia Sergeievna being bent over backwards toward the church floor. There were the professional rapists with their stone fists. There, when he opened his eyes, was a single file of ants plying the white tiles, mindless, and for a few minutes he despised this country with its Gestapo hospital clerks and duplicitous doormen, its torturers and murderers and secrets. Mikhail Lvovich was gone, but there were still five million Malovs loose in the population, State-sanctioned mobsters poisoning whatever looked like love.

He pulled the chain, sending all of them into the sewer, and as if the banging, shuddering pipes were his cue, Bobin opened the bathroom door. Czesich had his pants up, at least. "For God's sake, Slava, can't it wait until I get out of the fucking bathroom?"

Bobin seemed shocked at the word, and at finding himself on the bathroom threshold. He looked down at his legs as though they'd betrayed him. "I have one favor to ask, Anton Antonovich."

"You're drunk."

"Not exactly."

Czesich turned away. Against the swirling background of yesterday's horror, Bobin's drunken supplications were obscene and pitiful and repulsive. And the face that greeted Czesich in the mirror was no comfort. A purple half-moon hung under his right eye, the skin around it pencil-yellow and taut, and with the two-day carpet of stubble and the bloodshot eyes, and the lump just in front of his ear, he looked as though he'd spent a month on the streets. He stripped to the waist and lathered up.

Bobin had not moved. "Nikolai Phillipovich was kidnapped at three o'clock this morning," he said quietly, and Czesich sliced the blade into the skin of his cheek and watched himself bleed. He rested his weight on the sink and appraised his host in the orange-framed mirror. Drunk, Bobin seemed incapable of deception.

"Yefrem Alexandrovich was the witness. Three men caught him right in front of the hotel — miners, he thinks — and wrestled him into a car. . . ." Bobin faltered and peered at the wall as if expecting to see a disfigured ear there. "It was not long after the militia brought you back here. Three o'clock A.M. Nikolai was coming to see you, I think, to see if you were all right, and they kidnapped him. That's what's going to happen now that Lvovich is gone. There'll be no order now, no discipline, no . . . *respect*." Bobin leaned and caught himself against the doorframe.

Czesich stared in the mirror, then turned and faced him. "What about Lydia?"

"Home from the hospital," Bobin sputtered. He sought a word, squeezed his lips together in frustration, said: "Damaged."

"Damaged?"

Bobin looked confused. "Injured. They put her father in custody to keep him from . . . The chief of militia is a friend. . . . It is commonly done."

Czesich was having a difficult time following Bobin's mutterings. Julie upstairs. Lydia alive. Malov kidnapped. He tried to make a hopeful whole of these pieces, but his natural Slavic pessimism resisted.

"We heard you and Sergei delivered the food to the demonstrators," Bobin said. Czesich expected a lecture on discipline and order, but Bobin paused, lowered his head slightly, and looked at him out of the tops of his eyes. "It was the right thing to do, Anton

Antonovich. Hungry . . . the men and women there. . . . Certainly the correct thing."

Czesich stared in disbelief. Had Bobin been charged with symbolizing seventy-four years of the morality of convenience, he could not have played the role more perfectly. Still, he saw a shimmer of hope. People could change. All Bobin needed was to be trampled, beaten, to have a young woman raped before his eyes, and he might find himself partially purged, battered and afraid, but slightly less fake.

"Your Deputy Ambassador is very dignified — "

"I want to be alone now, Slava."

Bobin shrugged and swayed. "One favor, Anton Antonovich."

"Ask."

"I was wondering if you might . . . if you might mention to the Deputy Ambassador that I played some small role in, in the new situation coming to be."

"You're joking," Czesich said, but he could see otherwise. The political winds had shifted, and Slava Bobin was bringing his squat little vessel about.

"We have plans for a hard-currency tourist complex here," he said. "If it could be mentioned in Moscow . . . to the other Americans there, to your *beeznessmini*." Bobin fumbled around in the pocket of his shiny suit jacket, brought out a sky-blue business card with silvered Cyrillic type, and placed it very carefully on the edge of the sink.

Czesich bent over and read it aloud. "Slava T. Bobin," he said. "*Menedzher.*"

Bobin smiled.

Impeccably dressed and badly bruised, Anton Antonovich Czesich went out the door of his suite and found a militia captain waiting there, awake. The captain saluted him stiffly, and they started off down the narrow hotel corridor, Czesich a step in the lead. The *dezhurnaya* smiled at him, a secret smile, cryptic as Russia, and Czesich smiled back, nurturing one tiny green shoot of hope. He had survived, at least. Lydia had survived. It was possible, just possible, in spite of all the pain, that one small blow had been struck for the beleaguered Russian masses.

He had a flash of memory of two militiamen supporting him in the hotel's jerking elevator not so many hours ago, and he avoided the plywood box in favor of the stairs. He climbed very slowly, the captain at his side, the pulse pounding in his bruised temple, his knee crying out. He reached the eighth-floor landing and rested there, breathing hard.

"*Zhit' buditye?*" the captain asked. "You're going to make it?"

Czesich said he thought so. He pushed through the fire door. Eight-eighteen, another *dezhurnaya* informed him, was six doors down on the left. He smoothed his lapels, tugged on his cuffs, and started forward. The corridor smelled strongly of insecticide; the runner beneath his feet was tattered; the doors to either side looked too heavily shellacked, almost sticky; the wallpaper was new and already a bit ragged at the seams. Just the surfaces, he reminded himself, just the mask. He went along at a dignified pace, in keeping with his position, in some fair degree of pain.

He and his bodyguard stopped in front of room 818. Czesich knocked, nervous now, stomach growling. The lock clicked, the door swung open, and standing in front of him was a beautiful woman about his own age, dark hair, pale eyes, a fine mouth set in a mold of slight dissatisfaction. He thought he could see beyond the beauty now, at last, beyond the nervous disapproval. With Julie, you could never be sure at first, but he thought she might be happy to see him.

// EPILOGUE

WATCHMAKERS and bureaucrats, students and miners and aging chauffeurs — it was an odd mix of friends that squeezed into the Propenko home that same night. The visitors, come to draw Lydia back from her solitary terror, inhabited the cramped kitchen and living room without pretending to be who they were not, with secrets but without secret agendas, without competition. In keeping with ancient Russian tradition, they were at peace with their fate, evil and terrifying though that fate had turned out to be, and it was their resilience — illogical, Russian resilience — that drew Anton Czesich and Julia Stirvin to October Avenue and held them there until the small hours of morning.

Lydia emerged from the back room and sat with her mother, grandmother, and father for a time. She seemed transfixed by an unimaginable horror playing over and over again on an inner screen. Czesich and the other friends who had come to comfort her found they could not reach the level at which she suffered. Their kind words sounded shallow and hollow, and Lydia did not seem to want to be touched.

After midnight, when most of the visitors had gone home, and Lydia and her grandmother had gone to sleep together in the back bedroom, Propenko and Raisa and Czesich and Julie found themselves at the kitchen table for a few minutes, pouring from the same bottle. It was the first hour of August 19, 1991, and later that morning, Boris Puchkov and his fellow patriots would spill their hatred once again into Moscow's streets. There would be the usual show of armor — tanks and personnel carriers — the usual array of suit-and-tie thugs, the usual lies told by bullies. And, for a day or two, the past would rear up, cast its pall, claim a few more lives, then fall back, bringing with it an empire.

None of the four people at the kitchen table knew that yet, of course. They drank and talked in quiet tones, working on a difficult farewell, a kind of delicate, anguished hymn for the thing they had seen extinguished in Lydia Sergeievna and in themselves. If hope meant the expectation of a painless life, then they had no hope left, no Glorious Socialist Future, no Heaven on Earth, no blissful, unblemished love to look forward to. What they had instead was a cargo of history, good and bad, and another chance to rearrange themselves beneath it so that the load might be more comfortably borne.